Eva Glyn writes emotional wo[...]
beautiful places and the stories th[...]
but finds inspiration can strike just[...]

She cut her teeth on just about every kind of writing (radio journalism, advertising copy, PR, and even freelance cricket reporting) before finally completing a full-length novel in her forties. Four lengthy and completely unpublishable tomes later she found herself sitting on an enormous polystyrene book under the TV lights of the Alan Titchmarsh Show as a finalist in the People's Novelist competition sponsored by HarperCollins. Although losing out to a far better writer, the positive feedback from the judges gave her the confidence to pursue her dreams.

Eva lives in Cornwall, although she considers herself Welsh, and has been lucky enough to have been married to the love of her life for twenty-five years. She also writes as Jane Cable.

www.janecable.com

twitter.com/janecable
facebook.com/EvaGlynAuthor
instagram.com/evaglynauthor
bookbub.com/authors/eva-glyn

Also by Eva Glyn

The Missing Pieces of Us

The Olive Grove

An Island of Secrets

THE COLLABORATOR'S DAUGHTER

EVA GLYN

One More Chapter
a division of HarperCollins*Publishers*
1 London Bridge Street
London SE1 9GF
www.harpercollins.co.uk

HarperCollins*Publishers*
Macken House, 39/40 Mayor Street Upper,
Dublin 1, D01 C9W8

This paperback edition 2023
1
First published in Great Britain in ebook format
by HarperCollins*Publishers* 2023

A catalogue record of this book is available from the British Library

ISBN: 978-0-00-855327-2

Printed and bound in the UK using 100% Renewable Electricity
by CPI Group (UK) Ltd

For John and Joan, and with fondest memories of Marjorie

Chapter One

Dubrovnik, 14th September 1944

The glowing orb of the sun sinks towards the sea as he takes his newborn daughter in his arms and carries her to the open window. Below him red-tiled roofs spread untidily in every direction, pierced by the towers and domes of the city's many churches; churches which cast their shadows long over the narrow streets. He knows that as soon as she is able, his wife, Dragica, will slip into Sveti Vlaho to light a candle in thanks for the child's safe delivery.

He will not go with her. It is not his way. This is his moment of silent communion with the world, with all that he wishes for Safranka flowing through him. There is peace at this hour, when the air is soft and the shutters close, the salt breeze carrying snatches of conversation and laughter, just as it always has done.

Yet this is not his Dubrovnik. Not the city he grew up in,

the place he cherishes in the very core of his heart. It is a city under occupation, from outside and from within, its streets and alleyways ringing with the empty spaces where his friends once lived and dreamed. Gone now, and who knew if they would ever return.

Should he have left too, to fight with the partisans? Not with his wretched leg. He cannot march, let alone fight. He would have wasted his life for nothing. Whereas here, perhaps, he has been able to do at least one thing that was good.

He had not wanted his child to be born in a city at war, but Dragica had told him that god decides when we enter and leave this world. Her god, that is. But now his daughter is in his arms, everything has changed. Everything. He can feel her warmth through his shirt, imagines her heartbeat in time with his. She has strong lungs at least, given how she wailed in those first few moments, and he smiles at the memory. They told him that would happen, that it was normal, but no one had warned him love like this was even possible.

He wonders if, after all, the time is right and Safranka's arrival heralds a new start. The Germans are pulling back from the islands and there is a thought, a whisper, that victory might be almost within the partisans' grasp. Oh, to be able to leave behind the subterfuge and deceit that sickens him. Turn his back on this ugly chapter of his life and look forwards.

The sky beyond the city walls is streaked with orange and purple, the streets below him falling into the velvet silence of the night. The old moon creeps and crawls from behind the mountain, its crescent like a cup, a cup full of wishes for his daughter. Too many for one man on one night. He hopes that she will grow to love this city as he does, that she will grow to be fearless and brave. That there will be laughter in her life, and love. And that she will never, ever know the evils of persecution and war. Above all things, he wishes her that.

Chapter Two

Sussex, December 2009

As the closing bars of 'Jerusalem' died around them there was a moment of silence in the church, then the undertakers moved forwards to take the coffin from the trestles in front of the altar. The polished oak gleamed under the lights. Behind her someone coughed, and Fran clutched the end of the pew, the smoothness worn by generations of hands strangely comforting.

Now the pallbearers were on the move, the sickly scent of hothouse lilies filling the air as they passed. She took a deep breath and stepped out to follow them, but suddenly she couldn't do it. She couldn't go first, couldn't stare at the end of the box, all but seeing his head through the grain, so she stood back to allow her brother Andrew to pass, then followed him.

Around her people were gathering gloves and buttoning coats, no doubt steeling themselves for the ordeal in the churchyard. Somehow she would have to find it in herself to

4

pick up the clod of cold earth and trickle it into the grave. She had to be strong for Andrew, Patti and Michael. Set an example. She concentrated on the solid shape of Andrew's shoulders beneath his black overcoat. She couldn't fail Daddy now.

The church doors opened, light and air flooding in, and in the same moment an almighty shove from behind sent her sprawling to the floor, the corner of the font flashing dangerously close to her eyes. The air was knocked from her body. She couldn't breathe. Couldn't think.

Patti stood over her, her thin mouth twisted into a ribbon of hatred. "How dare you push in front of me? How dare you! He's not even your real father."

The silence around them was absolute, intense. The pallbearers stopped, the coffin swaying slightly between them. Fran wanted to say something, but she knew if she opened her mouth the only sound would be a howl of absolute desolation.

Andrew turned, as if in slow motion, his grey face full of a fury that Fran had never seen before. "Patti! How could you? It's Dad's funeral, for god's sake."

"You two ... you always gang up on me ... you always take her side." Patti's knuckles were white as she clutched her handbag to her, then she ran from the church, heels clipping on the flagstones, her order of service fluttering to the floor.

After a moment Andrew reached for Fran's hand, helping her up then wrapping his arm around her shoulder. "Come on, Sis," he told her, loud enough for everyone to hear. "We can do this. Just the two of us. He'd have ..." He glanced after Patti. "He'd have understood."

• • •

Fran stayed at Daddy's wake until the bitter end. It was the right thing to do, she knew that. After Patti's dramatic exit she could hardly leave Andrew to cope with it alone. But once the last guest had left, and she had waved off her son, Michael, and daughter-in-law, Paula, back to London to collect their girls from school, she had gratefully accepted Andrew and his wife Alice's offer of a lift home.

"You'll be all right, won't you?" Alice asked as they dropped her at the kerb outside her neatly white-washed terraced house. "That bloody woman has to make everything about her."

"Don't worry. I'll be fine."

Andrew leant across from the driving seat. "Put Patti out of your mind. I reckon it was him leaving you a little extra money for caring for him so well that sparked her off."

"I won't take it if you think it will help."

"Don't you dare even think about it. You've earned it, Fran. You gave up two years of your life for him."

"I couldn't have done anything else."

She waved until the car disappeared around the corner then unlocked the door. Her own space closed around her, and she kicked off her shoes. Truth be told, she had really missed her little home when she'd moved in with Daddy after his stroke, but now she was back it seemed unbelievably empty and cold.

She'd always called him Daddy, right through adulthood, because he'd preferred it and because she was so very grateful to him for treating her like his own. Fran could barely remember the time before he had been in her life. There was something; a farmhouse kitchen with a table that went on forever. Standing on a stool to roll out pastry with old Mrs

Daly, pans popping softly on the range while chickens clucked in the yard outside. And sitting on Mama's lap as she drove the tractor, the wall of the South Downs towering above them, seagulls wheeling as the plough cut into the earth.

Most of her memories began in the house with a tiny square of lawn at the back and bedrooms under the eaves, where they had lived when Mama and Daddy first married. And school. She remembered school. After the isolation of the farm, at first it had seemed too busy, too huge. But she had felt a whole lot better once she'd realised she was far from the only child with a daddy who wasn't her real father. Mama said that after the war they were lucky to have him, had to be the very best they could be to deserve him, and she'd been right.

She'd tried to be a good daughter, and for the most part she thought she'd succeeded. For the most part. But even when she hadn't, he had been her champion. He'd always called her his dark eyed child; different to the others, but his own in every other way.

It took a lot to repay a man for that sort of love, but she hoped she had. It had required no second thought at all to leave her job two years earlier when he'd had his stroke, and to move back into the family home. After all, Andrew had a business to run and Patti … Well, Patti would never have had the patience. Fran had been just a few years off retirement, and it wasn't as though she'd had a career as such, although she'd loved her admin job at the school. Michael had left home years before so she lived on her own. It hadn't been all that much to give up, had it?

She knew that in the blink of an eye she would do it again. She'd loved Daddy so much, with his quiet good sense and gentle humour. It still seemed impossible he wasn't there. Even so, there was no point moping. She'd spoil herself a little for the rest of the day and then work out what the hell she was going to do with her life now.

Once she'd changed out of the scratchy woollen dress she'd bought for the funeral she pottered around, enjoying the grain and warmth of the wooden floor beneath her bare feet. After watering the herbs on the windowsill she boiled the kettle to make a cup of tea. The pine doors of the kitchen units had seen better days, but very soon she'd be able to afford some new ones. Maybe a cooker too. She'd bought hers second-hand years ago, and one of the electric rings had never worked. But when had she needed all four of them anyway, when she'd only been cooking for one?

She reached into the cupboard and pulled out her favourite blue and white striped mug. Perhaps she'd have one of those nice biscuits Polly and Joe next door had bought her. Proper old lady present, biscuits, but she supposed that was what she was.

She didn't feel old, that was the thing. Her waist may have spread a little and her hair was definitely as much salt as pepper, but inside she was just the same. Michael had said sixty-five was the new fifty, but there was a part of her that felt forty, or thirty even. Not the part that ached just a little when she got out of bed in the mornings, obviously, but even so, was she really ready to settle down in front of the fire in a pair of fluffy slippers? For a start she didn't possess a pair of slippers, and she'd ripped out the fireplace a good many years before for a number of reasons. For any number of reasons.

She carried her tea and the biscuit tin through to the sofa and balanced them on the seat next to her before sinking back into the soft leather. She tucked her feet under her and opened her laptop. Since Daddy died she didn't feel as though she'd had a moment to herself, so now she could catch up with the *Dubrovnik Times* and the Croatian blogs she followed. At least it would take her mind off the empty spaces around her.

She still wasn't sure why her interest in Croatia had been kindled during Daddy's last months. Yes, Dubrovnik was where she'd been born, although she had left as a babe in arms. But after she had stumbled across an advertisement for a cruise around the Dalmatian islands in a Sunday colour supplement, she'd found her interest well and truly piqued. At first it had been something to do while Daddy dozed in his chair for increasingly long periods of time, but then, as it became inevitable his end was near, it had become a vital distraction. She had never told him, of course. It would have felt incredibly disloyal after all he'd done for her.

Straight away an article relating to a massacre that had happened during the Second World War caught her eye. Partisan forces had liberated Dubrovnik in the middle of October 1944 as the Nazi occupiers fled northwards. Fran imagined them being welcomed with open arms by the local population, especially as almost immediately they had rounded up about three hundred people who had been considered collaborators. In all honesty, she couldn't blame the partisans for that – the same had happened all over Europe, and quite rightly too.

It seemed these collaborators had wielded influence throughout Dubrovnik society, and priests, intellectuals, even the mayor, had been incarcerated to await trial. But there were no records of any trial being held, and a week later more than fifty of them were taken to the island of Daksa and shot, their bodies lying undisturbed for almost sixty-five years.

The reason the item was news now was that in September a team of academics had exhumed them in an attempt to identify the victims through DNA analysis. The problem was that no one knew who some of the men were; all they had to go on was a list of the names of thirty-six known Nazi collaborators the partisans had published after the event, and a few families who had come forward since because a relative had disappeared close to that time.

Fran put her laptop on the floor and sipped her tea. When exactly had her father died? She didn't know. All her mother had ever said was that his was a hero's death, so having been massacred by partisans seemed improbable. Far more likely he'd perished in the last desperate burst of fighting to free the city from the hated occupiers. The timing would have been about right; she'd been born on 14th September and she knew he hadn't lived for very long afterwards.

Her mother had always said they'd arrived in England in the depths of winter, and she had wondered if she would ever see the sun again, so they must have gone quite quickly after he'd died. Mama had never been entirely clear about why they'd left, but Fran knew it had been on an English boat and it had all been arranged by Mrs Daly's cousin, who was an officer billeted in the hotel where her mother had worked. Perhaps he'd helped them because the old lady had needed someone to work on her farm, and Mama had been too heartbroken to want to stay in a place that was so full of memories.

Her mother had seldom spoken about her time in Dubrovnik, and certainly not about the war, but that wasn't unusual – very few of her generation had. When she'd talked of Yugoslavia at all it was about the village where she'd grown up, the country recipes and customs, and folk stories that had entranced Fran as a child. As an adult, Fran had sometimes wondered about Mama's life in the city but had never liked to pry.

Peeling the foil wrapper from a chocolate biscuit, Fran returned to the article, scanning the list of collaborators. Her vision blurred. She looked again, coughing as a crumb lodged in the back of her throat. But it was there. It was definitely there, the name jumping off the screen as though someone had highlighted it: Branko Milišić, clerk, born Dubrovnik, 1919.

Her first coherent thought was that it wasn't necessarily her father. There could well have been more than one Branko Milišić living in the city at the time. Of course she didn't really know, but it didn't sound like an unusual or outlandish name. In fact there was another Milišić, a sea captain named Željko, so that sort of proved it. Her mother would never have called her father a hero if he'd been a Nazi collaborator. Would she? The very thought made Fran feel a little sick.

But why had she left Yugoslavia so quickly? Had she been afraid of repercussions if she stayed? It had never occurred to Fran that it might have been for their own safety. It would rip such a huge hole in her understanding of her own childhood …

No, Fran, calm down. That just cannot be. Really it couldn't. It didn't fit with a hero's death at all.

Fran levered herself from the sofa and stood in front of the photograph of her parents on the wall. The parents who had brought her up, not the shadow of a father she couldn't remember. The picture had been taken in the garden of their house at Aldwick on their ruby wedding, Daddy tall and slim in a checked sports jacket tucking Mama under his arm as she gazed up at him from behind her glasses, her salt-and-pepper hair newly cut and blow-dried for the occasion, her round face brimful of love. These were the people who mattered. These were the ones she had lost.

A tear slid down Fran's cheek. Pointless, so bloody pointless. She couldn't let herself wallow, however shitty her day had been. Couldn't let herself slide into that pit, because there was no one here to help her out of it. Biting her lip, she fought back a sob. She felt hollow inside; hollow, empty and exhausted.

She turned away from the picture and took a deep breath. Crying wasn't going to bring them back and she had things to do. Not important things, by any means, but things that would keep her busy. Pop to the supermarket for a start, treat herself to something nice for supper. And the way she was feeling right now, a bottle of wine to go with it.

Chapter Three

O utside the mayor's office the corridor is dark, the chipped green paint on the walls cold against his shoulders. Yet still his palms sweat as he strains to make out the voices inside. The mayor's normally strident tones are muted. Strangled, almost. The other man's, a verbal wringing of hands, a hectoring whine. Familiar, but he cannot place it. When the door opens he will know him soon enough.

The dread of discovery lives with him every moment of every day, but it is at its sharpest when he is about his work. The web of evil spins out from here, from the centre of the city, a traitorous cancer eating his beloved home from the inside out. And he is just a pathetic, wriggling fly. Summoned. Trapped. Waiting. Praying the inevitable will not come.

The longer he stands, the more his leg aches, the cold teasing his shrivelled muscles from the bone. He knows the pain well, he has carried it down the years. The fear he has not.

It is sharp, dangerous, new; born along with his daughter. What will happen to Dragica and Safranka if he has been found out? Will their twisted retribution rain down on his family as well?

The voices inside the room rise and shift into false bonhomie then the door sweeps open and a priest walks past without a second glance. The cripple invisible to the man who preaches vitriol and hate in front of his gilded altar. Branko's fists ball in anger. There is little worse than a hypocrite. Except, perhaps, a religious one.

"Milišić? Are you there?"

He steps into the room, blinking in the sunlight streaming through the window. "Yes, sir."

"I fear our German friends will soon be leaving us, so we are raising a fighting force to protect the city from the communist threat."

His heart stops in his chest. If they fight the partisans and win, the nightmare will never end. It has to end. For Safranka, for Dragica, for himself ... But the mayor is speaking again.

"I suppose your leg is still as bad as you continually claim it is? Even so I need you to return to your uniform."

He forces himself to look the man in the eye. "It is not possible, sir."

"Why not?"

His heart thuds again. Can the mayor hear it? There are a thousand reasons why not. But he must think, think. Think of one that will not give him away. "I would be a liability, sir. I move so slowly, I could not fight." He needs the bitter taste of deceit in his throat to expel the next words. "There must be ways I could be more useful for the protection of our city."

The mayor taps his pen on the blotter. "I do not like it when people refuse me."

"And I do not do so lightly."

The silence swirls around them, oozing from between the tomes in the bookcase, floating with the motes of dust, and coating every surface and the spaces in between.

At last the mayor speaks. "Very well. I need a messenger boy. Unless you're not even man enough for that?"

Do not rise to him, do not rise. There is no place for pride and anger here. If nothing else, his family needs to eat. "Yes, sir. I can do it."

The mayor nods. He is dismissed.

Chapter Four

Sussex, January 2010

S tanding in the car park behind Pagham Beach waiting for her best friend Parisa, Fran knew without a doubt she needed a walk in the fresh sea air to blow the cobwebs away. She hadn't planned to stay up to see in the new year, but given it was the start of a new decade too, one of her neighbours had decided at the last minute to hold a party.

It had been the best fun Fran had had in ages. In fact, it quite took her back. Naturally there had been a mix of people there so the music had been varied, but she liked to think her addiction to Radio 2 had kept her reasonably up to date, and it hadn't taken very much wine before she'd kicked off her shoes and danced with the other women and a few of the braver men for what had felt like hours, only stopping to refill her glass.

No wonder she felt rough. Even a couple of paracetamols hadn't put a dent in her headache, but she knew Parisa's company and being out in the open would probably help. Even if her friend was late. As usual.

Fran and Parisa had met on their first day at Chichester High. Parisa had been the only British Asian girl in the school and, although everyone generally assumed Fran was English because she had only ever used the anglicised version of her name, they had bonded over a shared sense of difference. Of course at eleven years old they hadn't exactly put it like that, but they had gravitated towards each other just the same.

While Parisa had been academic and highly driven, Fran had struggled along, but her popularity with the other girls had made it easier for shy Parisa to fit in, and in return she had helped Fran with her homework. And although their paths had diverged when Parisa went to medical school in Manchester and Fran to Brighton and then London, they had kept in touch and had rekindled their friendship when they'd both returned to Chichester in their late twenties. Fran as a single mother, Parisa as a respected GP.

A muddy VW Golf turned into the car park and came to a halt next to Fran's car. The moment the engine stopped, Fran could hear barking as Button, Parisa's Lhasa apso, strained at his harness to try to launch himself through the window in her direction.

Ignoring the dog, Parisa gave Fran a huge hug. "Happy new decade! Just think of all the adventures you can have."

"And you."

Parisa stood back and laughed. "You sound – and look – a little jaded. Good party?"

Button's yelping had reached fever pitch and Parisa turned back to the car to release him, her navy trench coat flapping in the breeze. Even to walk the dog she looked a million dollars, and Fran felt positively frumpy beside her, in the bright orange waterproof she'd bought when the camping shop had a sale.

Of course it was easy for Parisa to look elegant, she was a good five inches taller than Fran and slim with it. She didn't have so much as a single grey hair and her smooth skin and fine bone structure meant she still looked young enough to wear it in a loose ponytail, tied with a designer silk scarf in an exuberant bow, while Fran's unruly mop was rammed into a bobble hat.

The moment Button was free he barrelled into Fran's legs and she crouched to ruffle his soft ears, which she knew he loved. With his huge dark eyes and chocolate drop nose, he really was the most adorable little dog.

"Why don't you get one?" Parisa asked.

Fran straightened up. "You sound just like Michael. And no, you know I have an aversion to poo bags."

Parisa shrugged. "You get used to it."

"You spent your life working with icky stuff."

"Only occasionally."

"The answer is still no. What if I wanted to travel?"

"And do you?"

"If I can pluck up the courage."

They started to walk towards the beach, past the deserted amusement arcade and the closed fish and chip shop, its metal sign creaking in the breeze.

"How about one of those singles holidays?"

"Aren't I a bit old for them?"

"They do them for retired people too, you know."

Fran turned to her, scowling. "I am not old enough to sit on a coach for hours, only to be dumped at a shopping outlet as the highlight of the day. And to listen to other women go on and on about their brilliantly gifted grandchildren as though nobody else has ever had any."

"Good point. I don't think we'll ever be as old as that."

"And you love shopping." Fran rolled her eyes.

"Not at outlets." Parisa shuddered.

"Don't look at my coat like that! Not everyone has your pension."

"Ah, but you will have a bit of money once probate's been granted."

"For the first time in my life." Fran laughed. "It'll take some getting used to."

Parisa hugged her. "You deserve it. You've earned it."

"I couldn't not have looked after him. You know how good he's always been to me. He never once treated me any differently to the others. I remember … I remember, when I was tiny, it must have been not long after he and Mama married, we were in town and someone must have asked who I was. And he told them … he told them … I was his wife's daughter, but wasn't he lucky, because now I was his too."

Fran was glad the freshness of the breeze could be making her eyes smart, but Parisa knew her well enough to tell the difference.

"Come on, have a good cry if it helps."

"How can it? It won't bring him back. It won't bring either of them back, it won't make us young again. It's … it's all gone. Everything's just so sodding empty." And if she did let herself cry, she had a horrible feeling she would sink onto the pebbles and howl like a toddler. It was certainly what she was doing inside.

Parisa bent to unclip Button's lead, then put her arm around Fran's shoulder as he raced down the shingle bank towards the gunmetal waves to chase a seagull. "That's normal. It's called grief. And there's always an extra dimension to it when you've been a carer. You have a big hole in your life to fill, Fran, but perhaps you need to deal with everything you've lost first."

Fran shook her gently away and they began to walk along the beach. "It's not like me though, is it? To sit around moping and doing nothing. I need to get my act together. I thought I might go back to volunteering at the children's centre, maybe work in a charity shop a couple of days a week."

"Medium term that's a good call. I don't think you'll be happy if you aren't doing something to help other people, it's the way you've been brought up. What I'm saying is don't leap into any commitments while you're feeling so fragile, you'll only let people put on you and you'll regret it later. You know what you can be like and you deserve better than that. Allow yourself to grieve for a while, then work out what you really want to do with your life."

"I think that's the problem. I don't know."

"I didn't either when I first retired. Which is probably why I still find myself on too many committees. But then I got Button, joined the walking group, discovered silk painting. You need to take a bit of time to decide what works for you."

Fran tucked her chin into her scarf as they crunched along. Parisa was right, but it was just the emptiness that was so damn scary. She really needed something to do now, tomorrow, next week. She couldn't even get on with clearing her parents' house with Patti being so awkward. It was just too much of a risk to do anything until they got probate in case she decided to challenge the will.

It wasn't even as if she was lonely; she had plenty of friends, although she had to admit she'd lost touch with a fair few of them during Daddy's last illness. It was just … oh, she couldn't quite put a finger on it, but the weeks, months, and years ahead looked really empty. Even thinking about it felt like staring into a black hole and brought her out in a cold sweat. What would she do with all this time on her hands? Her life had always had shape and purpose, and now it hung loosely around her like a cloak.

But there was one thing, one thing that had been keeping her awake at night and was probably contributing to her fits of misery. She kicked a pebble with the toe of her trainer. "I did wonder about going to Croatia to find my roots, but now I'm not so sure."

"That sounds like an excellent idea to me. We used to talk about it a lot when we were teenagers, didn't we? Where we were born, where our families came from, those whole histories we knew so little about."

"You've been to Pakistan though, haven't you? Heaps of times."

Parisa nodded. "When my parents were alive, for family weddings and suchlike. But I have to say I found the whole thing a bit weird. It was my culture, my relatives, and Mum and Dad were obviously so completely at home, but to Kalima and me it was totally alien and we felt like fish out of water. All the same I'm glad I did it. Glad I found out."

"So perhaps there's no point after all."

"There's every point. It's part of who you are. Maybe one thing you could do to fill your time would be to take an online course to brush up your language skills."

"Convert my few phrases of rather rusty old-fashioned

Serbo-Croat into Croatian, you mean." For the first time in a long while little green shoots of enthusiasm stirred in Fran.

"Exactly that. You'd be using your brain for a start. And then you could book a trip, maybe for the spring when the weather's a bit better. Where would you go?"

"I read an article about a cruise through the Dalmatian islands, but I'm not sure about being stuck on a boat for a week with a load of strangers. I don't suppose you ..."

"No. Definitely not. I'd be throwing up the whole time. And what about Button? I wouldn't want to put him in kennels, and I can't ask my neighbours to have him for more than the odd night."

"Fair enough."

They walked on, Button rushing around their legs, then zooming off in a vain attempt to catch one of the avocets feeding at the water's edge. The sea was churning grey-green, the salt spray licking their faces even at the top of the beach. The Mediterranean wouldn't be like this. It would be calm, blue. Fran thought of the pictures she'd seen of Dubrovnik's red roofs glowing in the sun, and she could almost feel the warmth.

Perhaps she'd have been keener to go if her father hadn't shared a name with one of the men the partisans had executed. Oh, she knew it couldn't have been him – well, most of the time she did – but it had introduced just the tiniest seed of doubt. She'd wanted to go to Dubrovnik to find her father, and if she could, discover why he'd been such a hero in Mama's eyes. And at very least experience the place she'd been born for herself. It had seemed such a shiny dream when Daddy was ill, so now she was free to go, what was holding her back?

She turned to Parisa. "Do you really think I could find the confidence to go on my own?"

Her friend snorted. "Of course you can. Honestly, remember when we were in Porto and that woman fell down and needed stitches? Who was it took charge and got her to the local doctor? And at the children's centre Christmas party when—"

"I know, I know. It's just, I don't know, I don't really feel very strong at the moment."

Parisa hugged her. "And is that surprising? Give yourself time, Fran. He's only been gone a month and grief is a long old process."

Fran nodded. She supposed Parisa was right – she normally was – but somehow at the moment it didn't seem to help.

Fran threw the duvet from her legs and swung them off the bed before tying her dressing gown firmly around her and marching down the stairs. So what it was two in the morning? This business with her father had kept her awake one night too many as it was. She was going to email those researchers in Croatia right now.

But all the same she stood in the kitchen, hugging her arms around her as she waited for the kettle to boil. If she did this, there would be no going back. One way or the other, she would know. There was always the chance that, rather than setting her mind at rest, she would have to face the fact that her hero father had been a Nazi collaborator. But she'd never known him, so what did it matter? And if it didn't matter, why was she thinking of taking the test in the first place? Round and round and round. Quite frankly, she was bored with it.

Giving the DNA sample would at least make her stop wondering whether or not she should. At first when she'd read the article it had seemed a rather academic question, but then the thought had begun to take hold, popping up when she was doing the ironing, or raking frostbitten leaves from her tiny back lawn, niggling away at her. Should she, shouldn't she? And most of all, why?

The why was the biggest conundrum. Why should she want to find out about this man whose blood may flow in her veins, but whom she had never known? Especially as she'd had the most wonderful father for most of her life. She honestly couldn't have wished for anyone better, and she knew Mama had been right when she'd told her as a little girl they needed to be grateful every day that he'd taken them on.

Fran certainly felt ungrateful now. It was so disrespectful to Daddy, when he'd been gone from her life for so little time, to allow herself to be kept awake by this shadow of a man. She didn't even have Daddy's wise counsel to fall back on to help her decide what to do; he'd gone. They'd all gone. She was completely alone and it was making her so bloody miserable. A sob came from nowhere, but she swallowed it back down, because if she started to cry now, how the hell was she ever going to stop?

Only once before in her life had she felt so utterly empty and defeated, and that had been towards the end of her marriage. It was as though something deep inside was beginning to stretch and yawn, and she didn't much like the dark shape it was taking. At least having been there once before, she recognised it for what it was, but she just couldn't let herself sink that far again, even at two in the morning.

Gripping the edge of the table, she took a deep breath. She was not a negative person and she was damned if she was going to become one. What she needed was to sort out her future, and having the past hanging over her wasn't helping. She had to do this. Had to close the book. If nothing else, do it for this set of bones that might or might not be the Branko Milišić Mama had married. At the very least, then he could be buried with a name.

Her laptop was on the dining table and she opened the bookmark for the *Dubrovnik Times* article, copying the address into an email. She sipped her tea, scalding her lips, then typed 'Daksa' in the subject line.

What next? The simple truth, the bare facts:

My father shared a name with one of the men on the list of the men executed at Daksa, and he died at about the same time, so I am prepared to take a DNA test. Please let me know what to do.

She pressed send and sat back. It hadn't been so hard, not really. She'd imagined the relief running through her, then climbing the stairs and heading back to bed and to sleep, but instead her heart was pumping, her brain spinning into overdrive. When would she hear back? What would happen next? Would she even have to go to Dubrovnik to take the test?

Oh, she'd been a fool to think this was some sort of quick fix. Somehow, somewhere, this was all muddled up with missing Daddy, and she couldn't begin to untangle it. Certainly in the wee small hours of the morning. She powered down her laptop, but all the same she didn't move, just stared at the blank screen. As if that would tell her anything. After a while she started to shiver so she picked up her tea and carried it up the stairs. She'd read a little until she felt calmer, then try to go to sleep.

Before climbing back under the duvet she opened the top drawer of her old pine chest. There, wrapped in tissue paper yellow with age, was the necklace, stuffed into an old pair of socks. Fran unwrapped it a layer at a time. It was the only precious thing her mother had brought from Dubrovnik and Fran had always understood it had been important to her father. Which was why this Nazi business couldn't be right.

The pendant was rectangular, about an inch high. The gold filigree work was astounding in its detail; chiselled and chased until it was as delicate as lace. The outer frame was a series of interconnecting arches, a perfect round turquoise in each corner, which was echoed by four pink coral dots at the edge of the inner square. But it was the centre decoration in royal blue enamel that had got Fran thinking. A menorah and a Star of David. There was no doubt at all this exquisite piece of jewellery was a symbol of the Jewish faith. So if her father had been a Nazi, why would this have been so precious to him?

Right at this moment it was too much for her befuddled brain. So many questions, and pointless ones at that. Questions she would never know the answer to. Questions she wished she had asked her mother. But that chance had gone, almost seven years before, although tonight she missed her more than ever. A wave of black agony swept out of nowhere, catching her unawares so she was unable to stem the tide. Why now? Why feel like this now? Clutching the necklace in her hand, she curled under the duvet and howled.

Just when Fran thought things couldn't get any worse, Patti called. She'd heard the ringing from the garden where she'd been tugging the last of the washing from the line as the ominous grey sky turned to sleet, so she rushed into the house, dumping the basket on the dining table and grabbing the phone without screening it first as she'd taken to doing since her sister's abusive messages had started.

"I'm never going to forgive you for this."

Oh lord, no. Fran's hand felt frozen to the phone.

"It's … it's not the money … you took them from me as well. You stole my parents. From the moment you came back until the day they died … you never let me near Daddy when he was ill … never …"

"But, Patti, that's not true. I asked you repeatedly—"

"Everyone thinks you're so bloody perfect, but you're not. If it happened now, I'd sue you, so I would. You ruined my life." She was slurring her words badly, and it was only three o'clock in the afternoon. Fran stood silently, waiting for the rest of the onslaught. She knew she should hang up and walk away, but somehow she couldn't.

"If you'd done … if you'd done what Mama asked you, everything would have been different. Everything. No one would have laughed at me for being ugly, and all that pain … god, all that pain you put a tiny child through. You, the frigging family saint. I don't know how you can live with yourself. You're no frigging sister … you lost that right …"

Tears clawed at Fran's throat. She knew it wasn't true, not half of it, but all the same the hatred in Patti's words tore her apart. Now she did hang up, and sank onto the sofa, taking one shuddering breath after another, before unplugging the phone at the wall, just as it started to ring again.

Shakily, she pulled her mobile from her pocket. No. Andrew would be at work, she mustn't bother him. But he was the only one she could talk to about this, the one who would remind her it was all a pack of hysterical lies. But somewhere in the lies, Fran knew there was more than a kernel of truth, and that was what hurt her more than anything.

Ever since she could remember, right from when Mama first met Daddy, Fran had been told she had to be a good girl to deserve him. Then, when Andrew had been born, her mother had explained that, as the oldest, Fran should set an example. Be good, and kind, and patient with her brother, look after him. And the same with Patti when she came along. Only she hadn't always done that, had she? She'd let everyone down.

It was when they'd been living in the little house in Midhurst. Andrew had been ill in bed with chickenpox so, as a special treat while they'd waited for Daddy to come home from work, Mama had been toasting marshmallows over the fire with Patti and Fran. Patti had been almost three at the time, and Fran eleven, so when Mama had popped upstairs to check on Andrew, she'd been plenty old enough to keep an eye on her younger sister as she'd been asked.

Except Fran had been reading the latest Chalet School book and could hardly bear to put it down. With Mama out of the room, she had sneaked another couple of paragraphs, but then Patti had screamed and she'd looked up to see the arm of her nightdress in flames.

Even thinking of it now made Fran feel sick. In a moment of panic she'd started screaming herself, then had remembered a first aid talk at Brownies and had tried to roll a wriggling, hysterical Patti in the hearth rug. Then Mama had arrived, and she'd been yelling too; yelling at Fran to run down the road to the phone box to ring for an ambulance.

But when she got there someone was already inside. She knew it was an emergency and she should tell them so, but she wasted valuable minutes plucking up the courage, until their neighbour came along, asked what was wrong, and did it for her.

Poor little Patti had been in hospital for weeks and weeks. In fact she hadn't come home until they'd moved to Aldwick, and in the meantime the family had been split apart, as either Mama or Daddy spent time with her every day. At one point she and Andrew had been packed off to stay at Mrs Daly's farm, and she'd felt even more guilty because they'd had so much fun.

When Patti came home, still terribly scarred, it had seemed natural for Mama to protect her and spoil her a bit; after all, she'd missed out on so much. Andrew had been less than impressed, but to Fran it made sense, and as she felt so very responsible, she did her best to spoil Patti too. Nobody ever talked about what had happened that night; one of Mama's favourite mantras was 'least said, soonest mended', and for a very long time she stuck by it.

When Patti hit her teenage years that changed. Fran was living in London at the time, and not in the happiest of places herself. The first she knew of the approaching storm was when she received a letter from Mama, suggesting she might not want to come home for a few weeks. Patti was being called some awful names by boys at school, which had led to a long conversation about what had happened on that awful night. While Mama had been very clear to Patti that she blamed herself for leaving the room, Patti had decided the fault was Fran's and Fran's alone, and somehow over the years, things had gone from bad to worse between them.

Despite desperately wanting to, Fran had never found a way to put things right; in part because of the guilt she had always carried for what had happened, and also Mama's insistence that discussing it would only open old wounds. But Mama had been gone for seven long years, and if Fran had made an effort to sort it out, Patti might have felt able to visit Daddy more during his last illness, and she knew he would have liked that. The thought that it hadn't happened because of her was frankly heartbreaking.

Fran lay down on the sofa, staring at the ceiling as her head began to thump. She was exhausted from fending off her grief for Daddy, from worrying about the future. She couldn't take this as well, the constant reminders from Patti of her inadequacies as a sibling. Right now, she just couldn't do it. She couldn't do anything, truth be told. She couldn't seem to find a way to sort out her jumbled thoughts with everything closing in around her – it just wasn't happening. Parisa had said to give herself time, but already she was becoming impatient. If only she could summon the energy, she'd give herself a right good kick in the butt.

Remembering her conversation with Parisa, a thought drifted into her mind. Could Dubrovnik be the answer? The jump-start she needed? Or would it be running away?

The DNA test had dropped through her letterbox a week before and had stared at her accusingly from the window ledge for a good three days while she plucked up the courage to open it. Upstairs in the bathroom she'd swabbed the insides of her cheeks dutifully, sealed the brush back into its container and headed for the Post Office before she'd had the chance to change her mind. It would be a while before she received the results, but perhaps she didn't need to wait. Maybe she should just go. And go soon, while she was still trying to work out what to do with the rest of her life.

Fran sat up. That, at least, made a certain amount of sense. She didn't want to volunteer for things then suddenly announce she was taking a holiday. Particularly if she was going to help out at the children's centre – continuity was important. With some of the kids you needed a good long while to build up their trust and you didn't want to disappear the moment you'd done so.

Of course she'd have to ask Andrew what he thought. She was reasonably sure probate would be a while coming through, and in the meantime, nothing could be done about clearing the house. Fran gripped her hands together, fighting back tears. That was a very good thing, because she really wasn't sure she could face the house right now anyway. Perhaps a couple of weeks of winter sunshine, away from the ice and snow that had gripped the country on and off for weeks ...

She jumped up and ran to the dining area to turn on her laptop, dumping the basket of washing on the floor. Drumming her fingers on the table, she waited for the machine to spring into life, then checked the weather for Dubrovnik. It wouldn't exactly be T-shirt warm in February, but there would be plenty of sun. An average of seven hours a day in fact. The sleet was still beating on the window, the sky above an unrelenting grey. The weather had been so awful she felt she had hardly escaped the house for weeks. Perhaps that was part of the problem. She really needed a change of scene.

But before booking anything she would have to speak to Michael, to make sure he and Paula wouldn't need her to look after the girls at any point. She'd offered, now she was free to do so, and Paula in particular had been keen on taking her up on it so they could snatch the odd weekend away. She wouldn't want to mess up any plans they'd made in that direction. And she couldn't leave until the second week of February anyway, because Polly and Joe were going skiing and Fran had promised she'd feed their cat.

The idea was as terrifying as it was beguiling; to travel all that way on her own. She wasn't even sure her passport was still in date. No, it must be. It was only three years since she and Parisa had taken their last city break together, to Rome, and the memory made her long to wander through history in the sunshine, sip coffee outside street cafés and watch the world go by.

In some ways it seemed selfish and indulgent to go away now, but as long as it was OK with Andrew and Michael, what did it matter? Her old life had gone. She couldn't just atrophy here like some premature fossil, wondering what to do next. Something needed to change. In fact, she needed to change it. Could going away on her own be the first step towards a different future? If nothing else, she would give herself time to think.

She googled 'Dubrovnik old town' and flicked through the images. Red-tiled roofs, the azure Mediterranean, city walls rising and falling with the rhythm of the rocks that climbed above the sea then plunged down again around the harbour. Pretty churches, colonnades beneath elaborately carved arches, tiny alleyways packed with restaurant tables and chairs. It looked like heaven.

But it had become a hell for her mother, a hell from which she had run blindly into the unknown to escape. What had happened there, to her father? Was the green-clad island in some of the pictures Daksa? No, she wouldn't think about that. Not now she had found a straw of positivity to grasp on to. Provided it was OK with Andrew and with Michael, next week she would go to the travel agent.

Chapter Five

Dubrovnik, 19th September 1944

He turns up his collar against the rain and, leaving the shelter of the colonnade in front of Sponza Palace, walks as fast as he can towards the harbour. But his leg drags worse than ever, and he curses the wet wind from the south that makes it ache this way.

When he first saw Dragica it was raining, and he had been stumbling along on the slippery flagstones. She had glanced up from where she was scrubbing the step outside her uncle's shop and he had looked into her huge, expressive eyes and felt so very ashamed. This beautiful woman, with her soft, round face, would surely only pity half a man like him.

But he had his pride. Nothing if not that. So he managed a smile, lifted his hat and wished her good morning. As he had done for many weeks afterwards, while he plucked up the courage to ask if she would like to watch the sunset with him.

And by the most momentous of miracles, she had said that she would.

Now he must find some nourishing food for her supper. She needs to eat well to feed Safranka properly, and he is used to going without. Even so, hunger cramps his belly, but he hardly dares dream there will be enough for them both. The coins in his pocket would barely buy a single potato, should he be lucky enough to find one.

He can hardly remember what it feels like to have enough food; it is something in their life together they have never known. Oh, to be able to buy Dragica a paper twist of *kroštule*, drenched in sugar and warm from the street seller. Or to take home a slab of cheese that had been brought to the market from the countryside where she grew up, to savour with olive oil and fresh hard-crusted bread. But he must not torture himself like this; he must not dream, but focus on the reality that if there is not enough for his wife to eat, Safranka could sicken and die.

The harbour is full of gently rocking boats and he searches for Vido's among them. The distant white horses proudly ride the gunmetal sea, but here the fishing fleet lies in the crooked elbow of the bay, the towering walls of Svetog Ivana fort a final bastion against the wind and waves. Have the boats even gone out today? If they have not … if his friend has nothing … he cannot think about what he might have to do to feed his family.

Vido's sloop is moored in its usual spot, and his friend raises his hand when he sees him.

"I have been waiting for you. Now I can go home and get dry." He reaches into the bow and pulls out a package. "Bream. A big one. I saved it especially."

His mouth may be watering and his heart – not to mention his stomach – filled with longing, but he shakes his head. "You know I cannot afford bream."

A smile emerges from the depths of Vido's beard. "You can afford it because I charged that bastard priest three times the price for his sardines. It will be good for Dragica" – he looks him up and down – "and for you, my friend. You're so thin. You need to eat as well."

"You are too good to me, Vido, but I thank you. Thank you from the bottom of my heart."

"There is no need for that. We're comrades, you and I. Bound by more than friendship."

"And for that I am forever grateful too."

Vido looks serious for a moment. "Without your courage I would never have found my place in this war, and that is something I will not forget. Because of you, in the future, I will be able to look my children in the eye."

Branko shrugs. "Who else could I trust?"

Vido jumps from his boat and clamps his arm around Branko's shoulder. Together they walk through the arch beneath the walls and across the square in front of the cathedral, where they go their separate ways. The rain drips down his neck and beneath his collar as, clutching his precious parcel, he watches Vido run up the steps. There is one more wish he has for Safranka, a very important one. A friend she can trust with her life.

Chapter Six

Sussex, January 2010

A ndrew stood in the doorway, raindrops studding the turned-up collar of his overcoat.

"I brought you this."

Fran stepped aside to let him in and he hugged her fiercely. What would she do without him?

"You shouldn't be taking this shit from Patti," he continued, "but seeing as I doubt she'll listen to me at the moment I wanted you to have some protection."

"Protection?"

"Yup." He waved a small black gadget under her nose. "Unplug your answerphone and use this instead. When someone phones, their number pops up on the little screen so you can decide whether or not to answer it."

"So she won't be able to leave any more nasty messages?" Fran wrapped her arms tightly around her chest. Oh, not to have to feel sick every time she came home to see that little red button flashing.

"No. Of course the downside is that no one else will be able to either."

Fran managed a smile. "You mean all the people trying to sell me a timeshare or offering to invest my non-existent savings? Everyone who matters has my mobile number anyway."

"And Patti hasn't?"

"No. Nor my email. I don't even think she knows I have them. Thankfully."

Fran made two mugs of tea while Andrew fiddled around with her phone. She hoped he'd have time to stay a little longer. Of course, he lived on the other side of the county, and he was so busy running his estate agency she didn't expect to see much of him, but it was bloody nice when he was here.

Once he'd finished, he joined her on the sofa and helped himself to a chocolate digestive from the tin.

"Hopefully that's spiked Patti's guns," he said. "You don't need this on top of everything else. I know she's our sister and can be an attention-seeking bitch when she puts her mind to it, but all this is beyond unforgivable. I still can't really believe what she did at Dad's funeral."

"Me neither. But … all the same … she hasn't always had it easy."

"And neither have you," he shot back. "Fran, honestly, none of this is of your making."

"Yes, but I've always felt responsible for her accident. I was meant to be keeping an eye on her, remember? I let Mama down so badly."

"And did Mama ever say that?"

"No ... but I can't help the way I feel. And anyway, I should have nipped the bad feeling that started when she was a teenager in the bud ..."

"If I remember rightly, you weren't in too great a place yourself at the time."

It was ground they had covered tens, if not hundreds, of times before. Fran thinking she was, at least in part, to blame for Patti's disfigurement and Andrew never quite seeing it that way. But he was right that her own life had been heading off track when Mama's letter telling her to stay away had arrived, and it had been all the more devastating because of it. Newly married, stuck up a tower block with a tiny baby, and a husband who didn't want to be there any more than she did. No wonder it had all made her feel even more of a failure.

It had taken almost a further two years of misery before, having visited for Sunday lunch, Mama and Daddy waited around the corner until Ray had gone to the pub, then marched back into the flat, helped Fran to pack her and Michael's belongings, and taken her back home to Aldwick to heal.

She'd been in such a bad place she had hardly been able to look after her own and her toddler's basic needs, so, much to Patti's annoyance, Mama had stepped in. It had only taken one hissy fit from Patti for Daddy to come down on her like a ton of bricks, but then she had found more insidious ways to make Fran's life a misery. She had even dropped out of sixth form, saying she couldn't work with Michael in the house, but after a while her parents had sent her away to a posh cookery school near Woking, and peace had descended once more.

Andrew interrupted her thoughts. "So, what's all this about a trip to Dubrovnik? A holiday would do you good."

"Well it depends. If you need help with the probate or anything, of course I won't go."

"There's no need to worry about that. The last piece of paperwork is on the way so then I can file, and we'll be waiting weeks for it to be granted. It's the perfect time, while we can't do anything about the house."

"I'm not sure I could face the house at the moment anyway."

"Me neither. I took the auctioneer around to value some of the better pieces and it was grim. So bloody empty without him."

Fran covered his hand with hers. It wasn't the young boy's hand she had held so many times, taking him to the sea, or while he was learning to cross the road, it was a middle-aged man's with a smattering of dark hairs and slightly crumpled skin.

"Remember when we first moved in?" she asked him. "It was pretty empty then too. Our old furniture from Midhurst rattled around, and I don't suppose they had the money to buy much new to go with it."

Andrew laughed. "And we just sodded off to the beach. We were no help."

"Mama told me to take you if I remember rightly. I was quite awestruck with the responsibility, especially after what had happened with Patti, and then you went and ran into the sea with all your clothes on so I had to follow you."

"I was only four!"

Fran grinned. "We've had such happy times, haven't we? We were so blessed to have them as parents."

"I think we've been pretty good parents too, what with Michael already a partner in a successful business. I couldn't be more proud, you know. He may have followed me into estate agency, but he never once asked for a leg up."

"And your Nick in California, doing his high-tech stuff."

"It's a long way away ..." Andrew looked thoughtful, then smiled. "But it's bloody great for holidays. Talking of which, back to yours. Dubrovnik because you want to find your Yugoslavian roots? I'd be interested to know a bit more about Mama's early life too. She didn't talk about it very much, but then I suppose I never asked her."

"When I was small she told me a little about growing up in the country, but never about her time in the city. I guess talking about her first marriage might have felt disloyal to Daddy. I do feel a bit like I'm being disloyal to his memory wanting to go off there so soon."

"There's nothing disloyal about it. He was the lucky one, remember; he had Mama's and your love for most of his life. Your birth father had so little of it."

"I ... I've never thought of it like that. In fact until recently I've hardly thought about him at all."

"And have you done that DNA test?"

"Yes. I'm waiting for the results. But whatever they are, I've decided I still want to go, as long as you're sure it's all right with you."

"Of course it is. Fran, as a family we owe you so much for looking after Dad, and Mama before him. You've been an absolute rock over the years. You deserve to get away from us for a while." He winked.

Fran nodded. "Then tomorrow I'll book it."

She was rewarded with a gentle punch on the arm. "Attagirl, Fran. Have some fun for once."

It was all very well being brave sitting on the sofa with

Andrew beside her, but once he'd left, his words played heavily on her mind. Yes, she may have been the family's rock, but that was over, so who was she now? In the weeks since Daddy's funeral even her relationship with Andrew had flipped; he was the one looking out for her these days. And close as she was to Michael, he didn't need her. He had his own family, his own life, and that was the way it should be.

She picked up the mugs and carried them into the kitchen, rinsing them under the tap before setting them on the draining board. The terracotta-coloured feature tiles seemed to jump out at her from the wall, reminding her of Dubrovnik's roofs. Could she somehow manage to go there alone? Was she even that brave? But there was nothing for her here if she wasn't needed. Yes, at some point in the near future she'd have to build a different kind of life, but perhaps what she should do right now was to take a break. From herself, if nothing else.

Wiping her hands, Fran poured herself a glass of wine. There was a new mini-series starting tonight with Denis Lawson, and he was the very best sort of eye candy as far as she was concerned. She'd let him distract her for a while then, once she'd slept on it, she'd decide about Dubrovnik tomorrow.

Fran slumped into the low leather chair opposite Parisa.

"You look as though you need a double espresso," her friend said.

"I need a double brandy. I can't remember when I last spent so much money."

"Good. But all the same, I'll buy the coffees."

Fran closed her eyes, allowing the soft strains of some violin concerto or other to wash over her. The money wasn't the half of it. In fact, the crazy thing she'd done had actually saved her some cash. The travel agent had found the most wonderful little apartment in Dubrovnik old town, but it had only been available for a long-term let. All the same, it had still been just about the cheapest option, and she didn't have to stay for the whole three months, did she? Maybe Andrew and Alice could use it as well, after she came back. Or Michael and Paula could have a romantic break there while she looked after the girls.

Parisa placed a tray with two cappuccinos and a couple of chocolate muffins on the low marble-topped table.

"As they aren't licenced, I thought sugar would be a suitable alternative to booze. So spill – what have you booked?"

Fran pulled a couple of pieces of paper from her handbag and spread them on the table. The travel agent had printed them from her computer for her to keep and now she gazed at the pictures again, marvelling at the fact that in just three weeks she would be there.

"It looks very cosy," said Parisa.

Fran laughed. "I knew it wouldn't be your style but it's definitely mine. Small, plain, nothing fancy. But see that gorgeous little terrace? It looks right over the street so I'll be able to sit in the sun and watch the world go by."

"When are you off?"

"More or less as soon as Polly and Joe come back from Italy. Tenth of February."

"And for how long?"

Fran closed her eyes. "I've done something a bit crazy. I've taken it until the end of April. Only the biggest hotels are open at this time of year so it actually worked out cheaper than staying in one of them for three weeks."

Parisa punched the air. "Wow, you're not doing this by halves, are you? You're not just going to find your Croatian roots, you're going to live them."

"I didn't say I was actually going to stay that long."

"But why wouldn't you? You won't miss much here."

"Well if we get probate I'll need to come back sooner to start clearing the house ..."

"And where's the rush with that? If the others are desperate for the cash they can pitch in and do it. Come on, Fran, this is your time. You never do anything for yourself. Live a little for once."

"I have to say, there was a moment when I was sitting in the travel agent when I did feel a bit like when I left home to live in Brighton, the same kind of fizz of excitement. But then I had to hand over my credit card and I was just plain terrified. I mean, what the hell have I done?" She tried to smile. "Which, of course, is the difference between being nineteen and being sixty-five."

"There you go, banging on about your age again. Why should it matter? You're as young as you feel, and if this makes you feel like a teenager on the verge of life's great adventure, even ever so briefly, that can only be good and you ought to channel it."

Fran picked up her coffee. She knew when she sipped it she would end up with a chocolate moustache and Parisa wouldn't. She still didn't know how she managed it. "I think ... I don't know ... when I went to Brighton there was an incredible feeling of freedom, of not being responsible for anyone but myself. I was the oldest, wasn't I, always looking out for the little ones, having to set an example, but suddenly – bam – I could be me."

"Then you really need to find that nineteen-year-old you again, because for the best part of forty years your whole life's been about being the dutiful daughter, the responsible sibling. Not to mention the most incredible mother to Michael. If you think about it, your situation isn't all that different now."

"Except—"

"If you dare mention your age ..." Parisa wagged her finger.

"Sorry."

They sat in silence for a few minutes, then Parisa said, "So we have just under three weeks then? We'd better get started."

"On what?"

"New wardrobe, new make-up, hair cut ... and colour."

"But I can't afford—"

"That's what credit cards are for. Especially when you have a sizeable inheritance heading your way to pay them off. Come on, drink up. We'd better head around to Gorgeous George's and book. We'll go together the week before you leave. Have a manicure as well. It'll be fun."

Fran rolled her eyes, but Parisa was on a mission. "Then we'll pop along to Army & Navy. I noticed the summer stock was coming in. And we can stop at Country Casuals on the way."

"No! I don't shop in those sorts of places."

Parisa put her hand on Fran's arm. "Humour me. We'll just look. I won't make you buy anything you wouldn't wear, honestly. I'm far too fond of you for that. It's just I think updating a few of your clothes might give your confidence a boost. You need to start seeing yourself a little differently, Fran, and looking the part might help."

Sussex, February 2010

Fran poured herself a glass of wine then grated cheese on top of the cottage pie. Upstairs her cases were packed; two huge bags, one of which she'd borrowed from Parisa, mainly full of old favourites with a smattering of the new and alien clothes her friend had encouraged her to buy. She would wear them. One day. There was a denim skirt she liked, with big practical pockets, so she'd start with that.

Oh god, clothes were the least of her worries. The real issue was how the hell she would find the courage to get on that plane tomorrow. She'd never had to navigate an airport on her own before, and what if she turned up in Dubrovnik and there was no taxi to meet her? What if the apartment was a rat-infested wreck, or didn't exist at all? Now it came to it, the whole enterprise was making her feel physically sick.

She'd been nervous enough when she booked it, but right now she would give just about anything not to have to go. Except if she didn't, Parisa would kill her. Not to mention how disappointed Michael would be. It was just as well he was taking her to the airport so she couldn't back out at the last minute.

A key turned in the lock and the front door opened, letting in a blast of freezing air. Fran ran through to the living room and Michael enveloped her in a bear hug. At almost six foot he towered over her, his build and fair hair like his father's. Despite having a desk job he kept himself in good shape with regular visits to the gym, and there were laugh lines around his brown eyes.

"It's so good of you to come this evening."

He hugged her again. "I want to make the most of you before you go."

Fran stepped back and looked at him. "You're OK about it? Really?" Oh please, let him say he wasn't and then she could stay.

"Of course I am, but it doesn't mean I won't miss you just a little bit."

She put on her bravest smile. "I'll certainly miss you, especially our chats. Emailing won't be the same."

Michael disentangled himself from her arms and strode towards the dining area. "I've thought about that. You're taking your laptop, aren't you? There's this thing we use at work called Skype and I'm going to set you up on it so we can make video calls. Then you can see my ugly mug whenever you like and I can check you're really OK when you say you are."

"Honestly? That sounds wonderful."

"I'll do it now." He sat at the table and pulled the machine towards him.

"And I'll get you a beer. Adnams do you?"

He grinned at her. "My favourite. You're spoiling me."

"Just this once. And the cottage pie is ready to put in the oven too."

He sniffed the air. "Do I smell a hint of curried beans?"

"Now why would I leave them out?"

"Oh, Mum. There's nothing quite like being at home. Even when you're forty-two."

As Fran pottered around the kitchen, she thought about

what he'd said. He was right, she supposed. There was a strange and unique feeling about being back in the place you grew up; almost as if you could slough off your responsibilities and become a child again. She remembered it from when she'd first left Aldwick; coming back from Brighton for Sunday lunch, or for a weekend once she'd moved to London. But latterly the feeling of responsibility had followed her wherever she'd been. Even now she had nobody left to look after she seemed to be struggling to shake it off.

Michael broke into her thoughts. "I need to send you a link to verify your account. Is it OK if I log into your email?"

"Of course."

Fran began to rinse the broccoli. He'd probably notice the message, but ...

"I see the results of the DNA test came through."

"Yes. I thought as I was seeing you it would be best to tell you face to face."

Michael looked up at her. "I take it it was positive?"

Fran nodded. "Read the email for yourself."

She stood behind him, her hand on his shoulder, as he took it in. She didn't need to read the words again, she knew them almost off by heart. Her DNA had enabled the researchers to positively identify the remains of Branko Milišić, whose body had been excavated from a mass grave on the island of Daksa. She still felt a little sick reading those words. Whatever he had or had not done, this man's blood flowed through her veins. And Michael's. She may not be able to remember him, but the connection still felt strong.

After supper Michael remained at the laptop while Fran filled the draining board with houseplants to make it easier for Polly to water them. If she let herself think she'd be away until the end of April a kind of panic gripped her, making her palms sweat and her heart beat faster. She had never, ever, not seen Michael for that long. But of course she could come home whenever she liked. She'd promised herself she'd stick it out for the three weeks she'd originally planned, and then she would see.

Wiping her hands on a tea towel she wandered over to the table. "What are you up to? Working?"

"No. I wouldn't waste your last evening doing that. I'm looking up these Daksa executions."

"You're that interested?"

"Of course. But I can't find very much. Just this rather overblown story on a website about haunted Dubrovnik. Stuff like the monks dying singing praises to the lord. How the hell would anyone have known that?"

"Eyewitness reports?"

"I doubt it. It seems the whole thing was shrouded in mystery for years. Further on it says no one was allowed on the island. The one family who lived there was removed while the killing happened, but even when they went back, they didn't stay long before they left completely because of ghostly goings on and seeing human hands sticking out of the soil."

A shiver ran through Fran. "That's horrible. You'd never forget it."

"If it's true."

"Yes, if it's true."

"Will you try to find out more about what happened to your father once you get to Croatia?"

Fran sat down next to him. "I don't know, not now there's a DNA match. I mean, what if he was a fascist?"

"Do it, Mum. I'm curious, and if he wasn't, it would be

good to clear his name. There's something about it that doesn't quite fit. I mean, would Franciscan monks really be Nazi collaborators? It seems unlikely, so maybe other mistakes were made."

"And Mama's Jewish pendant. If my father was a Nazi, why would that be a treasured possession?"

Michael nodded. "Because if he'd looted it, he would have probably sold it. Is it valuable?"

Fran shook her head. "The stones aren't precious and there's no hallmark on the gold so it's most likely plate. It just means a lot to me, that's all, because it was hers."

"You're taking it with you?"

"I hadn't thought about it."

Michael grinned at her. "Wear it tomorrow. Then you'll be going back to your roots together."

Chapter Seven

Dubrovnik, 24th September 1944

He helps Dragica into her best Sunday wrap, the fine woollen one she brought when she came here from the country, then picks up his daughter. Safranka is all in white, her cotton smock embroidered by her mother as she'd sat at the window all the long summer, her belly huge and uncomfortable, her fingers pricked by the needle as she worked. He traces the delicate chain of flowers. It is a shame to cover it with the shawl that was once Dragica's cousin's, but the breeze is cool and it will not do for the baby to catch cold.

They walk down the alleyway together, a family of three for the very first time. Stopping to show Safranka to a neighbour, he cannot remember feeling so proud, taking his beautiful daughter into the city that will become her home. Good wishes and blessings from friends and acquaintances slow their progress until they reach the broad main street. Here sunshine floods the shining paving stones, the air softer and warmer than in the cramped alleyways, and fresh with the salt of the sea.

He pauses and looks at his wife. "You are not too tired?"

"No. And anyway, I will manage. I need to do this."

"Remember going home is up the hill."

She laughs, her face lit up with the smile that won his heart. The hill has been a joke between them ever since they found the apartment. Not only the steps and slopes of the streets, but the mountain inside the building, the wooden staircase that takes them almost to the roof.

"Don't worry," she tells him, "I can rest on the way if I need to."

Towards the harbour the street widens into a square, the tall finger of the clock tower piercing the crystal-blue sky. To their right is the church of Sveti Vlaho, its elaborate frontage cast in shadow. They stop at the bottom of the steps, Dragica's hand on his arm.

"I suppose it is useless to ask you to come with me?"

He shrugs. Looks away. "You know how I feel about religion."

"Not even to light our daughter's candle?"

"It will be purer if you do it alone. You can bless it with belief, whereas I ..."

He watches as she opens the door and the dark interior swallows her up, then he sits on the steps with Safranka in his arms, drinking in the beauty around him. Normally he would simply limp past, head down, but today is different, special. He can almost believe that soon there will be a new beginning for Dubrovnik and its people.

The pale sunshine reflects on the creamy stone of the Sponza Palace where he works, making it glow almost golden, highlighting the corbels that support the rounded arches of the colonnade with their intricately carved leaves and scrolls. In a city full of wonders, he thinks this is surely the most glorious building of all, one of the few to survive the great earthquake. Looking down at Safranka, he begins to murmur the story.

He knows his words will have no meaning for her now, but one day he will teach her about her birthplace and she will grow to love it too. He pictures her as a toddler, then as a little girl … holding his hand as they walk through the streets, listening in awe while he tells her tales of the city's triumphant past and its proud place in history. But not the shameful truth of this war. He shudders and grips her tighter. He will never tell her that. How could she ever love her home if she knew?

Chapter Eight

Dubrovnik, February 2010

F ran listened to the rain rattle on the bedroom window. The light was creeping through the cracks in the shutters telling her it was time to get up. Except she didn't want to. She really didn't want to. Coming to Dubrovnik felt like the worst idea in the world and she hadn't even been here twenty-four hours.

Last night, as she'd cobbled together a meal from the contents of the welcome pack, she'd decided she would start her stay by walking the city walls, but listening to the rain, that didn't seem such a good idea. She wanted sunshine, light, warmth. She could get rain at home, thank you very much. She burrowed under the duvet, close to tears. How the hell was she going to stick this out for the three weeks she'd promised herself? It was bloody tempting to book her ticket back home right now, but Parisa would be down on her like a ton of bricks and she'd never hear the end of it. Not to mention Michael's disappointment she'd thrown in the towel so soon.

She was missing them so much already. And what was she expected to do when it was too wet to go out and explore? How the hell did retired people fill their days? The emptiness she was facing for the next few weeks was nothing compared to the terrifying void that awaited her on her return.

Gripped by a sudden dread, she sat up, hugging her knees to stop herself shaking. Was this it, all of it? A vortex of nothingness spinning infinitely into the future? Absolutely no reason to get up in the morning? Before, she'd always had a purpose: work, Michael, her parents ... Now there was nothing. No one, but no one, actually needed her. If she didn't move from this spot all day, everyone else's worlds would keep on turning. She was completely irrelevant. Irrelevant and old.

Fran's heart thudded unevenly, as though it was struggling to climb into her throat. *That's it, have a coronary.* It wouldn't matter. Not to anyone. But of course that wasn't true. Michael may not need her, but he would certainly miss her. She knew only too bitterly how it felt to lose a parent, the wounds were still so fresh. She couldn't put him through that. She had to look after herself, keep herself going.

She took a deep, shuddering breath. *Come on, Fran, don't let yourself sink. Haul yourself out of the pit. Everyone retires. Everyone manages. Look at Parisa; she's always saying she's far busier than she wants to be. Take a leaf from her book. Find something useful to do.*

Still feeling shaky, she clambered out of bed and headed for the shower. The jets of water made her feel no better and the toothpaste, plucked from an unfamiliar glass shelf, tasted sour in her mouth. Glancing in the mirror she saw nothing but podgy cheeks and lines around her eyes. God, was that really her? It was tempting to curl up on the sofa in her dressing gown but she forced herself to put on proper clothes, albeit old and comfortable ones, all the time struggling to hold back tears.

Don't sink. Don't sink.

Tea. Toast. Marmite from home. No. Instead she opened the fig jam that had been part of the welcome box. It was rich and fruity, the almost sickly sweetness coating her tongue, and after a couple of mouthfuls she felt just a little more alive. It was amazing what sugar could do, she told herself. Except she couldn't keep filling her face with it or she'd be the size of a house.

She had a foothold. She had to keep hauling herself up. She opened the kitchen blind, gazing at the rivulets of water tracing the glass. She needed an inside project for the day and there was only one thing that came to mind. If she wasn't going to stay here long, she should at least get to Daksa and find out all she could about the executions. She might regret it forever if she didn't try to lay her father's ghost to rest.

First, find the island. She had bought an English guidebook before she left the airport, so she opened it at the map of greater Dubrovnik. The island outside the harbour she'd seen from the taxi yesterday was called Lokrum, so that wasn't it. But on the other side of the peninsular a whole chain of them stretched; Koločep, Lopud, Šipan. But no Daksa that she could see. How very odd.

Next to the narrow kitchen was a narrow living room, where Fran had left her laptop. Everything about this apartment was narrow, Fran thought. Narrow and ... stifling. No, that was too negative; it was compact. Yes, that was the word. Not an inch of space was wasted; the sofa exactly the width of the lounge, the bedroom just the right size for her to be able to walk around the bed and the old oak wardrobe fitted into a niche next to the door. Today the exposed stone walls seemed to press in on her, but she forced herself to remember how charming she had found it all, with its cosy throws and cushions, when she'd first arrived. Was that really just last night?

She should be used to living alone. Apart from when she'd been caring for first her mother and then for Daddy, she had been on her own in her house for almost twenty years. She even liked it. But she'd been working then, busy, her friends around her, her parents just down the road, her life so full she'd had no time to think. Was that the problem now? She was thinking too much?

The mental space had begun to open up during the last months of Daddy's life. Much as he'd needed her near him, he had begun to wear out, to sleep more and more, even in the day. She'd been pretty much trapped in the house with little to do, and once she had started to read about Croatia, it had become somewhere to escape to in her mind. It was almost as if the country of her birth had found an empty corner and begun to trickle into it.

She had always been a busy person so maybe there simply hadn't been the space for it to happen before. From school to secretarial college, partying in Brighton and then London ... and of course once she fell pregnant with Michael and married Ray ... those awful years when she'd all but died inside. She pulled herself up short. She couldn't allow that to happen again. Mama and Daddy weren't here to drag her out of any mess she made now. She had to do it herself.

Right, first she needed to find out where this bloody island was. She'd assumed it was close to Dubrovnik, but that wasn't necessarily the case. She opened Google and typed 'Daksa', but not a lot came up. Really only that article Michael had found, and she could come back to it in a moment. Hopefully if she searched the maps she would find the actual place.

A boomerang-shaped piece of land appeared on her screen, incredibly with three churches at its southern end. She broadened the view to find it more or less blocked the entrance to Dubrovnik's commercial port, Gruž, much closer to the mainland than the chain of islands on the tourist map. And much smaller. Perhaps that was why it hadn't even been named. It was so close it shouldn't be a problem to get one of the trip boats to take her there. She'd seen pictures of them lining the old harbour, and if it stopped raining later, she would walk down there and ask.

She flicked back to the article and immediately found out that in medieval times the island had been a monastery, so that at least explained the churches. There was a picture of it too, long and low in a churning grey sea, a rocky shore topped with thick, dark vegetation.

The language the writer had used was flowery to say the least, but Fran tried to ignore references to dark pines trying to hide bloody horrors and concentrate on the facts. If, indeed, facts they were. But at least it was a place to start, and she began to scribble a few notes.

Apparently the partisans had entered Dubrovnik on 18th October 1944. Who had been in charge before? She assumed the Germans, but it didn't say. Anyway, the partisans had rounded up three hundred people they assumed to be collaborators, or at very least had Nazi sympathies. On 24th

October dozens of them were taken from the prisons where they had been kept to Daksa, and for several days and nights afterwards they were executed. A few days later a proclamation had appeared with the names of thirty-six collaborators, including her own father's. Had her mother run away because she was frightened or because she was ashamed?

She stopped reading before the article descended into complete ghoulishness. She had the facts. A few of them, anyway, but of course she had no idea how her father had been implicated. On one hand, they had arrested hundreds of people and there had only been fifty-odd bodies found, so there must have been some sort of selection process, a collection of evidence, even if it fell far short of any sort of trial. On the other, had he just been an innocent man caught up in some general round up? It could have been the case, couldn't it? It had all happened so quickly, perhaps mistakes had been made. But with the rain lashing against the windows it was more than easy to believe the worst of him and wonder why the hell she had come here in the first place.

She kept coming back to it; why did it matter? She had no doubt she'd had a better life because of his death. If she'd grown up in this city, however beautiful it might be when it finally stopped tipping it down, it would have been under communism, and although Yugoslavia's particular brand of it had seemed pretty benign from the outside world at least, she wouldn't have had the freedoms she'd enjoyed in England. And of course she would have lived through the war in the early nineties, and Michael, or any son she may have had in this parallel universe, would have been of the age where he'd have been expected to fight. Fran shuddered. No, it was so much better the way things had turned out.

But that didn't mean she wasn't curious. What had happened to her father, the sort of man he'd been, was part of her history. And what was more, it was part of Michael's too. He'd been so interested, she couldn't let him down by coming here and doing nothing about it. She had to at least try to find out what she could.

Fran put her laptop on the coffee table and stood up to stretch. She had to admit she was feeling just a little bit more like herself. The rain was still streaming down the window so she wandered through to the kitchen to make herself another cup of tea. She'd email Parisa to tell her she'd arrived while she drunk it, then make a shopping list, and after that, complete the next module of her Croatian course. If she was going to do any serious research, she would need a better grasp of the language and it was comforting to have a plan to fill her time.

By half past four it had stopped raining and although a day of getting on with solid tasks had made Fran feel better, she was absolutely desperate to get out of the apartment and at least clap eyes on another human being. The slit of sky she could see between the buildings looked ominously grey, so she put on her waterproof and set off down the deserted street, the paving beneath her feet glistening and a little slippery in places.

The apartment was tucked into what was little more than a narrow alley that climbed towards the most inland tower in the walls surrounding the old town. Mostly it was made up of flights of steps cut from dark grey stone, contrasting with the creamy walls of the houses crammed together on either side. On almost every ledge and doorstep were pots filled with a variety of leafy green plants, some with delicate pink flowers, their heads too small to have been bowed by the rain.

Further down the hill, just before the main street, Stradun, the path levelled out and there was a small café. A waiter was working under its awning, wiping down the tables and chairs that all but filled the narrow street, bending his long skinny frame to clean the water from their metal legs.

He turned and looked at Fran, shaking a mop of brown hair out of his eyes. *"Dobar dan."*

"Dobar dan."

He switched into English, but she wasn't surprised her foreign accent was so obvious. "You would like a coffee maybe? Or some wine?" He consulted his watch. "It isn't too early for wine. Not when it is so wet it is almost dark outside."

It hadn't been part of her plan, but Fran was delighted at the prospect of someone to talk to, even if only to order a drink and pass the time of day. She started to pull out a chair but he shook his head.

"No. Inside. I am sure it will rain again so I have not put the cushions."

The interior of the café was dark but cosy, the unplastered stone walls and timbered ceiling the same as in her apartment. In one corner was the bar, its wood blackened with age and covered in heavy carvings that at home would have screamed Victorian. A red velveteen upholstered bench ran along the wall beside it, and it was at a small table here that the waiter gestured Fran to sit.

"I can clean the glasses while we talk. Now, would you like red wine or white? Or maybe even the local *rakija*?"

After the day she'd had, Fran didn't need too much tempting, although she decided it was best to keep off the strong stuff. "A glass of red, please."

"We have a small carafe. If you want two glasses it is cheaper." He grinned at her, his hazel eyes shining. Honestly, he looked far too young to be working in a bar, but perhaps everyone under thirty did these days.

"You are a good salesman."

He leant forwards conspiratorially. "I'll give you free olives. The boss is out."

"I wouldn't want you to get into trouble."

That cheeky grin again. "Don't worry, I won't. My name is Vedran, by the way. I'm a student at the university."

Fran took off her coat and settled onto the bench while he bustled around behind the bar. "Tell me, what are you studying?"

"Law. It is hard. Very hard. But it will be worth it because I will get a good job at the end."

"Is it harder because you work as well, so you have less time to study?"

"A little. But that is normal. I am lucky, better than most students anyway, because I can live with my parents, so I do not always have to cook and wash clothes when I get home."

He set the carafe of wine and a glass in front of her, then returned with a plate of olives, sitting down on the chair opposite. "But that is too much about me. You are visiting the city? We don't have many tourists at this time of year."

"Yes. I've taken an apartment just up the street. My mother

was from Dubrovnik. In fact, I was born here, but I left as a baby."

He tipped back his chair. "Really? This is the first time you've come back?"

"Yes. I didn't ..." – she struggled to find the words – "have the time or the money before."

"So now you've come home and I have a new customer. What's your name?"

"It's Fran. I was christened Safranka, but my mother only ever used it when she was cross with me."

"Well I am not cross so I will call you Fran. You plan to stay here?"

She shook her head. "In England I have a son, granddaughters, a brother I am fond of. I've rented the apartment until the end of April, but in truth I don't know how long I will stay."

"But why would you leave when you have paid for it?"

Only about a million reasons, but if she said she was lonely it would sound like a cry for help, and anyway, how would a young man like Vedran understand the frankly terrifying sense of isolation she had felt that morning?

She shook her head. "I don't know. Perhaps ... I don't want to make too many plans." She picked up her glass and took a slug of wine. "But there are some things I want to do. Like a boat trip to Daksa."

Vedran looked serious. "It will be hard to find anyone to take you there. It's a bad place; haunted."

Really? He believed that? "There must be someone ..."

"Not the trip boat owners. To go there now would bring them bad luck for the whole season. Why do you want to visit?"

There would come a time when she'd have to tell someone, and awkward as it felt she might as well get it over with. Much as she didn't want him to think ill of her, it would be interesting to gauge the reaction of an impartial observer. "My father, although I never knew him, was executed on the island. It was why my mother left."

Vedran shook his head. "That was an awful time in our history, with Yugoslavian pitted against Yugoslavian. But that, I think, is the way in the Balkans. Perhaps we need to be divided as we are today to have peace."

"It seems ..." – she searched for the words – "a complicated place."

"Yes. So you will definitely need to stay more than a few weeks if you want to understand it."

"I'm not sure how I'd begin to do that."

"Living here will be enough, I think. You have begun by talking to me. Talk to other people as well. Your neighbours, the women who work in the shops and on the Green Market, although they are from the country, so perhaps don't have so much English."

"I have a little Croatian. I am trying to learn."

"That is very good. Talk to them, Fran. About their lives, their experiences. About the food they cook. Food is very important here. It's the right time of year to do it, because in the summer everyone is busier. Now there are opportunities for conversation.

"And the museums are open. You can visit those for the history, and perhaps the city archives. And once you understand enough language, watch the news on our television so you know what is important today." His eyes were shining. "You are so lucky, Fran. If I had been born in

England, brought here to grow up, then could go back, I would jump at the chance."

Fran felt herself smiling. "And I spent this morning wondering how to fill my days. But still, the language will be a huge barrier ..."

"No. Most people speak at least some English." He wagged his finger. "Don't make excuses."

She picked up her wine. It was all right for him to say all this, he wasn't sixty-five. But was that just an excuse too? Parisa would say so. As would Michael. And somehow the gloom of the day was slipping away just a little, a tingle of excitement taking its place. Could she shake off her misery and do this? Was it just about possible? There was only one way to find out.

Chapter Nine

Dubrovnik, 29th September 1944

Head down against the drizzle, he hurries around the corner into Ulica Žudioska. It looks no different to the other narrow thoroughfares that thread through the city, but here the buildings close in on him as if they are determined to shut out the sliver of mountain and sky beyond. He does not come here if he can help it. It is too full of ghosts.

But he is the mayor's lowly errand boy, delivering instructions and messages to the web of collaborators who poison every corner of his city, so visit the old Jewish quarter he must. And if he hates coming here, then he hates the nature of his business even more. And the weather, and the way his leg aches.

Oh, he is nothing but misery today. Rumours circulate of a German retreat, but still there is no sign of them leaving. And who would replace them if they did? The Ustaše is planning to fight on, and the city's walls are thick, its defences strong. Will the partisans even bother to take it, or will his dreams of fairness and freedom die like the leaves in the wind?

He stops outside the old synagogue to catch his breath. Its slender arched windows are empty of glass, the door splintered and hanging from its hinges. It says everything to him; everything about how the beautiful city he loves has become the darkest of places, filled with suspicion and fear.

The night the damage was done is not one he will forget. The night that belief in his fellow countrymen deserted him. That night he witnessed the hatred in their eyes; hatred of difference, of things they had never learned to understand. And Dragica wonders why he has no time for religion.

Before then he had simply ignored it, as had his father, which was probably what had allowed his friendship with Solly to flourish. He thinks back to when he first saw him, a gangly ten-year-old with round wire glasses, sitting on his mother's front step. The boy who had stood his ground to defend the child with the dragging leg when the other children teased him.

They lived on neighbouring alleyways just yards from where he is standing now. After his long illness he had wanted nothing more than to be like the other boys, but all his attempts to join in with their street games had brought at best laughter and at worst derision. Solly had shown him perhaps being like them wasn't possible, that because he was different too, he had learned there was more than one way of being accepted.

Theirs was a bond that had only strengthened over the years, the boy who couldn't run and the boy who looked at the world through thick pebble glasses. Their loyalty to each other had been absolute as they grew into manhood, so it was little wonder that Solly had turned to him in his hour of need. And he had done what he could. Everything he could. Only after the end of the war will he know if it has been enough.

Chapter Ten

Dubrovnik, February 2010

F ran knew she shouldn't have doubted Vedran's local knowledge, but a few calls to boat trip companies had put her in no doubt they were not prepared to make the trip to Daksa. Two had made excuses but the third had been blunt; the island was bad news and no amount of money would tempt him to go there. Perhaps once they all opened for business at Easter, provided she was still here, she might find someone, but for the moment her attempts to see the place her father had died were well and truly frustrated.

The only other lead she had was the necklace. Again she had sought Vedran's advice, as most of the jewellers on Stradun were closed in winter, and he had pointed her in the direction of an old-fashioned family business opposite the Imperial Hotel. It was where his uncle took his watch to be serviced, he told her. They were honest and reliable.

Even though she'd been in Dubrovnik for almost a week,

Fran had yet to venture through the famous Pile Gate, so it was probably about time she did. So far she had really enjoyed the compactness of the old town; it made her feel safe. It was easy to see from one end of Stradun to the other, and she loved threading her way up flights of steps and down narrow, sloping alleys, pausing to peep into courtyards that in summer would be covered with vines, and gazing across to the rust-coloured rooftops cascading down from the seaward walls. If nothing else, getting to know every twist and turn of this beautiful city was filling her days.

It was a short and familiar walk to Onofrio's fountain, but this time she passed it and went through the arch beyond. She was momentarily plunged into darkness and she shivered, almost running up the steps on the other side. Goodness, she never ran anywhere, but emerging into the sunshine she was pleasantly surprised she wasn't out of breath. Maybe she could take up jogging and lose a bit of weight.

Outside the gate she was in another world. Beyond the elegantly balustraded bridge over the moat was an open plaza surrounded by modern buildings. Traffic cruised past on a road to her right and a couple of buses idled nearby, belching diesel fumes into the still morning air. It was as if someone had broken a spell and she had tumbled back into the twenty-first century.

As she crossed the bridge she'd glanced to her left where the sea sparkled in the morning sun, and although it would take her out of her way, Fran turned her back on the traffic and headed towards it. The stepped path she took followed a wide stone staircase that hugged the wall of an old Italianate house, its plaster chipped but shutters freshly painted, terracotta tubs of leafy green geraniums guarding the front door.

This time last year she'd been planting geraniums into pots herself in the greenhouse, with Daddy wrapped up in his coat and scarf issuing instructions both of them knew she didn't need. Grief gripped her and she felt herself well up. How come it could spring from the smallest of things? She scrubbed her eyes with her fist then carried on down the steps.

At the bottom was a short concrete promenade which ran along the edge of an enclosed bay completely dominated by an enormous rock and the ruins of a castle high to her right. Its grey bulk was perched hundreds of feet up on an outcrop, dark green vegetation spilling from beneath its walls almost to the sea. The sea that was so clear that Fran could make out every stone beneath the shimmering surface, every fish darting silver between them.

It was so very peaceful here, and beautiful, with just the wash of the waves and the bobbing wagtails for company. She walked out along the stone-built jetty then turned back to look at the shore. In summer the place would be buzzing, but now the cafés and bars were boarded up, the kayak hire operation nothing but a battered sign. Wouldn't it be fun to explore the city walls from the water? She guessed she would have to wait until April, when Vedran said everything opened.

Would she still be here? A large part of her longed to be at home, watching the snowdrops she'd planted along the edge of her borders come into flower, bringing with them the promise of spring. But for the next few weeks at least she needed to stay where she was and make the best of it; she just couldn't let everyone down by turning tail and running away without giving it a decent shot. They expected better of her – a family rock should at least exhibit a degree of backbone.

Her enthusiasm for learning all things Croatian ebbed and

flowed, but it was certainly a good way to pass the time and she made sure she spent at least a couple of hours each afternoon working on her language. It gave her life some much-needed structure. It was fun to try out new words and phrases on Vedran, and he had taken to bringing newspaper clippings to the bar, which they read together. He was such a lovely boy, if only she could do something for him in return.

So at times she had a purpose, but at others, especially during the long evenings, she felt she was in a strange kind of limbo with Dubrovnik as a staging post between two lives. The life she'd had before was closed to her now and she had to forge a new one. She still couldn't begin to imagine what that might be.

Oh, of course she had ideas. In a practical sense she had come to realise that when she went home she could fill her days in exactly the way Parisa did. She would take on a few volunteering roles, continue learning Croatian. Maybe even join a sea swimming group to keep herself fit. There would be plenty to do, all right. But somehow it didn't feel enough. She could be busy left, right and centre, but where would she really be needed? That was the problem with Mama and Daddy gone, and Michael grown up; nobody actually needed her anymore, and she was coming to understand that this, more than anything, was making her feel like a rudderless ship.

Fran sighed. This wasn't getting her anywhere. She'd best go and find that jewellery shop. So she retraced her steps and set out along the traffic-filled street. Vedran had said it wasn't far, and she could already see the imposing Imperial Hotel on the other side of the road. It really was breathtaking, rising high behind its strip of manicured garden like an elaborately decorated pink and white layer cake. She knew her mother had worked in a hotel; had it been somewhere as swanky as this?

The jeweller was in a row of old stone buildings, its window display a pleasing mixture of modern and antique, although the prices were fairly eye-watering. Fran was neither buying nor selling, but it did make her wonder if she would need to pay for their advice. Well, it wouldn't hurt to ask, and she had been rehearsing the Croatian words to herself for most of the morning.

The woman behind the counter was about forty, her brown hair swept stylishly into a chignon. As soon as Fran closed the door behind her, she smiled and asked how she could help. Taking a deep breath, Fran explained she had an antique necklace she would like a professional opinion on, but please could she speak slowly so she could understand.

The woman put her head on one side. "You are English?"

Fran blushed. "Yes. I'm learning Croatian, but—"

"Then please do not think me rude. It is just with so many English and American visitors it is important to speak your language and perhaps it will be easier for you."

Reassured by the woman's friendly manner, Fran took the necklace out of her bag and unwrapped its tissue paper nest. She had ignored Michael's exhortation to wear it to travel here. In fact she had never worn it. It felt far too precious for that.

The woman picked it up. "It is Jewish, certainly. Do you know anything of its history?"

"Only that my mother took it with her when she left Dubrovnik in 1944. My … I think my father gave it to her."

Sympathy filled the woman's eyes. "So your father was a Jew?"

"No … no. But he died all the same."

There was an illuminated magnifier on the counter and the woman switched it on and put the pendant under it, turning it over and over to examine it from every side.

"I can see no hallmark, but perhaps it is too old. I am certain it is gold, probably twenty-two carats."

"Really? I always assumed it was plate."

"It would be hard to work plate this finely and anyway, why would you bother?" She shrugged. "But on the other hand the stones are semi-precious, although they are often used in Jewish pieces. Have you asked at the Jewish museum?"

"I didn't know there was one."

"Oh yes. It is in the same building as the synagogue in Župioska Street. You know it?"

"I'm sure I can find it."

The woman nodded as she handed the necklace back. "It's easy. You walk down Stradun almost as far as the Sponza Palace and the road is on your left."

The fact there was a Jewish museum in Dubrovnik both fascinated and frightened Fran. Had the city been an important Jewish centre? What had happened to them during the war? Although, she was fairly sure she could guess the answer to that one and the thought of it made her feel rather sick. If her father had been a Nazi collaborator, had he played any part in the holocaust? Even though she had never known the man, that would be too much to bear. Not least because her mother had regarded him a hero.

It couldn't be. Her mother could never have admired

someone like that. Her mother had been gentle, kind, and never to Fran's knowledge remotely racist. She had always welcomed Parisa into their home, never once mentioning her different background or the colour of her skin, which many people would have done at the time. Then in the late seventies she had worked tirelessly to help Vietnamese boat people who arrived in England as refugees. Fran just couldn't believe the mother she knew and loved would have thought a fascist a good man.

She may never discover the truth of it, but it might help her if she could pin down a few more facts. Go to this Jewish museum and take a look around. There may even be other jewellery like the necklace, although where that fitted into the picture she couldn't even begin to understand.

After lunch she headed back down the steps to Stradun. The sun glistened from the shiny paving stones and illuminated shopfronts tucked behind asymmetrical arches, half window and half door. Most were shuttered to the world, but the minimarket was open, although Vedran told her the food shops beyond the Ploče Gate were cheaper, especially outside the tourist season. She would go there after the museum, but what would she make for supper tonight? So far it had been the same things she cooked at home, but one of these days, she promised herself, she would try some new ingredients.

Stradun led towards a white-grey, square stone clock tower, pointing like an elegant finger into the sky. Beyond it rose the hills she had skirted in the taxi from the airport, hills that plunged into a silver-blue sea topped with foamy white horses, spreading so far into the distance it merged with the grey line of the horizon. It was odd, within the walls she was barely aware of that great expanse of water; there was something about the place that made her feel cocooned from the real world and she didn't know if that was a good thing or not.

At the end of Stradun, tucked just within the city walls in a small square, was the Sponza Palace with its delicately arched colonnade, the first-floor windows above it looking as though they had been stolen from a medieval cathedral. The quiet calm of the open space in front only accentuated its delicate beauty, but as she looked carefully, she noticed the arch nearest the walls was smaller than the others. That asymmetry again, like the frontages of the shops. It looked perfect at first glance, but it wasn't, not quite, and somehow the thought made her smile.

She turned away to look at the baroque church of Sveti Vlaho opposite, with its broad flight of shallow steps. Its huge wooden door was weighed down by an arch supporting a figure of a man and two flamboyant chubby cherubs. Impressive as it was, it really wasn't to her taste. Maybe if she'd been brought up to be religious then she would have seen it differently.

She started to walk along the plain side wall of the church, towards the street behind it and the irregularly shaped square where the Green Market was. She had been there a couple of times after Vedran had mentioned it, but now it was too late in the day and the row of trestle tables where three or four women sold their wares would be packed away. And anyway, she needed to stop prevaricating and locate this Jewish museum, not wander off in the opposite direction.

Fran had little trouble finding Žudioska Street, although she was surprised the synagogue was such an anonymous building. She remembered the imposing one in the centre of

Brighton, with its polished pink marble columns flanking each window, topped with red, black and blue bricks. Here in Dubrovnik its location was only given away by the notice on the front door.

All the same, that door was open, and Fran peeped around it. Seeing a sign for the museum pointing up the stairs she climbed them, her footsteps echoing on the polished wooden treads.

There was no one at the desk on the tiny landing halfway up, but it was clear this was where the museum was, so Fran left her entrance fee tucked under a stapler next to the till. The first room was cramped and dominated by two display cases, one filled with an enormous Torah scroll, which the English version of the card below told her dated from the fourteenth century. However had it survived?

The other cabinet contained a number of religious artefacts, including some in a similar style of traced gold to the pendant, albeit on a grander scale. One resembled a large crown, elaborately decorated with zigzags, circles and curlicues, all beaten out from behind in tiny perfect points. The embroidery on the vestments next to it was astounding too.

Fran walked into the second room, which was almost as small as the first. Immediately her attention was drawn to a yellow armband in a small black case, the sheer horror of seeing an artefact from the holocaust era, a symbol of such hatred, took her breath away. To steady herself she peered at the documents surrounding it, wondering if she had enough Croatian to make any sense of the words.

"You are interested in our culture?" Fran hadn't heard the man approach and she jumped, swivelling around to face him.

He was perhaps a little younger than her, bald and painfully thin, with paper-fine skin and piercing grey eyes.

"I know little about it. Your history—"

"What is your first language?" he snapped.

Goodness, had her attempt at communication been that bad? She felt herself blush. "English."

"Then I will speak to you in that. My English will be better than your Croatian." Fran must have been open-mouthed, as he shrugged. "I did not mean it badly. It is just the truth."

"Oh. OK."

"So is this what you want to know about?" He gestured towards the case with the yellow armband. .

"Yes. I ... er..."

"So many tourists do, because persecution is all they have heard of our faith, which you could say is a little insulting. But I will tell you anyway, then you will perhaps appreciate the treasures we have here, and what a miracle it was we managed to hide them before the Nazis arrived. Although of course not all of them were returned to us, but that's as may be. There are always people who seek to profit from those who are persecuted in times of conflict, people who should not have been trusted.

"When the war started, we had eighty members in our community and twenty-seven died. Their names are on this memorial scroll." He tapped the frame.

"That's so sad."

"Of course it is sad, but it was better here than in many places. In other parts of Yugoslavia, even at the beginning of the occupation, the Croatian Ustaše were in charge. They were here too, everywhere, spreading their hatred, and we had our own Kristallnacht when the synagogue was damaged, but then the Italians arrived to occupy the city and they left us alone.

"For a while our numbers even grew as people fled from other parts of the country, but in November '42 they were told to intern us. Some in the harbour at Gruž, but many on the island of Lopud. The next summer they started to transfer our people to the camp at Rab, so by the time the Italians surrendered in September '43 there was no one left.

"It was being at Rab that saved us, because before the Germans could properly take control of the area, the partisans freed many Jews to fight and work with them. Only around two hundred were left in the camp and they were sent to Germany, so of course they did not survive."

He had clearly come to the end of his practised spiel, but despite his matter-of-fact manner his words left Fran feeling chilled to the bone. The fascist Ustaše had been everywhere in Dubrovnik. Perhaps her father had been one of them after all? She bowed her head. "Thank you for explaining it so well."

"It is important to educate people so these mistakes do not happen again. The far right are gaining influence in our country. Everyone must understand what that could mean."

As Fran nodded, she thought of the necklace, buried deep in her handbag. He was just the sort of person who might know about it, but it was beyond her to admit her father might have played a part in the bad things that had happened to his community. The very thought of it made her want the floor to swallow her up. But now she was here, she might as well bite at least part of the bullet.

"I … I have a necklace. I think it's from Dubrovnik and dates from that period or earlier. I'm told it's Jewish and I would like to know more about it."

He was leaning against the wall, his arms folded tightly across his chest. There was a translucency to his skin that was almost frightening, his cheekbones stark beneath his shining eyes.

"Show me."

Fran fumbled in her handbag, removed the necklace and unwrapped it, holding it in the flat of her hand.

"May I?" He picked it up without waiting for an answer, his fingers cold against her palm.

Fran watched as he examined it, turning it over and over.

His head jerked up. "Where did you get it?"

"My mother gave it to me. Why?"

"It looks like part of our missing treasure." His hand started to close around it, but Fran was quicker, grabbing it back by its chain. They stood, glaring at one another.

"Give it to me," he said. "I need to consult someone."

"I'm sorry, no." Fran stuffed it into the depths of her handbag.

"But it is important to our community."

Fran felt as though her heart was in her throat. This was the only link she had that took her back to the Dubrovnik her mother had known. There was no way she was letting it go.

"Not as important as it is to me," she told him tartly. Clutching her bag she stalked past the display cases in the outer room then down the stairs, but once she was outside, she all but ran along the narrow street until she reached the wide, sunny expanse of Stradun.

Fran's visit to the museum had left her shaken so she was more than usually delighted to receive a text from Michael asking if she fancied a Skype call tonight. It would be good to share her newly jumbled thoughts about her father; perhaps he might even be able to help her to sort them out.

After her flight down Žudioska Street Fran had stood for a while in the harbour, the wind ruffling her hair as she watched a couple of about her own age wash down the deck of their yacht. It was called *Petite Liberté* and was registered in Nice so she guessed they must be travelling the Med. How glorious to have someone to embark on such an adventure with.

There had been a few times in Fran's life when she'd regretted her single status, but not many. When Michael had left home she had considered dating, and a colleague had even asked her out a few times, but they had never moved beyond friendship because it hadn't felt right to her. She'd been far happier sitting at home, falling in love with the heroes in the romantic novels she read, or watching Sean Connery or Tom Jones on TV. Celebrities she'd grown up with who were still pretty damn sexy. It was such a shame that women like her didn't stand the test of time as well, but when all was said and done her fantasies were so much safer.

She didn't need a man to go out and about with, as some women seemed to. She supposed it was easier because her best friend was single too. But it was having that significant other, a person who needed you and loved you pretty much unconditionally … When Daddy had died, that was what she had lost. And although she knew Michael would do anything for her, as she would for him, he had his own life, his own family. They were his priority now, and that was the way it should be.

Perhaps if things hadn't gone so very sour with Ray she would have felt differently about dating. The whole thing had been such an awful mistake and had got all caught up with Patti starting to blame her for her accident too. She'd been too low to feel anything but horribly responsible for everything bad that had happened around her, and although she understood the reasons for it now, it was a feeling she'd struggled to shift down the years, to ever rediscover the happy-go-lucky teenager that once she'd been.

Much as she loved her family, at nineteen she'd been desperate for a taste of freedom, and when one of the girls she'd been at secretarial college with asked if she'd like to share a flat in Brighton where they both worked, Fran had jumped at the chance.

Brighton in 1963 had been everything staid and parochial Chichester wasn't. There'd been a slightly edgy undercurrent beneath the holiday town image, which Fran had found thrilling. They'd seen – but not heard – The Beatles play at the Hippodrome, although they had felt far too grown up and cool to scream themselves; bought daring above-the-knee skirts in The Lanes, and wore them to parties held in flats belonging to people they'd met in the pub.

At first it had felt strange to only care about herself, but after a while it had become liberating, and she had even stopped going home to her parents for Sunday lunch every week. Then after a year or so the finance company where she worked as a secretary had asked if she wanted a transfer to London. A room was free in a shared house where another college friend lived so it had seemed as though fate was calling her.

Perhaps fate had been. The house was in Parsons Green on

the less fashionable end of the King's Road and they spent their free time either there or in the bars of Soho. Fran had been young, with a bit of money in her pocket, so had been determined to have a good time.

Even before she met Ray, one of her favourite places had been the Marquee club in Wardour Street. Looking back she marvelled at the artists she had seen; The Who, David Bowie, and her favourites, The Kinks. Watching Ray Davies growl out 'You Really Got Me' had certainly brought a tremble to her knees. It still might now, to be honest. At the time she'd been in the middle of the sixties' music revolution and hadn't even realised. It had just been what they did.

She'd seen her own Ray in the club a few times, and as they were leaving one night he'd asked if she would go for a drink with him sometime. When she'd gazed at him from afar, admiring his shock of blond hair and sharp mod suit, he'd seemed like the coolest man alive, but he'd been quite nervous about asking her out and that had endeared him to her even more.

They'd shared a love of music, and in those heady days that had seemed to be enough. Ray was a motor mechanic who'd grown up in Battersea and worked for one of the swanky car dealerships in Mayfair. It had opened his eyes to another world, one he claimed to aspire to, but rather belatedly Fran had realised he didn't have either the brains or the work ethic to reach it. But by that time they were married and living in a high rise flat south of the river, and it was far too late to do anything about it.

Fran had lost her virginity in the house in Parsons Green about three months after she met Ray. They'd been a little drunk, but it had felt all right, and after all, everyone was doing it, weren't they? Ray had used a condom, but he didn't much like them, and being a single woman meant Fran didn't have access to the pill so when after a while they'd become a little careless, the inevitable had happened and she'd found herself pregnant.

She had been more than a little relieved when Ray had suggested they married. Far too ashamed to tell her parents the reason for their hasty decision, she didn't even invite them. They had booked a slot at the registry office on the King's Road with two of Fran's housemates for witnesses, and pretended to themselves they were minor celebrities on the run from the press. It was one of the last times Fran could remember them actually having any fun together.

Once Fran finished her supper, she poured herself a large glass of wine and settled on the sofa in front of her laptop, waiting for Michael's face to appear. When he did, he was sitting at his kitchen table and for the first part of the call the girls joined him, excited to see their gran on the screen and ripping a huge hole in her heart because she couldn't hug them. After a while Paula ushered them away, saying it was Belle's bedtime, blowing a kiss to Fran before leaving her and Michael alone.

"So, was the jeweller able to tell you anything?"

Fran rolled her eyes. "There's a whole long story about the necklace, but first a bit of good news. When I was coming back today, Vedran, the young waiter I told you about, stopped me. His uncle has a boat and he's willing to take me to Daksa."

"Wow – that's a big result. When are you going?"

"Next week sometime. There's a problem with its radio he needs to fix first apparently."

"I hope it's not some old rust bucket …"

"So do I. But really, the island isn't far."

"Well just don't take any risks."

Fran laughed. "Honestly, you sound just like I did before you went on your first ski trip."

"They do say roles reverse."

"I'm not that old!"

"You're not old at all, Mum, and don't you forget it. Anyway, what's happened with the necklace?"

Fran told him about the visit to the jewellers, and the less than pleasant encounter at the Jewish museum.

"That was pretty uncalled for," Michael said.

"I know, and it freaked me out. I thought he wasn't going to give me the necklace back. But thinking about it since, the poor man actually looked quite ill, so maybe that was the reason he acted so strangely."

"That's typical of you, making excuses for other people's bad behaviour. Just don't take any shit from the barman's uncle, OK?"

Fran hadn't even considered what kind of person her boatman could be, but it would only be for a few hours so it didn't much matter. It would be a means to an end.

"Enough. I can look after myself. But I do have a theory I want to run past you."

Michael took a sip of his beer and nodded. "Shoot."

"The necklace is more valuable than we thought, and that could back up your theory it had some personal meaning for your grandfather, or he would surely have sold it. But what if … what if …" The words stuck in Fran's throat. "Say it was part of the Jewish treasure. What if he was one of the fascist Ustaše who took part in that Kristallnacht the guide mentioned, and he took loads of it to sell and just kept the necklace because Mama especially liked it or something? She mightn't even have known where it came from. Or what he'd done to get it."

There. It was out. The thought that on top of everything else her father was at best a looter, at worst a thief.

Michael sat back in his seat and smiled. "Now that is quite a plausible theory. Well done, Mum, I think you've cracked it."

Oh no. She hadn't really expected him to believe it, and his doing so somehow made it seem like the obvious answer. "But it's awful, having a father like that. I'm not even sure I want to see where he met his end right now. It sounds as though he bloody deserved it."

"Yes, but don't forget, he may have been your birth father, but Grandad brought you up. It's kind of like me and my dad really. I may have his genes, but I haven't seen him for thirty-five years and he's had no influence on my life at all."

Fran leant forwards. "Don't you sometimes wonder what happened to him though? Where he is, what he's doing?"

"Only if I'm south of the river and it crosses my mind I might run into him. But I don't think I'd know him now anyway, and he certainly wouldn't know me. He didn't want to know me, did he, Mum, once he had a new family? And that's pretty stinging when you're seven years old. But with Grandad, bless his soul, I didn't need Dad after all. And I guess it was the same for you."

"I couldn't have wanted a better father." Fran felt choked inside but fought the emotion from her voice.

"Well there you go. This Branko Milišić is just an interesting bit of family history, that's all. Think of him as that and you won't go far wrong."

But for Fran, it wasn't that simple and she was beginning to grasp why, although she could never have put it into words for Michael. Milišić wasn't just history; her mother had loved him, married him, considered him a hero. And that's what made the sort of man he'd been very important. All her life she'd had total and complete faith in her mother's judgement, done as she'd told her and followed her advice. Mama's guidance and opinions had shaped her; the oldest child, the responsible one, the sister who was supposed to look after everybody.

And if Mama had fallen for and married a fascist, well, didn't that bring her beliefs into question? And if she'd been wrong about that, wasn't it possible some of her other views had been misguided? Views that Fran had held dear and lived by as well? She wrapped her arms tightly around her chest, squeezing back tears. No, it didn't bear thinking about. There must be some other explanation, one she was missing right now. If only she could ask Mama … A sob rose in her throat. What a stupid, stupid, thing to think after all this time. It only made everything hurt all the more.

With a sigh she powered down her laptop, turned off the light and, willing herself not to spend hours weeping into her pillow, decided to have an early night.

Chapter Eleven

Dubrovnik, 2nd October 1944

He wakes in the small hours, the moonlight streaming between the cracks of the shutters, Dragica's even breathing beside him comforting and real. He counts in its time; one … two … one … two… But still the dream remains vivid in the corridors of his mind; all the more haunting because it was born from truth.

Safranka stirs in the wooden drawer that serves as her cot. He wants so much better for his daughter than this, but after the war, please, after the war … He prays to a greater being he doesn't believe in that life will become a little easier.

The stirring becomes mewling and he slides out of bed to pick her up. As long as she is not hungry he will not wake her mother. Already Dragica is working in the hotel again, leaving each morning with the baby strapped to her back. He feels completely worthless it has to be so, but he ruined any chance he had of a better job when he refused to carry on wearing that hated uniform. But she understood. Even now she tells him again and again he did the right thing; he owes her so much more than a paltry few hours of sleep.

In the other room of the apartment, where they cook, live, and even sometimes laugh, he stands at the window with Safranka in his arms. Beyond the terracotta rooftops, below the city walls, he can almost hear the restlessness of the sea and it brings back the dream; Vido, Solly and him, the boat weighed down with pirate chests of treasure as it sank lower and lower into the waves, their frantic attempts to bail it with tiny silver cups counting for nought.

The reality had been equally frightening, but Solly had not been with them. Solly had been subject to curfew, so had hid in the synagogue during the afternoon with the rabbi, where they had packed the sacred treasure into wooden crates small enough to be disguised and carried to the boat.

Across the bay are many islands. Islands where no one lives, where no one would go. Only five men would know the location: the rabbi, his son and Solly from the Jewish community and two outsiders. Branko because Solly trusted him, and Vido because he was Branko's friend and he owned the boat.

Long after darkness they had stolen into the synagogue and taken the first of the boxes to the harbour, slipping from shadow to shadow like ghosts. They had gone a second time and had intended a third, but lights appeared in Svetog Ivana fort, an Italian patrol emerging onto the quay. There was little point in hiding, so while Branko held the swaying lantern, Vido made a show of checking his nets for holes. As the first rays of dawn broke over Mount Srđ they left the harbour. Only on the open sea had they truly felt able to breathe.

Safranka shifts in his arms and he looks down at her. Opening her eyes she gazes back, balling her tiny hands into fists and wriggling like a fish. He runs a soothing finger across her forehead. Will he ever be able to tell her the things he has done? He bends his head to kiss her. No, never. The things he has had to do – and the things he has failed to – are his and his alone. She must be allowed to grow up without the stain of war.

Chapter Twelve

Dubrovnik, February 2010

F ran stepped onto the harbour and looked around. Directly in front of her a stone quay projected into the crystalline water, and as she looked down fish darted between the moored boats, silver arrows in a translucent green-blue world.

Fran had expected bustle at the waterside, but all was quiet, the only movement coming from the restaurant that filled the three stone arches nearby, as one waiter shook out crisp white tablecloths and another polished glasses. She stopped and gazed out to sea. To her left the coastline curved, scattered with modern hotels lapped by the waves and nestled below the steep hills that surrounded the city. To her right a solid stone fort built into the walls sheltered the harbour behind the imposing circle of its tower, and straight in front the island of Lokrum emerged from the blue, dark green and mysterious. Would Daksa look like that?

Vedran had told her to meet his Uncle Jadran in front of the middle arch of the restaurant at ten o'clock, describing him as a serious-looking man, tall with broad shoulders and grey hair. It wasn't quite five to, but he was there already, gazing into the middle distance, and it gave Fran a moment to study him.

She immediately saw what Vedran meant by serious. There were no laugh lines around his eyes and his lips were pressed tightly together. But what a bone structure ... he must have been very good-looking in his youth. In fact, he wasn't half bad now, and Fran only just had time to slap the thought back down when he turned and noticed her.

He strode across the paving, hand out in front to shake hers. "You are Fran?"

"Yes. Jadran?"

"Indeed. The boat is moored under the castle wall. May I carry your bag?"

"Thank you. Vedran suggested I bring a picnic for lunch."

"Vedran can be very persuasive. But it is kind of you to give in to him."

They started to walk along the quay. What did he mean, Vedran could be persuasive? Had he talked him into this against his better judgement? Should she say anything? Oh, this made it impossibly awkward, if it wasn't bad enough already that he was so good looking ...

She took a deep breath. "I'm really sorry if Vedran has talked you into something you don't want to do."

Jadran stopped and looked over his shoulder. "My apologies if I gave that impression. I am happy to take you." Then he continued walking, with Fran trailing behind.

Did he mean it? It was impossible to tell. To change the

subject Fran said, "Your English is very good. I mean, I know everyone here speaks it, but yours is perfect."

"Thank you. I worked in the maritime industry until I retired so I used it every day. I am a little rusty though, if you will forgive me. Now, this is my boat."

The motor launch was bigger than Fran had expected, the size of a small yacht and made of pristine white fibreglass with a roofed cabin and an open deck at the back. But when she saw the name, *Safranka II*, she couldn't help but gasp.

"Is everything all right?" Jadran asked.

Oh, how stupid. She was making a right fool of herself. "Yes, it's just the name … it's my name."

He frowned at her for a moment. "Of course, you were born Yugoslavian so Safranka … Fran … it is sensible if you have lived all your life in England."

"Why did you call the boat …"

"It had the name when I bought it, but it is a pleasant coincidence. I'll jump on first, then I can help you."

His hand was warm in hers as he guided her onto the platform at the back then across the deck, edging past the built-in table to the cabin.

"If you sit up front with me I can point things out as we pass. Or you can stay outside and enjoy the sunshine."

"No, I would like to know where we are. I was only thinking the other day how much I'd love to see the city from the water."

"Then I can make that wish come true at least." He gave her a small, tight smile.

The engine started with a throaty roar and they nudged between the fishing boats on either side and away from the harbour. Jadran pointed out Svetog Ivana fort, saying it was built in the sixteenth century but now housed a maritime museum and aquarium. As they rounded the breakwater in a sweeping arc, Fran gazed at the walls of the old town rising to their right, climbing and falling with the rhythm of the surf-tinged rocks below. She could just glimpse the terracotta roofs beyond, glowing red in the morning sunshine and she lifted her face to meet its rays.

"You like it?" Jadran asked.

She nodded. "It really is the most beautiful city."

"On a day like today, it is. Vedran said you were born here?"

"Yes, but I left as a babe in arms so obviously I have no memory of it."

"So you have come to find out what it's like?"

"Yes."

Fran was pleased he didn't question her further, but pointed out the fortresses of Bokar and Lovrijenac, built to guard the bay she had visited on her way to the jeweller. The spray from the boat's prow flew into the air on either side of the cabin, rainbow prisms appearing and disappearing in the blink of an eye as they bounced gently along.

Now the old town was behind them and they cut across the mouth of a wide bay where the trees grew down to the edge of the rocks, the rugged shoreline dominated by the sharp concrete angles of an enormous hotel, falling in terraces towards the sea. Would this be how most visitors experienced the city? Fran thought fondly of her little apartment – she was luckier than she had known. Maybe she shouldn't rush home quite yet, anyway.

More green, more hotels, more sea and spray. The salty freshness of the air tickled Fran's nose as Jadran pointed out the hospital, and the suburb of Lapad, where he said the smart people lived.

"Are you smart?" Fran teased, and for a moment she thought he was going to laugh, but instead he smiled vaguely and shook his head.

"I belong in the old town," he told her.

"You've lived there all your life?"

"There was a brief time when I was younger ... but yes, it has always been my home."

"Perhaps when we are young we need to spread our wings. I went to work in London."

Jadran nodded, but didn't elaborate on his own experiences, perhaps because he was navigating a relatively narrow channel between the mainland and an arc of small islands, some no more than rocks. The largest and furthest out to sea was home to a lighthouse.

"That is Grebeni," he told her once they had passed it, "and in a few moments you will see Daksa straight ahead."

The mainland to their right was dotted with more hotels, their swimming pools an unnatural blue against the ever-changing colours of the sea. Then they rounded a final headland and in front of them was a narrow island, covered in thick vegetation.

"Is that it?" Fran asked Jadran, and he nodded.

With no reliable descriptions of the island readily available, Fran hadn't known what to expect. Her first impression of Daksa was dark, pine trees and overgrown shrubs descending to the rocky shore, but as they approached she could make out the blank walls of buildings, hewn from the island's stone and seeming to grow out of it.

"It's the old monastery," Jadran told her.

"Have you been here before?"

"Never. But I tracked down the man who brought the archaeologists and he told me the jetty's at the other end, by the lighthouse."

Jadran slowed the boat as they nudged closer to the shore. From this distance Fran could see aloes and vicious looking cacti, and she was glad she'd chosen to wear thick jeans and trainers. All the same she hoped they wouldn't have to battle very far through the undergrowth.

As if reading her mind Jadran said, "He also told me they cut a path through to the dig site, and I am hoping that as it's been winter it won't be too overgrown."

When they reached the tip of the island Fran could just see the tower of an old-fashioned lighthouse peeping through the trees. A rocky outcrop was marked by a modern beacon and Jadran edged around it, before bringing the boat in next to a jetty that was no more than a pile of stones. He brushed past Fran then jumped out, securing *Safranka II* to a rusting iron staple embedded in the rock.

His athleticism surprised Fran. From his face she had thought he was about her age, maybe even a little older, but his quick and easy movements were that of a younger man. She found herself imagining the muscles beneath his navy jumper and a tingle passed through her, a feeling so unfamiliar she had to look away. Good god, she needed to get a grip. Looking at the poor man like that was so inappropriate; she was here to see the place where her father had died, not act like a hormone-fuelled teenager in the presence of the first decent-looking bloke she'd come across. What had got into her this morning? Was it her nerves?

She gathered herself, and before he could offer his hand

stepped onto the rocks and into the shade of the trees. There was a strange feeling to the island, a stillness, that was hard to define. Jadran must have felt it too, as he reached onto the deck for the picnic bag then put it back down again.

"I think it would be better to have our lunch on the boat afterwards."

She nodded and they clambered up the rocks until they were standing in front of the lighthouse. It was far more of a ruin than it had appeared from the sea, with empty windows and ivy trailing through the cracks in the wall. Next to it was a path that seemed to lead into the island's heart.

Not far away stood the shell of a small stone cottage. They peeped inside to see mould growing up its walls and a rough floor strewn with bird droppings. A wooden cupboard stood in the corner, its door hanging off its hinges, the epitome of abandonment bringing a lump into Fran's throat. These people … they must have thought the war had passed them by on their tiny island, and then …

Jadran broke into her thoughts. "Where the lighthouse keeper lived, I guess."

"I read somewhere on the internet they came back for a while after the executions but … but their children … well, it was probably just making it seem more gruesome than it was, but anyway, they left."

"What happened here was gruesome."

He led on, through what was almost a tunnel of thick foliage, dark-leafed laurel closing in on either side.

Jadran stopped. "I am sorry, I left the water on the boat and it would be foolish to go far without it. I won't be a moment."

Fran nodded, listening to his retreating footsteps on the soft earth as she gazed around her. Had her father walked this path, or one very like it? Had he had to guess why they had been brought here, or had he actually known what was about to happen? For a moment she felt as though she could reach out and touch him, then a rustle in the undergrowth jolted her back to the here and now.

Even so, the terror of the place gripped her and she shuddered. She understood now why boatmen did not like to come here; there was a heaviness to the island, an atmosphere that brooked no intrusion. But that was crazy, it was only the narrowness of the path, the encroaching bushes, the fact she was completely alone. For one mad moment she wondered if Jadran planned to abandon her here, but then he appeared around the corner, a bottle of water in each hand.

The path wound its way past the larger trees, the deeply creviced bark of the Aleppo pines illuminated by shafts of sunshine that found their way through their open canopies. At times they were walking between high walls of glossy-leaved shrubs, their feet scrunching on leaf litter and small twigs. After a while they began to glimpse battered masonry structures through the gaps.

They emerged in front of a square stone building with one large doorway and a row of small, barred windows close to the eaves. The steps leading to it were all but overgrown with grass and weeds, and ivy spread upwards in an untidy triangle from the corner closest to them.

Nearby was a low stone wall and Jadran perched on it. "What exactly have you come here to see?"

Fran shook her head, unable to look at him. It was a very good question. Wanting to see Daksa had been something that Michael had suggested, but what she hoped to gain from being here …

"I ... I don't know, really." What an idiot she must seem.

"You have a personal connection to the island." It was a statement, rather than a question.

"Vedran might have said. My father ... my father was one of the men executed here. But please, don't think badly of me because of it."

"Why would I do that?" There was genuine surprise in his voice.

"Discovering your father was most likely a Nazi sympathiser is not an easy thing. Especially when you've been brought up to believe he died a hero."

"In my experience men are not one thing, they are many things. And you, Safranka, have not been shaped by your father. You must have been far too young when he died."

At the use of her given name she turned. "No one's called me Safranka since I was a child, and only then when my mother was cross with me."

"Do you mind me using it?"

She thought for a moment. "No, actually, I don't."

He nodded then levered himself away from the wall. "Well if you do not know what you are looking for, then I suggest we find it."

She followed him up the steps and into the building. Above them was a barrelled ceiling, with stone lintels and traces of wooden joists where an upper floor had once been. The ground beneath their feet was damp in patches, and there was a musty air to the place, despite the breeze trickling in, stirring the dust. Jadran sneezed and the sound echoed through the arches.

"This must have been part of the monastery," he said. "A storeroom, perhaps?"

Fran looked up at the barred windows. "Or a prison."

"Or maybe for defence against pirates."

All the same Fran could not help but stare up at them. Had the floor been in place in 1944? Had her father gazed from those high windows, across the treetops towards the mainland? No, it was too fanciful, thinking these things about him. She couldn't even picture him; whether he was tall or short, fair or dark, yet here his presence was all around her.

Her eyes adjusting to the light, she noticed there was graffiti on the walls and she bent to take a closer look. While some was clearly fairly recent, lower down were letters scratched roughly into the surface. Initials, or names, and swastikas. Her stomach churned. These men had been fascists all right. And it seemed in more recent years it had become a place of pilgrimage for those who believed the same. She closed her eyes.

Jadran was behind her. "So much for no one coming here. But then someone must have found the remains and alerted the archaeologists."

Fran crouched down. "Some of it seems older." She tried to stop her finger from trembling as she pointed. "And look ... look at the swastikas."

She felt his heat as he dropped to his haunches next to her. "Shall we see if we can find your father's name?"

"I want to, and yet I don't." How could she explain to a stranger? Finding a swastika next to his initials would be the final, incontrovertible proof that her father had been a Nazi collaborator. And much as now she knew in her heart it was true, she wasn't ready to be faced with it just yet.

Jadran's touch was light on her shoulder yet comforting at the same time. "We can come back another day. No pressure."

"I wouldn't want to trouble you."

"It's no trouble. I'm retired, remember. Time on my hands."

They stood and returned outside, Fran blinking in the bright sunlight. Once her eyes had adjusted, she followed Jadran around the side of the building, unwilling to be left alone in this strange and silent place. He stopped at the corner.

"You may not want to see this. It looks like where the archaeologists were digging."

"Then I do."

He nodded and stood out of the way to let her pass. Behind the barn was an area where the vegetation had been cleared, surrounded by jumbled stone that looked very much like the remains of the walls of another building. The area was filled with loose earth, which a few straggly weeds had been brave enough to colonise, but there was no doubt that this was the grave site.

Fran dug her fingernails into her palms. It didn't matter. She hadn't known him. But all the same there was something about the place that was squeezing her skull and making her temples begin to throb. Something evil and dark.

Jadran was running his hand along the barn wall. He turned to her and shook his head. "Bullet holes. If you have seen enough, I suggest we go back to the boat." Even he was looking a little pale.

They retraced their steps along the path in silence until they reached the abandoned cottage.

"There was no trial, you know," Jadran told her. "Not all these men would have been collaborators. Some were probably just anti-communist."

"You're kind to say it."

"Yugoslavia … it's always been complicated. Always bitterness and hate. If you like I will explain, but not now. I don't know about you, but I need to feel the sun on my back, so I suggest we head to a little bay I know near the city and eat our picnic there."

Trying not to wonder how much sending a text to England would cost, Fran stopped halfway up Stradun and typed,

I don't suppose you could load something called Skype on to your computer?

It was just a few moments before Parisa replied.

Sounds ominous. You went to that island today, didn't you? Just walking Button then I'll do it. Will text again when I have.

Good. Fran desperately needed to talk to her. What she couldn't deal with right now were Vedran's inevitable questions about the day so, feeling more than a little guilty, she took a less than direct route back to the apartment, winding her way through a series of alleyways to avoid the bar.

Once inside she poured herself a glass of wine and flopped onto the sofa. She knew it was only four o'clock but sod it. Today had shaken her in more ways than one, and what was worse, they were beginning to jumble together in her mind. And it was Jadran who kept popping to the surface.

She hadn't felt a jolt of attraction like this since she'd been in her twenties. It had started the moment she'd seen him on the harbourside, and much as she had tried to ignore it during the boat trip, seeing him leap onto the rocks, agile as a puma, it had ripped through her again. What the hell was wrong with her? She hardly knew the poor man. But he'd been so nice about everything, so reassuring, although having spent the best part of a day with him, she knew what Vedran meant about him being serious. It wasn't that he didn't smile in that thin-lipped way of his, there was just something very guarded when he did. As though he was wondering whether it was the right thing to do.

Of course he could just have been being polite. That was probably it. After all, Vedran had talked him into today so he'd probably been fulfilling his obligation and she would never see him again. In which case it didn't matter that she was feeling like a hormonal schoolgirl with a massive crush. Just at the point in life when her hormones ought to have got used to behaving themselves.

But why was she feeling this way now? Was it to do with Jadran himself, or because she was suddenly open to new possibilities? For a moment that felt like an exhilarating thought but she slapped it back down. There was absolutely no way she wanted another relationship in her life. It was a decision she'd made a very long time ago and for excellent reasons.

Already the wine glass was empty. This was no good. She needed to eat. Or perhaps email Michael about the really important business of the day. The swastikas on the wall had told her everything she had needed to know but had feared knowing. It was one thing Michael saying Milišić was an interesting footnote, but he was her father. And Mama had loved and married him.

She was relieved that before her mind could spin too far down that particular vortex, Parisa texted.

I'm up and running. Let's talk.

It was wonderful to see her friend's face, although the first few minutes of the conversation were drowned out by Button barking because he could hear Fran but couldn't work out where she was. In the end Parisa had to shut him in the kitchen, but the moment she returned to the screen she was on Fran's case.

"So, what happened?"

"It wasn't so much what, as who, and I need you to talk some sense into me."

"Who? That sounds promising."

"No it's not, it's awful, because I should have been focusing on my father, especially as … But anyway, the problem was my boatman was bloody gorgeous and I can't stop thinking about him instead."

"Fran Thomson, what are you like? Lusting after some young man." Parisa laughed.

"No, not young – at least not that. He's Vedran's uncle. You know, the barman I've become friendly with."

"Is he single?"

"What, Vedran?"

"No, his uncle, you idiot. Stop being obtuse."

"No one's ever mentioned a wife and he doesn't wear a ring … to be honest, I hadn't even thought about that. It wasn't relevant before I met him and it didn't occur to me today. God, that makes it even worse."

"So what's this Adonis like?"

"Nice looking … hell of a body. Thoughtful. Considerate."

"Then if he does turn out to be unattached, what's the problem?"

"The problem is I'm sixty-five and feeling like a sixteen-year-old with a massive crush."

"So what? It's attraction, pure and simple. It does happen you know."

"But it hasn't to me, not for years ..."

Parisa looked thoughtful for a moment, but there was a sparkle in her dark eyes. "I take it you've kept everything in working order, though."

"What do you mean?"

"Regular masturbation."

Fran felt the heat rise up her chest and then her neck. Honestly, sometimes she was just too blunt.

Parisa laughed. "It's all right, I don't expect you to answer that one. Just remember for men of a certain age things aren't always as easy in that department as they once were."

"Whoa," Fran spluttered. "You are going way too fast here."

"Just looking ahead, that's all. I wouldn't want you to think any lack of intimate enthusiasm on his part was due to your lumps and bumps. Far more likely to be his testosterone levels."

"Enough. How can I talk to you about this if you keep reducing it to sex?"

"Sorry. I thought that was what you'd be worried about."

Fran shook her head. "I hadn't even got to that point. I was feeling so ashamed of myself for lusting after him. He's been the perfect gentleman all day. I bet he'd be horrified."

"You might be pleasantly surprised. Your problem is that you think you're past it, but let me tell you, you're not. You're a pretty woman, Fran, with your peachy complexion and those great big eyes, you just can't see it. Personally I think a little fling would be good for you, give you a bit of confidence. Then, when you get home, you'd be more receptive to anyone nice who happened to cross your path."

"I … I hadn't thought of it like that."

"But you probably are overthinking it, that's the trouble. If something happens, just relax and enjoy it. And if you never see him again, well, you have a nice new fantasy to keep you warm at night."

Fran nodded. She knew Parisa was right, about the last bit at least. But as she was getting ready for bed and climbing into her oh-so-sensible brushed cotton pyjamas, she wondered if it was even possible to have a sexual relationship after so many years. Especially a fling. She'd never so much as thought of having a fling, even in her fantasies. What would it be like? Fun? Exciting? Or just impossibly embarrassing, taking her clothes off in front of someone she barely knew. Someone nice, like Jadran, at that. But there was something about him, something hidden and guarded, that made her think he wasn't the flinging type either.

Bugger this for a game of soldiers, she was going around in circles again. Parisa was right, she probably was overthinking it. Maybe she had too much time to think here, that was part of the problem. Too much time to think and to feel. But today, out on the water, she'd found she'd barely missed Daddy at all. His constant presence in the back of her mind had been whipped away by the wind and the waves, and although it made her feel just a little guilty, it had to be chalked up as progress, didn't it?

Chapter Thirteen

Dubrovnik, 11th October 1944

Hearing Dragica's footsteps on the stairs, he stirs the thin liquid in the pot. At least there is something worth eating in it tonight: potatoes, two large tomatoes from her aunt's terrace and some octopus Vido has given him. When he had started to say that he didn't want charity, he was told in no uncertain terms he was only poor because of what he'd done, and to shut up.

If rumours are to be believed, in the countryside the partisans are edging closer and the Germans beginning to retreat. But there is no sign of that in the city. There are still patrols, checks, searches, and now the Ustaše march alongside them. That is perhaps the most terrifying sight of all.

He opens the door to his wife, bent almost double and clinging to the banister to haul herself up. He takes the baby from her back, gathers her to him and she rests her head on his shoulder.

"Oh, that mountain of stairs. I am not as fit as I was six months ago."

"I am so sorry. I wish you didn't have—"

She silences him with a kiss. "It is not your fault. What you did was right and I will not hear it spoken of again."

They stand in the centre of the tiny room, leaning together with Safranka in his arms, fast asleep. The scent of Dragica's hair fills his nose, salt with her sweat but rich with the very essence of her. Outside dusk falls, a lone bird chirping in a nearby roost. He closes his eyes as time slows with his heartbeat, the moment etching itself deep into his soul. When he is old and Safranka brings him a child of her own, he knows he will remember it.

The baby shifts and begins to whimper.

"She must be hungry," Dragica tells him. "I will feed her, and then we will eat."

Tonight there is almost a proper meal, but he knows even if the partisans liberate the city there will still be shortages and hunger. At least there will be freedom. But he cannot rid his mind of the kernel of fear. At the end of it all, will the home-grown fascists somehow be able to cling to power?

If that happens, he will be forced to take a risk, take his family away, penniless refugees with an uncertain future. Leave the city of his birth, the city he loves. But he will do it if he has to. In his heart he knows that under the jackboot, whoever is wearing it, this is not his city. And more than anything, Safranka must grow up in freedom and without the taint of fear. That, and a father's love, are the most important gifts he can give her.

Chapter Fourteen

Dubrovnik, February 2010

Fran was momentarily covered with confusion when she saw Jadran sitting outside the café two days after their trip. She had been cooking before she came out and she was sure her hands still smelled of onions, and if she'd known she would have brushed her hair, put on a little lipstick even... She stopped. It was too late for that. She must have looked like she'd been pulled through a salt-covered hedge backwards after a day on his boat.

He stood, smiling, to greet her. "I hope you don't mind, but Vedran told me you normally come at this hour and I wondered if perhaps we could enjoy an aperitif together."

She tried to sound calm, keep the absolute delight from her voice. "Yes, I would like that."

Did a knot of tension disappear from his jaw, or had she imagined it? Certainly she hadn't imagined the smile, although it had now disappeared and his face had returned to its usual neutral but interested look. Hark at her ... usual ... she'd only met him once before.

Vedran came out and stood by the table. "Red wine for you, Fran? Another beer, *Tetak*?"

"Not until I have finished this one. You will have me drunk." He sounded gruff, but his hazel eyes were soft as he looked up at his nephew.

"He's a lovely boy," Fran said once Vedran had gone back inside.

"He is. Although he could be trouble when he was a teenager. So, Safranka, what have you been doing these last days?"

"I've spent them in the kitchen. I found a book of traditional Croatian recipes in the shop by the fountain and I thought I would try some. One of the ladies on the market had some beautiful cabbages so I've been making *arambaši*." She laughed. "I'm sorry, I might smell a little of onions."

"My mother-in-law used to make it and the apartment would stink of onions and cabbage all day, but it certainly tasted good. Did your mother cook many Yugoslavian dishes?"

Ah, so there was, or at very least had been, a wife. "Only cakes, and I don't need recipes for those. We had *krofne*, and *mađarica*, and always *pinca* at Easter. If I am still here then I must make some."

He sat back in his chair. "How long do you think you will stay?"

"I have the apartment until the end of April. At first I thought I might not be here that long, but I'm beginning to feel more settled."

"Then perhaps, if you will permit me, I could show you a

few more places. I have a car as well as the boat and the weather is improving all the time."

Fran couldn't help but grin at him. "That would be lovely."

"Have a think and let me know where you would like to go. But I am afraid I will insist on there being home-made cakes for the picnic."

Vedran brought their drinks and looked as though he was about to join them, but two elderly men made their way down the street and into the bar.

Fran fiddled with the stem of her wine glass. "I haven't seen you here before." God, what an awful, bland thing to say. He'd think she was an idiot.

"I don't normally drink an aperitif. Or drink very much at all, to be honest. But it is a beautiful sunny afternoon and I think I promised you a history lesson. As long as you don't think that would spoil it."

"No, I'm interested. You said Yugoslavia was complicated and I've learned a little from my reading, but it would be good to have an inside track."

"Perhaps it is complicated because there never should have been a Yugoslavia in the first place. Tito did very well to hold it together for so long. That needed communism I think, but also the right leader. Before him we were too fragmented. Owned by other nations. In fact, the country only began when the Austro-Hungarian Empire collapsed after the First World War.

"The problems were religion, cultural identity, political factions even. We had Muslims, Catholics, Christian Orthodox. We had Croats, Serbs, Slovenians, Bosnians, Herzegovinians … not to mention within that Istrians to the north who were more than half Italian. And here in Croatia people always felt under-represented and hard done by. And very independent."

"My mother always referred to herself as Yugoslavian, if anyone asked. But I suppose nobody had heard much of Croatia then."

"Also, during the Second World War the name of Croatia was tarnished by far-right politics. The Chetniks, who were largely Serb, were the royalist resistance and the partisans the communist resistance, and they were just as likely to fight each other as the Germans or Italians. But in a little Croatian corner, right from the moment the Axis powers invaded, there were any number of fascists who supported them, and a so-called 'independent' state of Croatia was created and they began their own mini-holocaust."

"So my father could very easily have been one of them."

"I'm afraid so, although they didn't gain too much of a foothold in Dubrovnik until after the Italians left."

Fran sighed. "You didn't tell me that on the island."

"No. But what I said on the island was true as well. Not everyone who was executed would have been a fascist, and the families of many of the victims denied it. If you wanted to prove or disprove it, we would need to find other evidence."

The evidence was the necklace, but should she mention it to him? Her experience in the museum still smarted. And why did it matter? Her father was dead, long gone. She took a deep breath, feeling the late afternoon sun on her back. No, she wouldn't think about him now. She was on holiday, in the company of a handsome man, and she was going to set her worries aside and enjoy the moment. Parisa would be proud of her.

She took a large slug of wine and smiled at him. "Well, that's quite enough about my family," she said. "Tell me about yours."

Did she imagine a shadow pass across his face? But he nodded, sipping his beer.

"There's Vedran, as you know. My younger brother, Rajko, is his father, and we have a sister, Viviana, but she lives in Šibenik with her husband and two daughters so we don't see them as often as we would like. That's it really. You have a family in England too?"

How quickly he'd put the focus back on her, and Fran was more than a little intrigued. The seriousness about him, the way he held himself in check ... something had happened to hurt him, and hurt him badly, Fran was sure. Looking at Jadran, her heart ached just a little, but on the outside she smiled, then opened her phone.

"You'll wish you had never asked. I have so many pictures of my granddaughters on here you'll be bored to tears."

∼

Fran set off early down the steeply stepped streets, the sunshine just beginning to reach the upper storeys of the houses, making the tiles glow. The scent of baking bread and coffee drifted from someone's kitchen but hers were the only footsteps and she walked slowly, pausing to admire the pots of plants outside the painted front doors, and drinking in the Saturday morning stillness.

She had been intrigued when Vedran had asked her to come to the café early because he wanted to talk to her. Intrigued, then rather worried. Jadran had wanted her number, but hadn't called. Perhaps he had changed his mind and had asked Vedran to break it to her gently. If it mattered to her this much already, maybe it would be a good thing to end it, whatever it was, before it started to matter even more.

The café didn't open for half an hour but the door was ajar and inside the radio was playing, so Fran peeped around. Vedran was at the sink at the back, washing glasses, so she slipped inside.

"*Dobro jutro*"

He turned around, grinning. "*Dobro jutro,* Fran. I knew you wouldn't let me down."

She approached the bar. "You made it sound important."

"I wanted to talk to you yesterday, but it was too busy. It's about Uncle Jadran."

"I thought it might be."

"He's asked me to tell you something, but first I'll make us coffee."

Fran shrugged, trying to look as though she didn't care. "It's all right, you know, if he's changed his mind about taking me out and about. It was kind of him to offer but I wouldn't want him to feel he had to."

Vedran looked serious and she could suddenly see the likeness to his uncle. "It isn't that at all. But there's something he wants me to tell you first. Something he finds difficult to talk about himself. I guess because it's so long since he had to, because everyone knows." He waved in the direction of the corner table. "Sit down and I'll bring the coffee."

So Jadran did want to see her again. As a friend, obviously. She knew he couldn't be attracted to her; she was a bit too tubby, had let herself go, really. She didn't colour her hair like Parisa, despite her pleading with her to do so before her trip. She didn't even know how to wear clever make-up, and she'd barely looked at any of the new clothes her friend had made her buy. Except the long denim skirt with the embroidered pockets, which for some reason she'd put on this morning.

A cappuccino landing in front of her interrupted her chain of thought, then Vedran sat down opposite, nursing an espresso.

"Uncle Jadran lost his wife and daughter in the Siege of Dubrovnik, so it is uncomfortable for him to talk about family."

For a moment Fran struggled to grapple with the thought of something so awful happening, but then she managed to stutter, "Oh no ... and I went on for ages about Michael and the girls. It must have been terrible for him."

Vedran shook his head. "I don't think so. I mean, I cannot be sure. I am closer to him than anyone, but he does not share everything ..." Vedran shrugged. "But he asked me to tell you about Leila and Kristina so he doesn't have to."

"What happened?"

"I do not remember myself, because I was a baby, and anyway my father made my mother take me to her parents on Korčula , and we lived there for several years until the war was over. As I understand it, Uncle Jadran wanted Leila to take Kristina as well but her mother was here so she wouldn't go. He told my father the biggest regret of his life was not making her.

"Dad and Uncle Jadran joined the Dubrovnik Defenders and one day while they were manning an artillery post the apartment where Uncle Jadran lived was destroyed by mortars, then went up in flames. He came home to find people digging through the wreckage with their bare hands, but there were no survivors."

"Oh god, the poor man." Fran's throat was full of tears and

her voice shook. Life was shit sometimes. More than shit. "How old was his daughter?"

"Thirteen."

Fran sniffed. "Oh god. I can't imagine ... I have just one child too, and to have lost him ... to lose him ... it would break me."

"I think it broke Uncle Jadran too. When the city was freed he joined the army. Dad said he won medals for bravery but you cannot ask him about that time. Once the war was over, he came back here and moved in with Leila's mother, and he still lives in that apartment, even though she died eight or nine years ago."

"Oh, the poor man." Even to herself she was beginning to sound like a broken record.

"He would not want you to pity him, Fran. That is not why he wanted me to explain. He only wanted you to appreciate there is a part of his life you must not ask about, because it would be hard for him to tell you."

She nodded. "I understand." After all, there were also parts of her life she didn't share with anyone, although having heard Jadran's story they seemed small and insignificant and she felt thoroughly ashamed of even thinking of them right now. She drained her coffee and stood up. "It's gone eight o'clock and you should be open. Thank you for telling me, Vedran. Please let Jadran know that I understand. Really, I do."

Leaving the café, Fran walked on towards Stradun. Of course the part of her life she didn't talk about was nothing like the tragedy Jadran had suffered, nothing at all. Her silence was rooted in shame. The shame of a disfigured sister, of a failed marriage. But after this morning's revelation about Jadran's family, even thinking about it seemed rather overdramatic, something Andrew would say had a touch of Patti about it.

And he was probably right. He'd always maintained that Patti was an attention-seeking bitch who had done her best to kick Fran when she was down, to deny her her parents' support when she needed it. But when Mama had written that letter telling her to stay away, Patti couldn't have known …

Fran took a deep breath. She mustn't let the doubts seep back into her mind. Not here. Not in this beautiful city where her sister couldn't reach her, not with the sun on her back. But somehow its rays didn't warm her, and it had little to do with her own miserable griping.

Rather than heading for the market as she had intended, Fran turned right towards the Pile Gate. She knew on the wall inside was a metal plaque which showed the bomb damage during the siege. So far she had only glanced at it in passing, but this morning she wanted to know more. She had been completely wrapped up in a conflict sixty-five years ago, when there was a far more recent one that had impacted the lives of people still living here today.

She remembered only too well watching the television news with her mother, and her mother weeping. To her it had just been another far away war. She had never imagined she would come to know someone who had been caught up in the thick of it and had lost so much.

Fran stood in front of the plaque, which was titled 'Map of damage caused by the aggression of the Yugoslav army, Serbs and Montenegrins'. There was no doubt who the people of the city were blaming. Did Jadran still carry blame in his heart? Had it fuelled his belief that a united Yugoslavia should never have been? Fran had assumed his telling of its history had been neutral, but if you thought about it, was anyone's, ever?

It turned out the area where she was staying in the north-east corner of the city had been one of the worst hit. Had that been where Jadran and his family lived? But the damage was almost everywhere, the whole map covered with little black triangles and dots. Her nails dug into her palms. It was just too awful, too awful to contemplate. She couldn't even imagine what it must have been like living here then. She didn't actually want to.

Fran turned away, back through the archway, past the fountain and down Stradun. The sun had gone behind a cloud taking with it all the calm of the early morning, leaving her feeling wrung out and ragged. She kept trying to remind herself it wasn't her war, her loss, but somehow the pain of the people who had lived through it seeped into her own grief for Daddy, building into an ugly ball of emotion that threatened to overwhelm her.

Avoiding the café, Fran all but ran up the side streets and alleyways until she reached her apartment, trying to keep the storm inside her at bay. She fumbled the key in the lock, then slamming the door behind her, threw herself down on the bed and wept. For Jadran and his family, for Daddy, and everything she herself had lost.

Wave after wave of emotion gripped her as she sobbed. She just wanted to go back through the years, back to when both Mama and Daddy were alive, when she could hug them, talk to them. When, on a wet Saturday when she had nothing much to do, she could jump in her car and head to Aldwick and be assured of the most loving of welcomes. There was nowhere and no one like that for her now. Everyone else had their own lives, whereas she …

Come on, Fran, come on. Get a grip. She told herself that several times before she finally managed to release her rather damp pillow from her clutches and roll onto her back, empty and exhausted. Even here, just when she thought she was beginning to heal, there was no hiding from her grief. No hiding at all.

The words trickled into her brain, slow like icy water, sparking an entirely new train of thought. Shafts of sunlight from the half-open shutters broke through the gloom as the idea began to take shape, almost as obvious as it was alien. Could hiding from her pain be wrong? If she ran away from it, buried it, how could she ever look it in the eye? How could she ever deal with it and heal? From the loss of both her parents.

Thinking back to when Mama died, how had she managed then? By putting all her energies into supporting Daddy, that's how. And not only Daddy, but Andrew and Michael as well; checking in with them, listening to them, she'd become the family shoulder to cry on. As Andrew had said, the rock. But where had her own tears been? Of course there had been moments, but she'd brushed them aside. She'd had to be strong for them. Now, on her own, hundreds of miles from home, there was no one she had to pretend for anymore.

It was OK to cry. She'd said that to Andrew often enough. She just hadn't taken her own advice. *Let it happen, Fran, weep, wail, rage against the hurt. At least if you try something different, you might be able to move on.* But instead of crying, there was a smile around her lips, a feeling that she was perhaps finally getting somewhere. And she certainly wasn't going to waste the day. Just as soon as she'd washed her face she'd head out of the Pile Gate, past that gorgeous little bay she'd discovered and on until she found the viewpoint beyond which Jadran had shown her while they were picnicking on the boat. And if she felt like crying on the way, well, she'd bloody well do it, and sod what anyone might think of her.

Chapter Fifteen

Dubrovnik, 13th October 1944

He stumbles down the wooden stairs, breath ragged, high spots of colour burning his cheeks. The peeling paintwork flashes past, the smell of cabbage from the other apartments, piss and human sweat. Faster and faster, until inevitably he trips, wrenching his arm on the banister to avert disaster.

And here he sits, head in hands, the pain in his leg searing into his hip. He was right, but he was wrong. No, he is right. He is. But he is not proud. Not proud of his behaviour at all.

He opens his fingers and gazes down at his trousers, the fabric shiny, all but worn through at the knee. He knows the situation is worse at the back, but he hopes his jacket will cover it in the street at least. In the mayor's office, he is used to being laughed at.

But he will not, will not, wear any part of that hated

uniform again. Dragica yelled at him, told him it was a waste, that no one would know. But *he* would, and that is the point. She'd folded her arms, refused to mend the tear, refused him access to the needle even, so he'd pulled his battered trousers on anyway and run from the apartment like a slighted child.

Before, they would never argue, but hunger, fear and exhaustion are wearing them down, dripping and nipping away at them. The war, this awful destructive war, it has to end soon. It must. But whenever it is, it will be in the future. Now he should go back, hold her in his arms, apologise … but his leg trembles when he tries to stand and he knows it will not hold his weight. Certainly not to climb the stairs. It will be hard enough to drag himself through the streets to work. Oh, how he despises himself; less than half a man.

He closes his eyes and leans against the wall while he tries to control the pain. He would never have worn the uniform of the Ustaše at all, but how could he have refused to help Solly? His brother in all but blood.

It has been two long years since he last set eyes on Solly; years of not knowing if he is alive or dead. Two years since the rumours began to spin and fly, rumours that the Jews were to be interned. And his friend had sought him out, told him he was stealing away to join the partisans, begging Branko to do what he could for his wife and child.

He had failed at the first attempt. He had not been quick enough to hide them and they had been taken away to the island of Lopud. All of fifteen kilometres across the sea, it might as well have been the moon. The one thing, one thing, Solly had asked him to do, and he had let him down.

Filled with despair he had worried at the problem day and night, the early days of his marriage blighted by his guilt. But then, in the course of his work, an answer had presented itself. An answer as unpalatable as it was perfect. But he had had no choice. He had promised Solly. Yet much as it had been necessary then, he will never, ever wear that wretched uniform again.

Chapter Sixteen

Dubrovnik, March 2010

T he first text Fran received from Jadran was brief and to the point:

Do you like gardens?

At least it made it easy to reply.

Yes, I do.

If we go tomorrow, will you have time to make some cake?

Fran smiled to herself. Of course she had time, she always had time. And what was more she would love to do it.

So now they were driving away from the old town on the main road that skirted the modern city, the solid rock wall of Mount Srđ disappearing into the distance above them. On the seaward side, through gaps in the apartment blocks, she could glimpse the commercial port of Gruž, a long tongue of water reaching into modern Dubrovnik's heart, and she wondered if that was where Jadran used to work. She was about to ask him but he began telling her about the elegant Franjo Tuđman suspension bridge they were starting to cross, named after the first president of modern Croatia.

The road skirted the coast, running behind luxury villas with incredible sea views. Beyond them Daksa seemed to hunker down in the water, from this distance nothing but a blur of dark green against the blue. Fran looked away, unwilling to let shadowy thoughts of her father spoil her day.

It was only twenty minutes later that Jadran turned off the road, past a gnarled plane tree so huge it dwarfed the benches around it, and wound down the hill until he came to a shaded area where half a dozen cars were parked.

"Welcome to Trsteno Arboretum," he said. "Some people call it Dubrovnik's garden."

Fran looked at the metal gates. "Is this the entrance? It looks a bit closed."

"No on both counts. I have a friend who volunteers here and we are visiting as his guests. Ah, here he is."

Jadran got out of the car to greet a man wearing baggy blue trousers and a battered straw hat and Fran followed, picking up the cool bag that contained their picnic. Jadran took it from her immediately, then introduced Kristo, who shook her hand then led them through the gate before leaving them to explore.

"Kristo comes most days now he's retired. I suppose it fills his time. I do sometimes wonder if I should do something like this."

"I think ..." Fran paused, uncertain how to best phrase this.

"I mean, I retired a few years ago but I've been caring for my father. He died in December and, well, I'm not really sure how to fill my time either."

Jadran nodded. "It's a problem. I retired fifteen months ago and I haven't solved it yet. At first I had the boat to do up and that was a big project. But now it's finished. I'm just not used to having leisure time. I used to work such long hours, into the evenings because sometimes I needed to talk to associates in America. But now ..." He shrugged.

Fran smiled up at him. "I'm glad it isn't just me. I see people all around me making the most of retirement, but I'm struggling, to be honest. I mean, I have plans to volunteer once I get home, but even that ... Oh well, let's not spoil a beautiful day worrying about it."

"I agree."

The gardens were perched high above the sea and as they crunched along a broad gravel path shaded by trees, Jadran told her how the Gozze family had had them designed around their summer residence five hundred years before, and how the aqueduct they built to irrigate the land was still working today. It didn't just water the plants, but also fed babbling fountains and the pond in front of an impressive grotto guarded by a muscular Neptune. The water cooled the air, making Fran wrap her cardigan more firmly around her as they watched the goldfish shimmer between the waterlily pads in the greenish light.

They strolled along terraces lined with palm trees interspersed with classical stone columns supporting wooden trellises, the summer vines beginning to wind their way upwards, their thick, twisted stems belying their age. The lush greenery rustled in the breeze, a splash of deep colour provided by the glowing purple bougainvillea that colonised the front of the house, and the air was filled with the scent of privet and rosemary from the small and slightly overgrown formal gardens.

A straight paved walk led them to a red-roofed pavilion overlooking the sea.

"I had thought about eating our picnic here," Jadran said, "but it is perhaps a little too cool with the wind."

"The view is spectacular though." In front of her the Mediterranean was almost turquoise, dotted with humps of islands. Perching on the parapet Fran could see that below them was a small harbour with a long breakwater and an arched building that seemed to grow out of the rock. "Oh, that is so pretty."

Jadran half smiled. "Of course we could have come here by boat, but it's a little choppy out there and the car is much quicker."

"It was interesting to drive, to see the coast that way."

He nodded. "And up here again you have a different view of the Elafiti Islands. Technically Daksa is the first one, but the others are larger. If you look beyond those cypress trees to our left, that one is Koločep, then directly in front with the hill in the middle is Lopud, and to the right is Šipan. It may not look it from this angle but it's the biggest by far."

Lopud. The name rang a bell with Fran, but where had she heard it? Of course, at the Jewish museum.

"Wasn't Lopud where the Jews were interned during the Second World War?"

"Was it? I had no idea."

"Yes, I went to the Jewish museum and the guide told me."

"That's an unusual place for the casual visitor to go."

How much to say? She didn't really want to spoil their day with her tale of woe, and her trip to the museum wasn't exactly a pleasant memory. "Long story," she said. "Probably best told when we find a place for our picnic." Hopefully in the meantime Jadran would forget all about it.

They climbed down some steps next to the pavilion onto a wide path, where old stone benches and pillars peeped from overgrown foliage, then through a small citrus grove, the glossy-leaved trees laden with oranges, which she told Jadran how much she loved. All the time Fran was aware of the humped shape of Lopud across the sea. *What dark secrets these islands held*, she thought. *With their beauty they seemed to slumber so innocently in the sun, but underneath the surface…*

Fran was relieved when the track turned inland past some buildings and they were able to peep through an open door to see an old wooden olive press. Surrounding the villa and the formal gardens in an arc was a veritable forest with a huge variety of trees, many of them neatly labelled.

Jadran explained that the Gozze family had been merchants and had instructed their captains to bring back plants and seeds from wherever they could find them. Shafts of sunlight burst through the lush foliage, cicadas chirped, and even the occasional bird sang on the branches above, the gentle breeze carrying a sweet fragrance Fran did not know.

They emerged from the trees onto a grassy footpath that led through a meadow towards an olive grove.

"Now this is more how I imagine a Mediterranean landscape," Fran said.

Jadran nodded. "And I imagine England is full of rose

gardens, but I do not expect that is entirely true either."

"Then you would be disappointed in my little plot. I have one rose bush, and to be honest it's a struggle to keep it alive, what with the white fly and blight."

They sat in the sun on an old stone wall between the field and the trees to eat. Just feet away from them the grasses rippled in the breeze, studded with blue and white flowers and a liquorice-like scent perfumed the air, which Jadran explained came from the olive flowers.

Fran had filled two plastic boxes with pasta salad; the ripe tomatoes and peppers may have come from the supermarket, but she had bought the olives and the local cured sausage from the Green Market behind Sveti Vlaho church and made her own dressing. It had been fun to cook for someone other than herself for once.

Mindful of Jadran's insistence on cake she had decided on *čupavci*, little sponge squares covered in chocolate and coconut, because she had reckoned that with those she couldn't go far wrong. She watched as he bit into his slice with a sigh, then closed his eyes. His face seemed more relaxed today, and he had even smiled a few times, although Fran was beginning to wonder if he gave more away with his eyes. There was such a sparkle to them at times.

"So, Safranka. Tell me what happened at the Jewish museum."

Oh, so he had remembered, which meant there really was nothing for it but to tell him. To brush him off would be rude, and she certainly couldn't lie. She swallowed a mouthful of cake. "The only thing my mother brought from Dubrovnik was a necklace that had been precious to my father, and it has

Jewish symbols on it. I took it to a jeweller first, but she suggested the museum might know more."

"And did they?"

Fran fiddled with the lid of the plastic box on her lap. "The man claimed it was part of their missing treasure. He wanted to take it from me. It was all … rather awkward, actually."

"I hope you didn't give it to him."

"No. I couldn't ever part with it. But it did make me wonder if perhaps my father, if … well, how he came to have it, really."

"One would suppose that if he was a fascist, he wouldn't have wanted anything Jewish anywhere near him."

"Unless he'd looted or stolen it to sell."

Jadran's hazel eyes were intense. "You don't seem keen on giving your father the benefit of the doubt. Not about the necklace, nor when we were on the island."

Fran looked away. "I don't know why what happened to him is even important."

"And yet it is."

She'd already shared too much, and if she even tried to voice her vague doubts about her mother's judgement and why that mattered, she'd sound like a crazy woman.

"You do want to know, though?" Jadran persisted.

"I suppose so. My son, Michael, is very interested and it would be a shame not to at least try to find out everything I can while I'm here."

"How would you feel about going back to the museum?"

Fran shuddered. "I know I shouldn't be so pathetic, but the guy was very intense and he did freak me out a bit."

"Would it help if I came with you?"

"I couldn't ask you to …"

Jadran smiled. "I'm retired, remember. All those empty days to fill."

Fran rolled her eyes. "I know what that feels like. All right, if you really have nothing better to do, please come with me."

She would have far preferred to follow Jadran up the museum steps, but when he stood back politely for her to go first it would have been churlish – or perhaps even childish – to refuse. To bolster herself for the occasion she'd worn her denim skirt and it swished uncomfortably around her legs as she climbed. At least, given Jadran was behind her, it didn't make her bottom look as huge as her jeans did.

When she saw the same man sitting behind the desk she would have turned around if she could, but his face lit up when he saw her.

"You came back. I hoped you would." He looked less pinched and there was even a blush of colour to his cheeks. Fran didn't know what to say, but he carried on. "I was perhaps less than polite to you and I apologise. I can only blame my arthritis. It was not a good day."

So it hadn't been her after all and she felt her shoulders relax. "You know, I said to my son afterwards you looked ill."

He bowed his head slightly. "Thank you for your understanding. I am Eli, by the way."

"I'm Fran. And this is Jadran."

They shook hands then Fran reached into her purse for the entrance fee, but Eli waved her away. "I do not think you have come here as tourists."

Jadran peered into the first room. "No, but I'm feeling a bit ashamed. I've lived in Dubrovnik all my life and I've never even thought of visiting."

Eli shrugged. "Like many people. Please, look around while you are here. I can answer any questions." He turned to Fran. "Do you have your mother's necklace with you?" She nodded. "May I see it again? I have talked to someone about it and he has an opinion, but needs more information if possible."

Fran was somehow glad of Jadran standing behind her. What other information could she give? She reached into her handbag for the tissue package and set it on the desk. Before unwrapping it she said, "I would like to understand more about it too."

Eli nodded. "I can at least explain some of the iconography."

Fran's fingers felt fat as they fumbled the tissue. Oh, she was making such a meal of this, and in front of Jadran too. How embarrassing. But eventually the necklace was laid out on the desk where they could all see it.

Eli pointed to the pendant. "First, the Star of David. You probably know it. It has come down through the generations from King David's shield to Israel's national flag as a symbol of our struggles for freedom. And the menorah below it ... well, people have written whole books about its meaning, but it represents the seven days of the creation, and the six lights of human knowledge leaning towards the light of God in the centre."

"What about the stones? Do they mean anything?" Fran asked.

"They are both very traditional and are mentioned in the

bible, so often used in our jewellery. Some people see them as good luck, but in my view that is just superstition."

"So is this a religious piece or not?" Jadran asked.

"When I described it to my friend he said it was more likely to have belonged to an individual. Without seeing it he could not tell the age, but sometimes jewellery was passed from mother to daughter, or it could have been a more recent gift."

"So not part of the missing treasure?" Jadran persisted.

Eli shook his head. "My friend thinks it unlikely. But how your mother came by it, Fran … these things, with such symbolism, are rarely given outside the faith."

"It … it came from my father. Mama always said it was important to him."

"And he was Jewish?"

Fran shook her head, gazing down at the necklace. The chain had become tangled in her battle with the tissue paper and she began to unwind it. If the necklace wouldn't have been given to someone outside the faith, as Eli had put it, then someone – most likely her father – must have taken it. The necklace, for all her mother had loved it, was tainted, but had she known? Had she guessed? Oh, this was just too awful to even contemplate.

"Do you want me to tell him, Safranka?" Jadran's voice was soft.

She scrunched the necklace back into its wrapping and returned it to her bag. Her voice sounded strangely high-pitched, almost angry when she spoke. "What? That my father lived in Dubrovnik? That's no secret, in fact, I think I mentioned it to Eli before. Anyway, we mustn't take up any more of his time."

"You know no more about the necklace?" Eli asked.

"My mother left for England after my father died in 1944, so it is older than that. But nothing else. I am trying to find out a bit more about their life here if I can ..."

"Then please tell me if you do. And come back any time."

"Thank you. I hope you stay free from pain."

He shrugged. "That is unlikely, but it is kind of you to wish it."

Jadran followed her down the stairs and along Žudioska Street in silence. They were almost at the corner with Stradun when he stopped outside the shuttered window of a gift shop and said, "I am wondering why you didn't tell him the truth about your father. It strikes me the more he knows, the more he might be able to find out."

"How could I do that? My father was probably implicated in the death of his people, maybe even his family members for all I know. And he more or less said he thought he stole the necklace ..."

Jadran frowned. "Did he? I don't recall that."

"He said pieces with religious symbolism weren't given outside the faith. It's the same thing." She folded her arms.

"*Rarely given*, I think were his words. Safranka, it's almost as if you want to believe ill of your father."

Why was he sounding so arsey about it all of a sudden? What did it matter to him?

"All the evidence points that way, doesn't it?" she replied. "He had blood on his hands, blood, Jadran, and that's nothing to be proud of."

He took a step back, his eyes narrow and his jaw clenched. "Then you won't want to be standing on a street corner talking to another man with blood on his hands, will you? Good day to you, Safranka."

She watched as he turned onto Stradun, his footsteps echoing on the paving stones. The set of his back was rigid, his arms military straight at his sides. Of course, in the war he had been a soldier ... how could she have let her emotions get the better of her and said something so stupid? His situation wasn't the same at all. He had been fighting to defend his city, his country ... her father's actions had been driven by racial hatred. She wanted to call after him, but what could she say?

Slowly she followed the direction Jadran had taken, heading for the side street that climbed the hill to her apartment. Well, she'd blown that good and proper, hadn't she? The one man she'd met in years that she'd really liked and ... how many times had she seen him? Four? And she'd messed it up already. Still, a week or so ago a relationship had been about the furthest thing from her mind so it shouldn't be hard to forget it again. It wasn't as though he'd been anything more than friendly anyway. Like Parisa had said, it had been a nice little fantasy, nothing more. *Nothing to see here, Fran. Move on.*

Outside the café Vedran was serving drinks to two women while their children played in the street next to the tables. Fran raised her hand in greeting, intending to walk straight past, but he called after her.

"Where's Uncle Jadran? I thought you were going to the Jewish museum this afternoon."

"He ... he went straight home." Tears pricked the back of her eyes.

"Really? Why? He told me he'd see me here later."

"We had ... a disagreement." She tried her best to sound breezy as she carried on. "Nothing for you to worry about though."

"Oh, but it is." He grabbed her elbow. "Come inside for some wine and tell me."

Damn. Why had she even come this way? The truth was, she'd been on automatic pilot, just heading for home to lick her wounds. Now she would have to tell Vedran how insensitive she'd been and she wasn't sure she was up to doing that right now.

He piloted her to the corner table nearest the bar and almost before she'd smoothed down her skirt there was a glass of wine in front of her, and he pulled out the chair opposite.

"Tell me what happened."

There was no way she could lie. "I said something really tactless, that's all, and he probably realised how stupid I am."

"That isn't an explanation."

"Look, it's sweet of you to worry, but there's no need."

"I think there is. Uncle Jadran hasn't looked at a woman in twenty years and he's relaxed with you, happier than I've seen him in a long while. He was even whistling the other morning when I stayed over at his apartment. So of course I am worried you have argued."

Fran rocked back in her seat. This was the very last thing she'd expected Vedran to say. She felt as though her eyes were on stalks, her mouth open, so she quickly composed her face and took a sip of wine.

"I ... I didn't realise. Didn't even think. Are you sure it's me? It can't be ... he's only being friendly and I'm nothing special."

"No, I can't be sure, as you put it, but the circumstantial evidence is strong, so you'd better tell me what happened so we can put it right." He faltered, uncertainty filling his eyes making him look even younger than his twenty years.

Disappointing him too would be like kicking a puppy. "I mean ... I hope we can put it right," he continued.

All the same she had to hold firm. "I think your Uncle Jadran is a lovely man, but there's no point if I'm just going to keep saying stupid things and messing it up."

Vedran stood up slowly, shaking his head. "I need to check the tables, but please Fran, think about what I've said."

Glad of the respite, Fran sat back, cradling her glass in her hands. Had she really made a difference to Jadran? If nothing else, she supposed she had filled a bit of his time, and she knew how important that was when the days and weeks did nothing but stretch interminably ahead. And until today they had got along fine. It had been relaxed between them, easy. Until she'd gone and spoiled it all.

It had been fine with Ray at first too. Making a home together in their little flat had been so much fun, and at first their lives hadn't changed too much from before they married. They still went out to gigs, to the pub with their friends, some of whom were quite envious they had their own place to go back to. And as her belly and boobs had grown throughout her pregnancy Ray had seemed to find her even more attractive, so she'd had no complaints in that department either.

When had the rot set in? There'd been a bit of a dodgy patch after Michael was born, but then they had rubbed along all right. It was never easy, was it, with a baby around and less money because she'd had to give up her job. But they'd managed. Or rather, they could have done, if Ray had gone to the pub a bit less often. She'd tried to go back to work when Michael was a year old, but it hadn't lasted long because he had somehow hit his head at the nursery one day and they hadn't done anything about it. Having to run to the phone box to call the ambulance that night, with his limp body in her arms, brought all the horror over Patti back. As did the two long days and nights spent at his hospital bedside. Her parents had gone through this for weeks on end, and it had all been her fault. She couldn't allow this to go wrong too. What was more, she needed to find a way to make it up to her family, to put things right with Patti. But it was hard with Mama warning her to stay away, and being so perpetually exhausted. Sometimes it felt as though all the fight had gone out of her.

Her priority after that had to be to keep Michael safe and she threw in the towel at work. Ray had told her not to be selfish and to find another nursery. She had told him if he spent less money she wouldn't have to, but he said if he was the earner, he'd do what he liked. Then everything went wrong, and it was always her fault. If she hadn't trapped him by falling pregnant; if she lost a bit of weight she'd be more attractive; if she spent as much time and energy looking after his needs as she did Michael's …

Vedran sat down opposite her again, interrupting her train of thought. If he wasn't so young she would have tried to explain to him how useless she was with men, how she'd only hurt his uncle, but he'd never understand.

He leant back and folded his arms. "So, what did you argue about?"

Clearly he wasn't going to let her off the hook easily. "It was this business with my father. I didn't tell the man in the museum he was a Nazi sympathiser and Jadran thought I should have. But how do you say something like that to someone whose family might have been affected by his actions? Anyway, as it turned out, I used a really unfortunate turn of phrase. I told you I always put my foot in it. I said I was ashamed because my father had blood on his hands. So Jadran said I wouldn't want to be seen with him then, would I? It was only afterwards I remembered he'd fought in a war."

"Oh wow. Of all the buttons to push. He hates being reminded of that time because of what happened to Leila and Kristina." The wind looked well and truly knocked out of Vedran's sails.

"So you do see then, how badly I've messed this up? The hurt I must have caused … he isn't going to forgive me for that, is he?" Tears were filling her eyes again, and to her horror one spilled over and she wiped it quickly away. She stood, pushing the money for her wine and a generous tip across the table. "I'm so sorry, Vedran. Good luck with your studies and thank you for everything."

"Fran, wait …" But luckily as he followed her through the door a group sat down at the last free table outside so she was able to make her escape, the pink and white flowers in the pots on the doorsteps blurring behind her tears as she stumbled up the steps towards the sanctuary of her little apartment.

Fran could chart the labyrinthine progress of her evening by the glass of wine. It really had been a mistake to open a bottle, but by the time she'd finished sobbing and hiccupping, and had washed her face, she'd thought it would calm her down.

Of all the buttons to press. That's what Vedran had said, and he was right. For Jadran, everything about the war would be tangled up with the loss of his wife and daughter, and she must have hurt him so badly. He never even talked about it, but what had she done? Thrown it all in his face.

Initially she'd still been sober enough to realise that probably wasn't quite the truth, that he was the one who'd become angry, but as she set aside her third glass so she could make herself a sandwich for dinner she was almost paralysed by the pain she must have caused. She slumped back down at the table, picking at the corner of the label on the wine bottle.

Jadran was a lovely man who had been nothing but kind and thoughtful, and what had she done? It wasn't just that she didn't know how to handle men, this was an epic fail simply on the basis of his being another human. She hadn't thought for a moment about how he might feel, being confronted with her obsession about another war, another marriage ending in a violent death. How selfish was she?

It wasn't as if she didn't know the right thing was to put other people first. It had been Mama's mantra and what she had always tried to do. It just went to show; getting so terribly wrapped up in herself only led to upsetting other people. Experience should have told her that and she shouldn't do it. She didn't want to hurt anyone, especially Jadran.

If – and it was a big if – Vedran was right and being with her had made Jadran a bit happier, then it was doubly awful. If he really hadn't so much as looked at another woman in twenty years, how must he be feeling about her gender in general right now? Oh lord in heaven, what had she done? Stifling a hiccup she grabbed her glass and took a generous slug of wine.

Yet all the same there was a devil on her shoulder, whispering that she'd come here for time on her own, time to be free of responsibilities and think about herself and her future. She wasn't responsible for Jadran, how could she be?

She hadn't asked to be part of his life, hadn't wanted to … But she had. She really had. She enjoyed his company.

Sod it, sod it, sod it.

She stood and walked around the kitchen table, her arms wrapped tightly over her chest to stop herself from drinking any more wine. It wasn't helping. She needed to sober up. No, she needed to talk to Parisa. She'd sort her out. But as she was reaching for her phone she realised she was far too ashamed of what she had done to admit it to anyone.

Putting the stopper back in the bottle she took what was left in her glass through to the living room and lay down on the sofa, picking up the TV remote control. She'd left it tuned to a Croatian channel she'd been trying to follow, but now the words jumbled up in her head and she muted the sound. It was Vedran who'd given her the idea, dear sweet Vedran, whom she'd probably upset too. She was just one big liability. No use to anyone.

She downed the rest of her wine and lay on her back, staring at the ceiling. The lampshade began to sway, then spin a little, but no, it was actually the room that was moving. Bloody hell, she was drunk. There'd be hell to pay in the morning, but it served her damn well right. She closed her eyes, trying not to cry.

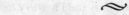

It was only a few hours later that Fran woke with a thumping head and a mouth like sandpaper. She sat up cautiously, lowering her feet to the floor. At least the room seemed relatively stable now so she stood and made her way to the kitchen, filling a mug she'd left on the draining board with cold water and glugging it down, followed by another. She filled it again and headed for the bathroom to hunt out the paracetamol.

She managed to find them and was sitting on the edge of her bed trying to wriggle into her pyjama bottoms when she heard her phone ping. She stared at it with incredulity. The message was from Jadran, and she read it out loud, but she could still hardly believe it.

Vedran tells me I have upset you.

No, the boot was certainly on the other foot. Or at very least, part of it was. But how should she reply, especially as she had downed the best part of a bottle of wine. It's just what everyone told the youngsters not to do, wasn't it? Text while drunk. And yet she couldn't leave it unanswered. She had to put him right. It wasn't fair, otherwise. She stared at the screen, waiting for inspiration, but instead another message appeared.

Perhaps he is correct and I shouldn't have said what I did. I apologise.

Sod this not texting while drunk malarkey.

No. It was me who was thoughtless and I'm sorry too.

She exhaled, feeling unsteady. OK, that was fine. They'd cleared the air. Then if they did bump into each other again it wouldn't be so awkward. She still wasn't sure how she'd face Vedran though, but that was easy. She just wouldn't walk past the café. It was probably time she made some plans to go home anyway. She'd discovered far more than she'd ever wanted to about Branko Milišić already.

She was halfway to the bathroom when her phone pinged again.

I would still like to help you find out more about your father.

What if she'd decided she didn't want to? But of course Jadran didn't know that, and it was really nice of him to offer. Beyond nice, actually, it was closer to saintly. Unless he was a glutton for punishment. More words appeared.

If you will permit me.

Permit him? What a crazy way of putting it. Despite the hurt she'd caused she really wanted to see him again, perhaps have the chance to put things right. Even if it did mean digging a little deeper into her father's unpalatable past. Besides, he was a lovely man and …

Fran, no, you can't go there. It was the drink talking. Or at very least thinking. Carefully she typed,

That is more than kind of you. I don't really know what to do next.

Coffee tomorrow to make a plan?

Why, oh why, was she feeling so close to tears again? These were nasty, horrid things too, not like the cleansing ones she still sometimes cried for Daddy, the ones that left her smiling once they were spent, with happy memories of him wrapped up as though in a hug. No, the prickles behind her eyes felt ugly and harsh and she didn't have a clue why.

Oh, for god's sake, Fran. What she really needed was to sleep off all that wine and pray she didn't feel – and look – like death warmed up in the morning.

Come here at eleven. I need time to bake you a cake.

She typed her address then pressed send. A cake was the very least she could offer him after what she'd put him through.

Chapter Seventeen

Dubrovnik, 13th October 1944

S he waits for him at the corner of the street, baby on her back and a package in her hand, saying nothing as she watches him limp towards her. They speak at the same moment.

"I am sorry."

"The Germans are leaving."

They try again, but it is the same.

"What did you say?"

"I am sorry too."

Then they laugh, and it is all he can do not to sag against her, but she links her arm through his and they walk up the hill together, as though it is his strength supporting her.

"What do you mean, the Germans are leaving?" he asks.

"Some of them are. The higher officers at least." She waves the parcel under his nose. "Which is why we have ham for the stew, and bread to go with it. There was too much ... can you ever imagine? Too much. So cook shared it out between us." She looks at him from beneath her long lashes. "Unless you are going to be stubborn about this as well and not eat German food."

"I am too hungry to be stubborn, and anyway ..."

"Anyway what?"

"There is a difference."

"Explain."

He senses that despite her words, he is not entirely forgiven. "The food ... it is not personal. The uniform ... that is my shame."

"It should be your pride. Oh, Branko, all those lives you saved ..."

"No! There is little I can do in this war, but at least I managed to help just a few people. Such a small thing ..."

Safranka stirs on her back as Dragica hugs him. "One day, I will tell our daughter ..."

He shakes his head. "Like everything to do with this wretched war, it is best forgotten. I did what I had to, that was all."

"You are a strange man sometimes. But I love you with all my heart."

Later, much later, after they have savoured the stew, and once Safranka is sleeping deeply, they make love. She wants him, welcomes him, for the first time since the baby was born and he marvels at the tenderness between them, unblemished by the harshness of the life they lead. And afterwards he gazes at her, stroking her cheek.

"I want so much more for us than this," he says.

"It will soon be over. I told you, the Germans are leaving. Perhaps there will not even be a battle for the city."

"Perhaps the partisans will walk straight by if there's no one to fight." He gazes into the dark pools of her eyes. "If the Ustaše take over, we will have to leave. There will be other parts of Yugoslavia where there is freedom and fairness, and I will not have Safranka grow up in a place where there is none."

"But you love this city," she murmurs.

"I love my daughter more."

Chapter Eighteen

Dubrovnik, March 2010

By quarter to eleven, Fran's Victoria sponge had been sandwiched together with the last of the plum jam she had bought at the market, and the filter coffee jug she had found at the back of one of the kitchen cupboards had been washed and stood ready for use. She could do no more but wait for Jadran, and she decided to sit outside to do so.

At this time of the morning the sun was high enough for it to creep over the stone wall that separated the long narrow terrace from the street and bathe the small metal table and chairs in light. Really, they were not very comfortable, but sitting here felt slightly more like neutral territory than having their coffee inside. She couldn't quite put her finger on it, but that would seem just a little too intimate.

She propped her book in front of her and pretended to read, all the time listening for footsteps. What would she say to him? Would it be impossibly awkward? She clasped her fingers tightly together then unwound them again. *Relax, Fran. Just relax. He wants to help. You want to make amends. As long as you think before opening that great big mouth of yours, everything should be fine.*

As it happened, she had dashed inside to check she had boiled the kettle when Jadran arrived. She heard the creak of the outer door and rushed back onto the terrace in time to see him standing on the bottom step, smiling uncertainly.

"Good morning, Safranka. How are you?"

"Very well, thank you. You?"

"If I am honest, a little nervous. I was hasty yesterday and I regret it."

Oh, god, he was worried too, bless him. "And I was thoughtless." Fran smiled. "So we're probably quits. Shall we just forget it ever happened? Life's too short."

He nodded. "Especially at our age." But as he said it, there was a twinkle in his eyes.

"Then I'd better not keep you waiting for your cake. Why don't you sit down and I'll bring it out here? It's a shame to waste the sunshine."

Fran felt better while she was bustling around in the kitchen with mugs and plates, and tried as hard as she could to carry the feeling of domestic competence and calm with her onto the terrace. Jadran exclaimed over the sponge, and Fran apologised for the coffee, which seemed terribly weak compared to how Vedran served it in the café, but a moment came when they were left looking at each other.

It was Jadran who filled the silence. "We need to make a plan of how we find out more about your father. If you can give me some basic information, I can look in the city archives, and perhaps you can contact the archaeologists to see if they have any more detail about Daksa and the events leading up to it."

"What information do you need?"

"Everything you have. Although I do realise it mightn't be very much." He pulled his phone from his shirt pocket, and Fran recognised it as a BlackBerry, just like the one Michael had. Jadran gesticulated with it. "I needed it for work, but at least I can make notes and email them to myself."

"OK. Well, my father's name was Branko Milišić. He was born in Dubrovnik in 1919 and the archaeologists told me he was a clerk."

"And what about your mother? If I can find her, it might lead me to him if there are marriage records."

"I don't know when they married. She wasn't born in the city either, she talked about growing up in the country, but not where. I do have a date of birth, though; it was 17th July 1921. And her name was Dragica, although all her life in England she called herself Milly."

Jadran smiled sadly. "Then she must have loved your father very much, to take her name from his."

"Do you know, that hadn't really occurred to me." God, she must sound so stupid again. "That ... that makes it worse."

"Makes what worse?"

Her bloody big mouth. When, oh when, would she learn to think before she opened it? "It's hard to explain ..."

"I'm listening."

And he was. He was looking at her intently, his head on one side and his hazel eyes focused on her face.

She owed him this. Owed him the truth, the truth she had barely dared to put into words for herself. But if he was going to carry on helping her, he needed to know why it was so important. Why, for her, the stakes were so high. And that it wasn't all about her father.

She took a deep breath. "For a while, when I found out the way my father's life ended, it niggled me why it felt important. It was at complete odds with what my mother had always told me, which was that he died a hero, and I realised perhaps that was the reason. It just didn't fit, and I didn't want to believe it." She paused, and Jadran nodded encouragingly.

"Since the evidence has begun to stack up against him, Michael and I have been trying to come up with reasons for it. Perhaps Mama had right-wing leanings too, but that certainly didn't play out in her later life. In fact, the exact opposite. But maybe she'd had her fingers burnt. Or maybe she hid it all so she could make a new start in England. When she met Daddy she always told me I had to be good so that we deserved him, so maybe she felt the same applied to her.

"But I can't second guess it, and it makes me wonder how well I really knew my mother at all. I think that's what hurts. I've spent most of my life looking up to her, trying to follow her example, behave in a way she thought was right … and what if … what if … I never knew her at all."

There. It was said. Fran sat back and picked up her mug, her hand trembling slightly.

"Then it is even more important we try to find out the truth, Safranka. On Daksa I told you that you were not shaped by your father, and that is right. But I can see perhaps you are your mother's daughter through and through."

Fran nodded, taking a gulp of coffee. It was cold. She leapt up. "Let me make another pot. Stronger, this time."

"Good idea." A thin smile played around Jadran's mouth. "But remember, Safranka, whatever we discover about your parents, from where I'm sitting, apart from your coffee making skills, your mother did a pretty good job."

I've got something. Where are you?

Apologising to the stallholder she'd been chatting to, Fran stepped away, read the text again, then typed her reply.

At the market.

See you outside Sponza in five minutes.

It must be important and Fran felt slightly sick. What couldn't wait until they met at the bar later? All the same she knew Jadran had been incredibly enthusiastic about the research project, although she suspected it was most likely because it was something new to fill his time.

As she rounded the corner of Sveti Vlaho she saw him step from under the delicately arched colonnade, his grey hair glinting in the sunshine as he looked around. Despite the knot in her stomach she couldn't help but smile, waving as he strode towards her.

They met at the corner of the church.

"It's something important?" Fran asked, then inwardly cursed for forgetting the social niceties.

"Yes. Links between your father and the Jewish community."

"Good or bad?"

He put his hand gently on her arm. "Safranka, please. Don't

judge him. Let facts be facts at the moment. This could just be the beginning. I have a lot of material left to go through."

She nodded, looking down at the paving stones between them. "All right."

"So, they have records of the city's employees over the years and I wondered whether, given your father was a clerk, he worked for the municipality, and I was right. He started in 1934 and his address at that time is in the ledger. Here, I wrote it down." He handed her a scrap of paper. "It's Kovacka Street, which is in the area of the old ghetto, so it's highly likely he would have had Jewish neighbours." He gesticulated behind him. "It's that street there, the one that runs up the side of the palace, but I think this address is close to the other end."

"That's amazing. I never thought ... never thought I would find where he actually lived."

"It was an incredible stroke of luck. But, Safranka, there is something else. At the beginning of 1943 he went to work at the internment centre on Lopud for six months."

"So he worked in the prison camp? Well that just about seals it, doesn't it? He was a Nazi so no wonder he was executed."

"You're judging him again."

"I'm sorry, but what other conclusion am I meant to draw?"

"He could have been sent there. He mightn't have had a choice. They'd have needed administrative staff too."

Or he might have jumped at the chance. Having Jewish neighbours didn't necessarily mean he'd liked them; sometimes proximity could work the other way.

Jadran looked down at her with that almost smile and Fran felt something inside her ripple. This was ridiculous, and so inappropriate. And yet … No, she must consign that thought to the dustbin right now.

"Thank you so much for doing this for me."

"It's fun. I've never solved a mystery before. And of course, it fills my time." That sparkle just beneath the surface again, although his voice was perfectly serious. "Will you look for your father's house?"

Despite the fact she was uncertain, it would seem very ungrateful not to. "Yes. In fact, I think I'll do it now." There, she'd committed herself. And the way he beamed at her was all the reward she needed.

Leaving Jadran to go back to his research she turned up Kovacka Street. Most of the small roads leading inland from Stradun ran parallel to each other, and to Fran's eye looked fairly similar. She passed two boarded up bars, a chemist, and further on, a small hotel, which at this time of year had a slightly neglected air. She checked the numbers on the doors – Jadran was right, she had a way to go yet, and with every step she became less and less certain she wanted to get there. Her father had been a fascist. What Jadran had discovered this morning had made her more certain because surely the administration would only have sent people it could trust to work in the camps.

The road marked the beginning of the slightly broader Prijeko Street, which ran parallel to Stradun, and on the other side it began to climb so steeply it was almost all flights of steps. Above her, air conditioning units jutted out and washing hung from balconies, a television blaring from deep inside a building. The smell of coffee and of roasting spices mingled in the air and a cat that was stretched out on the paving stones stopped licking its paws to watch her pass.

She must be getting close. Fran stopped and turned, looking back the way she had come. The street was so narrow that if she stretched out her arms she could almost touch both sides, the golden-grey stone seemingly pressing in. The buildings towards the corner below her were bathed in sunlight while those nearer were darkened by shadow. She hadn't realised, but she'd become quite hot climbing, and now she had stopped she started to shiver. For the first time she was going to see somewhere intimately tied to her parents' history. Maybe her mother had visited this house, maybe even lived here. Perhaps … perhaps … it was where she herself had been born.

Fran closed her eyes and tried to imagine her mother going about her daily business in these narrow, stepped streets. What she had told Jadran was right. She genuinely knew nothing about what her life had been like here; not when she came to the city from her village or why, not how she met Fran's father, whether they were rich or poor. Nothing. All she had of her mother's Yugoslavian roots were her colouring, a smattering of language, a few recipes and the necklace.

If only she could talk to her mother now, hear her voice, watch the careful way she polished her glasses when she was thinking. Just one more hour with Mama, that's all she wanted, and not just to ask all those unanswerable questions, just to be in her company, comfortable together in the way they always had been. The stab of yearning was almost too much to bear.

How come her grief was so sharp after all this time? But now she knew it was because she'd buried it for far too long; it wasn't Dubrovnik that was bringing it back; it was more that she was allowing it in. She had to learn to move beyond it somehow, but right now it seemed such an impossible task.

She reached out her arm and steadied herself on the metal balustrade of a set of steps leading up to someone's front door. She needed to ride this wave of emotion, find a sense of proportion. Her father had lived in this street when he was fifteen, that was all she would ever know about it. *Come on, Fran, get on with finding the bloody place.* Then she could finish her shopping and go home with a clear conscience for a nice cup of tea. And a little weep, if that was what she needed.

When she reached the house there was something subtly different about it and its neighbours. White plastic doors and windows with square posts on either side and the lintels above made of concrete. The stones themselves were regular, lighter, although the rows closest to the ground were dark and not quite so square. She frowned. Why …? And then it dawned on her. They must have been bombed in the war in the nineties. Just like Jadran's home had been.

How on earth would she tell him her father's house had been razed to the ground too? The answer was clearly that she wouldn't. She'd pretend she hadn't noticed. That was it. Instead of taking a picture of the house itself she snapped a few of the street in general that she could send to Michael and show Jadran and made her way back down the hill.

After thirty or so yards she stopped. That was a real cop out. She turned and retraced her steps then took another picture at an angle. There. She'd done it. She could always say she hadn't wanted to take a direct photograph of someone's home.

As she put her phone away, she began to wonder why she was going to such lengths to protect Jadran's feelings. She didn't want to hurt him again, that was for sure. But could it be more than that? If she was honest with herself she knew it probably was. Somewhere along the line there'd been a subtle shift in her feelings; she wanted not only to protect him, but to care for him, look after him, in a way that meant more than just baking him cakes.

But that was what she did, wasn't it? Took care of people. Of Andrew and Patti when they were little, then of Michael, then Mama when she'd fallen ill, and Daddy ... Having no one to look after was what had made her feel so damned empty and useless. But it was no good expecting Jadran to slot in and fill that gap. For a start, he lived here and she lived, well, thousands of miles away, and she was only here for another seven weeks or so. More importantly, though, she was beginning to wonder if replacing one person to care for with another was actually the right thing to do. Mightn't it be better to try to break the caring habit?

That was just one uncomfortable thought too far. *That's quite enough introspection for one day, Fran.* She needed to stop all this rubbish and finish her shopping, or she'd have nothing to eat tonight.

Her route took her down Žudioska Street, and outside the synagogue she stopped. She'd promised to let Eli know if they discovered anything else about her father. It seemed such a simple thing, but all the same her stomach churned. However benign the Italian regime might have been, an internment camp was an internment camp in anyone's money. But on the other hand, she didn't have to say too much, just where her father had lived. Maybe only mention Lopud if Eli was in a good mood. Yes, that sounded like a plan.

Her legs felt quite weak as she climbed the stairs, but there was a hint of something else propelling her on. A desire to test herself, maybe, to see how brave she could be. She didn't know why, it just felt important after the emotional upheaval of the morning, like courage was something she was going to need to move her life forwards. After all, this was quite a small way to start.

When Fran reached the desk there was a woman behind it, who told her that Eli wasn't in that day. Pushing a piece of paper towards Fran, she asked if she would like to leave him a note. Fran felt the knot in her stomach relax. The perfect solution. Quickly she scribbled down where her father had been living in 1934, and then that he had worked on Lopud for six months and he was a clerk. Perhaps it was a little disingenuous linking the two, but ... Finally she added her phone number and, thanking the woman, headed out into the sunshine.

"So, how's your hunky Croat?"

Much as Fran loved her Friday night video chats with Parisa, and as long as she had known her friend, she still wasn't always ready for her direct approach.

"Hello, Parisa. How was your week?" she asked pointedly.

"Nothing to write home about. Taking Button to the groomers was probably the highlight, so stop changing the subject and spill."

Fran took a sip of wine. "We had a bit of a disagreement, actually."

"Sounds ominous."

"No, we set things right. Well, to be honest, Vedran sort of banged our heads together. Which is a bit embarrassing, given he's all of twenty."

Parisa laughed. "He's playing Cupid, then?"

"Perhaps. He said his uncle's happier since he met me, and of course he's close to him, but initially I didn't possibly think he could be right. Then I started to worry that if he is, it's a hell of a responsibility. I'll be coming home at the end of April."

"And how old is this Jadran?"

"Early sixties?"

"And he knows your plans?"

"Yes."

"Then you're not pulling the wool over his eyes and he's quite old enough to make up his own mind. Fran, honestly, there you go, worrying about someone else when you ought to be concentrating on your own needs."

Fran took a sip of wine. "Do you know? I was thinking along those lines yesterday afternoon. I was worrying about Jadran, about saying something else that could hurt him and then I thought ... you know ... is this all about me needing someone to look after?"

"Only you can answer that, Fran. But he's a grown man, remember. You said he's been a widower for almost twenty years, and he's survived, so he clearly doesn't need protecting. It may well be what you're looking for in him, but it certainly isn't what he'll be looking for from you. I'd put money on it."

"Another reason we'd be doomed before we started. Anyway, I'm pretty sure I don't feel ready for a relationship." Her friend opened her mouth to speak, but Fran carried on. "And don't say a fling, because something I do know is that it's not for me."

Parisa sat back. "Well I'm pleased you've made a decision about something." She paused. "And I really hope that didn't come over as patronising as it sounded."

"It's all right. I'm used to you." Fran laughed. "I knew it almost straight after we talked last time too. It just felt completely wrong. I'm not like you; I know you enjoy it, but I don't want casual sex."

"But do you know what you do want? Setting aside your lifelong habit of caring for someone, that is. What do you want for you?"

"I don't know. It's been ages since I've even thought about it."

"Then it's time you did. But you know that, don't you?"

Fran nodded and sipped her wine.

"I totally get that a fling isn't for you, but what do you want from a relationship? It sounds like a degree of commitment at least, but what else?"

"I … I don't know. I don't even think I want a man in my life. I mean, I know I dated a bit when Michael first left home, but I can't say I ever felt comfortable with it."

"Ray damaged you, didn't he?" Her voice was softer.

"You can't blame Ray for my personal foibles."

"Are you sure about that, Fran? I mean, I'm not, because you've never really talked to me about it, but I reckon it's time you gave it some thought if it's holding you back. I was in Manchester at the time, remember, and when I came home some years later, I assumed you were over it, living in your little house with Michael and happy as anything, but hearing you talk now I'm not so sure."

"I don't think *damaged* is the right word," Fran started slowly, "but he wore me down. He was always on at me about something I'd done wrong, and I was stuck halfway up a tower block with a toddler. I suppose … I had no other point of reference. After Mama and Daddy brought me home, they used to talk a lot about building up my confidence, so I suppose that was how they saw it. I just felt so guilty and ashamed that my marriage had failed. I didn't want to risk it again."

"So it's the idea of taking a risk that's putting you off? Do you know what you're frightened of? Rejection? Because from what you've said I don't think that would be an issue with Jadran."

"No, it's not exactly that, it's … it's … oh, I don't know, maybe it's getting it wrong again, hurting someone when I don't need to … oh, god, I don't know."

How could she put into words all the swirling doubts about her motivations and feelings, even to Parisa? She'd come here to give herself time and space to work out what to do next, but these new thoughts and ideas that were beginning to whirl around her head just made everything seem impossibly complicated. She didn't even know how to start unravelling it.

"But there is something I want to pick your brain about, and it does involve Jadran."

"All right."

"Whatever I decide I want, however I may or may not feel, at the moment there's a mouse in the room, but I have the feeling it has the potential to grow to the size of an elephant. Top up your wine and I'll tell you about our argument."

The seeds of this train of thought had been niggling Fran for a day or so now, and she explained to Parisa that several times Jadran had accused her of judging her father, and given the nature of their row, what really concerned her was whether he was worried she was judging him for his part in the war in the nineties.

"Well, I think you just have to make it clear to him that you're not," said Parisa.

"Not so simple. He doesn't talk about the war. He even got Vedran to explain that to me before we started to meet regularly. It's definitely a no-go area."

"Hmm. That does complicate things a little. If there's a whole great chunk of his life he won't talk about, that in itself will stop you from getting close."

"Exactly. So what with that and the fact we live in different countries, it really is a non-starter. He's just a friend, so we'd best leave it as it is."

Parisa shrugged. "It's a shame, but plenty more fish in the sea. If that's what you decide you want, of course."

Except there weren't. Certainly not fish like Jadran. Fran thought about it later, as she pottered around the kitchen, washing up. Much as Vedran had implied Jadran hadn't looked at a woman for years, she hadn't looked at a man either, hadn't really wanted to spend time with one who wasn't a family member. Parisa had plenty of male friends, but Fran didn't, which meant she wasn't really sure how to handle this one.

And if she was entirely honest with herself, her feelings for Jadran were already deeper than she'd been prepared to admit. He took up far too many of her waking thoughts, and there was something about being with him that made her feel alive in a way she wasn't sure she had ever felt before. Even though it couldn't possibly be classed as a date, she was already worrying about what to wear on Sunday, because he was taking her for a posh coffee at Gradska Kavana.

It was just so bloody complicated. Why the hell couldn't she simply enjoy spending time with an attractive, thoughtful man in the way other women seemed to? What was wrong with her? Had Ray damaged her in some way, as Parisa seemed to think? No, that couldn't be it. It took two to break a marriage, much as it took two to make one.

But that wasn't always the case, and she knew it. There had been children at the centre where she'd volunteered who had lived in the local refuge with their mothers. Children who had experienced, or at very least witnessed, awful violence, and it had never even occurred to Fran to even remotely blame the women. But on the other hand, Ray had never hit her. Well, only the once, and he'd been very drunk at the time. The next morning he'd been so apologetic she'd actually thought things would be all right between them again. And they had been for a while, although she'd always felt she was walking around on eggshells.

For the first time in a long time she thought about Daddy saying how 'that man' had sucked the confidence out of her. Was it true? Had there been something dark and coercive about his behaviour that had made her steer clear of men ever since? Well not all men, obviously. As well as being her brother, Andrew was one of her best friends, and if she'd met someone more like him; someone kind and loyal and honest, someone who made her laugh, things might have been very different.

Jadran was kind, though, and honest. Loyal too, she suspected. At least he had been to the memory of his wife. Things felt very easy and natural when they were together – it was only when they were apart that she started to overthink it all and get in a muddle. Were all the complications and contortions of her own making? Should she just go with the flow and see what happened?

Fran wiped her hands on the tea towel and folded it over

the back of the chair. That sounded all very easy, didn't it, but could she even do it? Should she even do it? *Oh, for god's sake, Fran, stop it. Don't start that again.* She looked at the clock on the wall. Almost time for the Croatian evening news. Struggling to understand it would be all the distraction she needed.

Chapter Nineteen

Dubrovnik, 16th October 1944

I t is the fear he remembers most about his time on Lopud. That and the waiting. Those times he had to remain motionless in the darkness under the trees in the garden next to the Grand Hotel, the damp cold seeping through the stiff serge of his uniform as he fingered the key in his pocket. He had no reason to be there. He felt like a fugitive himself.

He had started his slow march along the harbour when the monastery church chimed the hour. If anyone was watching him, so much was normal. Down the steps, around the harbour, past the shuttered buildings as the breeze whispered the drizzle from the sea. A patrol he had exchanged with an Italian soldier for food. They used to laugh at him because he seemed to be always hungry.

The white concrete ghost of the hotel loomed between the trees as the moon showed itself from amongst the clouds, illuminating the building's sharp angles with an eerie light.

Not the best of moments to have heard a boat approaching the shore. If he had dared, he would have cursed, but perhaps it was not Vido after all.

The engine cut. Burst into life again. The signal. It was time. All needed to come together for his plan to work; the Ustaše guards drunk on the rakija he had 'found' for them; Solly's family on the other side of the door … He had one chance, one chance only to get this right, or they were all as good as dead.

He limped from the shelter of the holm oaks and orange trees towards the building. The key in the lock, the click of the mechanism loud as gunshot. *Breathe, Branko, breathe.*

He stopped, checked left and right. Listened and looked, then pushed the door open. The faintest of rustles as two dark shapes emerged hand in hand, the larger one clasping a bundle to her chest as the child stumbled sleepily behind. He willed her not to fall and cry out as they ran to the shelter of the trees. If she had, all would have been lost.

The woman began to speak, but he silenced her with a shake of his head. They crept behind him, through the gardens until they were in sight of the jetty where a fishing boat creaked and rocked. Without a word he turned and marched on, past the hotel towards the far end of the bay. He could do no more for them. It was up to Vido now.

Chapter Twenty

Dubrovnik, March 2010

When Fran arrived outside Gradska Kavana on Sunday morning, Jadran was sitting on the impressive stone balustraded terrace wearing a linen shirt with a navy cotton jumper tied around his neck. The tables were in shade but the sun was already creeping along the street, illuminating every last creamy brick of the side wall of Sveti Vlaho church opposite. She could just hear the faint strains of organ music drifting from inside.

Jadran stood to greet her. "I am so glad you could join me, Safranka. Sunday coffee here is a proper old Dubrovnik tradition. Of course, we really should have gone to church first, but that is not something I have done in a very long time."

"Me neither. I wasn't brought up to it – my parents weren't religious at all."

He pulled a canvas director's chair away from the table so she could sit down. She was pleased she had finally plucked up the courage to wear the fancy embroidered cardigan Parisa had talked her into, and even more delighted when Jadran complimented her on it.

"This is actually the same place as the restaurant on the harbour front," he went on to explain. "So this side is for drinks, and the other for meals. In summer it's impossible to get near it, but this time of year it is perfect. Like it used to be before we had so many tourists."

"Do you resent how many there are?"

"No. The city is beautiful and historic, so of course people want to come. And many local businesses would not exist without them, and many jobs. But all the same I am pleased Vedran is studying for a proper career. Too much work here is seasonal, and the old town is becoming far too expensive for most people to live in, so very soon the sense of community will go."

"You said you've lived here all your life. You must have seen many changes." As she said it, she bit her tongue. *What a stupid, stupid thing …*

Jadran put his head on one side. "Well, yes, but sometimes the old becomes the new. Listen."

Fran had barely been aware of the background music on the terrace but it seemed to be some sort of folk ballad which plodded along, accompanied by an orchestra but with some fairly spectacular harmonies. She was glad there was something to distract him from her crassness.

"What is it?" she asked.

"It's a band called Dubrovački Trubaduri and they were very popular when I was a teenager. They disappeared for a while, but now they are back. Older of course, grey hair, like me … but still beautiful music."

"Yes." Fran didn't really know what else to say – they weren't exactly The Kinks or the Stones, but she was saved by the sound of her mobile phone ringing. She was so astonished that she fished in her handbag without even wondering how rude she might appear, and answered the call.

"Is this Fran?" The accent was Croatian and she thought she recognised the voice.

"Yes."

"It is Eli, from the museum. Thank you for your note. It was most interesting your father worked at the internment camp at Lopud."

"I … I hope it didn't shock you."

"At first perhaps, but we do not know if he had a choice. And anyway, his choices are not yours, Fran. It does not do to hold grudges from one generation to another."

Fran felt a weight lift from her shoulders. She'd lost quite a few hours of sleep over Eli's potential responses to her note. "Thank you so much for saying that. I was really quite worried and I wondered if I should have told you."

"Well it was a good thing you did, because I have mentioned it to a few people and there is someone in our community who was sent to Lopud with her family as a child, and if the story is right, they escaped from there."

"Oh wow, that's incredible."

"I wondered if you would like to meet her? At the moment she is in Israel celebrating Purim with her daughter, but I could ask when she returns next week."

Fran swallowed. "She might not want to meet me if she has bad memories."

"Oh no, Elvira is a very positive sort of person, so I am sure she'll help if she can. But it is up to you if I ask her."

She felt sick at the thought. Sick that perhaps, just perhaps, someone might remember her father. And her father as a Nazi sympathiser at that. "Can I think about it and let you know?" But if she thought she knew the truth already, why the hell was she so frightened of it?

"Of course. Enjoy your day."

Fran was halfway through saying thank you when he hung up. She looked up to see Jadran watching her, his head on one side.

"That was Eli," she explained. "I left him a note telling him my father had lived near the Jewish community and that he worked on Lopud. He knows someone who was imprisoned there as a child."

"But Safranka, that is wonderful news."

"Is it? What if she does remember my father and he was a bad man?" As soon as she said it, she regretted her words. "I'm sorry," she rushed on, "I'm not giving him the benefit of the doubt again, am I?"

He looked at her as if he was trying to weigh her up, then almost started to sigh before he said, "Maybe you should just give him a fair hearing? The hearing he never received at the time? I think everyone at least deserves that."

"Yes … yes … perhaps you're right. Well, I know you are. Gather the evidence and then …" She shrugged. "I suppose I need to be brave enough to face the truth, whatever that turns out to be."

"The past cannot hurt you, Safranka, because it is not your past. And before you think I was not listening when you told me about your mother, I do not think it changes the woman she was either. Whatever decisions she made when she left here during the war, I don't believe anyone could have lived a lie for fifty years."

"No … no, I do get that. But all the same, I am worried about what I might turn up."

"But didn't you come here because you wanted answers?" He was frowning, his hazel eyes unusually dark against the light.

"Oh, I know. I'm being silly. But I guess there are always things you'd rather not know about people, aren't there? None of us have led entirely blameless lives, after all." She smiled at him.

"Of course not. We're human. And human beings can be very weak." He looked at her for a long moment, then suddenly stood, brushing his hands on his trousers. "I am sorry. I am expected at my brother's for lunch. I have to go."

Fran scraped back her chair. "Thank you for the coffee."

"My pleasure."

She followed him through the tables, but his smile was a small, tight thing as they said their goodbyes at the bottom of the café steps and went their separate ways. She looked at her watch. It was only eleven o'clock. Had her prevarication over her father irritated him that much? It certainly seemed to have touched a nerve. Oh well, there was nothing she could do about it now. And with that thought she walked in the direction of the market to see what she could cook for lunch.

For the second time in as many days, Fran's phone ringing surprised her. Surely it wasn't Eli again? It was only eight in the morning. She put down her toothbrush and raced to the bedroom to answer it.

"Hello, Mum."

Michael. "What's wrong?"

"I don't want you to worry but …" His voice was tentative, nervy.

"But?" Fran held her breath. Was he ill? Had one of the girls or Paula had an accident?

"Auntie Alice phoned. Uncle Andrew was taken into hospital overnight. They think he's had a stroke."

Fran dropped onto the bed, her free hand groping for the corner of the duvet. "How bad?"

"She doesn't know. They're still doing tests and the like, but she'll keep us posted. She was in two minds about bothering you, seeing as you're away, but I thought you'd want to be told."

"You're absolutely right. Oh god, I wish I was at home, then I could do something."

"Don't be silly, Mum. There's nothing any of us can do right now, other than wait."

"Oh yes there is. I can book my plane ticket back."

"There's no need to be hasty. Let's see what the hospital says."

"No! I want to see him and I'm coming home."

Michael sighed. "I get that, but I am sure you'd be better off waiting. Why not … why not … just email the travel agent to see what your options are? Then when we know exactly what we're dealing with you'll be in a position to act."

"That does sound … sensible."

"Good. Sorry to rush this, but I need to get the girls'

breakfast sorted. I'll call back the moment I hear from Auntie Alice."

"Thank you."

He rang off, leaving Fran perched on the edge of her bed. Slowly she unfurled her fingers and gazed at the network of creases on the duvet cover where she'd been gripping it. *Please, please, let Andrew be all right.* He was her little brother ... he was so young ... if this had to happen to any of them, it should have been her. She was the oldest. Oh, god.

It must be the stress of everything that had caused the stroke. He'd called her the family rock, but she'd taken that support away just when he needed it; just when he was grieving for Daddy too. If only she hadn't come on this indulgent adventure. She should have stayed and helped him to sort out the probate, try to deal with Patti instead of running away ... all the extra things she'd put on him by not being there. Whatever Michael said, she needed to go home. To take it all over so Andrew could recover. *Oh, please, let him recover. Let him get completely well.*

But whatever happened, this was definitely a wake-up call to sort things out with Patti. They were sisters, after all, although she suspected that these days if Patti referred to her at all she would call her a half-sister. With the emphasis on the half. All the same, they shared their mother's blood and had been brought up by the same parents. That had to mean something. Had to mean it was possible to finally put this right.

However had it all gone so very wrong in the first place? She knew, of course she knew. If only she had actually watched her next to the fire as Mama had asked, and not been reading her book. A momentary lapse and her sister had been disfigured for life. She couldn't blame Patti for hating her once she'd discovered it had all been her fault.

The right time to have stopped things from escalating further would have been when Fran had come home when Michael was a baby, but at first she had been too exhausted and low to do anything. Even looking after Michael properly had become an impossible chore. It was hard to really believe those dreadful days had happened now, but they had and had probably gone on far too long.

Fran could remember the exact moment she had woken up from her depressive stupor and the first thing she'd seen had been the hatred in Patti's eyes. It had been over such a small thing too. Ever since she'd come out of hospital, Patti had wound the clock in the hall with Mama on Sunday mornings, and she'd come downstairs to find her mother lifting Michael up to do it. Looking back Fran knew it had been a huge overreaction from a sixteen-year-old, but Patti had become so used to being the centre of attention perhaps it had been inevitable.

Of course Fran knew that all Patti's woes in life were not her fault; her missed chances with her education, her unfortunate marriages, her half-hearted attempts at her private catering business. These were Patti's life choices, not hers, but all the same it had been her failings as a sister that had started the whole sorry train of events.

Daddy had known it too. When he'd been helping Fran to move into her house he'd warned her against overprotecting and spoiling Michael as they had Patti. He explained they had fallen into it after her long illness without even realising it, and had inadvertently created 'a bit of a monster'. It was the best parenting advice anyone ever gave Fran but made her feel even worse that her mistake had been at the heart of it all.

Even years later it had made family life a bit awkward at Christmas and the like, when either Patti or Fran would visit, but rarely do so together. That had all changed when Mama had been diagnosed with her first cancer. But Patti had found her mother's illness hard to cope with, although she had later blamed Fran for keeping her away. Just as she had done with Daddy, now she thought of it. But back then it had been down to Andrew to try to broker an uneasy truce, bless him, although he'd told Fran he wanted nothing to do with Patti either.

Andrew. Darling Andrew. What was he going through right now? She glanced at her phone, but it was only fifteen minutes since Michael called. This was going to be the longest, longest morning. She'd arranged to meet Jadran to walk around the city walls. Would it be a good thing to be distracted? Or should she just wait here? She wasn't exactly going to be great company. She couldn't put this misery on him as well.

Still, it was early yet. She would sort herself out now so she wouldn't be in the shower when Michael called back, then try to decide what to do about Jadran while she had her breakfast. But whatever happened, her first priorities would be to email the travel agent, then try to compose a suitable form of words to send to Patti. The rift between them may have been a lifetime in the making but now it was time to put it right.

The fact Fran's toast stuck in her throat like a dry old piece of cardboard made up her mind that it would be a bad idea to go

EVA GLYN

out with Jadran. She didn't want to eat, dress, do anything
except wait for the call from Michael. She hadn't even taken
her breakfast onto the terrace, and she normally loved feeding
the sparrows that appeared the moment she sat down.

Instead she cut her abandoned toast into tiny pieces and
scattered them across the outside table. At least the birds
would be happy this morning. Before turning back inside she
paused to listen as they chirped in the branches of the tree with
the strange windy trunk that seemed to grow out of the wall.
There were footsteps in the street outside too, the sound of
voices. Everyone else's life was going on as normal, while hers
was on hold.

Back inside she texted Jadran, telling him there was a
family emergency in the UK and she needed to wait for a call.
His reply, asking her what had happened, was immediate.

My brother Andrew's had a stroke. Waiting to find out
how bad.

Safranka, I am so sorry. Do you want company or would you
rather be alone?

What did she want? If Jadran were to come over she'd have
to change out of her jogging bottoms, and she wasn't sure she
had the energy. And what would she say to him? She couldn't
face making conversation, that was for sure, and he'd have a
miserable morning too.

I'm too anxious to be good company.

That wasn't what I asked.

176

No, but it had been her answer. She felt that despite his perfect English, sometimes things were lost in translation between them. It had nothing to do with language, more the way they were, just slightly out of kilter with each other, a hair's breadth away from mutual understanding. The way he'd got up and left so suddenly yesterday seemed to underline it.

It really didn't matter. She'd be on the plane home later today or tomorrow. Well, she would be if she got her act together to email the travel agent. First things first. And then she would try to work out what to say to Patti while she still had the courage to do so.

Even the email about her flight took a while to compose and Fran felt thoroughly wrung out afterwards. Everything was like wading through mud, which wasn't surprising, given all she could think about was Andrew. It was a good couple of hours since Michael had phoned, but it would still be only just after nine in the UK. Not very long to assess a stroke patient. She knew when Daddy'd had his it had taken most of the day, and there'd been the very real risk of him having another one. But she'd been sitting by his bed practically the whole time; she'd been able to talk to the doctors, hold Daddy's hand. Now she was absolutely no use at all. At least if she'd been at home she could have supported Alice.

Rather than sitting here worrying, she decided to start tidying the apartment ready to leave. She opened the fridge. There was far too much food to finish in one day, but she could always give it to Vedran or Jadran. She gazed at the packet of prawns from the supermarket, the slightly limp lettuce, the lump of cheese. There was no point in cleaning around it. Perhaps there was no point in doing anything at all.

Her phone rang and she made a grab for it, sending it spinning to the floor. Seeing it was Alice, Fran couldn't stop her voice from shaking when she said hello.

"It's OK, I'm just waiting to take him home."

"You're what?" This was quite frankly unbelievable news.

"I'm taking him home. They're pretty sure he had a TIA, not a stroke, and he's right as rain now. Even ate his hospital breakfast. They've booked him in for some scans on Friday to try to work out why it happened."

"Oh, Alice, that's wonderful."

"I know. It's been a bloody awful night, but they've been marvellous. Once I get home and he's rested up a bit, I'll get him to give you a ring to put your mind at rest."

"Only if he's up to it."

"Honestly, you wouldn't think there was anything wrong with him now. Except he's pissed off he's not allowed to drive for the moment."

"I bet. Thank you so much for phoning me, Alice. Have you told Michael?"

"I dropped him a text. And there's no need at all for you to come home, so don't even think of it."

"But I could take some weight off his shoulders with the probate and everything, help you if you need to ferry him about."

"There really is nothing to do. We're still waiting on the probate office. Enjoy your holiday, Fran, lord knows you've earned it, the way you looked after Bob."

So Andrew was all right, but she wasn't needed. Fran

didn't know whether to laugh or cry. She stared at the blank screen of the phone for a while, then realised a tear was trickling down her cheek. Relief, she supposed. Relief, and thankfulness. Huge thankfulness. If she'd been a religious person, she might have gone down to Sveti Vlaho to light a candle, but it seemed a little hypocritical.

There was a gentle tap on the door. "Safranka?"

Oh god, she looked an absolute mess. But she couldn't pretend she wasn't here.

"I brought you some oranges from my tree. I'll leave them outside if you like," Jadran called.

She stood with her hand on the door. "Thank you. I ... I've just heard. Andrew's all right. But ... but I ... I haven't got around to getting dressed so ..."

"I quite understand. If you feel up to it, we could always walk the walls this afternoon. Or tomorrow?"

Just hearing his voice made Fran feel calmer, as though there was a small patch of peace and light creeping into a corner of her world. "This afternoon?"

"Perfect. I will meet you at the Pile Gate at half past two."

Jadran was waiting in the shadow of the wall, next to the entrance tower. When he saw her, he stepped forwards and rested his hand gently on her arm.

"How are you?"

"Much better now. And thank you for the oranges."

He shrugged. "I remember you saying you liked them. The alternative was a cake, but to buy one would have seemed insulting, somehow."

"Would it be insulting to use some of the fruit to bake a marble cake?"

"Not at all. It sounds intriguing. And if you make it, delicious."

"Then that's what I shall do. Oh, and Jadran, before this happened I was thinking about what you said about my father; I am going to find out all I can about him, and as for a fair hearing … well, who am I to judge? Who am I to judge anyone?"

He squeezed her arm more tightly and his warmth flowed through her. "I am so pleased that is your decision."

Fran followed him up a flight of stairs hunkered next to the church wall, to a kiosk where he paid the entrance fee before they climbed even higher. Out on the parapet she blinked in the sunshine. To their left was the tranquil bay beneath Lovrijenac fortress, its waters the palest azure under the clear blue sky, and ahead of them the busy street that led past the jewellers where she had taken the necklace.

Jadran followed her gaze towards the sea. "Most people go around that way, but I prefer to head inland first. Perhaps it is because I like saving the best until last."

To Fran it seemed as though the wall sliced between two worlds. On her left the parapet was too high to look over but peeping through the arrow slits she could glimpse the modern city with its clamour of traffic and she could certainly hear its roar. The view to her right was an uninterrupted vista of the roofscape of the old city, and from here she noticed that the terracotta tiles were far from uniform in either colour or shape. Some were pale and moss covered, long rows of rounded tiles sloping with the gradient of the buildings; others were squarer and richer in colour, cascading from elaborately topped ridges; and in this corner of the city at least, the corner where she was staying, a great number of the roofs were smooth and shiny with very little sign of age at all.

As they climbed the steep steps towards the Minčeta Tower, Fran would have loved to have asked Jadran about it, but the war was a taboo subject. She paused and gazed down again. If the results of the conflict were so obvious to her, how was it for him, living in the city every day? Or did you, over the years, cease to notice? She would be hard pushed to remember the colours of her neighbours' front doors, or when they'd had new windows put in, but on the other hand the street where she lived hadn't been scarred by mortars.

Whatever Jadran felt he appeared unfazed, and once they had passed the tower, he leant on the parapet to point out the street where Fran's apartment was, although it proved impossible to locate the actual building in the jumble of roofs, walls and even small gardens below.

A little further along they stopped to watch the builders working on the cable car system that would carry tourists to the top of Mount Srđ, and Jadran explained it was due to open later that summer.

"We had one before," he told her, "but it was destroyed in the war. It's taken this long to replace it, but there have always been other priorities."

"It must have been difficult to rebuild."

He nodded. "In so many ways." But rather than it being an opening, Fran had the impression that any conversation in that direction had been closed down.

As they descended towards the Ploče Gate, the outer reaches of the harbour came into view, and Jadran tried to point out *Safranka II* in the rows of small craft moored behind the protective mole.

"We should perhaps take another boat trip soon," he said. "Unless of course you will be going home to see your brother?"

Fran twisted around to face him. "I was going to, but I spoke to Andrew just before I came out and he says there is no need. I felt so guilty, though, leaving him to cope with sorting out Daddy's will and everything. I'm sure his TIA was probably stress induced."

"You can't know that, Safranka. He seemed OK when you spoke to him?"

"Yes. To be honest I think he's a bit embarrassed about all the fuss."

"Well then."

Well then indeed. But somehow it didn't feel as simple as that, although she wasn't entirely sure why. She tried to focus on the sun on her back, the beautiful views, and Jadran's company, telling herself to enjoy the moment. The navel-gazing could come later, when she was alone.

As they rounded Svetog Ivana fort, the path broadened out. They could now walk next to each other and the views became even better. The island of Lokrum rose lush and green, the gentle swell washing the golden rocks on its shore.

"In this light it looks as though it has its own mini walls," Jadran said. "Although of course they are the natural stone. There are beautiful places to swim there." He turned to her. "Do you like to swim?"

"I used to. One of the things I'm thinking of doing is joining a sea swimming group to keep fit. Or rather get fit. But of course in England most of the year I will need a wetsuit."

"Here you would not. Even, I think, in April. So perhaps towards the end of your stay we will go."

Which only gave her six weeks to be able to get into her swimsuit. She had packed it, as an afterthought, but the very idea of exposing that much flesh in front of Jadran made her feel a little sick. She glanced at his muscular arms, the hint of a tan line below the sleeves of his polo shirt. No, she could not do it.

"Perhaps," she said.

They carried on, the sea rippling turquoise below to their left and the city's roofs glowing to their right. Fran was fascinated by the jumble of buildings, some with washing strung between their windows, others with quite extensive gardens tucked under the walls, several of which boasted orange trees bursting with fruit.

"Are they common here?" she asked Jadran.

"Yes. It was a tradition that a couple would plant one when they married. My oranges come from the tree my parents-in-law were given in 1946. I would guess that straight after the war, it would have been a precious thing indeed."

Now the path narrowed again, running between low parapets, and Fran marvelled at a tabby and white cat stretching out in the sun, perfectly balanced on top of the wall. After a while they came to a point where the walkway widened once more. There was an ice cream stall with a rack of postcards next to it, and a little further on, a café on a rugged stone bastion sticking out over the sea. It was in an ideal position, with Lokrum seeming so close you could almost touch it, views across the bay to Lovrijenac fortress in the other direction.

"I thought perhaps we could take our aperitif here for a change," said Jadran.

"That would be perfect. But first I need to find a card to send to my sister."

"Then I will sit down and order our drinks. Not that they seem particularly busy, but I am thirsty. What would you like? Red wine?"

"White please, and a glass of water as well."

It proved more difficult than Fran had thought to choose a card for Patti, but she didn't want to keep Jadran waiting so picked up one of the harbour. In the end what was in the picture didn't matter; it was the wording that would be important.

Jadran was at a table next to the parapet with a wonderful view back to Lokrum. Fran joined him just as the waiter brought their drinks and they chinked glasses, the drops of condensation on the outside mingling then dripping down Fran's wrist. She set the card on the table.

"You haven't mentioned your sister before," said Jadran.

"No. We're not close. But I thought, after what's happened to Andrew, perhaps I should try to make peace."

"It is not always easy to make the first move."

"No, and I barely know what to write. But I'm the oldest so it's down to me. And if I'd been a better sister in the first place, none of it would have happened."

Jadran raised an eyebrow as he picked up his beer. "I find that hard to imagine. You seem so gentle, Safranka, so kind."

"It's complicated." Fran traced her finger around her glass, making a trail across the beads of condensation. She hoped Jadran would say something, change the direction of the conversation, but instead he sat silently waiting. But did it really matter if he knew? She couldn't have him under the illusion she was some sort of paragon of virtue. No wonder Vedran thought she'd made a difference to his uncle if he was labouring under that sort of misapprehension.

"It goes right back to our childhood." She explained what had happened with the fire and shrugged. "It was worse because at the time it really kicked off I was struggling with my marriage … I couldn't make that work either."

Jadran looked at her. "Safranka, do you know how much you blame yourself for things?"

She shook her head. "It is what it is."

"I am not so sure. I may be speaking out of turn, because I hardly know you, but I do think that over the years I have become good at seeing people how they really are. There is so much falsehood in this world, and you are not false."

"Then why do you doubt what I am saying?"

He sighed. "Earlier you blamed yourself for your brother's illness and from what you have told me that cannot be the case. Then a few moments ago you said that *you* could not make your marriage work, when in my experience it takes two people to do that, not one."

"Oh, I …" Put like that, it did sound as though there was a pattern and Fran could see why he thought it, but it didn't change the way she felt. Yes, over the years she had come to see that she and Ray had both been to blame, that his behaviour had been unacceptable, but she had always wondered what might have happened if she'd been able to stick it out a little longer …

Jadran cleared his throat. "I am only saying this because I know how destructive blaming yourself can be. It can eat away at you inside, and you barely notice it, or you mistake it for something else entirely even. Believe me, Safranka, I know. You need to move beyond it."

Still she felt unable to speak. There was a lump in her throat almost the size of one of Jadran's oranges and she didn't know why. She took her hand from the stem of her glass and rested it in her lap. Even a slug of wine wouldn't wash the feeling away.

He spoke again, slowly. "On the other side of the city, not very far from the street where your father lived, was my apartment. The one my wife and I moved to when we were married, where Kristina was born and where we spent our life together. Everything that was ours, that was us, that we had saved for and cherished, was within its walls, but in the end, things were not important. Things were nothing.

"When the war came, I begged Leila to take Kristina to Korčula. Vedran was a baby and his mother had family there, and there was space on their small holding for my family too. But Leila did not want to go, because her mother was in Dubrovnik. And in the depths of my selfish heart I did not want them to leave either. I could have done so much more to persuade her. I could maybe even have made her go, although she would have hated me for it. But at least she would have been alive."

Fran sat silent and still.

"And they were killed. Both of them. A mortar hit the building while I was manning a gun that was meant to protect the city from such attacks. And for years I blamed myself: if I had shot that mortar down; if I had made Leila and Kristina leave. If only, if only. And later in the war, other if onlys. Far too many.

"Safranka, what I am saying is do not blame yourself.

Blame will eat you away if you let it. Don't make my mistake. It will take so much longer to heal if you do."

There was a choke in his voice, and Fran looked up to see his hazel eyes swimming with tears. She put her hand over his in comfort, and after a few moments he turned his fingers upwards and squeezed hers.

There was stillness between them, and a feeling that wasn't quite peace but an inching towards it. The thought surprised Fran, she had been barely aware of the tension, and yet it had been there, all the same. The tension of words unsaid, of questions that could not be asked. She had recognised its importance, of course she had, but not how it affected the way they were with each other. Now the door to change that was open.

She glanced at his face in profile. His lips were pressed even more tightly together than usual, his strong chin set firm. From this angle she noticed a slight bump in his long straight nose, as if at some point it had been broken. The whole of Jadran had been broken, and the thought made her want to weep. But he was here. He had survived. And his hand was warm in hers.

"Thank you for telling me," she said. "Vedran said you don't talk about what happened."

He frowned. "Not exactly that. I hadn't talked about it for years because I hadn't needed to. Everyone I know knows about Leila and Kristina. And they all have their own sad stories too. The scars you still see on the buildings are what's visible, but they are not the only scars, that's for sure. But over the years you rebuild. Inside and out. And I've found it's harder to do that when you blame yourself. You have to accept what's done is done and you cannot change it."

Fran nodded. She could change how things were between her and Patti though, but she did not mention it, because it seemed so insignificant next to Jadran's loss. You couldn't compare it on any level, and she had the chance to put things right. A chance that life – and death – had denied him completely.

His gaze followed hers to the postcard, seemingly reading her thoughts. "Do you know what you will write?"

"I think ... keep it simple. Just that life is too short, that what's happened to Andrew made me think we should put the past behind us. We're sisters, after all."

Jadran nodded. "I think simple is always good. Life can be complicated enough without us making it more so." He gave her hand a final squeeze then let go. "But perhaps I am becoming too philosophical. And as I said at the beginning, we have saved the best part of the walls until last and they will close soon. It would be a pity to rush."

At first as they continued the path was too narrow and too stepped for them to walk side by side, and Fran was glad of the opportunity to gather her thoughts. Jadran had opened up to her. Yes, he had done it to help her, but all the same it had removed a barrier between them.

A barrier to what? He may have held her hand, but it had been for mutual comfort, nothing more. The comfort of friends. And yet she was aware there was some sort of path and they were moving along it. Should she let it happen? It would probably only lead to hurt for both of them, and yet in a way she felt powerless to stop it. Powerless because she wasn't sufficiently brave, or because she actually didn't want to?

They stopped at the fort of Bokar and Jadran perched on a canon to tell her about the history of Lovrijenac fortress, high on its rock on the opposite side of the bay. The moment of intimacy may have passed, but to Fran it felt as though there was an easiness between them as she teased him about how he'd have to carry her up all those steps if he wanted her to visit it, and when he tipped back his head and laughed, for a fleeting moment she saw him as a much younger man.

They returned to the walls proper through another tower, then Onofrio's fountain was below them and they began their descent, first to the level of the roofs, then to windows, and finally past the top of the tree next to the Pile Gate.

They were standing in its shade when Jadran took her hand. "Thank you, Safranka. For your company and for listening."

"Thank you for telling me about Leila and Kristina. And for your wise words."

"I'm glad I could help. And I think talking to you helped me too."

He dropped her hand and she watched as he walked away, but just before disappearing down a side street he turned and waved at her. She waved back then set off down Stradun, smiling to herself.

Chapter Twenty-One

Dubrovnik, 18th October 1944

Not a shot has been fired, at least, not one he's heard, and yet in the late afternoon two men in partisan uniform arrive in the Sponza Palace. Their red-starred caps tilt low over their foreheads, their battledress jackets unadorned with insignia. They walk past the mayor's door and into the main office.

"*Smrt fašizmu!*"

There is a scrambling of chairs as the workers rise to their feet and for once he does not stumble.

"*Sloboda narodu!*" He joins the chorus, and hope swells in his heart. Death to fascists, freedom to the people. Now; now, they will be safe. Safe, and free.

The partisans release them from their labours and together they surge down the stairs. Some, he knows, will not be happy about this development, but in the main his colleagues share his joy. Their war is over, a shiny bright future full of hope just around the corner.

Across the square, along the harbourside, partisan soldiers take their rest. Vido sits on his boat watching them, a bottle of *rakija* at his side.

"I waited for you," he calls over the hubbub. "We must celebrate together."

Branko scrambles to join him, the deck swaying beneath them.

He takes a swig of his drink, raw alcohol burning his throat. "Where did you get this?" he asks.

"I kept it for today. I have always known in my heart it would happen."

"I wish I could have shared your faith. But now ..." He gesticulates, then falls into silence. In the arches of the old arsenal partisans lounge, their guns propped against the wall. Others stroll across the waterfront in the fresh autumn air, pausing to pass the time of day with the fishermen, the breeze carrying familiar words but spoken in strange accents from the north, the east. But they are Yugoslavs one and all, in charge of their own destiny.

"It is the future we have dreamed of."

Vido nods. "Even the Ustaše did not dare oppose them here – they walked straight in, with no bloodshed in the city at all. Perhaps there may be places where it is not so easy. Perhaps we are still a little way from peace. But it will come."

"And more than that, we will be free. Our children will be free. I just wish I could have played my part."

"You and I, we have more than played our parts. No, for different reasons we could not fight, but we did not stand by and let innocent women and children go to their deaths as many others have done. We should be proud."

"I think of them often, you know, and wonder ..."

"Branko, enough. You risked your life. More than I did, certainly. One day you'll be recognised for the hero you are."

He shakes his head. "I think it is a time I would prefer to forget. There has been too much hatred, too much sadness. But let us not think of it now. Let us drink to a peaceful future."

Chapter Twenty-Two

Dubrovnik, March 2010

As Fran emerged into the bright sunlight on Stradun after buying the stamp for Patti's postcard, her phone started to ring, Eli's number appearing on the little screen. Swinging her bag higher onto her shoulder she answered it.

As ever, there was no preamble. "Elvira has returned from Israel and she invites us to her apartment for coffee tomorrow."

"That is so kind. Does she remember anything?"

"A little, but perhaps even that will be useful. I will text you her address, but you might need your friend to bring you, or take the bus. She is my neighbour in Lapad."

Fran wandered towards Sponza Palace and the harbour. As they had drunk their usual aperitif yesterday Jadran had said he would be working on his boat this morning and she wanted to find him, tell him her news. But all the same something made her hang back, and she stood for a while gazing at the intricate oak leaf patterns on the corbels of the building, lost in thought.

She could very easily find the right bus to get her to Elvira's apartment, but somehow she wanted Jadran with her. Without her even realising it, finding out about her father had become a journey they were taking together. Yet it was her journey, nothing to do with him really. Except with every step, and twist, and turn, he had become more involved, and without his enthusiasm for hunting through the city records they would never have known about the Lopud connection. Would it even be fair of her not to tell him?

She simply wasn't used to doing things as part of a pair. Looking back, she couldn't remember having that sort of relationship with Ray, not even when Michael was a baby. It had always been her job to stay at home, and his to go out to work. It had been the way of things then, but she had never really felt they were undertaking the big adventure of parenthood together.

Yet with Jadran, doing things together felt right. Maybe a bit *too* right? The thought made her feel a little giddy and she tipped her head back and gazed up into the clear blue sky. There was no point in them falling for each other, and yet it was happening. Something deep inside told her Vedran was right and his uncle was becoming fond of her. But how could she allow herself to reciprocate when she was only here for another six weeks? And anyway, whatever Parisa said, she was far too out of practice with men to want one in her life that way ever again.

This was getting her nowhere. To buy a little time she wandered along the side of Sveti Vlaho to the Green Market. It seemed that every week more women turned up to sell their wares, but she still frequented the ones who had been there right from the beginning, who now greeted her by name. At Vedran's suggestion she had asked a little about their lives and they had been glad to tell her, so now she knew whose husband's health to enquire after, and whose daughter had another baby on the way.

Salad crops were beginning to appear and Fran bought a succulent lettuce and some radishes. Her hand hovered over an artichoke. She'd never cooked one before, but sod it, she was sure she could find a recipe online. Time to experiment. *Live a little, Fran. If only in the kitchen.*

Safranka II was moored under the walls of the castle, close to where she had been when she first met Jadran. It seemed a very long time ago. There was no sign of him now, but the way the boat rocked told her he was on board somewhere and she called his name.

It took him a moment to appear, wearing navy overalls and with a smear of grease down the side of his face.

"Safranka! This is a lovely surprise. Have you come to interrupt me?"

"Only if you can be interrupted." She grinned back at him.

"To be honest, not for long. This is proving a bigger job than I thought. But to sit in the fresh air for ten minutes with you would be a pleasure." He held out his hand to help her on board then pulled it away. "I am covered in oil."

"It's fine. I can manage." She jumped on the step at the back of the boat then onto the deck. "I won't keep you long anyway. I have news from Eli."

"Good news?"

Fran considered. "I think so. His friend is back from Israel and has invited me for coffee tomorrow. Us, if you would be interested in coming."

"Of course I would. It's exciting, isn't it?"

"I … I haven't really had time to think about it." No, that wasn't true. In the time since Eli had called she'd been thinking about something else entirely. "I was out shopping when Eli phoned so I came to find you."

Jadran's smile was the broadest she had ever seen it. "Then perfect. I will come with you tomorrow. Safranka, I really feel we are getting closer. I don't suppose you've heard back from the archaeologists yet?"

"Only to say they have no more information but hope to send out full autopsies in due course. I'm really not sure I'm ready for that." She grimaced.

"Don't worry. I can always read it for you when it arrives."

"Thank you. It's … it's … well, I thought this would be a bit of a lonely search for the truth, but you have made it anything but."

"I'm glad, Safranka, really glad."

Elvira's apartment was in a modern building overlooking the forest park of Velika i Mala Petka. The heels of Fran's pumps clicked on the white-tiled floor, but the clinical look it might have given the living area was softened by rich red rugs and throws, and a packed bookcase lining one wall.

She guessed Elvira was just a few years older than her, and with her glossy dark hair and fresh lipstick she reminded her a little of Parisa. She greeted them warmly then disappeared to the kitchen to make coffee, which she poured from brass *dzezva* into tiny cups the colours of jewels. Finally she set down a plate of fluffy *krofne* and sat on the sofa next to Eli.

"You had a pleasant trip?" Fran asked her.

"Yes, thank you. It is a good time of year to visit Israel; not too hot, and my grandchildren are growing by the day. It was wonderful to be able to spend so long with them."

Fran rolled her eyes. "I know. Mine do the same." Although she was smiling, she felt a stab of envy. This was the longest she'd ever gone without seeing Michael and the girls and despite their frequent Skype calls she was missing them even more than she'd thought she would.

Eli cleared his throat. "As I told you, Fran is trying to find out about her father and has discovered he worked at the internment camp on Lopud. It might help her to know what you remember."

Elvira shook her head. "No names of the guards, and that is certain. I was only four years old. Was your father Italian?"

"No. He was a local man. Jadran found out he was a clerk in the city offices, but for a while he was on Lopud. We don't know why."

"The prison was run by the Italians and given what we learned after the war, that was a very good thing. And I use the term *run* loosely. My overriding memory is of playing in the fields while the adults tended their vegetables, but I guess we must have been shut in somewhere, at least at night. There were certainly guards around because I do recall being told to avoid some of them and it puzzled me because they were the ones who spoke our own language. I learned later these were Ustaše, Croatia's home-grown fascists."

Fran put down her coffee cup. She'd been brave enough to

send the card to Patti, she could be brave enough to say this too. "I am a little afraid my father was a Ustaše," she said.

"They were not all bad," Elvira told her, shaking her head. "In fact one of them helped us to escape. Not only my mother and me, but other families too."

"You escaped? Eli said he thought you might have, but how?"

"I remember very little, except it was at night by fishing boat." She put down her cup and frowned. "But the guard who let us out ... he was a small man I think, and walked with a limp, which was perhaps unusual for a soldier. Later my mother told me he was a friend of my father's, and the fisherman a friend of this friend. Apparently we were taken to an uninhabited island to meet another boat, and then on to another and finally to somewhere in North Africa. The war in that part of the world was more or less over so after a while we were able to travel to Israel. I grew up there, but after my mother died I wanted to come back.

"Like you, Fran, I was looking for my father. He escaped to join the partisans just before we were interned, but much later we learned he was killed. I guess I wanted to make sure it was true, and of course it was. His name is on the memorial at Bihać. But while I was here I met my late husband, so of course I stayed."

"You said there were other families who escaped from Lopud. Is there anyone else alive who might remember?" asked Jadran.

"None of the older generation, but there are others who were children there. I can send a few emails if you like, to see if anyone knows more."

"And the necklace," added Eli. "Fran has a necklace that's

clearly Jewish but she doesn't know how her father came by it. If he was on Lopud perhaps it was there."

Fran hung her head. This again. This implication her father had stolen it. And yet it was probably true. "I'm not sure I want to know."

There was silence in the room until Jadran said, "Then that is your choice." He reached out and squeezed her hand.

"But it would be a shame," Eli persisted. "After all, it is an interesting piece. Do you have it with you?"

"I always have it with me. It was my mother's after all. The only thing she brought to England with her, so it must have meant a great deal."

"Would you permit me to take a photograph to send with my email?" asked Elvira. "I really do appreciate how precious these heirlooms are, but sometimes children remember such things."

"Especially if worn by their mother," Eli added.

Elvira shook her head again, making her earrings jangle. "You are so tactless sometimes, Eli, it beggars belief. Children remember jewellery because it's shiny."

Fran's throat felt too full to speak.

Eventually Jadran said, "There would be no question of Safranka parting with the necklace, even if someone claimed it belonged to their family."

"No, of course not," said Elvira, "it was her mother's. But it just might jog a memory somewhere. You never know."

"All right." Fran nodded, but her fingers shook as she took it from her handbag and laid it on the coffee table. At least Elvira understood, and she needed to do everything she could to close the book on her father for once and for all. However painful the truth might be.

After leaving Elvira's apartment Jadran suggested they walk in the forest park, under the shade of the Aleppo pines. Ahead of them the sea glistened jade-blue, and although they could still hear the traffic from the suburbs around them, with every step Fran felt just a little calmer.

Eventually the sound of the cicadas took over as the path wound steeply downwards past trees with yellow flag-like leaves that rippled in the warm breeze. Jadran stopped at a bench with a view through a gap in the canopy and they sat down.

"From the other side of the headland you can sometimes see Lopud in the distance on a clear day. It juts out into the sea a little more than Koločep."

"Hmm." Fran wasn't too sure she wanted to be reminded about the island just now. Coming face to face with someone who could have come face to face with her father had churned up so many feelings she'd thought she was beginning to put behind her. She curled her toes inside her pumps. "If I'd worn sensible shoes we could have had more of a walk now we're here."

Jadran shrugged. "We can come back another time. It is a good place to picnic."

"I'd like that. Jadran, thank you for being such a support back there. I feel awful that my father could have been one of those cruel Ustaše guards."

"Ah, but he could also have been the one who helped the families to escape."

"It's not very likely, is it?"

"Numerically the odds are against it, but of course he did

live in the Jewish quarter so maybe had Jewish friends. And besides, we don't even know in what capacity he was there. My gut feeling is he would have been some sort of administrator, so probably not in uniform at all. I don't think he could have become a soldier, because he went back to being a municipal clerk as soon as the camp closed."

"I suppose that's something." She looked up at Jadran to find him looking down at her. "Before you say anything, I'm not judging him. It makes me feel uncomfortable, that's all."

"And that can't be a nice feeling. I wonder ..." He paused, frowning. "I was going to say, I wonder if we went to Lopud could we find out more. But maybe it's a little disingenuous to put it like that when what I am really wondering is if you would like to take a short holiday with me. I know, already you are on a holiday of sorts, but I think it would be fun to go away together. Take the boat. Perhaps not sleep on the boat – it would be very cramped with two of us especially as we are not ... um ... intimate, but we could stay in a guest house or something."

A faint tinge of a blush had appeared on Jadran's neck. What was he asking her? To go away, certainly, but in what capacity? In the moments before panic gripped her, Fran's stomach had stirred in a not unpleasant way. *Oh, stop it, you silly old fool.* Hadn't he just said that they weren't intimate? Surely the invitation was innocent enough. But the colour creeping towards his jawline, and something about the way he was looking at her, made her wonder.

Oh lord, she was too unused to this. How could she possibly know what he was thinking? She didn't even know what to think herself. Should she go? What would happen if she did? But worse, what if she didn't? It would sound so ...

rude, so ungrateful. As if she was rejecting him. No, nervous as she was, she couldn't possibly turn him down. And besides, she wanted to spend the time with him. She really did.

And yet, and yet … would it mean coming face to face with her father again? She felt as though she was circling around him, closer and closer, and however much she'd played it down with Jadran, what she might find was more terrifying than ever.

She looked at him. He would be waiting for her answer. "That sounds like a wonderful idea. I'd love to come."

It was only when Jadran relaxed his grip on the edge of the bench and began to flex his fingers that Fran realised how taut his whole body had become. This really was important to him. Oh lord, it shouldn't be. She was going home. But then, as Parisa had said, he was a grown man, he knew the score.

Could she … could she take a leap of faith too? In a voice that felt far from her own she said, "It will be what it will be. Not about my father, I mean, about …"

He shook his head, but he was smiling at her all the same. "I know just what you mean, Safranka, but you are wrong. It will be what we make it."

Chapter Twenty-Three

Dubrovnik, 18th October 1944

D ragica is at her most beautiful, the embroidered blouse she wore on their wedding day buttoned to her throat, its dark fabric highlighting the rosy blush of her cheeks. He turns from her, reaches to the back of the drawer.

"Here, wear this."

"Are you sure?"

"I think … it is important. It means they are with us in a way, joining our celebrations."

She nods, closes her hand over his, and the corners of the pendant bite into his palm, taking him back to the moment the woman gave it to him, in the shadow of the hotel wall, wrapping it into his grasp as he had tried to push it back.

"Please," she'd whispered. "Give it to your wife. Then a small part of my heart will remain in Dubrovnik always."

And so he had understood.

Together they walk down the hill to the main street,

Safranka strapped to his back. He relishes the warmth of her sleeping body, her instinctive trust in him to take care of her. He has been careless with his life in the past, but never again. His daughter is too precious. And besides, now that the war has been driven from their city there will be no need to take such risks.

Stradun is thronged with people, a tide of them surging, as if of its own accord, towards the square. There is laughter in the air, a shared joy that has been buried beneath worry and hunger for too long. People dressed, like them, in their Sunday best, riding on a human tide of hope. Things will be better now, they will.

Dragica's eyes are glowing. "Oh, but this is a wonderful day. I was beginning to believe it might never happen."

He grips her hand tighter, his heart swelling with happiness and love. "Me too." But there are those who walk beside them in silence, lost in their own thoughts, and he realises that in peace, as in war, there are winners and losers.

All day the mayor's door has been closed. He has seemingly played no part in the preparations for the speech the partisan commander will make from the upper window of the Sponza Palace. Will he preach reconciliation – or retribution? A cloud darkens a corner of Branko's mind, but he pushes it away, grins at Dragica and kisses the tip of her nose.

They come to a halt some hundred yards from the palace and Safranka shifts on his back. A ripple of silence covers the crowd, spreading out from the square in front of Sveti Vlaho. Even so, they are too far back to hear every word, but there is talk of their glorious victory over the German oppressors, and that all Yugoslavia must now be united under communist rule.

His cheer dies on his lips as he notices partisan soldiers watching the crowd. Not everyone is celebrating.

Danger is a cold punch to his solar plexus, and he cheers all the more; shouting and waving his hat in the air so vehemently it wakes Safranka and she starts to cry. Dragica tries to comfort her as the crowd presses around them; unwashed bodies and the faint whiff of camphor from everyone's best clothes.

She whispers in his ear. "We should leave. All this noise, it's upsetting her."

He nods and they burrow back through the swell of people, a tide still surging towards the Sponza Palace. In the first side street they stop and she takes Safranka from his back to soothe her, rocking her in her arms, their faces close so his daughter can hear the lullaby sung only for her.

He tells himself that this is what's important; this is his heart, his soul, his life. A quiet life from now on. He owes them that. But somehow, he can't shake the thought he is being watched.

Chapter Twenty-Four

Dubrovnik, March 2010

F ran gazed at the clothes spread out on the bed. Three nights. They were going for three nights, that was all. Why was she making such a meal of it? Her denim skirt would do for the evenings, and she knew Jadran liked her embroidered cardigan, so she'd pack that as well. But what else? The Marks & Spencer knitted cotton jacket with the oversized unmatched buttons? She hadn't worn it yet so at least it was new, but she wasn't really sure it was her.

Despite the difficulties of packing, she had to admit she was excited. There was a frisson of something about the trip that took her back to being a girl again, back to the shared house in Parsons Green. This was what they'd do before a night on the town; lay potential outfits on their beds, then run from room to room in their underwear, giggling and squealing, borrowing a skirt here, a pair of tights there …

Oh my god. Underwear. Hers was utilitarian to say the least.

Sensible cotton knickers and well-constructed bras. But it didn't matter. It wasn't as though anyone was going to see them. Were they?

No, it was all right. Fumbling her phone she checked Jadran's text again. He had booked them rooms, plural, at a guest house owned by a friend's cousin. Her slightly tatty and greying knickers would remain her secret. As would the folds of flesh they strained to hide. Honestly, she could have at least tried to diet while she was here, but what with a glass or two of wine every night, and baking cakes for Jadran … But it was fine. He'd booked two rooms. Clearly his intentions weren't sexual at all.

The tiny lurch of disappointment surprised her. Yes, it was a lovely fantasy to want to be kissed and held in his arms, but the reality of going any further was frankly appalling. But that wasn't entirely true either. A tiny part of her, a part that had been hidden for so long she had almost forgotten it existed, wanted more. Alone in her bed at night, all sorts of more. But in the cold light of day even the thought absolutely terrified her.

Why? She knew damn well why. It had been too long and now her body felt too old, too unattractive. She didn't even want to look at herself in the mirror, let alone have anyone else – especially Jadran – see the roll of fat around her waist, the pasty dimpled flesh on her thighs. Never mind the way her boobs sagged with relief the moment they were released from her bra.

So why was she sorting through her clothes, working out which ones she would look her best in? Was it for her or for him? She'd never bothered too much about how she looked, not in years anyway, so why now? Parisa had said something about a new look giving her more confidence, but confidence to do what?

Fran picked up her phone. She was getting in a right old mess, and although a part of her shied away from Parisa's bluntness, she knew it was what she needed.

Can you talk?

Yes. Skype?

Please.

On her way to the living room Fran glanced at the bottle of wine on the kitchen table and her hand hovered. No, she needed her mind to be as clear as possible. No Dutch courage this time.

"What's up?" Bless Parisa for getting straight to the point.

"I'm packing for our trip to Lopud and ... well ... I'm getting in all sorts of muddles."

Parisa sighed. "And are any of those lovely new clothes you bought and probably haven't even worn yet under consideration?"

"Yes. And I have worn some of them. Quite a lot, actually. But they're ... not really the problem. Well they are but they aren't."

"My goodness, you barely sound coherent. What is it?"

"OK, hear me out. I started by prevaricating over the clothes, but then I began to think about my underwear. It's pretty utilitarian and ..."

"Oh, so are things moving forwards with Jadran?"

"No! He's been the perfect gentleman and booked us a

room each. And let's face it, why wouldn't he? We may get on perfectly well but my body is absolutely gross."

"Of course it isn't. What are you? A size eighteen at most, and that isn't even anywhere near fat, let alone gross, as you so delightfully call yourself." Her voice softened. "But I do get it. It doesn't matter what I or anyone else sees, it's how you feel. Take it from an over-height, bony old stick insect."

"But you have a figure to die for!"

"I rest my case. Fran, very few women are happy with the way they look when they undress, and very few men either, especially at our age. But the thing is, no one expects perfection."

"But Jadran's gorgeous. He's really taken care of himself ..."

"I'd still put money on the fact he has hang ups too. Look at it this way; even if her wasn't a looker, would you still like him?"

"Of course. He'd be the same person."

"Exactly. And I bet he feels the same about you. He'll see a warm, generous woman with a pretty round face, eyes like sparkling jet and curves he probably can't wait to get his hands on."

It was kind of her to try to bolster her confidence, but ... "I wish I could believe you."

"Time will tell if I'm right. But just in case, I'd get yourself some new underwear."

The reality of the situation she seemed to be getting herself into slapped Fran right in the face again. "No," she whispered.

"Why not? There must be a lingerie shop somewhere in that city."

"I didn't mean that. I meant … I'm not sure I can go there … the physical side of things … I'd just be too embarrassed."

"Not in the steamy heat of the moment, you wouldn't. You're overthinking Fran, worrying over what might or might not be. He's booked two rooms. He's not going to make a grab for you and force you into anything. If he does make a move, you need to take it forwards at a pace you're comfortable with and if he doesn't like it, well, he's not the man you thought he was."

"It's easy for you to say."

"I know, but that could be because I have more experience. And I'm here for you, Fran, any time you want to talk things through, day or night. I mean that. I have to say though, even a few weeks ago I couldn't imagine us having this conversation and I'm damned pleased we are."

After Parisa rang off and as Fran continued with her packing, she thought about what her friend had said. Was she really making progress? In some ways, yes, of course she was. The grief she felt for Daddy had softened to a dull ache, and even that she didn't carry with her all the time. Yes, it could be sharp as hell, like the moment she heard his favourite Mozart sonata drifting through someone's window, but on the whole she was coping with it pretty well.

She still felt guilty about Andrew, though, for all when they spoke or emailed he seemed as fit as a fiddle. But she had made a start at putting things right with Patti, although having sent the postcard it felt a little like an unexploded bomb, wavering at the corner of her vision.

She'd even made a little progress finding out about her father, although the biggest questions remained, as did the whole issue of her mother's motivation for letting her believe he was a hero. But as to what she might do with her future ... Whatever happened with Jadran, he was just a pleasant distraction, not a solution. All the same, if Parisa was right, he could be an important step on her journey. It was just ... it sounded so cold, put like that, and it wasn't the way she felt about him at all.

She glanced in the bedroom mirror as she folded her clothes to fit into her case. There was a sparkle in her eyes and the bags under them were certainly much smaller. And if she delved deep enough there was a sparkle inside too, a flicker of how she remembered being young and excited about life felt. For the next three days at least she would forget she was sixty-five and do her best to encourage it.

Lopud, March 2010

As they rounded the rocky shoulder of land that formed Lopud's northernmost tip, Jadran slowed *Safranka II* to a lazy crawl.

"We should enjoy the views," he told Fran. "It is always interesting to approach somewhere new from the sea."

She sighed. "The views have been spectacular all morning." Jadran had taken the most scenic of routes to get there, first idling along the coast of Koločep with its short, sheer cliffs and bright blue water that shimmered over the slabs of white stone beneath, before looping into the channel between the two islands, towards the mountains of the mainland, their rugged fingers reaching into the sky to gather the clouds.

Fran looked towards the shore, where scrub and stunted pines colonised a precipitous slope above sharply angled rocks that were washed by gentle waves.

"So this is Lopud," she continued. "Do you know it well?"

He shook his head but did not return her gaze. "I haven't been here for many, many years. But look, here is the first landmark, the church of Sveti Mihovil – so tiny and completely on its own, right next to the sea."

Fran gazed at it, a small grey box of a building with a stumpy tower, perched in front of the trees on a stained stone platform built out of the rocks. "I wonder who it was built to serve?"

"Monks, probably. There's been a Franciscan monastery on the island since medieval times, but it was abandoned years ago and left to go to ruin. However I have been wondering if it was where the Jews were interned. There are so few buildings on the island big enough and it has pretty substantial walls. It's a shame Elvira couldn't remember more. The only other option I can think of is a ruined fort, although that is perched high up in the hills, so perhaps not so convenient and certainly harder to guard. But we will visit both and see."

"I don't hold out much hope." The last thing she wanted was to sound negative when she had promised herself she'd have fun so she continued. "I am looking forward to seeing the island though and I'm sure we'll have a lovely couple of days. A little holiday. Anything we discover about my father will be a bonus."

Jadran nodded and turned his attention back to the boat, and it was only a few moments later he pointed out the monastery itself to Fran. "Look, here it is, above the harbour."

Fran followed the direction of his finger to see a forbidding grey stone wall rising vertically from the rocks on the water's edge. Shrubs, and even a small tree, sprouted from impossible positions both through and below it, and high above them, set a little back, was a long two-storey building, only partially roofed, but which was surrounded by scaffolding. The church to its right was in much better shape, but on the other side, a little further up the slope, was a fortified tower that was more or less a ruin.

"It looks as though someone is doing some work," she said.

Jadran frowned. "I did not expect that. I hope we can still visit."

Beyond the monastery was a wide bay, creamy-grey, red-roofed buildings lining the waterfront and snaking up towards the dark wooded slopes beyond. Unlike in Dubrovnik there were generous amounts of green space between them, gardens or even small vineyards or fields. As much as she screwed up her eyes, Fran couldn't work out which.

Jadran steered the boat into a small harbour almost beneath the monastery walls, which was protected from the elements by the long arms of two concrete moles. He moored up against one of them and turned off the engine so all Fran could hear was the gentle wash of the waves and distant birdsong.

"It's so quiet."

"No cars are allowed here, that is why. A small step back into the past." He jumped from his seat and onto the deck, leaning out to loop the rope through an iron ring on the quay.

Fran followed him out of the cabin. Looking over the harbour from its vantage point on a high wall was a huge villa that had seen better days, with roof tiles missing and shutters hanging off. It had a sad and dejected air, and Fran asked Jadran if he knew anything about it.

"Hotel Kuljevan. At least, it used to be." He glanced around, shaking his head. "And it's not the only building falling into disrepair by the look of it." He strode to the stern and attached *Safranka II*'s other line.

"Now we are secure," he said, brushing his hands briskly on his trousers. "I am afraid it is a ten-minute walk to the guest house, but I can carry your case."

There was no need for him to do that, she could easily wheel it. "It's fine. I can manage."

He ignored her and picked it up.

At first they walked in silence along the broad promenade, and Fran tried to work out whether it was a companionable one. There'd been times when Jadran had seemed a little preoccupied this morning, scratchy even, although at others he'd been fine. But he'd said he'd come here before, a long time ago. Had it been with his family? Were his memories flooding back to haunt him?

Oh god, this was already impossibly awkward and their trip had hardly begun. How were they going to manage for three whole days if he was going to be like this? But perhaps, as Parisa would say, she was overthinking it. Fran stopped and pretended to look around her at the narrow sandy beach to one side and the row of shuttered shops on the other as she took a deep, slow breath, filling her lungs with the salty air.

Jadran stopped too and turned to her. "I know, it feels a little empty and closed, but in summer it's always been very busy. We don't often find sand in Dalmatia, and for people who like it, this place is a magnet."

"I can imagine. But I like the quiet and it has a sort of faded grandeur that's rather beautiful."

"Hmph. *Faded* is the word." He pointed at an ugly concrete building behind a rusting security fence. "That's the Grand

Hotel. It was an icon of modern architecture in the 1930s, and just look at it now."

Shaking his head he shifted his rucksack further onto his back and moved her case to his other hand. "At least that restaurant back there was open so we won't go hungry. Let's hope it's all right."

Lord, he was sounding grumpier by the minute. "It seemed fine to me," Fran said. "And it had tables right at the water's edge. The sea's so clear and sparkling too; it's gorgeous."

Jadran nodded, but his smile was a shadow of its normal self. "Then while you are unpacking, I will come back and book the restaurant for tonight."

"I could wait while you do it now."

"No. I have some errands to run anyway so it is no problem. I believe your room has a terrace so you can sit and relax in the sun and enjoy the view of that sparkling sea." He set off along the promenade again, Fran trailing behind him.

In fact the terrace ran across the front of both their rooms, shaded by a large palm tree surrounded by low shrubs, beyond which the Mediterranean shifted and glistened. Having tossed and turned the previous night, Fran tried to feel grateful for the opportunity to relax on a sun lounger with her book, sipping the home-made lemonade the owner of the property had brought her. But she couldn't help wondering where Jadran had gone, and what he was doing. Clearly, whatever it was, it was none of her business.

She hadn't expected feeling excluded to hurt, but then she hadn't expected to be excluded at all. He had suggested they came away together, and now he had left her alone. Fran frowned to herself; that didn't seem like the Jadran she was becoming friendly with, but then, how much did she really know him? Perhaps it was nothing to do with her, maybe it was his memories after all. She needed to give him the benefit of the doubt. She'd let it ride overnight, but once they'd visited the monastery tomorrow, if he wasn't any better she'd suggest they went home.

Fran felt relieved for having made a decision. The lemonade was sharp and sweet on her tongue, and the rippling sparkles of sunlight on the water teased the edges of her vision. Closing her eyes, she listened to the bees hum in a nearby bougainvillea, and found herself beginning to doze. It was all right, she told herself, she didn't think Jadran would be back in a hurry, so it was unlikely he'd catch her snoring and dribbling down her chin.

Fran slept for longer than she intended. The sun had already dipped behind the promontory, although when she stood and stretched she could see that most of the village was still bathed in its light. The last lazy rays glowed on the elegant tower that topped the monastery church, the hills of the mainland rising behind in a smoky haze.

She glanced towards Jadran's room to see his shutters were still closed, but before she could wonder where he was, she heard the pump of a shower. Time for her to get ready too. Wash off the salt of the day, try to do something with her hair, and put on some decent clothes. Not because it was a date or anything, but because she wanted to feel her best in case it proved to be a difficult evening.

$\sim$

The night closed velvet around them as they walked along the promenade, past the church and the dark shadows of the Grand Hotel and the public gardens that wrapped themselves around its perimeter. Even so the breeze whispering through the palm trees was cool, and Fran was glad of the soft woollen wrap Parisa had given her before she left for Croatia. It was so much smarter than any coat she owned, and she had even managed to fling it stylishly over one shoulder, rather than bundling herself up in it like an old woman. It gave her just enough confidence to remember her vow that this trip would be fun.

From their left came the gentle wash of the waves on the sand and to their right the muted sounds of domesticity; a television here, a baby crying there. Families settling down for their evenings, as they would be everywhere in the world. As Jadran strolled next to her Fran was aware of the spicy scent of his aftershave, something she hadn't noticed before. Could it be he was making a special effort? Perhaps to make amends?

But he was still unusually quiet as they walked, only coming to life when they reached the restaurant. Something was bothering him, that was for sure, but Fran couldn't begin to work out how to ask him without ruining the whole evening. No, she'd stick to her original plan and in the meantime make the best of it.

It was too cold to sit outside, but the interior was cosy and there was only one other couple there.

"Perhaps on our other days we could eat at lunchtime instead?" Jadran asked her. "Then we can sit by the sea as you wished. And anyway, it is when we normally have our main meal in Croatia."

"Honestly? I didn't realise."

"Yes. Eating in the evening is more for the tourists, so of course the restaurants adapt."

The owner appeared with the menus and two small glasses of clear liquid, speaking to Jadran rapidly in their native tongue.

He translated for Fran. "It's their home-made herb *rakija*, which he's given us as an aperitif. It's a traditional thing to do, but this stuff can be very strong. It would be rude to refuse it though."

Fran laughed, trying to lighten the mood. "I'll try anything once." She raised her glass to his. "Cheers!"

"*Živjela!*"

Fran took a sip and it was all she could do not to gag. "Ugh … it tastes like medicine. I'm afraid I'm not too keen."

Looking over his shoulder towards the kitchen, Jadran drained his glass. "Quick – swap." When he grinned at her before downing the second drink, he looked just a little more like himself.

They both chose squid as a starter, then while Jadran went for a seafood black risotto, Fran decided on stuffed cabbage leaves, wondering if they would be anything like the ones she'd managed to make herself. Jadran ordered a carafe of local red wine, which he told her came from the island of Šipan opposite.

Once he'd poured it, he said, "When I was out today, I visited the monastery."

"Without me?" Fran was a little shocked.

"Only to see if it was possible for us to look tomorrow, Safranka. I didn't want you to be disappointed."

Damn her big mouth. "Thank you. That was very thoughtful."

"I spoke to the site foreman and he said we should go at about ten o'clock and he will show us around. Only the ground floor though because they are working upstairs."

"That's so kind."

"He wasn't too keen at first, until I told him you were visiting from England and your father had been on the island during the war."

"And what did he say to that?"

"I think he assumed he was a British soldier. They were in Dalmatia, you know, fighting alongside the partisans."

Fran nodded. "It was how my mother came to settle in England. She worked in a hotel where the British were billeted and one of the officers got us away. I don't really know how it came about, but we went to live on his aunt's farm because she needed workers, so that was probably why he helped."

"I did wonder how it happened."

"Well now you know as much as I do."

There was a pause in the conversation as their food arrived, the squid cooked in the lightest of batters and sprinkled with fresh herbs.

"This is delicious," Fran said. "It's so fresh."

"Fresh food, simply cooked. It's perfect."

"What do you cook at home?" Fran asked him.

"Cooking is new to me, I'm afraid. When I was first married it was traditional for the woman to cook, and Leila was good at it. Then after … after the war, I lived with my mother-in-law until she died, and she certainly would never allow me in the kitchen. But now I'm retired I have time to work at it a little, shop for good ingredients, follow recipes. Although, I don't know if you find it too, it is a lot of effort to cook for one person. I normally only do it when Vedran is staying with me."

"I'm the same. It seems rather pointless if I don't have anyone else to feed and I've become unused to it. Although I've lived alone since Michael left home, for the last couple of years I was caring for my English father, so I moved in with him, and he loved his food. Supper was the highlight of our day, really." She raised her glass. "He liked red wine too."

"Then we will drink to his memory."

Their glasses chinked. "And to your mother-in-law's."

"Yes. To all those we have lost." As he said it, Jadran seemed to nod to himself, then took another sip of wine. "Today ... the ones I have lost have been very close. I ... I did not expect it. I am sorry if it has made me distant."

So her instinct had been right. Thank goodness he felt able to talk to her about it. "You said you'd been here before. Was it with Leila and Kristina?"

"Yes. When Kristina was small we would come here quite often. My boss ... he had a house on the island, and a young daughter of his own, so we would stay with his family or as a treat in the Grand Hotel. I thought coming back would be all right after all this time, but then ... it was almost as though I could see Kristina and Ana on the beach, hear Leila laughing at their antics. It was almost as though they were really here."

"I'm sorry I've put you through this," Fran whispered.

"No, it's not your fault. More than anything, it confused me. You see I'd decided ... decided it was time. Time to finally let Leila go and move on, yet there she was, pulling me back. I just didn't understand why I was suddenly so full of grief for them all over again. But this afternoon, I have walked and walked, gone to all the places we used to go ... and I feel better. The memories I found are happy ones, and that is very good."

"It certainly is."

"And in a strange way it made me feel less afraid. When I first lost her, I was frightened that over time I would forget her, that she would fade and I wouldn't be able to reach her. And I was worried if I moved on ... with someone else ... it could still happen. Today, I think, she surprised me."

"But Jadran, you don't have to forget her to move on. Leila will always live in your heart and that is completely right."

"You are a very understanding woman, Safranka." He took a sip of his wine. "I talk to her in my head, you know. I guess some people, as they get older, they talk to themselves. Me, I talk to Leila. I think ... I would miss her if I stopped doing that, but I couldn't ask another woman to live with it."

"Honestly, Jadran, at our sort of age there isn't anyone without the odd wrinkle, quirk or scar. It's part of who we are now we've been around the clock a few times. You need to do what's right for you."

Fran ground to a halt. She had been about to tell him that a living woman shouldn't worry about one who'd been dead for nigh on twenty years, but it felt so harsh to say the words out loud and she was relieved when their conversation was interrupted by the owner bringing their main courses. As they ate, they began to discuss what else they would do on the island. Jadran seemed so much more relaxed, the smile that went right to his eyes returning. Talking about Leila and Kristina had surely helped.

Somehow one carafe of wine became two, then the owner brought out some small squares of something like Turkish delight and two more glasses of *rakija*. This one was myrtle flavour, and Fran liked it much better, but all the same she knew she'd had enough to drink and was glad of the strong, bitter coffee and the jug of water on the table. She didn't want to start tomorrow with a hangover; seeing the monastery could be very important.

It was something of a surprise that when Jadran stood he seemed a little unsteady. But he was smiling at her, and his eyes were filled with a warmth that made her feel just a little gooey inside. *Careful, Fran, you're drunk too*, she told herself. *Don't say or do anything you might regret in the morning.*

But Jadran clearly had no such reservations. Outside the restaurant the breeze caught Fran's pashmina, blowing it from her shoulder, and as he wound it back around her, he dropped his lips to hers and they kissed. It was a soft, gentle thing, full of tenderness, but all the same it made Fran's heart race, and she responded in kind.

After a few moments of bliss he pulled away and smiled down at her. "Thank you for a wonderful evening."

"No, thank you."

"More importantly, thank you for understanding about Leila. It means a great deal."

He took her hand and they strolled back towards the guest house in silence, but this time Fran knew what the silence was. It was the silence of two contented people, people who had made a small step closer to each other and knew that, for the moment, that step was enough. She felt so much more in tune with him than she had before, but somehow it wasn't frightening.

Outside the door of her room they kissed again in the same gentle way. Jadran ran his finger down the side of her cheek as he stepped back to look at her.

"Goodnight, my beautiful Safranka. Breakfast at eight? Tomorrow could be a very important day."

"Breakfast at eight. Sleep well, dear Jadran." She reached up and gave him another quick kiss, before turning to unlock her door and float into the room.

Chapter Twenty-Five

Dubrovnik, 19th October 1944

The mayor remains in his office. The market stalls are empty. People still hungry.

As he walks through the square in search of food there are two points of difference. The first is that prices are marked on each table, and they are lower than in recent months, but what is the point when there is nothing to buy? He wonders if, in fact, that is the reason; the tables are empty because now the few potatoes and onions are sold in secret elsewhere.

The second change he finds more chilling. Everywhere he sees partisan soldiers watching. Slouched on street corners, guns over their shoulders and cigarettes in hand, eyes flickering from face to face. Who is an enemy and who is a friend? The city feels divided, even to him. The Ustaše could still rise up, so who can blame their vigilance? He should feel protected, but somehow it is not that way.

He walks across the front of the cathedral, under the

shadow of the arch, where more partisans wait. His leg drags painfully behind him, reminding him how obvious a man with a limp can be. Despite the bluest of skies above the harbour, it tells him there are storms beyond the horizon and Vido should fish tonight before they arrive.

His friend is on the deck of his boat, mixing bait, the stench churning Branko's empty stomach. Seeing his expression, Vido laughs.

"So you have not come to help me?"

"Perhaps. The weather is changing, a storm on the way." He rubs his leg.

Vido nods. "I saved you some sardines. They have not regulated the price of fish, but hand me a coin in case they are watching."

"You feel it too?"

"Everyone is nervous, but that is the way of these things. It will be better once they have rounded up the collaborators, broken the Ustaše so they cannot rise up."

"You think they will do that?" His heart is thick in his throat.

"The commander said so in his speech last night."

"I was too far away. I could not hear. Vido, you know they will take me too."

Vido shakes his head. "No, I do not think so."

"But I was Ustaše. I wore that uniform."

Vido's lips are pursed tightly together. "Then you should find them before they find you. Explain what you did."

"Perhaps I would not be believed."

"Promise me you'll consider it. I can vouch for you."

"There is no reason for you to involve yourself. No one knows about your part."

"But we have a better story together."

"No!" He says it so loudly he is frightened the nearest partisan will hear. He drops his voice. "No. We cannot both be taken. Think about it, Vido, think about the worst. If I am in prison, I will need Dragica to have someone to turn to, someone she can rely on for protection and food. And when the Jews come back and I am not here, you are the only one who can show them where their precious artefacts are hidden."

Vido looks angry for a moment, but then he shrugs. "I do not like what you say one little bit, and yet I have to admit it sounds sensible all the same."

Branko puts his hand on his arm. "You are my dearest friend, but if I am arrested you do not know me. You must promise me that, at least. If nothing else, to ease my mind." Without waiting for an answer he turns and limps across the harbour.

Chapter Twenty-Six

Lopud, March 2010

After breakfast they strolled hand in hand along the promenade towards the monastery at the far end of the bay. The warmth of Jadran's palm against hers, the gentle pressure of his thumb on her knuckles, felt so strange. Strange, yet good, like a slow coming together that had been waiting to happen for a while.

She had wondered what to expect this morning, but over coffee and hot bread rolls straight from the oven, their conversation had been so easy as they made their plans for the day. Their kisses had changed things, of course they had, but only by half a degree and she marvelled at it, although she had been a little nervous when he'd suggested that tonight they should have a picnic on the boat to watch the sunset.

She'd told him it sounded lovely, which of course it did, but inside she wondered if it was perhaps just a bit too romantic. Even as they strolled together she was nervous about what might happen next, all the time Parisa's voice resonating around her head, saying she was overthinking it. It was all very well for her; Parisa'd had partners from time to time, but this hadn't happened to Fran for the best part of forty years.

There was no opportunity to ponder it now because they had passed the harbour and were at the bottom of the broad shallow steps leading to the monastery. The tower of the church rose above the trees, a grey finger against the palest of blue skies. It was a reminder that she needed to focus back on her father, but in her heightened emotional state she was more uneasy than ever about what she might find.

A crenellated wall seemed to grow out of the side of the church, barring their way, but in the centre of it was a square stone entrance, the treads of the steps buckled with age. The wooden doors were wedged open and, as they passed through the shadow created by the arch, Fran noticed a dusty cement mixer languishing under a tree that seemed to be trying to grow through the exterior wall of the complex. A muscular man appeared from a building abutting the far end of the church, wiping his palms on his multi-pocketed workman's trousers before shaking their hands vigorously and speaking to Jadran in Croatian.

"Stefan welcomes you to the monastery and apologises his English is so poor. But I have told him it is all right, I will translate if needed."

The man spoke again, and Fran found she could pick out the occasional word. Not nearly enough to understand, and it hit her again how grateful she was that Jadran was helping her. It was clear from Stefan's gestures he wanted them to follow him, and he led them through a vaulted room then down a rubble-strewn corridor, the uneven flagstones beneath their feet covered in grit and dust as the sound of sawing echoed from above.

Light flooded through a large, square gap in the wall to their left, and suddenly they were in the cloistered walkway surrounding a raised courtyard. In some places the walls were blackened with age and in others, covered in ivy, but the beautiful plain corbelled arches shone creamy-grey in the sunshine, making Fran gasp at their beauty. Speaking through Jadran, Stefan explained that they had been restored first to see what was possible, and the result was stunning in its simplicity.

Fran closed her eyes. Had her father seen these things? How long had this place been a ruin? She asked Jadran to find out and he told her the monks had abandoned it more than a hundred years before the Second World War, so she reasoned it was probably in better condition now than it had been when her father had been on the island.

So had they really interned the Jews in a ruin? It seemed more than likely, unless they had created some sort of tented camp in the fields as Jadran had suggested when they'd talked about it over breakfast. But that would have taken a great deal of effort to build and secure, and the walls surrounding the monastery and its fort were high and unbreached. Fran's heart bled for the families incarcerated here, their lives open to the elements and with no way of knowing what the future might bring. Families like Elvira's. Families like hers. Except her father had been on the other side.

Wherever they had been imprisoned, the fact that innocent people had been locked up purely on the basis of their faith was barbaric in itself and the injustice of it began to burn inside her. Her father had been here, and whatever the whys and wherefores of his exact role, he'd been supporting the regime, for god's sake. It was vile, absolutely vile, and the place it had happened didn't matter a jot. His reasons for becoming involved in this abomination were far more important, and just why he'd thought it was right to incarcerate innocent children like Elvira. Why hadn't she seen it before? Had meeting a woman who'd been caught up in it made it all the more real?

Stefan had already moved off and they followed him through more long-abandoned rooms, including one with a strange stone platform that had apparently been the monks' pharmacy. Fran tried to feign interest as Stefan explained this and Jadran translated, but it was hard when her head was so full of those poor Jewish women and children.

Jadran broke into her thoughts. "Stefan says there is something else he wants to show us, but we must be careful because it is upstairs where they are working."

At the end of another corridor was a stone staircase, the treads worn by age and with no banister or handrail. As Fran started up it Jadran grasped her hand.

"I want you to be safe," he said, with a smile that brought her right back to the present.

For a moment she was able to regain a sense of proportion. Elvira had said this had not been a cruel place; maybe those guarding it had not been fascists after all. Maybe it had just been a job like any other; her father simply a clerk who had been made to come here.

At the top of the stairs was another hallway with shafts of daylight illuminating the dark ceiling timbers through holes in the roof. Fran could glimpse the courtyard below her through the windows on one side, but on the other, empty doorways gaped.

Fran peeped through one. "They could have kept prisoners here," she said. "They look just like cells." How many families in each tiny room?

"Monks' cells most likely," said Jadran, but somehow his words did not comfort her. Maybe that had been their original purpose, but what had they been used for during the war?

Light streamed through holes in the roof and patches of mould stained the walls. Even sixty years ago, this would have been no place to house human beings, and whichever way you looked at it, her father had been part of this. Angry tears stabbed the backs of her eyes, leaving her momentarily stunned. Where was this fury coming from?

She followed the men into a narrow room with a deep-set window at one end, its thick glass still intact. The walls were plastered and painted with some sort of distemper, and although they were discoloured by years of damp, the graffiti was still plainly visible: 'IL DUCE' written crudely in two lines of huge capital letters, crammed between the window and the wall.

"So that seals it. The Italians were here. This must be the place."

"It's evidential, but not conclusive. Maybe this was just where the soldiers were billeted," Jadran replied. He was just too bloody reasonable at times.

"Soldiers who were clearly committed fascists," she shot back.

Jadran put his hands in his pockets. "Well at least one of them was." He spoke to Stefan, then said, "So far this is the only thing like it they have found. He says he is sorry there is nothing British here for you to see."

"You'd better tell him my father was Yugoslavian. I wouldn't want him to change the monastery's history on the basis of a misunderstanding."

"No, you are right. There are more than enough shadows here as it is."

"You see though, don't you? You understand?" The backs of her eyes were burning again.

He looked at her, head on one side. "I'm not sure I do."

She needed to get a grip on her emotions and explain properly. She took a deep breath. "It's because … I can't accept my father because he was a fascist. Not a soldier like you were, defending your country. That I completely understand. If it was simply that, there would be nothing for me to forgive. But to hate someone enough to imprison or kill them on the basis of their ethnicity … it's … it's a … well, in truth I don't know what to call it. It's barely human. It's vile and I'll never forgive him for that. Never." She choked back a sob. "I'm sorry … I'll see you outside."

Blinded by tears she all but ran down the stairs and back into the courtyard. The sunlight fell in prisms onto the cleaned parts of the stone, hurting her eyes. How come seeing that brutal graffiti on the wall had unleashed all this emotion? What had she expected to find?

She gripped the rough stone edges of the well to steady herself. *Calm down, Fran, calm down.* She could already see she had overreacted, perhaps in part because her emotions had been stretched to the limit by everything that had happened with Jadran since they had arrived. His disappearing act, his explanation, his total openness about Leila, that kiss. The ups and downs of it all and the way it had made her feel. The way he made her feel. It was little wonder she was all over the place.

By the time Jadran appeared at the corner of the cloister she had recovered most of her composure and apologised for embarrassing him.

He nodded briefly but didn't look at her. "You have seen enough?"

"Yes."

He turned and she followed him along the corridor and out onto the parapet overlooking the bay. She started to apologise again but he raised his finger to silence her.

"It doesn't matter. Perhaps you would feel better if you went back to the guest house to wash your face? I need to check the boat so I will join you later."

As she watched him stride off, Fran felt about three inches high.

Despite the feeling she'd been well and truly dismissed, Fran was glad to escape to try to put her thoughts in order and control her emotions. The further she walked from the monastery, the more her sense of perspective grew; there may have been at least one Italian soldier who'd been a committed fascist, but according to Elvira there had been at least one Ustaše who hadn't been, and had helped the Jews to escape. And of course it was possible, although unlikely, her father had been that man.

By the time she reached the guest house she was feeling even more embarrassed about her behaviour. She had completely overreacted so of course she had shocked Jadran. It wasn't like her, she knew it wasn't. But of course Jadran didn't. What must he think? That the moment he kissed her she'd turned into some sort of screaming harridan? No wonder he'd sent her back to the hotel.

She sank onto her bed, fingering the tassels that edged the counterpane. Within little more than twelve hours of being kissed for the first time in forty years, she'd managed to blow it completely. Oh, it shouldn't matter, she was going home soon after all, but somehow it did. As they'd become closer, she'd begun to wonder if, even though they couldn't be together, perhaps it wasn't too farfetched to imagine herself in a relationship at some point in the future.

But was she really capable of it? This fuss she'd caused was all, and only, to do with her inability to deal with her growing feelings for a man, and very little to do with her father. Even last night, as she'd snuggled into bed thinking it was all wonderful, she had also felt deeply unsettled, and it had only taken one little thing this morning to knock her completely out of kilter.

Her first priority when Jadran came back would be to apologise and try to explain. Yes, it would mean putting her feelings out there in a way she really didn't want to, but she owed him that at least. He'd clearly already decided she was a hopeless case, so it wouldn't change the outcome, but it felt like the right thing to do.

She washed her face as he'd suggested and she did feel a little better. She sent a text to tell him so, then stretched out on her bed to try to read another chapter of her book. She found herself going over the same couple of paragraphs again and again, so after a while gave up and flicked through the tourist brochure that had been left on the dressing table instead.

At one point she thought she heard movement in Jadran's room next door, and the patio doors open and close, but it must have been the maid because there was no knock on hers. But as the time stretched endlessly onwards, she became a little concerned. Where was he? Was he all right? It was so unlike him. He hadn't even replied to her text … yet who could blame him for not wanting to be anywhere near her after her emotional outburst.

Setting the brochure to one side she decided some fresh air might clear her head. And of course, if she went for a walk, she might just bump into Jadran. Lopud was a small place after all. Out on the terrace she realised it must have been him that she'd heard after all because the sand came right up to the wooden boards and she could see his footprints on the path that wound between the shrubs to the beach. A stiff breeze had sprung up and she was glad of her fleece as the sun disappeared behind a bank of ominous clouds threatening the hilltops behind her.

Jadran's footprints led her away from the village towards the slopes where an enormous hotel was being rebuilt. The sand was soft and cool beneath her feet, the water in the bay shimmering like bronzed glass in the stormy light. She stood for a moment and gazed over the narrow channel towards Šipan wondering what she would say if she caught up with him. Apologise, that was the first thing, and depending on his response, take it from there.

She spied Jadran sitting on the sand next to a rocky outcrop a hundred or so yards ahead of her. He was so very still.

Something stopped her from calling out, waiting until she was almost standing next to him before saying hello.

When he looked up his face was wet with tears.

"Whatever's wrong?" Oh, lord ... she'd never even envisaged she might have hurt him like this. "I am just so sor—"

"Safranka, please go away. I do not want you to see me like this."

"I just wanted to say ... I'm so sorry for the way I behaved back there, truly I am."

He covered his face with his hands. "It isn't you. Please, just go."

Then it must be about Leila. Awful as his pain was, right now it made things easier for her. Feeling a twinge of guilt, she sat down next to him. "There's no shame in showing your grief, you know. No shame at all. Especially when you were brave enough to suggest coming here."

There was a long silence before he said. "But what if the tears are not grief, if the tears themselves are shame?"

Was he talking in riddles, or was his emotional state muddling his English?

"I don't understand."

"This, I cannot expect you to." He rubbed his sleeve across his eyes in a gesture so like Andrew as a small boy when he'd scraped his knee, Fran felt her own tears threatening. "This thing that has come between us, just when you have shown me it is possible to move on. That makes it all the harder to bear, but one day, one day, I will learn to be thankful to you, and to accept the reason you do not want to be with me."

Fran dug her fingers into the sand, then lifted her palms to let it trickle through. Yes, she understood they could not be together, they had always known that, but not why she wouldn't want to be. What on earth had she said back at the monastery to make him think it? She watched the grains of sand complete their slow descent, then picked up some more.

"I don't understand what you mean. I was overwrought back there, far too emotional, but I never meant to give you the impression ..."

"You spoke the truth, that is all. The truth about how you feel."

His words made no sense. "I may not be recalling things too clearly, but all I remember is talking about my father."

"Yes, and the things you can't forgive." The familiar frown creased his forehead.

Fran wanted so much to smooth it away, but instead kept trickling the sand through her fingers.

"I had hoped ... hoped you could forgive my war, or at least we could forget about it, but what you said this morning..." He sighed. "If you cannot forgive your father then you will not be able to forgive me, and we will never be able to move beyond that."

At last Fran felt able to look up and smile at him. "If that's it then there is no need to worry. I was in such a muddle back there I was barely coherent, but what I'm really struggling with is the fact my father was probably a committed fascist, that he did what he did through ethnic hatred, and your situation is completely different."

Jadran shook his head. "But it isn't, not at all. Whatever your father's story, I went to fight with hatred in my heart. Hatred of the Serbs who had killed Leila and Kristina. But more than that, hatred of each and every Serb."

"That's understandable ..."

"Perhaps your father had his reasons too, but we shall never know. I am not proud of my war, Safranka, which is why I do not talk about it. Not even in my head to Leila, because she would not have been proud of me either. In fact, she would have been ashamed. It was the darkest time of my life, and I made it more so by my actions."

"Vedran said you were decorated for bravery—"

"Pah! For brutality, more like." He gazed out over the bay again, but Fran sensed he was unaware of the beauty around him, and what he was seeing was long in the past.

She stopped sifting sand and put her hand over his.

Eventually he said, "You need to know what I did and then you can decide whether you forgive me, although I fear I am clutching at straws. You need to think about it too, not tell me now that it is all right, just to be kind; because you are, more than anything, kind. But this is not the time for kindness, Safranka, it is the time for honesty."

She sensed it was important she didn't answer too quickly, so waited a few moments before saying, "Yes, I promise."

"Then I will tell you."

She looked up at him, but he could not look at her.

"The first thing you need to understand is this was not a war like others. It was a civil war, driven by old arguments that only Tito had managed to keep at bay. Nor was it especially disciplined, when people like me who were not professional soldiers formed most of the fighting forces." He took a deep breath and Fran became aware he'd been garbling his words, although on another level they sounded automatic and rehearsed.

"You have doubtless heard of the massacres at places like Srebrenica. They came to the attention of the whole world and rightly so. But perhaps they also fuelled misunderstandings. There were actually three sides in the conflict, not just the Bosniaks and Serbs, but a Croatian army too, and although we started out by helping the Bosniaks, we ended up fighting everyone."

"And were you involved in a massacre?" Fran's voice was almost a whisper.

"No. Nor in the concentration camps. But perhaps ..." he faltered. "Perhaps only because my war did not take me to those places. I do not know what I might have done if it had so. It does not make my own behaviour any better. Safranka, I killed men with vengeance in my heart. Killed when I did not need to. You have to understand that."

His hand was trembling beneath hers as he carried on, his tale gathering pace with every sentence. "It was not a war fought on strict military lines. For most of the time my unit was in the mountains skirmishing. Disrupting supply lines, hunting out the enemy by day and night, living off the land and from what we could loot, because there was not enough food for anyone. Most often we were hungry and cold, and no doubt many men were scared, but I was not afraid of dying. For me death would have been welcome, so I was reckless in my killing, careless even.

"I cannot tell you how many lives I ended, but I can tell you when it changed. It was at a time when we were protecting our own supplies, and we came across an enemy unit camping nearby. A threat we had to wipe out. We hid further around the mountain until nightfall and then we went in. I slit a sentry's throat." He stopped. Looked down at her. "Yes, Safranka, the killing could be that brutal and I expect it will shock you. But by that time I was numb to it.

"We surprised them, overwhelmed them, and some of them started to run away. Not many; we could have let them go, but I did not. I shot one in the back. Often they had arms we could use so I went to check his body, and when I turned him over ... when I turned him over ..."

Jadran's voice was shaking so Fran squeezed his hand, but he snatched it away.

"He was nothing but a boy, Safranka, just a boy. He looked younger in death than perhaps he was, but to me he was just like Kristina and I knew the grief I had caused another father. Countless other fathers." He shrugged. "After that I could not do it and walked to the nearest command post and told them. All they did was transfer me to an artillery unit, but at least I could not see the faces of the people I murdered."

He'd been right when he'd said her first reaction would be to be kind, and tell him it made no difference, but that wasn't what he wanted. He wanted her to properly understand, to think this through. But although she was shocked to the core, she did kind of get it. He'd lost his wife and daughter, everything that mattered to him. It was little wonder he'd hated the Serbs.

"And do you ... I mean, how do you feel about Serbians now?"

He turned to face her. "Since the war I have tried not to see people in terms of their ethnicity because it is not helpful. We are neighbours. Quite literally because there is a Serbian community in Dubrovnik, so we need to be able to tolerate each other at very least. Not all Serbs wanted the war, any more than most ordinary Croats or Bosnians did. What is important is to accept each individual human being as you find them. For who they are, not what they are."

Fran nodded. So he had at least learned from his experiences. Would her father have done the same if he'd lived? That she would never know. "Thank you. Thank you for telling me everything. Thank you for trusting me."

"And you will think about it? Really think about it?"

"Of course. It is what you want me to do. Although you were right, my first instinct is to say it doesn't matter."

"When of course it does."

"It matters to you, Jadran, and that is something I will respect."

He sat for a moment longer, then raindrops began to fall, patterning the sand with tiny circles. "Come on, we need to get back."

He heaved himself up and Fran followed, trailing after his long strides as he marched in the direction of the hotel.

Chapter Twenty-Seven

Dubrovnik, 19th October 1944

S he is breathless as she reaches the top of the stairs, her face flushed, hair escaping from her scarf. He looks up from cleaning the sardines Vido gave him.

"There are English officers in the hotel." Her brow is creased in a frown and he kisses it.

"That is perhaps to be expected. They are the partisans' allies, remember. They have helped them to win back the islands." He unties the shawl that binds Safranka to her back, the sweet milky warmth of his daughter enveloping him as he takes her in his arms.

"But, Branko, I do not understand. If they are their allies, why do they keep them prisoner?"

He tears his eyes from his daughter's face. "You are sure?"

"Yes. They have been given rooms on my floor and there are guards outside."

"To protect them, perhaps?"

She shakes her head. "I saw them remove the Englishmen's guns. And when I took their food at midday, although they thanked me politely, they did not look happy."

He rocks Safranka in his arms. There must be a reason for this strange behaviour, but it unsettles him almost as much as the partisans' perpetual watching. The mayor was still in his office today and that unsettles him too. Are their liberators not quite the heroes he imagined? But no, they have fought so hard to free the country, that cannot be the case.

He knows his conversation with Vido will keep him awake tonight, one more thread to the exhaustion that runs as deep and as constant as the ache in his leg. How will he cope in prison? How much more can he take? But running away is impossible with Safranka so small, so take whatever comes he must. For his family's sake. He needs to be strong, and brave. But just how brave he can be, now he is not so sure. Sometimes it feels as though his reserves of courage are all used up.

He buries his face in Safranka's dress and she wriggles in his arms. He draws Dragica into the circle and holds them both. Time stills. A shutter slams below them. The last rays of sun dapple the wall. Moments like these transcend everything; moments of love like he has never known before. Moments that sustain him and that he will remember down the years; the years when what they are going through now will fade into insignificance.

"I am a lucky man."

Dragica looks up and kisses him. "We have each other. And because of that, we will survive."

Chapter Twenty-Eight

Lopud, March 2010

It was late the next afternoon and Fran was sitting outside a bar on the promenade, waiting for Jadran to join her after refuelling *Safranka II*. Near her feet was a cool bag that held their picnic. Yesterday's rain had persisted into the early evening, so they had postponed their boat trip, instead sharing a pizza for supper in a small café then having an early night. It had been a blessing really, as things had been very awkward and strained between them.

This morning Jadran had looked drawn, older than his years, and she had truly felt her heart was breaking for him. But he'd been resolutely cheerful, and after breakfast they had climbed to the island's other fort, high in the hills, and although the view across the narrow band of water to the mainland had been spectacular, Fran doubted it was where the Jews had been held as it had clearly been a ruin for generations. Goats wandered between stunted trees and what remained of the walls, their bleating mingling with the chirp of the cicadas and the scent of wild rosemary.

They'd perched on a rocky outcrop in the shade of an olive tree, discussing the possibilities of where the camp had been again and again, as though there was nothing else for them to talk about. And perhaps there wasn't, because although Fran already knew her answer to the one question that mattered, she had worried telling him too soon would make it seem as though she hadn't thought it through enough.

Of course, it would all be easier for him once she'd explained she could accept what he'd done in the war. And it wasn't only what *she* felt that mattered, because after all she would be going home soon, but her answer would make it easier for him to love any woman who came after. If she could accept his past, so could anyone. And a Croatian would have most likely gone through the war too and would carry her own scars.

She was surprised how disturbing she found the thought of Jadran with another woman, of giving someone else his serious small smiles, taking them out on his boat, sharing an aperitif, kissing them even. And it was wrong of her, because she couldn't have him, she had a whole life back in England to resume. Whatever shape and purpose that would end up taking, Jadran could never be part of it, because his life was here.

And there was something else too; something that was to do with her and her alone. That niggling worry that in Jadran she was just looking for a replacement person to care for. She had managed to bury the thought for a while, but yesterday on the beach the need to comfort and protect him had been almost overwhelming.

But that wasn't love; not the sort you wanted between a man and a woman anyway. In Mama and Daddy's marriage she'd witnessed balance, equality. Neither one subjugated to the other. Fran was beginning to realise that what was frightening her most about all this was that she could easily lose herself in Jadran's feelings, Jadran's wants, Jadran's life. She couldn't let that happen. She needed more; something for herself.

She glanced across at the monastery. She knew about Mama and Daddy inside out, and in many ways they'd been perfect role models, but what had her mother's first marriage been like? How had she come to love a man like her father? But there she was, judging him again. He wasn't necessarily a bad person, despite his unpalatable beliefs, which after all had been more common at the time. And perhaps her mother had fallen for him without even knowing.

That Mama had loved Branko Milišić was beyond any doubt. As Jadran had pointed out, why else would she have called herself Milly for the rest of her life when her name was Dragica? Why else would she have treasured the necklace? Why would she have brought up his daughter to believe her father was a hero? Perhaps he even had been a hero. Could he have been the man who helped Elvira's family to escape? Someone had, after all. But a man who'd done that would have been feted by the partisans when they arrived, not executed by them. Unless, of course, the partisans had made a terrible mistake.

For the first time Fran began to wonder how much the war had scarred her mother and it seemed so obvious it felt surprising she hadn't thought of it before. Had Mama been so insistent she and Fran had to be the best they could to deserve

Daddy because she had dark secrets like Jadran's that haunted her? Perhaps she carried the burden of her husband's guilt, had even believed that Fran was tainted by it too. Or had she left because she wanted to put as much distance as possible between herself and the partisans?

Oh, this was pointless, pointless speculation. She could never know what her mother's war had been like, or what her love story with Branko Milišić had been, but she had witnessed most of Mama's life with Daddy. Of course the early days were from a child's point of view and hazy to say the least, but there was something about her parents' love that had always seemed solid, and grounded, and right. No dramas or screaming arguments, no spiteful words or hurtful games. Whatever had happened in the war, her mother had moved beyond it and hopefully Jadran could too. It was just such a shame it couldn't be with her.

It wasn't only the place that was wrong, it was the time. Of course she had feelings for him; feelings so alien and uncomfortable they frightened the life out of her on so many levels. If she let herself, she could love him, of that she was sure, but how could she when it would mean losing so much of her life. Her newly emerging self, even. It was just too big a risk.

But although he knew she was going home, he hadn't held back, he'd made his feelings clear. He had as much to lose as she did, in fact he probably thought he had already lost it by telling her the truth. But whatever the uncertainties fluttering around her own head, she wasn't judging him for his actions during the war and she had to make him understand that tonight. If nothing else so the poor man could sleep.

As to what else might come of it ... could she do what

Parisa had said? Forget her convoluted thoughts and go with the flow? Was she brave enough to stop worrying and find out what might happen? A tingle of excitement radiated from deep in her belly, but what surprised her more was the thought that perhaps, and despite everything, her precious seeds of confidence might have grown enough to make the first move.

When Fran looked up, Jadran was walking towards her, his athletic stride at odds with the downward slope of his shoulders. But when she waved, his smile was instinctive and broad, although it quickly retreated back into his face, and that told her everything she already knew.

She stood and grabbed the cool bag, weaving through the café tables to meet him. "Shall we go?"

"In a moment. There's somewhere I want to show you first."

He took the bag from her and strode down the waterfront in the opposite direction to the harbour, past the small park. To Fran's surprise he stopped in front of the security fencing that circled the Grand Hotel.

"It was here. The Jews were interned here," he told her.

Fran gazed up at the concrete edifice, once white but now stained black with age. Weeds and grass had colonised what no doubt used to be terraces, almost covering the steps towards the entrance. So not a ruin, not a tented camp. In a hotel, and what had been quite a new one at that.

"How did you find out?" Fran breathed.

Jadran shifted the cool bag to his other hand. "By chance. I mentioned what we were doing to the harbour master. His uncle used to be the restaurant manager here in the sixties and took an interest in its history." He looked at her sideways. "How do you feel about it all now?"

"I'm thinking about what Eli said, that the camp was crowded, but not cruel. I suppose, if you can set the horror of being interned to one side, there would have been worse places to be."

Jadran nodded. "And your father's role?"

She knew this was far more than the simple question it seemed, so she looked up at him and smiled. "I'll tell you on the boat."

The rattle of the anchor came to a sudden stop and *Safranka II* swung lazily around on the chain until she settled with her bow facing into the small bay. Now all Fran could hear was birdsong drifting from the stunted pines that grew above the slabs of grey rock on the shore and the sloosh and slop of the water beneath the boat.

"It's so peaceful here," she said.

"I thought it would be. And a perfect place to watch the sunset. Out to sea, just to our right, is the tip of Mljet, then nothing but the Adriatic until Italy." He hauled the cool bag onto the table. "So, shall I open the wine?"

"Yes, I hope it's all right. There wasn't much choice. In fact there was hardly any choice of anything, so there is just bread, cheese, salami and a jar of olives. The salad they had looked rather tired."

Jadran delved into the bag. "But there is also chocolate."

"How could I forget your sweet tooth?"

"And it is Dorina with hazelnuts – one of my favourites." He smiled, but all the same looked slightly wan.

"Sit down for a minute, I have something to tell you."

He hesitated, bottle and corkscrew in hand. "Wine first? I might need it."

"No, you won't. I've been thinking so much about what you told me yesterday, Jadran. In fact, almost all of the time. But my first view has not changed. It makes no difference to me at all."

He sank onto the plastic bench next to her. "Thank you. Thank you so much, Safranka. But all the same, I do not understand. The way you are about your father ... why is it different with me?"

"For any number of reasons. First, I know why you acted as you did; the Serbian soldiers had killed your wife and child, and while that does not make retribution right, it makes it understandable. Particularly as I imagine you were so grief-stricken you weren't even thinking straight. And of course, when you realised what you were doing was wrong, you stopped."

"You are making excuses for me," he mumbled.

"No. Not excuses, reasons. There is a difference. An excuse would be something like, 'It was war and everyone was doing it,' but you never once said that and I don't suppose you thought it either."

"Maybe at the time, but not for many, many years."

"Well then."

"But your father could have had his reasons too."

"Yes, he could have, and we will never know. That's something I've been thinking about too. But in the overall context of the times it is at least a strong possibility that he acted as he did because he believed the ideology of fascism – that some people, some races, had less value as human beings than others. That's what's abhorrent to me. And nothing you have said has made me think you ever bought into Serbs being racially inferior."

"No! Of course not." He looked shocked, then began to busy himself opening the wine.

"As I thought. You see, that wouldn't fit with the man I have come to know at all. And this is perhaps the most important thing. I can accept what happened in the past because of the man you are now. We have all done things we are not proud of, but not many of our generation have had to live through a war. Yes, here in Croatia you have, but in Britain our experiences have been very different, so who am I to judge you?"

"You said the same about your father, but yesterday morning—"

"I was overwrought. Emotional. As soon as I got back to the courtyard and took a few deep breaths I realised." She took the wine glasses out of the cool bag and set them on the table. "I cannot ever come to know him, come to understand his actions and motivations as I can yours. I will never know who he was, or why he did what he did, even assuming that he did anything wrong at all. What I need to do now is come to terms with my own past, not his. Then I might be able to move forwards."

"Your own past?"

"Oh, nothing as life-changing as yours, but there are things I have not seen clearly, maybe because I didn't want to. Because it was easier not to, if I'm honest. It was easier to be the person everyone wanted me to be, and not perhaps the person I was inside. Like many women of my generation I was brought up never to rock the boat, and in today's world that seems rather outdated."

"And do you want to rock the boat, Safranka?" Although his voice was perfectly serious the sparkle had returned to his eyes, the last rays of the sun highlighting the flecks of grey amongst the hazel, making them dance.

"Yes, I think I do. Well, at least a little." She was reaching for her wine, but then she changed her mind, cupping the back of his head in her hand and tipping her face up to kiss him. Gently, softly, as they had kissed before. There was an impulsive craziness to the moment, nothing she had planned, a deep spark of joy filling her from head to toe as he responded.

But the moment he sat back to look at her, her courage vanished.

"I'm not sure why I did that really, except I wanted to very much," she stuttered.

"And I am very glad you did. A kiss needs no reason, Safranka. A kiss is a beautiful thing." He cupped her face in his hands, holding her gaze. "We both know the reality of our situation, that you are going home soon. It is a fact we must both accept, but in the meantime, let us see where our feelings take us."

Fran swallowed hard. There was one thing she had to be very clear about. "I don't feel ready to do any more than kiss, and perhaps cuddle a bit too. You know what I'm saying?"

"Yes, of course, and I agree. To become lovers would be a very big step for both of us, I think, and not to be taken lightly. I … I have only ever known Leila in that way. We grew up in different times."

"And I've only ever known Ray, Michael's father."

"Then we are the same, my beautiful Safranka, and we will find our own way, somewhere between being friends and being lovers, a place that is just our own."

"That's what you meant in the park, wasn't it, when you said it would be what we made it?"

He nodded. "But then it was just a hope rather than an expectation. Now, you have made me happy, as long as you are happy too."

"Very happy, but I have to say, a little cold."

"I can remedy that."

While Fran took the bread and cheese from the cool bag, Jadran disappeared into the cabin and came back with a soft red-and-blue-checked blanket.

"I thought we could share," he said, and wrapped it across both their shoulders before putting his arm around her waist and pulling her close.

And they sat, in the gently rocking boat, as the birds fell silent and the orange orb of the sun shot purple streamers across the horizon, then finally sank into the sea.

It was a moment Fran would cherish forever.

Chapter Twenty-Nine

Dubrovnik, 20th October 1944

He walks home through the backstreets to think. They came for the mayor at noon. Raised voices from behind his door, words muffled and indistinct. The silence in the office outside was palpable: no rustle of paper, not a murmur, not a cough. They did not look at each other, but there were those among them that could not fail to hide triumphant smiles. And those who had turned a little pale. Into which camp should he fall?

There are rumours some priests have been taken too, known collaborators. The clean-up has begun. Should he go to the partisans, as Vido suggested? But perhaps it is already too late to tell them a story that might sound like an excuse.

He stops outside the synagogue but cannot bear to see the broken windows and splintered door. If Solly was here he would know what to do. But he isn't and might never be again.

He turns his back on the street where they had once played and trudges up Ulica Prijeko as the fine mist of rain darkens the uneven flagstones beneath his feet.

The buildings loom on either side, the golden-grey stone of the city he loves stained with age. Once wealthy merchants' houses, with solid stone lintels above their doors, now the wood beneath has an uncared-for quality, the formerly polished steps drab after years of war.

Ahead of him two partisans stand on a corner, watching and waiting. Waiting for him? Sickness rises in his throat. *Please, no, don't let it be now.* He needs to hold his wife and daughter one more time to give him courage. He needs to warn Dragica, tell her who to turn to, what to do. Head down, he limps on, cursing the impossibility of making himself invisible. Cursing his inability to run.

Is running an option? Not in the physical sense, of course, but to pack their few possessions and leave Dubrovnik? He comes back to it yet dismisses it time and again. In his heart he knows that casting his family into a hungry and uncertain future is not the answer. Not with Safranka so tiny. And anyway, leaving would be seen as evidence of his guilt. How far would they have to go? How long would they have to hide?

He is yards away from the partisans. They have not moved and he senses their gaze. The silence of the street engulfs him. If he is taken, no one will know. In all the long years of war he has trusted these people, trusted them to bring salvation and peace to his country. Can he still trust them now?

As he draws level he raises his hat and bids them "*Dobra večer*" as he would anyone else. They reply civilly enough but they do not move, their eyes burning into his back until he reaches the corner. Tonight he must prepare Dragica for whatever might come next.

Chapter Thirty

Dubrovnik, March 2010

There were two parcels propped outside the door when Fran got back to the apartment, which was intriguing in itself. One was no more than a smallish Jiffy bag really, but the other was a neat flat box wrapped in brown paper and the handwriting on it was definitely Parisa's. What was she up to now?

Fran turned the Jiffy bag over and over in her hand. She knew the scrawl on the front of it, and the postmark was Brighton. So this, whatever it was, was Patti's response. A strong sense of foreboding gripped her. Why had she ever, ever, sent that card? But she knew in her heart of hearts she'd done it because she'd had to and perhaps, just perhaps, her sister's response was positive.

Right. Action. Cup of tea first, then open Parisa's parcel, because that was bound to contain something nice.

The note inside the wrapping was written on plain white card.

If they don't fit, I can return them when you come home.

Fran lifted the lid, only to be confronted by layers of creamy tissue paper, embossed with the name of one of the very exclusive boutiques where Parisa shopped. The box was too small to contain a top or anything like that, and how might a scarf not fit?

Peeling back the final layer of tissue Fran was confronted by a peach lace bra and a pair of matching French knickers. Honestly, what was Parisa thinking? Well actually she did know, but it wasn't going to happen. Not only was it not what she wanted right now, but what she and Jadran had agreed … Except Parisa didn't know that. So much had changed during their short trip to Lopud. It was as if the final door that had stood between them had been opened, and it led to honesty and trust.

Even so, Fran fingered the underwear. The lace was so fine, the silk so soft. She checked the size; they would fit all right, as well Parisa knew. It was just she wouldn't have occasion to wear them, and that was a bit of a shame. But she knew from their time spent in endless shop changing rooms that Parisa always wore this sort of lingerie, and there was certainly no permanent man in her life. Clearly her friend was wearing it for herself. Could she do the same?

Was Parisa trying to tell her something? Way back when they had been shopping for this trip, she had said she might feel differently about herself inside if she updated the way she looked. Sort of walking the walk before anything actually changed. But there had been no blinding moment of transformation when she'd put on a new cardigan or looked in the mirror after the haircut, although gradually the new and once alien clothes had become part of her daily wardrobe and she was comfortable with the way she wore them.

It would doubtless be the same with the underwear. She picked up the bra. It was light as a feather and beautifully stitched. Of course it was hand wash only, which would be a pain, but with care, something like this would last her for years, so if she liked it enough to buy a couple more it would be an investment. And she wouldn't be wearing it for Jadran or anyone else, she'd be wearing it for herself.

She sent Parisa a quick text to thank her and check she was still on for their regular Friday night Skype, then turned her attention to the Jiffy bag. Whatever Patti had to say she would have to face it.

She tore open the end of the bag and tipped out the contents. Fragments of card rained onto the table: the postcard she had sent Patti ripped into tiny shreds. Fran sighed. Well, what had she expected? But as she fished a piece of it out of her tea, she still felt disappointed. She'd been hoping for at least a small step towards reconciliation. It would make things so much easier for Andrew if she and Patti weren't at war.

Stuck in the bottom of the bag was a note, on a small square piece of paper that looked as though it had been torn off the sort of pad you kept by the telephone.

How dare you rub it in you're living it up in the sun? He's not even cold yet and you're spending his money. I hate you.

Fran turned it over in her hand. It was the sort of thing a

child would write and it occurred to her that in many ways Patti had remained stuck in childhood, still desperate to be the centre of attention, and blaming everyone else for her failures. Had she simply never grown up? After all, no one else was ever going to treat her as her parents had done after the accident. They had certainly spoiled her, all right, and Fran had too until they had fallen out.

So it wasn't surprising Fran had felt responsible, although now she was finally accepting that perhaps her parents should shoulder some of the blame too. Whatever the rights and wrongs of the matter, it was clearer than ever there was nothing she could do to put it right. The thought lay heavy on her as she pottered around unpacking and putting her dirty clothes in the washing machine. She couldn't even talk to Andrew about this final straw because she hadn't told him about the card, hadn't wanted to build up his hopes. She would just somehow have to learn to accept the fact that this particular chapter of the book was closed and move on.

She sank onto the edge of the bed, the mattress sagging beneath her. It was like grief, really, except this had been playing out for years. There had been anger, bargaining, misery … somehow she needed to find acceptance. She was close to it, she knew. There'd been no shock of pain as she'd tipped out the bag or read Patti's note; there had been something close to relief that constantly trying to put things right was over.

It was odd, but almost without noticing it, acceptance was the point she had reached with losing Daddy. The sharpest of the pain, the barely controllable tears, were no longer part of her life. Of course she still found herself thinking she must tell Daddy this or that, but now she could tell him in her head with just the dullest of aches in her heart, and sometimes even a smile. It had been his time; he'd wanted to be with Mama. She'd had to let him go.

And what about Mama? That wasn't quite so simple. While the distance of being in Dubrovnik had helped her to grieve for Daddy, it had brought her mother and the pain of losing her closer, brought unanswered questions to the fore, and there was definitely unfinished business. But that wasn't for now. She wouldn't even know where to start looking. Maybe Mama's ghost wasn't even here.

Fran stood and went in search of her handbag. Closing the book on Patti was quite enough for one day. Right now she needed to pop to the supermarket to buy something for supper, then email Michael to tell him about her visit to Lopud. She'd tackle the Mama issue properly when she was good and ready, and not before.

~

"Ah, Fran, I am glad you could come, and so soon." Eli was perching on a stool behind the welcome desk at the museum, but although he sounded cheerful enough, his face was pinched with pain.

"Is it not a good day?" Fran asked. "You don't look well."

"Let us just say I hope no one stretches my patience." He grimaced.

"I'll try not to. You said you had some photos to show me."

He nodded, and slid down, bending stiffly to fetch an album from a drawer. "The cruise ships have started again for the summer and an American tourist brought us this. His grandfather emigrated in the 1930s and when he died a couple of years ago, he found it amongst his possessions. He has no children of his own to leave it to, so he thought he would bring it home to Dubrovnik."

"How kind of him."

"Yes. And it will be interesting for you to see the city your father grew up in. Of course a lot of the pictures are just of people but there are some more general ones too, including Sponza Palace, where your father would have worked, and some of the streets around here too. You can take it away to look at if you like."

"I'm not sure I'd dare."

"No, really. And today I would prefer it. I am not feeling sociable."

Fran nodded. "I understand. Can I get you anything though? Bring you a coffee, maybe?"

He shook his head. "I will be fine. Now go."

Fran picked up the photograph album and put it in her shoulder bag. She had intended to take it back to the apartment, but there was a table free in a patch of sunshine outside one of the café bars that had now opened for the season further along the street, and drawn by the waft of freshly ground beans, she settled herself down and ordered a cappuccino. She would certainly miss the café culture when she went back home, and that date was beginning to loom. It would be Easter on Sunday and then she would have just three weeks left. Maybe less, because she really wanted to be back in England for Belle's birthday on the 23rd.

She needed to make a definite decision. She marvelled now at how, when she'd first arrived, she never thought she would last two weeks. And yet she had been here close to two months. And it wasn't only Jadran who had made it possible for her to stay; it was Vedran, Eli, the friendly women in the market, the neighbours she now knew by name, the city itself, all embracing her.

It was almost as though a tiny part of her belonged in Dubrovnik and she had never expected that. She had thought her experience would be akin to Parisa's on her visits to Pakistan; interesting, but alien. Yet it wasn't. Of course, her home would always be in England and not just because Michael and Andrew were there, but because it was where she had lived all her life. She was British, end of. But at least now she knew that this was somewhere she would always come back to. Maybe for a few months every winter, take the same apartment, catch up with her friends …

But she knew that was a glossy version of how things might be. When she went home, saying goodbye to Jadran would be painful. They spent so much time together it was inevitable, and it would take her a while to get over it. Would she really want to come back next year and go through the whole process all over again? Or worse, come back and find him with someone new?

A smiling waiter delivered her coffee and once she'd taken a sip, she took the photograph album out of her bag. It was bound in what looked like dark green leather but probably wasn't, wide rather than tall, with three pictures next to each other on each page.

At first there were formal portraits of what Fran assumed were family members; women wearing embroidered blouses, men and boys in stiff collars and ties with hair plastered neatly down. But then the photographer had clearly ventured outside and views of the city followed, including, as Eli had said, the Sponza Palace, with a man walking past in a homburg hat.

Some of the pictures were easier to place than others. Sveti Vlaho taken through an arch somewhere; the Pile Gate; a group of women walking down Stradun, arms linked and smiling, as though on a day out. Others were street scenes, fairly anonymous, but although it was hard to tell, from what Eli had said Fran took them to be in the area close to where she was sitting now. She was delighted to find one of the market where she bought her vegetables, looking more or less the same as it did today. She'd have to ask Eli if she could take the album to show the stallholders.

She flicked through the pages. A middle-aged woman, severe in an impressive fur stole, stood next to a little girl dressed almost as an adult, apart from her thick white stockings. Blurred pictures of boys playing football in a narrow street. A young man in an almost cartoon-sized flat cap standing outside the walls, the Minčeta Tower, the one closest to where she was living, rising behind him.

Next came a picture of two boys sitting on the steps outside someone's house, one clearly a few years older than the other, about twelve or thirteen maybe, and grinning at the camera. But it was the youngster who grabbed Fran's attention; shy, glancing away, his face partly in profile, looking so much like Michael at the same age.

No, she was imagining it. It couldn't possibly be. This child's hair was dark, not fair, and his frame was small, undernourished even. But his nose, the prominent cheekbones … She turned the pages of the album feverishly, fingers fumbling, searching for another picture of the boy, but there was none. Nothing at all, just that single glimpse into the past. Her past, maybe.

Fran sat back, the album closed on her lap, trying to stop

her heart from thumping. There was no way this child could be her father; the chances were infinitesimally small. But god, for some reason she didn't quite understand, she wanted it to be so much. Of course it was rubbish really; Michael had always looked more like Ray, not her side of the family. But was that just because he was blond and tall? The first time her mother had seen him as a baby she'd told Fran he had her nose. Did he? Even if she was the sort of woman who carried a mirror around with her, she wouldn't have taken it out in the street to peer at herself.

She went into the bar to pay for her coffee and ask where the toilet was. In the gloomy yellowish light she angled this way and that, but still she couldn't be sure. Her face was an entirely different shape, round and fleshy like her mother's, no trace at all of cheekbones and her nose rather insignificant and lost.

She walked back to the museum, deep in thought. Was she seeing something that wasn't there? She must be, but even so she'd welcome a second opinion. She couldn't ask Eli now when he was clearly in so much pain, but perhaps another day she would.

He was not at his desk but she soon spotted him, cleaning the glass front of the cabinet containing the Torah scroll.

"Ah, Fran. Anything of interest?" His face was closer to its normal colour and when he walked towards her he was moving more easily.

"You look better."

"The drugs have kicked in. Some days they don't, but today I was lucky. Anything of interest in the pictures?"

"I don't know, really. There's a photo of a couple of boys ... you'll probably think I'm crazy, but one of them reminds me of my son at a similar age. I took a picture of it with my phone. I … I hope that was OK."

"You have a photo of your son with you?"

"Not when he was eight or nine, but there's one taken a few years ago in my purse. Of course he's a grown man now, but it's the nose I'd like you to compare."

"Well that won't have changed. Let me see them both."

Fran's fingers fumbled as she took the photo of Michael, Paula and the girls from her purse, then flicked through the album.

Eli took the picture between his fingers. "A handsome family. You must miss them."

"I do, I really do. But I'll be going home in a few weeks."

He pulled a magnifying glass from the desk drawer as she set the album down, open at the right page. "Well," he said, "let's compare noses."

Eli seemed to take forever to examine the pictures, while Fran tried to distract herself by looking at the cabinet containing the ceremonial objects. There was silence in the room, the footsteps in the street outside seemingly amplified by it, the clock tower tolling the hour in the distance.

Finally Eli said, "That is very interesting. Not so much the noses, although I can see a little of what you mean. But the other boy. I can actually identify him. He's in this picture, here."

He led Fran to a group of photographs on the wall near the desk. "They show the life of the synagogue earlier in the century, and this one is of a Bar Mitzvah. There he is, in the middle, surrounded by his male relatives outside the synagogue door."

The caption below it read 'Tefellin of Solomon Goldstajun, March 1928'.

"Wow. That's some coincidence," Fran said.

Eli looked at her, his head on one side. "And what you, Fran, need to decide is whether one coincidence makes another more or less likely."

Dubrovnik, April 2010

Fran had been very touched when Jadran invited her to spend Easter Sunday with his family. Last year Andrew's son Nick had been back from America and they'd had a family gathering at Daddy's house; everyone together, even Patti, who had at least stayed long enough to toy with her lunch and be reasonably nice. Fran was pretty damn certain that wouldn't happen again.

She had spent most of yesterday making *pinca*, the traditional sweet bread her mother had baked every year. Jadran had assured her that his sister-in-law, Gora, would be delighted, because she worked in a bank and didn't have time for home baking.

Pinca was particularly time-consuming too, as the dough had to be kneaded and left to rise three times. When Fran was small she had helped – or more likely hindered – her mother to pummel the sticky mixture, thick with raisins and candied peel, and as it had proved, her mother had told traditional Yugoslavian folk tales, then finally the Easter story of Christ rising from the dead.

When Andrew and Patti came along they'd helped too, and the kitchen had been filled with even more fun. As Fran kneaded in the narrow space of her apartment, she could almost hear them again, feel the warmth of the sunshine through the picture window that looked out on to the garden, filled with daffodils and tulips. It had gone, all gone. This year the house at Aldwick would be standing empty, cold and unloved, and a tremor of grief travelled through her, causing her to stop pounding the dough for a moment to gather herself. Maybe next year another family would be living there, making their own memories.

But the family she'd wanted at that moment had been her own. Last year her granddaughters had helped with the *pinca* in Daddy's kitchen, Claire slapping the dough down with delight as Belle got into a sticky mess, their laughter filling the house. And Fran had ached for them; to be with them, to hug them. Even their Easter Skype hadn't helped. In fact it had left her feeling decidedly shaky because it was becoming increasingly clear it was time to go home.

Now, later in the morning, the *pinca* was wrapped in a clean tea towel on Fran's lap as Jadran parked outside a white-painted, three storey apartment block on the hill behind the seaside town of Cavtat. Fran had become so used to old Dubrovnik she found its stark modernity almost shocking, with harsh black railings making the building look like a stranded cruise liner, softened only by the dusty purple bougainvillea trying to colonise one corner of the wall.

Jadran parked the car then squeezed her hand. "You are very quiet."

"I was thinking about my mother, actually, and the memories that came back while I was making the *pinca*."

"Good ones, I hope. But all the same, I know even good memories can hurt."

She leant across to kiss him. "I'm all right. But thank you for caring."

This was just the sort of moment that made Fran wonder if there was a way they could be together and for an instant she felt so torn it was all she could do not to curl up right there and weep. But that simply wasn't an option so instead she smiled and, on slightly trembling legs, got out of the car.

Vedran opened the door and took them through to an enormous lounge with a stunning view over the rooftops far below to the bluest of seas. In the distance across the bay the red tiles of Dubrovnik provided a muted glow, tucked between Mount Srđ and the green hump of Lokrum island. Directly in front of them was a small olive grove, the air filled with the murmuring chirp of cicadas.

Outside on the terrace Jadran's brother, Rajko, was laying the table but he came in to greet them. He was a little shorter than Vedran, but with the same ready smile and a busy sparkle about him as he pumped Fran's hand. A moment later his wife appeared from the kitchen, her glossy dark hair cut short into a soft, spiky style that suited her tiny snub nose. Her eyes were tired but the warmth in her embrace felt genuine.

"At last, we meet you," she said. "Vedran, he tell us so much. And Jadran too, but he say only a little."

"It's lovely to meet you as well," Fran told her. "Thank you for inviting me."

"Easter is a time for family. We did not want you to be alone."

Rajko poured the drinks while Jadran showed Fran the beautifully painted eggs that adorned a rough-hewn piece of olive wood in the centre of the glass coffee table.

"They are traditional," he said, "and made as gifts for family and friends. The designs are drawn with wax and then the eggs are boiled in water with red or white onion skins to make the colour. I do not know if Gora had little time or if it is her preference for a limited palette that makes them all purple."

Vedran laughed. "I think perhaps it was both. Purple matches the cushions and curtains, but all the same Mama was still finishing them as I came home from work last night."

"I hope I haven't put her to any extra trouble," Fran said. "Jadran told me she has a busy job."

Gora reappeared with a tray of olives and slices of cheese in oil. "It is no trouble, Fran. One extra mouth is nothing."

"All the same, is there something I can do to help?"

Gora smiled. "Only come to the kitchen with me so I am not alone. Bring your glass and a dish of olives so we can talk while I finish preparing the vegetables."

The kitchen was at the back of the apartment, away from the sunshine and views. The units gleamed white, as did the worktops, and it would have felt very clinical if not for the terracotta tiles on the floor and the row of red storage jars that ran beneath the cupboards on the far wall.

"This is beautiful," Fran said. "Have you just had it done?"

"We have lived two years here, from when the apartment was built. We move always to modern places; we are not like Jadran who does not move at all. He is so stuck in his ways, don't you think? His flat is too old."

Fran didn't quite know how to answer. "I haven't been there."

"I expect you are more comfortable in Vedran's bar. He tell me you have aperitif there – at the same time every day. Are you like Jadran? Always the same?" Gora laughed, although up to that point Fran had thought she sounded a little aggressive, but perhaps it was just the way she was translating her Croatian into English.

She shrugged. "It's convenient for us both."

"Do not think I criticise. He is a good man."

Fran nodded.

There was a short silence, then Gora asked if Fran had family in England. "Yes, my son, his wife and two granddaughters. And a brother I am fond of too."

"How old, your grandchildren?"

"Claire is eleven and Belle just eight. She's nine later this month and I think I will probably go home in time for her birthday. We had a video talk this morning and she invited me to her party. Not that supper in McDonald's is really my thing but I do miss the girls and I'm flattered she wants her old gran there."

"Will you come back?"

Fran shook her head. "There would be no point. I only have the apartment for a week afterwards."

"No, not after, another time."

Fran took a sip of her wine. Now the reason behind Gora's words was becoming clear and although she couldn't blame her for wanting to protect her brother-in-law, for some reason it made her feel a little rattled.

"I would like to think so, yes." Worried she sounded too defensive she ploughed on. "I have surprised myself and I feel quite at home here," she added.

"Because of Jadran?"

How should she answer? In part, yes, of course it was, but she didn't want to give Gora the wrong impression, didn't want her to think …

"Did I hear my name?" Jadran appeared at the kitchen door.

"Would that be unusual?" asked Gora.

"I don't suppose so." He shrugged and smiled. "Safranka, I love Gora like my own sister, but she is a naturally curious person. However she will not be offended if you choose not to answer her questions."

Gora tipped back her head and laughed. "Jadran Novak, can I not even gossip now?"

"There is nothing to gossip about."

"You cannot say that. You have not brought a woman here in twenty years."

"And perhaps I will not bring one for another twenty if you are going to be so nosey."

To Fran's great surprise he dropped a kiss onto her lips before retreating to the living room.

Gora gazed at Fran. "So this is good news for Jadran. Good and perhaps bad."

Fran wrapped her arms tightly around her chest then rapidly unfolded them again. "Jadran always knew I was here for a limited time and my home is in England."

"But you are a little Croatian too? You said you feel comfortable here."

Fran nodded. "I suppose so."

"I think you will need to be. You know Jadran does not travel? Since the war he leave Dubrovnik only when his work make him, or to visit Viviana in Šibenik."

Fran was surprised by the strength of the disappointment that flooded through her. Some of her fantasies had been about showing Jadran her little house in Chichester, the beach at

Aldwick that had played such a large part in her childhood, introducing him to Michael and Andrew.

A timer standing next to the sleek built-in oven began to ring.

"The lamb. It is ready," Gora said. "Please tell the men and sit at the table. Rajko will need to open more wine."

Fran and Jadran wandered onto the terrace, leaning on the rail to take in the incredible view. For once, she didn't know what to say to him.

"Gora means well," he told her.

Fran considered her reply. "She seems very nice, but it was a bit of an awkward conversation at times, probably because she is concerned about you, given I will be going home so soon."

He put his arm around her shoulder. "It is not for her to worry about. I always knew … we always knew, Safranka, but I will not let it spoil the weeks we have left. We cannot tell how we will feel about each other when we are apart, so there is no point worrying about it. Agreed?"

"Agreed." She turned to look at him, the flecks in his hazel eyes glowing with warmth. "I don't want to think about saying goodbye just yet either." Because now she was even more certain it would be goodbye.

"It will be hard. We have been spending so much time together."

"Do you regret it?" Something inside her was making her push him, something she didn't much like.

"Not at the moment, but who knows? But I certainly would not change it. Would you?" His smile had turned into something hard, although his voice remained even.

Or was she projecting her feelings on to him? *Fran, stop overthinking it.*

She wrapped her hand over his on the balcony rail. "I suppose, when you have suffered the worst of possible hurts, nothing can ever be as bad again."

"If you believe that, you must also believe that nothing can ever be as good. I lived like that for almost twenty years, Safranka. I do not want to go back there."

"I know I—"

He released her from his embrace and turned to face her, his voice low and urgent. "You cannot understand everything so please do not try. All I ask ... all I ask ... is that we enjoy these next few weeks together and let the future take care of itself."

Because he already knew there was no future for them? But really, what did that mean? It didn't change anything because it was something she had always known as well. And if she'd let her feelings for him get a little out of hand, whose fault was that?

Gora bustled in behind them, accompanied by the delicious aroma of roast lamb. "Come and sit down, it is time to eat."

Fran put on her best smile as she turned. "Thank you. It smells absolutely wonderful."

Chapter Thirty-One

Dubrovnik, 20th October 1944

D ragica is resting on the bed feeding Safranka when he returns. He stirs the thin stew on the stove as he waits for her to finish. The scent of onions, his wife singing a lullaby, his hopes and dreams tied up in this moment. But he needs to tell her what is happening, or she will be frightened when they take him.

If only he had ham to put in the pot, or even better, a fig to present to her afterwards. There is so much in this world he wants to give her, so much that is beyond him and his means.

As they eat, he holds her hand and tells her of all the wonderful things they will have on their table after the war; not only figs and ham, apricots and cherries but also the rich, flavoursome cheeses from Pag. How there will be sugar, flour and eggs so she can bake …

And she tells him what she will make for him, their fantasy wrapping them closer with every word. Rich, flaky strudels, bursting with fruit, *krofne*, and even spiced *medenjaci* when honey is plentiful again.

And they laugh, because they have made each other even more hungry, but inside he wants to cry because he knows he must shatter the moment.

He can never tell her about the watchers, the eyes on street corners, the feeling that something is far from right. Instead he speaks of the mayor's arrest, that others will follow, and why he will be one of them. She listens in silence, barely able to meet his eyes.

"They cannot do this to you," she whispers.

He would give worlds to reassure her, sell his soul. "They will, and it is right they will. But once I have cleared my name, I will be free. The partisans are honourable people, not like the Ustaše."

"You sound so sure."

He takes both her hands in his. "I am sure. Trust me."

He has never lied to her before.

Chapter Thirty-Two

Dubrovnik, April 2010

F ran bought her ticket at the Pile Gate and climbed the steps to the top of the wall. It was late in the afternoon, yet still the narrow space thronged with people. Had it been a mistake to come here now? She hadn't told Jadran her plans, further than she couldn't meet him for their usual aperitif, so they'd taken coffee in the little bay below Lovrijenac fortress that morning instead. Maybe she'd deliberately wanted to shake things up a little, given what Gora had said.

Initially she made slow progress along the wall behind a solid line of tourists, but eventually the crowd thinned out as some stopped to gaze, others to take photos. The sea was a deeper shade of azure than she had ever seen it, and a warm breeze rippled the multi-coloured flags outside the kayak hire shop below her. In recent weeks the city had yawned, stretched, and finally in the days before Easter, positively sprung to life. The small streets off Stradun had become all but impassable as tables appeared, the ancient stones themselves ringing with accents from all over the world.

It was little surprise there were no free seats at the café where Jadran had told her about Leila and Kristina, so Fran bought a bottle of water at the ice cream kiosk and continued her walk. A couple of cruise ships were moored off Lokrum, gleaming white in the sun. Vedran had told her that from now on the city would only become busier, and already the atmosphere had completely changed.

Fran found a place where the path broadened over one of the towers projecting into the sea, and perched on the inner parapet, unscrewing her bottle of water as she gazed along the line of the wall at the buildings and gardens tucked below. She had come up here alone to think so she'd just have to ignore the hustle and bustle around her and get on with it. She needed to set aside her inner turmoil too; separate the emotion and properly reason this out.

That was the frustrating part of it, not being able to grasp the thoughts that fluttered around her like moths in the small hours of the morning, both questions and answers shape-shifting and teasing her. She needed to pin something down. The practical, the feasible, the ultimate resolution of what the hell she was going to do with her life when she got back home. Because all of a sudden, going home was in only a few weeks' time.

The one thing she had slowly begun to realise was that it was her life, and nobody else's. It sounded so silly and a little bit obvious, but the way Parisa had cheered when she'd told her on their latest Skype call had helped Fran to recognise this had been at the heart of her problems. For years she had lived for other people; first for Michael, then for her parents. But now her parents were gone, and Michael, thankfully, didn't actually need her. He'd been far more successful in his marriage than she had been in hers.

And as it was her life, it was up to her to find the solution to what she should do with it. Not ask Parisa, although she obviously had a few ideas, nor Jadran either, who had put no pressure on her at all. She knew he would listen, nod, understand, and she knew if she talked to him it might just help her to untangle things. But it would also mean confessing that he was part of her problem and that she would never do.

She would have to face it herself though, but that was a step or two further down the line. She agreed whole-heartedly with his strategy of enjoying the next few weeks together, as there seemed no sense in spoiling their time with what ifs and worries. She may well need a will of steel to do it, but she would find the strength from somewhere. She'd coped with far worse in the last six months and the recognition of her own strength buoyed her.

Jadran had said they wouldn't know how they really felt until they were apart, and that was probably right. But quite what would happen then ... Clearly, if he didn't travel, he would expect her to come back here and that was something she didn't think she could do on any sort of permanent basis. But being practical, that would leave him free to find someone more suitable, and although the thought of it unsettled her, she knew she ought to be pleased she had helped this lovely man to move on. He didn't deserve to be lonely.

A voice inside told her that neither did she, but she set the thought gently to one side. She would deal with it later. Considering it now would only complicate matters. She was coming to realise that working out what *she* wanted from life had to be done through a lens of something close to selfishness. She had been brought up believing that being selfish was one of the very worst sins. But could it be useful as well?

Putting herself first felt completely alien, and yet she was learning to do it. In small ways, like telling Jadran she couldn't see him this afternoon, and in bigger ones too. Like finally realising she had to remove Patti from her life for her own happiness and sanity.

Patti's absolute rejection of her had actually helped a lot. Once she'd recovered from the shock, she had begun to understand it was better for them both, and more importantly, better for her. She did not need that poison. It was awful to think her sister hated her so much, but there was no way she could change it so she had to move on.

Perhaps all these years Andrew had had a point. This was not her fault. Yes, of course Patti's childhood accident had been the catalyst, but now she was able to see things more clearly Fran knew that her sister could have chosen a more positive way of dealing with it as an adult. Like Jadran had said, blame stopped you from moving forwards. Things would never improve for Patti if she couldn't let it go, but the decision whether or not to do so would have to be hers and hers alone.

Here there was a parallel. Fran's life needed to change as well, and of course that was also up to her. She was where she was because she had put herself here too. Looking back, there wasn't even a great deal she would alter, but the question was, what did she want now? She took a sip of her water and gazed down into the garden below; at the pink buds of the oleander, and the orange tree covered in tiny white blossom, its scent rising to mingle with the salty freshness of the breeze, at the child's bicycle abandoned next to the kitchen door, the sunlight flashing against the upstairs windows ... It was just so beautiful, but she couldn't allow herself to be distracted.

She finally understood that Patti's accident had changed her life as well. It had planted the seeds of guilt and blame inside her, the feeling she had to make up for what she had done. Her selfishness in picking up her book again on that fateful night had taught her well and truly that it was easier and far less painful to do as she was told. It had been drummed into her enough, from when she was tiny, that she had to be good to deserve Daddy, and she supposed her selfless nature had come from that as well.

But it seemed quite a big leap of logic to go from putting others first to her deep-seated desire to be needed. Why did she crave it so much? That she really couldn't work out and it was scary because the problem of nobody actually needing her might never go away. It wasn't under her control at all.

Yes, she could try to fill the void with volunteering at the school or the children's centre, and that would be a satisfying – not to mention time-consuming – thing to do. But if she didn't do it, then someone else would. They didn't need *her*, per se, as Daddy had done, and Mama before him. Anyone with time on their hands and the necessary skills would do.

But Daddy and Mama could have had paid carers ... no, it wouldn't have been the same, because there wouldn't have been the love. The love that had flowed both ways and made it all bearable. The love that only family could give, and that she had given freely. She wouldn't change that for the world, so why, oh why, did it matter?

Oh, she was back where she started. She had to stop wanting to be needed, but who was she without it? She would never forget the urge to comfort and protect Jadran on the beach at Lopud and the way it had made her feel about him, but even without the practicalities that stood in their way it was just no good him replacing her parents as someone to be cared for. Not on any level at all.

Having realised this danger she'd been careful not to let herself fall into the trap, and as a result theirs seemed a very equal relationship. Of course they did things for each other, like she baked and he drove, but they spent time together because they *wanted* to. And she was perfectly happy with it. In fact, when she really thought about it, she was happy, full stop; whether it was spending time with Jadran, or shopping in the market, dropping into the museum to chat to Eli or just pottering around the apartment, reading or baking ... Could that be a lesson she carried back home?

She was also coming to accept, in theory at least, that in the same way she had opened the door to Jadran having other relationships in the future, he had probably done the same for her. Although she didn't want to think about the emotional fallout from saying goodbye right now – and the thought of being part of a couple was frankly terrifying in any manner of other ways – it was a possibility, if that was what she wanted. An avenue opened that she had believed to be closed forever. Were there any other sacred cows she could rid herself of while she was at it?

Like her father being a hero, perhaps. The jury was definitely out on that one. He was certainly implicated in the internment of the Jews, but there was still this tantalising story of the Ustaše who helped them to escape. That would make him a hero in anyone's eyes and there was a part of her that ached to be able to believe it.

Fran stood and stretched, gazing across the roofscape,

inland towards Mount Srđ, the dark band of trees on its slopes reaching down to wrap the city in its close embrace with the sea. Had Mama looked out towards the mountain? Or had her life been focused inwards on the city? She hugged her arms around her chest. How she wished she had asked her about her life in Dubrovnik while she could.

No, she mustn't let herself well up; she needed to keep a clear head. Even though the loss of her mother was once again a vicious open wound. Her discovery of her father had raised so many questions it was impossible to answer; nothing to do with what he had done – that really didn't matter, it was too far in the past, too remote from anything to do with her future … Except she was finding it hard to make sense of so many of the beliefs she'd held close all her life, without understanding her mother.

The breeze from the sea felt chilly on Fran's shoulders as the sun disappeared behind a cloud. It was time she was going back. Or going on. She bent to rub the stiffness from her legs then looked from side to side. No, she wouldn't return the way she had come; she would head on towards Lokrum, then past Sveti Ivana fort and the harbour to the Ploče Gate. She might even buy herself an ice cream at Peppino's if the queue wasn't too long. *Onwards, ever onwards.* It was the sort of thing Daddy would have said, and she had the feeling that right now he'd be quietly proud of her.

∾

Fran looked at herself in the mirror. Jadran had said he was taking her somewhere special for lunch and she might want to dress accordingly, so she had finally plucked up the courage to wear the only smart dress she had grudgingly agreed with Parisa she should buy. Back then it had seemed a pointless luxury, now she was really glad she had it.

She was also wearing her new underwear. Not that anyone else would see it, but she knew it was there, and the bra in particular made her boobs seem to sag a little less under the broad blue and white stripes of the tailored dress. She just had to hope there wasn't any flesh bulging out at the back like a couple of hamsters, but she hadn't been so stupid as to buy anything tight-fitting, so she'd probably get away with it.

She twisted and turned, trying to get a better view. She had meant to use her time in Dubrovnik to lose a little weight, which clearly hadn't happened, yet on the upside she hadn't gained any either. And the gentle sunshine had given her skin an extra glow, although it was still next to impossible to tame her hair, especially after spending yesterday afternoon on Jadran's boat.

Fran heard the creak of the gate and his footsteps on the terrace before he knocked on the kitchen door. She crossed the room to meet him, and he held her at arms' length for a moment before kissing her on the cheek.

"Safranka, I do like that dress. It's very smart." He himself was wearing navy chinos and a linen jacket, so she knew she had pitched it right.

"Thank you. They say stripes are flattering for the … um … fuller figure."

"Well, as I said, they look very good on you too." He winked, something Fran would never have imagined him doing when they first met. She wasn't quite sure whether it suited him, but if it meant he was happy, she wasn't complaining.

As they walked down the street towards Stradun she asked where they were going.

"To the Hotel Imperial. Is that all right?"

"It's wonderful. It's ... it's not your birthday or anything and you haven't told me?"

"No, that is in July. But I do have a special reason for taking you."

"What's that?"

"I'll tell you when we get there."

Fran's excitement was tinged with trepidation. More than tinged, if she was honest. The Imperial was an incredibly smart hotel and was as old as Dubrovnik's tourist industry. She was sure she had read in a guidebook that Edward VIII and Wallis Simpson had visited, along with most of the princes, dukes and counts from the rest of Europe. It wasn't somewhere she'd ever dreamed she'd go herself, let alone for a special reason. What on earth was Jadran up to?

She already knew the outside of the hotel was impressive, but as they climbed the gleaming white stone staircase that bordered its restaurant terrace and gardens, Fran gazed up at the pink and cream frontage in awe. The shutters on the bedrooms were painted a deep green, and gilded rosettes decorated the balconies. But in her smart new dress, and with Jadran's cool hand in hers, she actually believed they would let her through the shining swing doors ahead.

Once inside their footsteps echoed across the sand-coloured tiles in the lobby. Light reflected from the polished wooden panels that framed a stylish seating area around the concierge desk, and she couldn't wait to see what glories lay at the top of the short staircase. She wasn't disappointed. The elegantly arched windows of the corridor they found themselves in looked through a bar furnished with sumptuous sofas, towards stunning views of the leafy, manicured garden and, in the distance, the sea.

They followed some marble steps down to another floor, where Jadran stopped outside the entrance to the restaurant. "I think, Safranka, this hotel is where your mother worked."

Fran felt her mouth fall open like a goldfish so she snapped it shut again before he could notice. "Really? How do you know?"

"I don't, but the circumstantial evidence is strong. I've discovered this was where the British officers were billeted in late 1944, so as you told me one of them arranged for you both to travel to England, then it is probable this is where she met him."

Fran gazed around her. "Somewhere this smart? But then, I suppose she was only a maid of some sort."

"All the same, there would have been opportunities for contact. We will never know how the conversation came about, but this is by far the most likely place."

Jadran turned as a woman in a navy suit spoke to them in Croatian. He replied, and they were led across the light and airy room to a table next to a brass-arched window looking over an outdoor seating area studded with pot plants.

"I thought it best to lunch inside," said Jadran, "as the weather forecast is not so good. But if you would prefer the terrace ..."

"No. This is fine. Perfect in fact."

"A glass of champagne to begin?"

"Jadran, I ..."

"You don't like it?"

"Yes, but it will be so expensive."

"Well I am not suggesting we make it a habit, but once will not hurt."

Fran grinned at him. "Once would be very nice."

A waiter brought their drinks and some leather-bound menus, and after they toasted each other, and once Fran had got used to the tiny bubbles fizzing through her nose, she asked Jadran how he had thought to look into the hotel's history.

"It was puzzling me how she left. It could not have been easy to do so at the time, and when you said she worked in a hotel I began to wonder. This place was in use throughout the war; first by Italian officers, then by Germans, and finally the British."

"So she would have worked for the Nazis too?"

"Don't start jumping to conclusions. She would have had no choice. Money was money, and perhaps here she even had access to food. Life would have been incredibly hard for ordinary people at the time."

Fran fiddled with the top of the pepper mill on the table in front of her. "I wonder … could it have been hardship that led my father to collaborate?"

"It's possible. But we shall never know."

"No, we won't. And Jadran, I am comfortable with that. It's taken me a while, but now his story is less important to me. We only have the vaguest idea of what he did, and why he did it is even further away." Suddenly she was conscious of sounding ungrateful. "But this, discovering more about my mother, this is so very precious."

"I am glad." He put his hand on top of hers. "Does her part in this still trouble you?"

"Yes, but I need to work it out for myself." She gave his

hand a little squeeze. "It's not that I'm shutting you out, I would never do that, it's just I've realised I need to do it on my own." She sighed. "It's like climbing a slippery rope. Sometimes I feel I'm getting somewhere and then I slide back down. But I'll make it to the top somehow."

He twisted her hand over and intertwined his fingers with hers. "I'm happy to do whatever you want, even if it is nothing at all."

"I want …" Could she say it? Could she actually put into words what she needed from him right now? Did she even know? "I want … to enjoy a lunch with one of the loveliest men I have ever met."

There was a shyness in his smile as he looked down at their hands, his deeply tanned with his squarely cut nails and sprinkling of dark hairs, hers a little podgy and pink.

"You make me happy, Safranka, you know that."

"And you make me happy too." This wasn't a conversation she felt remotely ready for, even though she had started it. She laughed, but even to herself it sounded a little false. "But right now I am hungry as well. What shall we eat?"

Although the weather had turned a little blustery, after lunch they walked down to the bay below Lovrijenac fortress. As they strolled onto the stone jetty, the low rocks in the water on either side were awash with seaweed rippling in the swell, and the flags next to the kayak hire stand cracked in the breeze. Jadran tucked Fran cosily under his arm as he pointed them out.

A long-ago memory stirred, but then she realised it came

from watching her parents, not from anything she had ever experienced herself. Was this what it was like to be a couple? Together, warm, and right, completely in tune with each other? Like Mama and Daddy had been. But were she and Jadran? She probably felt like this because they'd both drunk just a little too much wine, yet the way he kissed her ear as they stood there, watching the spray cascade over the rocks at the mouth of the bay, moved her physically in a way she had never thought she would know again.

She wanted him so completely she was sure he would feel the catch in her throat, her heart beat faster. For a moment he was all she wanted, and to hell with the consequences, but she somehow managed to haul on the last threads of her common sense before she lost them completely. She wasn't a carefree girl in her early twenties, she was a woman of sixty-five, with more hang ups than she cared to think about right now, although under the circumstances perhaps she should.

Even so, ensconced in the warmth of his body with his breath tickling the side of her face, she closed her eyes and played the scenario forwards. If she turned to kiss him, slipped her hands under his jacket as she so wanted to do, it could only lead to one thing. They'd go back to her apartment, sit on the sofa, kiss some more, and then he'd unbutton her dress, and she, his shirt. And he would ask her if it was all right, and she would say yes because she had let things go that far and she wouldn't want to disappoint him …

No. Wait. What she was saying to herself was that she would go with what he wanted when it wasn't right for her. She had come so far, she couldn't let that happen. Yes, perhaps she wanted him, but not now, not like this. Neither of them were young anymore, and even if she could pluck up the courage, making love would be a significant act of commitment. A commitment she just couldn't make.

She turned in his arms, but instead of reciprocating his embrace she took a small step away. "I like how you're making me feel. Very much. But I think if I responded it might lead to more. More than I'm ready for at the moment, anyway."

He looked at her gravely. "I understand, Safranka. We have already promised we will not become lovers, but you are an attractive woman and I let myself get a little carried away. Perhaps it is partly the wine making me forget myself. To take that step, and then for you to go away ... it would not feel right."

Then she did hug him, burying her face in his jacket and squeezing so hard for so long she was sure his button would leave an imprint on her cheek.

"You are so damned perfect," she whispered.

She felt, rather than heard, him laugh. "I am very far from it. Nobody is. But what is perfect, or at least very important, is that we both see things the same way. Safranka, I may not have known it, but I have waited almost twenty years for a woman like you; a woman who is honest, and kind, and does not hide her beautiful face behind layers of make-up. So I do not mind waiting longer. In fact, I think I need to wait longer as well. There is much to consider ... or perhaps there is nothing between us at all, but we will not truly know until you return to England. Then, the space where we have been for each other will open up, and we will be able to see what is there. We just have to hope it will be the same for us both."

When she looked up there was sorrow in his eyes, and it ripped at her heart in a way she couldn't bear. How easy would it be just to say … But no, she had to stay strong, make herself her priority.

"Come on," she told him, grasping his hand, "we probably shouldn't drink anything else, but let's at least go back to the café for a coffee, then we can tell Vedran about our wonderful lunch."

Chapter Thirty-Three

Dubrovnik, 21st October 1944

The next afternoon they come for them; nine in all from the mayor's office. A detachment of troops appears in the doorway and a swarthy man with an accent from the north barks their names: Barbir, Dobud, Krečak, Kubes, Milišić … It is almost as though someone has given them a list. One by one they stand and walk towards the soldiers, Krečak's noisy protests silenced by a rifle butt.

On the stairs his leg gives way and he falls.

A boot in his back. A hiss in his ear. "Don't try anything funny, fascist shit."

He scrambles to his knees and the boot knocks him back. "Get up, you bastard."

Fear grips him like a fist and he clenches his guts to prevent its escape. Now he knows the hatred the Jews must have felt. Now he can see where all this might end.

The people in the square stop to look. A few of them jeer,

but mainly there is silence. Different eyes watching his shame. He hangs his head. Even if he survives this, how can he stay? He cannot stand by and watch Dragica abused as well.

Past Sveti Vlaho, towards the cathedral, then under the arch to the harbour, his eyes fixed on the flagstones beneath his feet. One after the other, the tramping of boots, the shuffling of shoes, the fresh sea air stinging their faces.

As they near the boats he hears Vido's voice. Despite himself he glances up, his friend's expression filled with anguish and indignation. He moves to speak to the guard closest to Branko, anger burning in his eyes.

Branko stops. Turns. Spits. Spits at his dearest friend. "Must you torment me, even now?"

The walls of Svetog Ivana fort have never seemed so high, the doorway so dark. He cannot think of them, of Safranka and Dragica. As the shadows of the castle's entrance engulf him, he knows he must turn his back on them as he has done on Vido. His sanity and their survival may depend on it.

Chapter Thirty-Four

Dubrovnik, April 2010

Fran slipped out early to the market, intent on finding something delicious to cook Jadran for dinner to thank him for yesterday's lunch at the Imperial. She had emailed Michael the photographs, including one a waiter had taken of her and Jadran together, and told him that most likely his grandmother had worked there. She'd been in part amused and in part horrified when he'd replied that Paula thought her date was dishy, and why hadn't she told them she had a man in her life?

Clearly the world had different expectations of herself than she did, but it was comforting to know her family didn't consider her past it in any way. She had wondered what Michael might think if she found herself a partner, but she was pretty sure his main concern would be to reassure himself she'd chosen wisely.

Even so, over breakfast she'd been about to email him back

explaining she and Jadran were just good friends, but she stopped herself in time. It wasn't true. They were more than that. Maybe even significantly more. Or at least, perhaps they could be. One day. Perhaps. God, was she talking herself in or out of this?

It wasn't just because they lived fourteen hundred miles apart (she knew because she'd looked it up): even if by some miracle she'd found him in the next street, she still wouldn't be ready for a relationship. And it was nothing to do with being worried about the sexual side of things, although of course she was, this was to do with something much closer to home.

When she'd been sitting on the city wall trying to figure things out, she had kept coming back to the suspicion that her feelings for Jadran were simply because she needed someone to care for in place of Daddy. And she knew that wasn't what he wanted from her. It wasn't what she wanted for herself, come to that, but she couldn't rid herself of the thought that however well it had started, that was how it might end up. Her newfound sense of self felt just too fragile to risk, although how she could make it stronger, she did not know.

To fall straight into a relationship would mean she wouldn't have the chance to explore being her own person fully, give herself a proper chance of making it work. If she didn't, she had a shrewd idea what would happen and it bothered her; she would start needing Jadran to need her, she'd begin living just to please him, and that wouldn't be healthy for either of them.

It was a strange thought that in order to be with someone else, first you had to learn how to live for yourself. For many people it probably wouldn't be an issue, but for her it was. She had only just started to find her wings and they were pathetic stubby things with very few feathers. They needed to grow, along with her confidence, so she could begin to find out how far she could fly.

As she walked down Stradun towards the elegant finger of the clock tower rising to meet the chalky-blue sky, she felt a little shaky. Was she on the verge of a breakthrough? Could she finally work this out? She paused at the bottom of Sveti Vlaho's steps, its facade bathed in morning sunlight bringing the cherubs into sharp relief and gleaming from the golden mitre adorning the saint's head.

Morning Mass was over, and a trickle of people were leaving. Fran climbed the steps to find herself inside a pillared church with a high vaulted ceiling, completely dominated by a gilded organ, so high above the marble altar it extended into the domed roof.

Blocks of coloured light filtered through the modern stained-glass windows above the side doors, illuminating the white-painted columns and walls. Fran sat at the far end of the back pew, the faintest tang of incense swirling around her as she closed her eyes. What on earth had possessed her to come in here? Yet in doing so she felt calm and able to think.

All her life she'd been taught to be selfless; to put other people first because it was the right thing to do, to be grateful for the chances she'd been given, and to behave in such a way that made sure she deserved them. Could her mother have been frightened that Daddy would somehow be snatched away, in the same way her first husband had been? She'd lost almost everything in Dubrovnik; she wouldn't have been able to bear the thought of going through that again.

Mama had found love, not only for herself, but for her child. Another man's child. Perhaps a bad man's child. A child who maybe deserved love even less because of her father. A child who had to be good. Was that it? Maybe … maybe it was part of it, or perhaps she was completely wrong. Once again, the mother she'd thought she knew so well was eluding her, and the pain of loss was almost as sharp as it had been seven long years before. She'd believed she was finally beginning to get over it and now it was hitting her square on the forehead again and again and again.

She dug her nails into her palms, but still tears prickled behind her eyes. How bloody useless was she? *She's gone, Fran. You'll never be able to ask her what you need to know so deal with it. Bloody deal with it.* Closing her eyes she took one deep shuddering breath after another, trying to push the searing pain away while all the time praying that no one would notice.

Eventually she felt calm enough to stand and, on trembling legs, made her way to a side altar near the main door. In front of her, candles blazed beneath a plaster figure of a bearded saint clutching some sort of shepherd's crook and a model of the city; a saint she now recognised as Sveti Vlaho himself. She felt in her pocket for a ten kuna note and poked it into the wooden box before choosing a tall, slender candle, lighting it from another and sticking it into the sand. She had never done this before, but it somehow felt comforting, almost like Mama was at her side, promising her that one day she would understand.

Out in the open air again she berated herself for believing that a candle could change anything but nevertheless there was a calm, clear space inside her brain. Maybe she was finally accepting there were things she would never know about her parents, aspects of their lives that would always be shrouded in mystery. The father she couldn't even remember, and the mother perhaps she hadn't known as well as she'd thought. Maybe she didn't really know herself either.

But that was no longer true. She was beginning to learn who she was, and more importantly, who she could be. Here in these ancient streets some of the courage imbued in its walls by the hardships its people had faced was seeping into her bones. And she was learning how to use it to let go of the past and start to build a future.

Walking down the shaded side of the church towards the market she rolled the word selfless around in her brain. In Mama's world, selfless was good, and selfish was bad, yet selfish was probably what she needed to be to take the final steps.

Was there another word? One that better described her intentions? Something positive? Self-centred was no better, although it felt more accurate for the state of mind she was trying to achieve. To put herself at the centre of things, at least for a while. At least until she worked out what it was she really wanted. After that, perhaps she would be able to find a happy medium.

Slowly the strands were beginning to come together, twisting one over the other in a way that reminded her of her mother plaiting her hair when she was small. She had both loved and hated the morning ritual, because, although the sharpness of the twists and turns had tugged at her scalp, it had been a time for her and Mama alone. A special time, which would always end with a hug and a kiss on the nose.

Oh, Mama, Mama. The backs of Fran's eyes were red-hot again. This really was turning out to be a godawful day. Perhaps their visit to the Imperial had opened a forgotten wound? Jadran's words about the harshness of life in those days came back to her. She had never really considered it before. Perhaps collaboration with the hated occupiers had been the only way to eat, to live. Her mother had gone on to find peace and plenty in England. Her father had paid the ultimate price.

Even here, in the city where her parents had lived and loved, the past remained tantalisingly out of reach. No more than stories, shadows, scraps of information that made little sense. It was hardly surprising the future felt so uncertain when the past was shapeshifting just beyond her grasp.

Fran stopped and wiped her eyes. *Enough.* If she went on like this her head really would begin to spin. Besides, she had promised to cook a special meal for Jadran tonight and already some of the best produce on the market would have gone. She needed to stop this navel-gazing and apply herself to the task in hand.

On the first stall there were eggs and what was probably the last of the wild asparagus, so perhaps a *fritaja* to start. Fran had come to know the vendor, so asked after her pregnant daughter, and was given a small bunch of rosemary when she told her what she was cooking. Already something close to peace was settling back into a corner of her heart.

By the time Fran had finished shopping the old town was becoming crowded with tourists, cruise ship passengers in unwieldy groups following guides waving different coloured flags. She cut down the backstreets, dodging the tables that had appeared outside restaurants and bars, then, crossing Stradun next to the minimarket, she found herself almost crushed against the wall by a large sweaty man in a striped shirt who was trying to take a photograph.

Vedran was outside the café and Fran couldn't resist slipping into the cool interior, and having dumped her shopping bag under the table closest to the bar, she sat down. Outside, the place was buzzing but here there was still a sense of calm. Two men she knew by sight were playing cards in the opposite corner and they greeted her. Once she had responded she rested back against the banquette and closed her eyes.

Vedran touched her shoulder, making her jump. "Are you all right, Fran?"

"Yes. Sorry. Just nearly got mowed down in the tourist crush and I could do with a coffee to revive me."

He laughed. "Imagine what it's like in the summer."

"I'm not sure I can. Already it's completely different to a few weeks ago. I'm so glad I came in winter."

"I'm glad you came, full stop."

He disappeared behind the counter and Fran could hear him busying himself with the cups, the hiss of steam rising from the machine, rich with the bitterness of the coffee. She would miss this, she knew she would. She was going to miss lots of things, yet slowly but surely her thoughts were turning to home.

Her cappuccino landed in front of her. "I hear you're cooking for *Tetak* tonight?"

"Yes. It won't be anywhere near the standard of the Imperial I'm afraid." She laughed.

"He won't mind. As long as he's with you, he's happy."

Fran watched as Vedran took the tray of drinks and pastries he was carrying outside. It had sounded like a glib comment, but even so it was true. It would hurt Jadran when she went back to England, yet back she would have to go. Wanted to go. Already it had been far too long since she'd seen Michael, Paula and the girls, not to mention Parisa. And Andrew had put some money in her bank account yesterday because probate had been granted. She couldn't leave him to sort out their parents' house alone.

And anyway, she didn't want to. Not just because she was good old Fran who helped everyone with everything, but because she enjoyed her brother's company. They'd have a laugh, and maybe even a little cry. And somewhere amongst the years and years of half-forgotten possessions, she might even find some answers about her mother.

Of course she would miss Jadran, but something he'd said as they stood on the jetty came back to her; something about only really finding out how much they wanted to be together once they were apart. It hadn't made much sense at the time, in fact it had seemed seriously cockeyed, but now perhaps she was beginning to understand what he meant.

Fran picked up her spoon and stirred the foam into her coffee. Yes, she did know what she wanted to do. What *she* wanted. God, Parisa would be proud of her. She'd email her as soon as she got home, to tell her her plans.

Fran definitely had mixed feelings about the evening ahead. Much as she was looking forward to seeing Jadran, what she had to tell him was going to be hard. In the middle of the afternoon, while she had been making his favourite *madarica* cake for dessert, she had actually found herself shaking, and she'd had to stop building the delicate layers and sit down for a bit. How was he going to react to what she had to say?

But she'd emailed the travel agent to fix the date of her ticket home and now it couldn't be undone. The flight details were sitting in her inbox like some sort of unexploded bomb, and she herself was veering wildly between excitement and gloom. But it was what she wanted, she knew that. How had Parisa replied? 'You can't please everyone, Fran, so I'm glad you're pleasing yourself.'

It still felt completely alien, knowing she was about to hurt someone she was fond of, and moreover was fond of her. But she could not simply stay in Dubrovnik; never mind the practicalities, just now it wouldn't be right. All the same it still felt deeply uncomfortable doing what she actually wanted, rather than bowing to someone else's needs and expectations.

Did Jadran expect anything? Not as far as he'd made her aware. In fact, one thing he did expect was that she would go home. All right, maybe not as soon as Sunday, but he knew it was going to happen sometime before the end of the month. Even so, telling him was not going to be easy and, as she changed into a fresh top and sprayed on a little perfume, she honestly didn't know where she'd find the courage.

He knocked on the door at about seven o'clock, when it was still warm enough for them to sit outside on the sheltered terrace. The scent of jasmine wafted from the plant growing over the door of the next house, mingling with the citronella candle Fran had lit to keep the bugs at bay.

Jadran opened the wine he had brought and sat down opposite her.

"Olives and cheese in oil. Safranka, you are becoming a proper Croatian."

"At least in the kitchen." She laughed. "But perhaps in other ways too. I don't know. I certainly feel a different person to when I arrived."

"How is that?"

"It's very hard to pinpoint. In England I had a very sheltered life, and that made it difficult to appreciate the hardships people have gone through here. But now I do understand it better, and I hope just a little of the courage and fortitude have rubbed off on me. I certainly feel braver. More able to cope. But perhaps that's also because my grief for my step-father is fading."

Jadran smiled. "I am glad. But I think it is still quite soon."

"Yes, but for him the time was right; he was old and he wanted to go, and that makes it so much easier. He had no regrets, so neither should I."

"And your mother?"

"I think ... I think... Well, to be honest, at times it's even more acute. I actually found myself in Sveti Vlaho this morning lighting a candle and I've never done that in my life before."

"And did it help?"

Fran shrugged. "I don't really know." Oh lord, she was sounding so ... so bloody nonchalant, when inside her emotions were churning even more than her stomach. She needed to go for it, get it out of the way. "But I have come to a decision, Jadran, and I need to tell you. I've booked my ticket home for Sunday."

It was hard to read his expression in the dusk.

After a moment he said, "Would you like me to take you to the airport?"

"Can I have a think? Wherever we say it, goodbye is not going to be easy."

"So you are also telling me it is goodbye?" The tautness she had almost forgotten returned to his voice.

"No. Not goodbye like that. Goodbye like … well, I'm not really sure. I've been thinking about what you said, about not knowing how we feel about each other until we are apart. It's hard to explain. I came here to sort a lot of things out in my mind. I've done OK, I've made some genuine progress, but now I need to go home to finish the job." She picked up her glass then put it down again. "I'd struggle to tell you exactly why, but it's what I need to do."

Jadran sat forwards and clasped her hand. "And I suppose if you go home sooner … I will miss you, Safranka, but all the same, we will begin to know … to know…" He studied the olive pits in the bowl as though he had never seen them before, then took a deep breath. "To know if we have any future at all."

"Yes."

He'd said it. A future. His words made her heart beat faster, and yet …

They sat in silence for a while, holding hands. Was she beginning to love him? This really wasn't the moment to be asking herself that question, especially as it was probably true. But even if he felt the same, and distance did not make those feelings fade, how could they ever make it work? It seemed impossible, and yet a part of her knew she was leaving behind something so precious she might never be able to replace it. Oh god, she couldn't start thinking that now, she couldn't. She wanted to go home, see Michael and the girls, enjoy being with them, not feel so impossibly torn.

She was glad of the darkness so he wouldn't see she was blinking back tears. *Say something, you stupid old mare.*

"Well, if nothing else, over the next few days I will need to make a lot of cake."

He gripped her hand tighter. "No, Safranka, it's memories we need to be making before you go."

Chapter Thirty-Five

Dubrovnik, 23rd October 1944

When they come for him, he does not know if it is day or night. Six of them crammed into a stinking cell without a window, the autumnal dampness seeping through its walls. He is the fourth to be questioned. The second, a journalist to whom he once delivered a message, was dragged back bloodied and broken, slipping in and out of consciousness even now.

It is important he tells the truth. Nothing more and nothing less. Only by doing so does he have any hope of being released. And hope is a scarce commodity. Scarcer even than sleep, than freedom from hunger, thirst and pain.

With a guard in front of him and a guard behind, he limps as fast as he can, up stairs and along endless corridors, weaker with every step. In a room with closed shutters a bearded man sits behind a table, his cap next to a notebook in front of him. There is no other chair. Already his leg is burning but he must not let it distract him. Answer the questions. Tell the truth.

"Branko Milišić, clerk in the city offices." It is a statement of fact.

"Yes, sir."

"You collaborated with the fascists." Another statement.

He shakes his head. "I understand it appears that way, but it is not the truth."

The man leans back, the chair creaking as he does so. "We have witnesses who say you are a member of the Ustaše, others who say you delivered messages."

"For a short while in 1943 I wore the uniform, but not through any personal belief."

"That is what everyone is saying now."

"If you will permit me, I will tell you my story. Then you can decide."

The silence lies heavy in the room. His liberty depends on the man's answer, but he senses it would be wrong to plead. As he waits, he looks at the floor, wooden boards worn smooth by generations of feet, the long sweep of grain an improbable link between the partisan's booted feet and his own.

"All right."

He exhales, then fills his lungs with air. He must speak slowly, clearly, make sure he is understood. "I grew up in the Jewish quarter and have many Jewish friends. When rumours came of internment one of them, Solomon Goldstajun, asked me to help his wife and child. He was leaving to become one of your soldiers. I could not join him because of my crippled leg.

"I was not quick enough to hide his family and in November 1942, they were sent to Lopud. A few weeks later the mayor asked for a volunteer to work as a clerk there and I thought if I was close to them, I might be able to do something. I did not know it meant wearing the Ustaše uniform, but it would have made no difference if I had. I had promised my friend."

"So you put your loyalty to your friend above your loyalty to your country?" The man's voice is even-toned, flat. How will he judge his answer?

"I did not see it that way. If I could help one Jewish family to escape, then perhaps I could help more."

"And did you?"

"Yes."

"Can you prove it?"

"Only by finding the people who got away."

The man flicks his pencil. "How did you do it?"

"Most of the soldiers were Italian. They liked to gamble and drink. They would give me extra food to take their duties and I would be able to unlock the door of the hotel where the Jews were imprisoned so they could escape."

"Lopud is a small island. Even if you let them out as you say, where did they go?"

"There was a boat to take them away."

"Whose boat?"

No, he will not give them Vido's name. His mistrust already runs too deep and he needs Vido to be there for Dragica and Safranka, needs him more than ever now. "I did not see the boat. I think different people, but I do not know."

"Then how was it arranged?"

Silence. The words will not form in his head. His leg throbs and burns. Time. He needs time. "I was able to hide the disappearances. It was my job to keep a tally of the prisoners. More arrived every week. Nobody knew how many left."

"That was not my question."

Say something. Something plausible at least. "A sympathiser ... perhaps a partisan like you ... he found the boatmen."

"And how did he know he could trust you? Could trust a Ustaše?"

Think, Branko, think. "The Jews were allowed to work in the fields. He approached them ... one of their elders ... all I was told was when to unlock the door. The Jews ... they trusted me because they knew me. The ones who had grown up in Dubrovnik at least."

The man looks at him, arms folded across his chest. There is an eternity of silence before he says. "Give him some water and take him back to his cell. I need to consider his story."

Chapter Thirty-Six

Sussex, April 2010

Fran flipped her laptop open and stretched her legs under the kitchen table before rubbing her big toe along the oval knot in the wooden floor. Home. It was the little things, really, that made it. Comforting everyday things you barely noticed, like having a decent cup of tea. It was the little things she had to cling to now.

It was funny, some things you expected to miss, and others you didn't notice how much you had missed them until you came back. She wrinkled her nose. No, that wasn't right. She knew how much she'd missed her granddaughters, she'd just kind of been able to hold herself apart from the pain – probably as self-preservation, but it did perhaps indicate how resilient she'd become. She bloody hoped so, anyway.

She would never forget the moment she'd pushed her trolley into arrivals at Gatwick; the crush of people waiting at the barrier, the colour, light and laughter after the muted crump and thud of the baggage hall. She'd been scanning the crowd for Michael when Belle had slipped under the barrier and in a single glorious muddle of blurred fleece and squeaking trainers had wrapped herself around her grandmother's waist.

Fran had cried then, silly old biddy that she was, her face buried deep in her granddaughter's tousled hair, tears of pure joy cascading down her cheeks. The torrent of emotion she'd felt in that moment had swept everything else away, leaving her shaken and stunned, but all the same acutely grateful for the wonderful family she loved so much. How could she ever leave them again?

While Belle clung on to her hand all the way to the car, Claire had hung slightly behind, unable to meet her gaze. When she'd left, her older granddaughter had seemed such a child, but now she was almost a teenager, with a smart new haircut and cheekbones emerging from her once puppy-plump face. And it had happened in just a couple of months. Even when she eventually thawed out and gave her gran a hug, Fran feared it would take a while for them to get to know each other again.

Had she really become so detached from her granddaughter in such a short space of time? The thought had threatened to overwhelm her during the drive to Michael's house in Chiswick, and she'd struggled to concentrate on what everyone was saying. It was only as they ate their Sunday roast that everything began to feel normal again. She hadn't really become detached, just a little disjointed. The chatter and laughter around the table had been gloriously familiar, uniquely theirs, but if Claire had changed just a little in the time she'd been away, Fran knew that she herself had changed a lot.

Michael had sensed it too. As they cleared the mess in the kitchen while Paula made sure Belle was in bed and Claire was at least moving in that direction, he gave her a hug and said,

"You're positively glowing, Mum. I honestly think you look five years younger."

"I don't know about that, but I needed the break."

"I know you did. I was really worried about you after Grandad's funeral, but now you seem so sorted. It's ace."

Fran had smiled and nodded. She hadn't had the heart to tell him how wobbly she still felt about the future, so instead they had fallen to discussing what she'd found out about her father.

Of course, she'd kept him in touch with each and every development, his interest and enthusiasm spurring her on, but somehow it felt as though they had reached the end of the road with so many still unanswered questions, and she worried she'd let him down.

"You'd never do that, Mum. And after all, we know so much more about him now: where he worked, where he was born, maybe even what he looked like as a boy."

Fran had leant forwards. "Do you really think that photo might be him?"

"I don't have a clue, but I'd like to think so. I don't suppose Elvira tracked down anyone who remembered Gran's necklace?"

"Apparently not, but it was always a bit of a long shot anyway."

She'd spent a rather sleepless night at Michael's house and he'd brought her home this morning. To distract herself from her thoughts – never mind the way she was missing a certain someone – she'd decided the best policy was action, so since then she had unpacked, filled the washing machine, popped around to thank Polly for looking after the houseplants and to give her the bottle of duty-free gin she'd bought her. But there had come a point when she couldn't put it off any longer; she needed to email Jadran.

Her last few days in Dubrovnik had passed in a blur. They'd taken the boat to uninhabited islands, driven to the top of Mount Srđ to enjoy the incredible views, eaten in restaurants tucked away in the backstreets of the old town, all the time trying to pretend that she wasn't on the verge of leaving. At the last minute she'd decided to take a taxi to the airport so their farewell had been over breakfast in the café, with Vedran moping around as though it was the end of the world, making them even more determined to be cheerful.

As they went their separate ways afterwards, Jadran had squeezed her hand. "No goodbyes, Safranka."

"No. No goodbyes." She'd had to believe it to keep herself together as she'd walked towards the waiting cab, the chewed edges of her fingernails digging deep into her palms. She had to believe it now, but how on earth it could be true she really had no idea.

She opened her browser and started to compose a message.

Dear Jadran,

As I said in my text, I had a good flight and Michael and his family met me at the airport.

She paused. She wanted so much to tell him about Belle, and confide her worries over Claire, but would it be tactless when he would never have grandchildren of his own? If they'd been sitting opposite each other in the café of course she would have done, but somehow committing the words to the screen seemed impossibly difficult. He felt ... he was ... so far away.

She was saved from making a decision by the washing machine's spin cycle reaching a crescendo, and she unlocked the back door and stepped into the garden. Groundsel was making its way between the cracks in the patio, and the rotary drier was stiff from months of neglect, so it took Fran several sharp tugs to free it. Even then it was reluctant to stretch into life and pinched her fingers, making her yelp. Bloody, bloody thing. Her eyes smarted. *For god's sake – get a grip and deal with it.* She was back in her real life now. The extended holiday was over.

After hanging the washing she made herself another cup of tea then returned to her email. What could she say? Her battle with the rotary drier would hardly make interesting reading. Nor would news about her family. Jadran didn't know them, so why should he care? He knew nothing about her life, not really. Why was she even bothering?

The gap between them yawned huge. It wasn't just the miles, the differences between them loomed large and forbidding too. Their lack of shared experiences, for a start: his life shaped by a war she barely understood, his university education and responsible job, the sorrow he'd carried with dignity and courage. The only thing she'd ever done she could be proud of was raising Michael, yet she couldn't even write to him about her precious family because of what had happened to his.

She ached for him, his smile, his voice, his hand in hers. She remembered their last trip on *Safranka II*, when they'd sailed a little way out from the harbour and around Lokrum island to watch the sun set over the sea and drink a bottle of their favourite Plavac Mali wine, and they'd sat in contented silence in the middle of the Adriatic because there was nothing they'd needed to say.

She sat back and rubbed her eyes. *Come on, Fran, hang on to those memories and make them shine.* The way she was feeling was nothing to do with Jadran, it was because the euphoria of seeing her family had drained away, underlining the fact her extended holiday was over and there was nothing she could find in her heart to look forward to. Of course she was going to feel crap while she tried to adjust to the humdrum everyday of being at home.

Hugging her arms around her, she walked into the living room and stood in front of the photo of Mama and Daddy on their ruby wedding anniversary. Fran tried to search her mother's eyes for the comfort she needed, but Mama wasn't looking at the camera, she was gazing at Daddy with the adoring expression that Fran knew so well. She'd only ever had eyes for Daddy, and it had been so wonderful, how much love she had found after so much hurt.

Fran had never really related to Mama's hurt until now, not really. When she'd finally left Ray there had been nothing but shame, tinged with relief. Or had it been the other way around? She rubbed her temples. She couldn't fully remember, but being apart from Jadran was harder than she had thought it would be. What if she never saw him again? What if … But no, she couldn't remotely compare what she was feeling to what Mama must have gone through. What was she even thinking? She was way off beam and it made her feel further away from her mother than ever.

Right. She'd better get back to that email. What would she say if he was here? What would she tell him? Slowly she began to type, the words awkward and sticky on her keyboard.

In some ways it feels good to be home, but in others, strange. I think I have a Dubrovnik hangover! And of course there is so much to do. I am sure my garden in particular is going to make me pay for abandoning it. I know there are some tulips somewhere between the weeds but I will need to search them out.

She read it back. That was so boring, but what else could she say? She'd only been home five minutes, surely he wouldn't be expecting too much?

Taking a deep breath she typed,

Anyway, I need to finish unpacking now. Love, Fran.

No, he always called her Safranka. And what about using the word love? How would he read that? She deleted the last two words and although it felt rather alien, simply ended the email with a kiss.

She imagined her message winging its way down wires and across satellite links, finally floating down through the ether or up on some undersea cable into the walled heart of Dubrovnik. Of course, he had a BlackBerry. It would find him wherever he was, whereas she would have to keep checking her laptop for his reply. Like some lovesick teenager. No, that would never do. There were plenty of other things she should be getting on with. Like the shopping list to end all shopping lists, for a start. *Keep doing, Fran, keep doing. Then you won't have to think.*

My dear Safranka,

Please excuse my delay in replying. I saw Kristo, who you may remember we met at the Trsteno Arboretum, on my way home yesterday and he told me they are short of volunteers, so I went over there to try it out. I am sure I will ache tomorrow, but of course it helped to fill the time. I expect you will have similar plans, now you are back at home.

As I look around my apartment, I realise what a very brave thing you did coming here alone, where you knew absolutely nobody, leaving your own home for so long. I think I would have found it very hard to do that.

I find myself wondering what that home is like, how long you have lived there, where you eat your breakfast or watch TV, so please tell me more. Have you started on the garden yet?

That is all for now. Sleep well x

Actually Fran had slept particularly well and felt far less grumpy because of it. It was, at least, good to be back in her own bed. That was something she was absolutely sure about, although in just about every other way she felt on shaky ground. She'd get used to being at home, she knew, she just had to keep telling herself that. The party was over. It was time for her proper life to restart. After all, that was what Jadran was doing.

Maybe next week she'd find some volunteering to do as well. Perhaps not too big a commitment just yet because soon they would be able to start clearing Daddy's house, although right now there was another delay while Andrew tried to persuade Patti to visit and decide if there was anything she wanted.

It would be pointless having Patti and Fran in the same space and although it saddened her, there was no guilt attached to the feeling now. Fran knew she had done absolutely everything in her power to put things right and it was time to move on. Once the house was sold and the estate divided that would be the end of it and the sense of relief she felt was quite astounding. She had never really understood how much it had been weighing her down.

So that was one big tick in the box. Now she needed to sort out everything else. Not so easy when she was using up most of her willpower to try to keep that awful hollow feeling of missing Jadran at bay. But she had to do it. Had to keep her own needs centre stage. It was why she'd come home, after all. She needed to face what would realistically be her future.

So what did that future look like? She was buggered if she knew. But there were two things she was sure about: it was here, in England, with her family, and it wasn't going to be about pleasing everyone else. What she wanted was important. But what the merry hell was it?

It was easier to think about what she didn't want. Already Polly had assumed she would feed Morris the moggy while she and Joe were in Spain in June, which would be a bit of a pain, but in this case she couldn't say no because she owed her big time for the months of plant care. It was just that the thought left her feeling particularly miffed that all manner of this sort of small stuff was going to land in her lap and tie her down.

Wait a minute ... hadn't she been scared of no one needing her anymore? Of her life stretching ahead without reason or purpose? Now she was shying away from even the simple everyday commitments. But why? It wasn't as though she had anything better to do at the moment. Had she managed to come back from Dubrovnik even more screwed up than when she'd left?

Oh god, she was fed up with herself already and she'd only been home a few days. One part of her knew that being unsettled was natural, and the other was already close to full panic. *Get. A. Grip. Actually, get a coffee.* That's what she used to do when she was feeling a bit low in Dubrovnik; why wouldn't it work here?

There was absolutely no reason why she couldn't do it. There were tens of coffee shops in Chichester, sometimes it seemed a new one was springing up around every corner. Perhaps, on a cool and slightly damp morning, she'd have to sit inside but that wasn't the end of the world. She swept her handbag from the table and picked up her coat.

Ah, but there'd be no Vedran to talk to … *Come on, Fran, stop making excuses.* He hadn't been working every time she'd visited the café either, particularly on weekday mornings, when he normally had lectures. She could do this. She would walk into the city centre, find somewhere that looked at least reasonably friendly and give it a go. And if it wasn't welcoming, or if the coffee was rubbish, there were plenty of other places to try.

Despite her initial resolve, she found herself hesitating outside the smartly-painted windows of one of the newer establishments towards the end of East Street. She wasn't exactly sure the trendy olive-green interior, filled with long tables and wooden benches, was her, even though, when a young woman with a swinging curtain of blonde hair stepped out, the waft of coffee following her smelt delicious. For a moment she was tempted, but perhaps it would be better to look for somewhere with softer seats.

A place a block or two away seemed to fit that bill as there were plenty of small, round tables with comfy armchairs on either side, but even so she felt reluctant to go in. What was the point in trying to recreate something of Dubrovnik here? It could never be remotely the same. On the other hand, if she was brave then perhaps even in her home city she might stumble across something surprising and new.

She slipped through the open door and joined the queue, the cheerful banter of the servers and the friendly hiss of the coffee machine drawing her in. As she waited, Fran eyed the cakes and muffins behind the glass but decided to be good. She'd had her breakfast – a nice, healthy bowl of sugar-free muesli that hadn't stuck to the roof of her mouth too much – she wasn't hungry and it really was time she started to lose at least a few of her extra pounds.

"What can I get you?" a man with braided hair called over the counter.

"Skinny cappuccino please."

"Chocolate sprinkles?"

"No thank you."

Vedran had never even offered them, and the coffee was so much more pleasurable to drink without the risk of a chocolate moustache. Not to mention tasting better as well.

As they worked, the servers talked to each other and to some of the customers in the queue. Fran felt awkward and invisible. Was it her age, or because she was new here? Everyone else seemed to be buying takeaways, then rushing off to work. Perhaps they did it every day. She shouldn't be so prickly.

But the feeling of isolation continued as she sat in a corner and sipped her coffee. The young mum at the next table thanked her when she picked up her baby's toy rabbit from the floor, then returned to tapping on her phone. A man in a thick jumper, busy with his crossword, didn't even look up when she ventured a good morning. And the coffee, although it was piping hot, lacked the bitter punch she'd enjoyed so much in Dubrovnik.

How come she was feeling so homesick for a place that wasn't her home? She reminded herself that when she'd first arrived in Dubrovnik she'd felt so very alone as well, and it had been bloody scary, because she really had been. But it hadn't lasted long; the city had opened its arms and welcomed her, while at the same time letting her newfound independent life flourish.

As soon as her drink was cool enough Fran gulped it down and left. East Street was already busy with shoppers so she cut through to Priory Park. She'd told Jadran about Chichester's walls and this was a good place to take a photograph to send him. Not that they were much to write home about compared to Dubrovnik, but it would be something to say.

After his invitation to tell him about her house, her second email had been easier than the first. His curiosity made it seem strange that he had never invited her to his apartment, but perhaps Gora had been right; if it was very old-fashioned and unchanged since his mother-in-law's days, perhaps he'd been a little embarrassed.

There was no doubt Jadran had been stuck in the past, but meeting her had seemed to unlock something in him and she was glad. But how much could he change and move on? At the time she had done her best to brush aside Gora's comment about him never travelling but now she was back at home she couldn't get it out of her mind. If he wouldn't come to England there was no hope for them at all so she might as well forget it. Should she just ask him? No, because she wasn't sure she could deal with his answer just yet.

But here in the park it was her own past calling her. Daddy had belonged to the cricket club here, as had Andrew for a while, before he'd discovered girls. Fran remembered many happy hours sitting on the boundary near the white-painted pavilion, Mama in a deckchair, her eyes never leaving Daddy, looking so smart in his whites as he fielded or ran in to bowl. Patti had been quite tiny then, and Fran had amused her by making the longest daisy chains ever, while Andrew played his own game of cricket with the other boys. At teatime Mama would unpack a wonderful picnic with cakes and sandwiches, which somehow always got squashed but tasted delicious, and a big bottle of Corona pop.

As Fran replayed the scene in her head she was waiting for the surge of grief, the stab of longing for a past never to be regained, but it didn't come. Instead there was a vague unease as in her mind's eye she pictured her mother in her straw sun hat and bright summer dress. It was that feeling again; that sense of not quite knowing who Mama was. She may have come to terms with her birth father's life – and death – but all the same it had set in motion a train of thought that was turning over every aspect of a past she'd believed in. A past she had held so very dear.

Eyes smarting, she climbed the slope to the top of the walls and dropped onto a bench, running her fingers along the chipped paintwork. She'd had a wonderful childhood, and yet, when she looked back at it now, was there the faintest of shadows? A half-remembered fear of doing something wrong, upsetting the apple cart of Mama's hard-won new life with Daddy.

She'd told Jadran who her father was hadn't really mattered because they would never know. And that was right. The world over, women fell for unsuitable men and loved them to distraction. Look at her and Ray. He'd seemed fine at the time, but that hadn't exactly turned out very well. And Patti had two disastrous marriages to her name. Maybe it even ran in the family. Perhaps Mama had been the only one of them with sense enough to choose wisely a second time.

Even Jadran wasn't a sensible choice, was he? If he was a choice at all. Really, there had been little more than friendship between them and despite what he'd said, it was impossible anything more would survive their separation. Right at this moment the woman who'd strolled into the Imperial Hotel on his arm seemed a million miles away; she'd almost been too scared to venture into a coffee shop this morning.

She sat bolt upright. *Come on, Fran, sort yourself out.* Maybe she would have to give up on Jadran now she was home but there was no way she should give up on herself. She'd come so far, she couldn't allow herself to slip back into her old ways. When she saw Parisa tomorrow she'd call in the cavalry to make sure that didn't happen.

Once Button had calmed down enough to stop spinning in circles and clambering up Fran's legs, Parisa attached his lead and they set off along the rough path that topped the downs. Beneath the escarpment to their left spread the village of Harting, set in a patchwork of woods and fields, the distinctive copper-green spire of the church rising above the dun-coloured roofs of the cottages lining the main street.

"So, what's it like being back?" Parisa asked.

"Honestly? Bloody awful."

"Missing Jadran?"

"Of course." There was nothing else to say, no way to sugar-coat it. He was the first thing she thought about when she woke in the morning, and her last thought at night. And it hurt. It bloody, bloody hurt. But she had to believe it would fade, she just had to. She kept telling herself this was the worst of it because they'd only been apart a few days, because she knew there was no point wanting what she couldn't have. Or letting Parisa distract her from what she was determined to talk about.

"That's not the real problem though. Already I feel as though I'm losing ground. I made so much progress when I was in Dubrovnik and I feel like I'm sliding backwards, losing sight of the person I thought I could be."

"You can't let that happen, Fran, and you know it. But I think you need to give yourself time. You've been home for all of five minutes and you were away for two and a half months. What's more, it was your first real taste of freedom for more than forty years. It's going to take a while to get used to the humdrum everyday again."

Fran stuffed her hands into her fleece pockets. "I suppose if I'd come back with some clearer idea of what I wanted to do with my life it might have helped. I've just got to remember that whatever I decide, it has to be for me."

Parisa put an arm around her shoulder and hugged her tight. "Too right it does. It's the most important thing. Just remember it doesn't make you a bad person if you say no when someone asks you to do something."

"Even when I've spent my whole life saying yes. That's a lot to unpick."

"Especially when you're back in an environment where people will ask, but you can do it, I know you can."

"I wish I had your faith."

They followed the broad chalk path along the edge of the downs, Button scampering ahead on the close-cropped turf, then dawdling around rabbit scrapes, his nose to the ground. The lightest of breezes ruffled his fur and carried the distant bleating and earthy aroma of sheep. Above them the pale blue sky whirled with clouds and Fran was sure at one point she heard a skylark sing. It was glorious up here, and only a few miles from home, but that wasn't the reason she'd suggested they came. No, there was somewhere she wanted to see.

Just before the view over the escarpment disappeared behind a belt of trees Fran stopped.

"Look down there," she told Parisa, "those buildings sort of tucked into the angle of the road? That's where Mama and I lived when we first came to England."

"And is it a coincidence we're here?"

"No. I've spent weeks trying to get close to my father, now it's time to get close to her."

Parisa frowned. "I don't understand."

"I'm not sure I do either, but I feel I need to. And this was where it started, although I don't remember very much. Mama worked so hard on the farm while Mrs Daly looked after me. She was a lovely old thing with no family of her own. We came to see her for years after Mama married, right up until she died. You see, I remember living here as a happy time, but it must have been miserable for my mother and I've never really thought about that before. No wonder she drilled it into me … But that's getting ahead. I want to ask you something. How do you remember my mother?"

"As probably the kindest woman I've ever met. She was always so welcoming to me, and your house was so full of love. I mean, don't get me wrong, I grew up in a loving home too, but my parents were very strict. Achievement definitely came first and I sometimes wonder what would have happened if one of us hadn't been academic. As soon as we came in from school we had to sit at the dining room table until we'd finished our homework. I used to love going to your house, there was so much freedom."

"Freedom?"

"It was the small things, especially as we got into our teens. At home I was treated like a child right until I went away to university, but at your house no one was ever breathing down our necks. Your mum always wanted to know about our days as soon as we got in, but then she just let us go up to your room. She never checked we were actually working …"

"But we always were."

"Yes, we may have put on a few records, but homework still came first. We must have been the best-behaved teenagers on the planet. It's no wonder we broke out a bit when we left home."

"Except I got myself into trouble and you didn't."

Parisa rolled her eyes. "I think med students were a little more worldly-wise than most, but I was no angel … and my parents would have killed me if I'd had to give up my studies because I was pregnant."

"These things ... the rules we're brought up with ... they shape our lives."

"That's very philosophical."

"No, but it's true. I was brought up to be good, to deserve Daddy, to set an example to the others. They were Mama's rules and they've dictated my whole damn life. The only time I rebelled was when I left home and that didn't end well. So I came back and picked up the rule book again. Years and years of it, Parisa, never even questioning whether it was the right thing to do, or even why these things were important."

Parisa put her hand on Fran's arm. "You almost sound bitter."

"I think I almost am, but I don't understand why. I just have the vaguest feeling I might have missed out. It's not as though I've had a bad life, though, is it? As you said, I've had the most loving of families and more than anything, I gave the same start to Michael, despite his father. And it's worked out so well for him I wouldn't change that for the world."

"And as a parent, did you give him the same rules? Did he have to be good to deserve love, or was it there unconditionally anyway?"

"You know it was. All I ever wanted was for him to feel secure so he could grow up happy and independent. But Parisa ... you've just rolled two thoughts into one and I wonder ... I wonder if you're right."

"How do you mean?"

"I've always thought of being good for Mama and Daddy and deserving love as two separate things but perhaps deep inside they did kind of merge; if I didn't do as I was told, I wouldn't be loved."

Parisa shook her head. "That could never have happened in your family. Not with your parents. They loved each other and they loved the three of you to distraction. Like I said, it was a true joy to be there. You were properly blessed."

Fran nodded. "You're right, of course."

"You don't sound convinced."

"And now you're going to say I'm overthinking it."

"No, I'm not."

Together they gazed out over the patchwork of fields far below them, while Button nudged around the gorse bushes that were glowing yellow in the sun.

Eventually Parisa spoke again. "I think it's all part of the process of grief, this delayed reaction you're having to losing your mother. You need to work through it, that's all. Questioning is part of it." She gave Fran's shoulders a squeeze. "You'll get there. Despite your current wobble, you're really very strong."

Fran looked up at her. "I only hope you're right."

It was later that afternoon she remembered. She was weeding in the garden and stood up to find the knees of her trousers covered in grass stains. It didn't matter; they were old ones, but a memory stirred from when she was a child in Mrs Daly's farmhouse.

She was sitting in the window of the snug wearing her best green gingham dress, thick white tights and new shiny black shoes. She knew she had to sit still and be good, because Mama was upstairs getting ready to take her to meet someone called Uncle Bob. He wasn't a real uncle – she knew she didn't have any of those – but all the same she'd been told how much fun it would be and how much she'd like him.

As she gazed out of the window a rabbit hopped across the lawn. A rabbit that should have been in the run where Mrs Daly kept them so they were ready for the pot. Fran ran towards the kitchen, then remembered it was jam making day, and terrible things happened if you didn't keep stirring the saucepan. It was no problem; that rabbit was always escaping and she was normally able to chase him back in on her own.

This time, however, he seemed to think it was a game and to be honest, so had she as she pursued him in and out of the bushes, only stopping when she heard her mother's furious voice.

"Safranka! Your dress ... your tights ... what are you doing?"

She'd stopped, looked down, seen the grass stains on her knees and remembered she was meant to be inside waiting. "But the rabbit—"

"Don't *rabbit* me. Just look at you. How can I take you to meet Uncle Bob like that? I'd be so ashamed."

Fran had started to cry and from somewhere Mrs Daly had appeared, spoken to Mama, then walked across the lawn to take her hand.

"Let's get you cleaned up," she'd said kindly and led her inside.

Over her shoulder, Fran had seen her mother start to walk up the lane to the bus stop without her, and had howled even more.

Later, as she had helped Mrs Daly to bottle the jam, the

older woman had explained that Mama hadn't meant to be cross with her, it was only because it was important that Uncle Bob liked Fran, because Mama liked Uncle Bob, and didn't she deserve some happiness after all she'd been through?

The words echoed down the years, resonating around Fran's head. Of course Mama had deserved happiness, and thankfully Bob had given it to her in spades, but what was really disturbing Fran now was what her mother must have been through to get there. Suddenly it was thrown into sharp relief – and it was terrifying.

How had her father been taken away? Had her mother had to watch as he was dragged from his family, or had he simply not come home one night? How long must the hours of waiting have felt to her, all alone with a tiny baby? Had she hoped for his release, or always known she would never see the man she loved again? And how had she discovered he was dead? Read his name on that awful, awful poster? *Oh, Mama, Mama.*

Fran wrapped her arms tightly around her chest and tipped back her head to gaze at the sky. Clouds scudded above her, splitting the china blue, but she barely saw them, plunged into the swirling darkness her mother must have endured. She couldn't feel her pain, of course she couldn't, but she could imagine … reading Branko Milišić's name on the list of the executed collaborators, and in the midst of that terrible grief, finding a way to get herself and her daughter to safety.

Then, coming here, to the quiet farmhouse tucked under the South Downs. All she had ever told Fran was that she'd found it very cold, but it must have been far worse than that. How many nights had she cried herself to sleep? How many weeks and months had she simply lost herself in hard work until gradually, gradually, there'd been a chink of light in her grief? Never mind the practicalities of a new country, a new language …

Slowly Fran came back into herself, gave her knees a final brush and walked rather shakily across the lawn and into the house. Her thoughts in the garden had been truly agonising, yet she felt closer to her mother than she had done in years. But why this? Why now? Parisa's words about questioning being a part of grief came back to her. These were questions that would never be answered; she could never know the depths of her mother's despair. Her mother had never wanted her to, and that was the truth of it.

The happiness Mama had sought had been for them both. It had been hard won, forged from the scars of war, and she had protected it in every way she knew how. Some women might have wallowed in their grief, or become bitter, but not Mama. She might have been scared of losing what she had, but at least she had been brave enough to start again. Could her daughter somehow find the same sort of courage?

Chapter Thirty-Seven

Dubrovnik, 24th October 1944

The soldiers herd them to the boat in the quiet of dawn, a silent shuffling mass of fifty or so men, filthy and starving, blinking in even the pale grey light. He glances up, towards the jumble of roofs that rise in the east of the city. Dragica and Safranka. Wherever they are taking them, his heart will remain with them here.

He cannot allow himself to think he will not see them again. There are men in his cell who say the partisans will kill them, but he has to believe that one day he will come home. Home to his wife and baby daughter. Home to the city he loves.

The sun stays hidden; not so much as a glimmer above Mount Srđ. Robbed of its golden light, the walls around the harbour remain relentlessly grey. The boat pitches and rolls as more and more men are forced onto it, surrounded by partisan soldiers with guns. The engines throb in time with his leg as he is forced sternwards. At least here there is air.

They cast off and swing around the breakwater, white-topped waves churning against the rocks below the city walls. He cannot look up. Cannot bear to say goodbye. He pictures Dragica, curled in their bed, her face streaked with tears. At least Safranka will not remember this. But if he does not return, she will not remember him either.

The thought rips through him, jagged as the bluntest of knives. It floods the space where the flame of hope has been: hope he would be believed, hope he would be freed. Hope he can no longer cling on to.

The boat rises and falls. He senses, rather than sees, Lovrijenac and Bokar glowering above him. He cannot look back or he will be swallowed by darkness, even as the grey light around him begins to reveal the colours of the ocean.

Soon the city is gone, replaced by the pines and scrub that fringe the rocks. They seem so close, that if his hands were not bound by wire he could jump and make it to the shore. If his hands were not bound … if his leg would allow him to swim. He curses the sickness that made him this way. Half a man. The wrong half, at that. Would Dragica be better without him? Without a crippled fool who failed to put his own family first?

The boat ploughs on through the swell. Not even the guards, huddled with their guns near the engine house, speak. Only the seagulls wheel and call above them, their freedom all the harder to bear.

Past the tip of the mainland, past the Grebeni rocks. He cannot wonder where they will be taken. It does not matter. Not in the least. Another turn and there is an island in front of him. Daksa, its ruined monastery rising from the pines and cypresses, its stones appearing to grow from the very rocks. The boat stutters, slows. This is their destination. So close to the city of his heart. So far away.

Chapter Thirty-Eight

Sussex, May 2010

It was becoming far easier to email Jadran. *But it should be,* Fran thought. She'd been home almost a month and they wrote to each other every day. Although she'd chatted on Skype to Michael and to Parisa while she'd been away, somehow she didn't suggest the same to him; seeing his face, hearing his voice, just might make her miss him even more.

His latest missive was particularly chatty; he was renovating the apartment. A few weeks ago he had ordered a new bed, and now he was decorating the living room. He was at pains to point out it was nothing fancy; a fresh coat of paint, a different sofa – something more comfortable that didn't sag in the middle – and a modern rug to go with it. He was certainly investing in his home, which given his reluctance to leave it was understandable.

Of course Fran was glad, but it also made her feel unsettled. This was the man his sister-in-law said would never change, and yet he was moving on without her. Of course she was pleased for him. Or at least, she was trying to be. But what was really niggling her was whether she was making any progress at all.

Cradling her mug of tea in her hands she wandered out into the garden. The straggly rose that every year attempted a feeble show of blooms against the kitchen wall was in bud, and bees buzzed around the lavender bushes lining one side of the lawn, their scent released by the late afternoon sun. Jadran was still volunteering at Trsteno; she was doing precisely nothing of any use.

She had popped into a couple of the charity shops in town to offer her services on a casual basis, but the first one had been very sniffy about training her if she wasn't prepared to commit. Training? How hard could it be to sort through a few clothes and operate the till? The second had been more welcoming and had given her a cup of coffee then taken her number, but she still hadn't heard anything from them and if she was honest with herself, she wasn't that bothered.

The strange thing was, time did not seem to be spreading infinitely and depressingly around her as she had feared. She spent an hour or so each day online learning Croatian; she even composed parts of her emails to Jadran in his mother tongue, and he both praised and corrected her. She fiddled around in the kitchen and was developing a rather strange style of cooking, which she supposed could be called fusion. And she'd joined a women's swimming group so three mornings a week found herself shivering on Pagham Beach then enjoying a warming coffee in the yacht club afterwards with her new friends.

Morris, Polly's moggy, appeared on the fence then jumped

down onto the lawn and wound himself around her legs. She crouched to stroke him, wondering if perhaps she should get a cat of her own. Far less of a tie than a dog, and company too. Yet she wasn't lonely. In fact, apart from missing Jadran and fussing about the future, when she let herself stop to think about it, she had settled back at home quite nicely.

So why not just fix what was making her sad? But there was no way that she could see that she and Jadran could be together. One thing she was sure about, she didn't want an on–off romance with them living apart more than they were in the same place. She would only spend a good chunk of her life hurting like she was now and she wouldn't do it. And she couldn't move to Croatia full time; she would miss Michael and his family too much, miss Parisa, miss her little house.

By the same token, she couldn't expect Jadran to uproot everything either, even if he wanted to. He had his family, and he was especially close to Vedran. He had his boat, and his home full of memories too. But he was beginning to change things, despite what Gora had said. Fran was sure that decorating the apartment was more than just something to fill his time, and if he felt able to do that, then just what else might he be able to change? But how could she ask him something so deeply personal when his emails were so, well, factual?

Finishing her tea, Fran returned to the dining table and opened her laptop. Finally Patti had visited their parents' house and taken what she wanted, so the rest of the clearing could begin. That was something she could safely write about, even if their feelings for each other (or lack of them, on his part) were strictly out of bounds.

After all the waiting, the only thing she took was the clock from the hall. She loved winding it with Mama every Sunday when she was little so I guess that was why. Andrew said she was only really interested in the money, but all the same it can't have been easy for her going back, any more than it was for Andrew or will be for me. But at least now we can get on with it.

She prattled on for a while about her latest walk with Parisa then drew to a halt, scrolling down through the email trail. Before she'd left he had told her that once they were apart they would know how things really stood between them but in not one single exchange had they discussed their feelings. Perhaps his silence meant he felt nothing at all.

The thought rarely came in the daylight hours, but when it assaulted her at night it was torture. Even now she found herself hugging her arms around her chest and choking back a sob. *Focus, Fran, focus. Don't let this overwhelm you.* But all the same her doubts assailed her; he'd only befriended her to fill his time, she only thought she loved him because she needed someone to care for, round and round in a destructive vortex that made her forget everything good that had happened between them.

No! Stop it! The laptop screen blurred in front of her and she scrubbed at her eyes with her knuckles. Get some distance and see what's really there. That's what Jadran had meant, after all. But she couldn't. Right now, she really couldn't. She wanted him more than she ever had done before.

The truth of the matter was she'd never meet anyone like Jadran again, so what was she doing, letting him go? Yet how could they be together? Was there an answer she wasn't seeing because she was too caught up in the mess inside her own head? She couldn't keep drifting along like this, resolving nothing. She was even getting bored with herself.

Sitting up abruptly she signed off her email as she always did, with a single kiss, and pressed send. Tomorrow she and Andrew were making a start on their parents' house. It would be another line in the sand. And afterwards, afterwards, she would need to be brave as hell and sit in a darkened room until she'd finally worked out what on earth she was going to do next.

Actually, the house isn't too bad, Fran thought as she stood in her parents' kitchen. There was the faintest sheen of dust on the work surfaces and table, and a huge smear of bird shit down the window, but it could have been worse. Much, much worse. Like the garden. The bird feeding station lay on its side and weeds sprouted between the patio stones. It would take them a month of Sundays to sort it out and Fran groaned inwardly, dreading the toll on her back and knees.

The house wrapped itself silently around her, with no ticking of the clock in the hall to fill it. She'd wanted to arrive before Andrew to give herself time to adjust to being here, get over any tears. But she was surprisingly dry-eyed. She knew in her heart that Daddy had gone. There wasn't a trace of his gentle soul anywhere.

She set the kettle to boil and took a couple of mugs and plates from the cupboard to rinse them. She'd made *čupavci*, all the time remembering baking them for Jadran for their first picnic at Trsteno, but she knew Andrew would enjoy them too. He'd always been a sucker for a home-made cake as well.

There was nothing more to do until he arrived, so she wandered from room to room, wrapped in her memories. Mama's collection of china plates on the dining room walls; the family photographs fading in the conservatory: Andrew's wedding: Michael's and Nick's graduations; she, Andrew and Patti on the beach as children. They were all there.

Except Mama and Daddy. They were on the mantelshelf in the lounge: a black and white wedding photo of them leaving the church; silver and ruby anniversary celebrations; a formal studio portrait in evening wear, which Fran thought had been taken at her mother's insistence to mark Daddy's promotion to branch manager. They were a lovely collection. In each and every one, Mama was clutching his arm and looking at him with the same adoring expression. What a love, unchanging over the years. They really had been very lucky.

Standing in front of the photos, Fran was gripped by a wistful longing for her mother. It wasn't just the things she wished she'd asked her, things she wished she understood, she simply wanted to stand next to her in the kitchen as they baked, to laugh together, to hug. And yet it had been seven years. Sometimes the pain was sharper than it had ever been. It wriggled its way to the surface, normally at the most inopportune moments, like when she'd been chatting to Polly in her kitchen and Ken Bruce had played 'I Only Have Eyes for You' as the love song for the day. It had been Mama and Daddy's special tune and she had all but broken apart emotionally at the sound of it.

At least now she understood this sort of thing was happening because she was finally dealing with her loss. And overall things were getting better. Since the day in the garden when she'd been able to put herself in her mother's shoes, the undefined anger she'd felt at Mama had started to fade (well, except for a few screwed-up moments at three in the morning). She was actually quite content being in this house; and by and large the memories were happy ones. Looking at the photographs, more than ever she knew she had been blessed. Hearing Andrew's car in the drive she shook herself. It was no good navel-gazing, today was a day for getting things done. She reached the front door just as he was fishing for his key in his pocket and they hugged each other fiercely.

"Don't," she whispered, "you'll make me cry."

"You and me both. But that wouldn't hurt, would it?"

"No, probably not."

Over coffee in the conservatory they made their plans. First they would walk around together and decide if there was anything in particular they wanted. Andrew had a list of the items that would go to auction, so next they would clear and clean them ready to be collected. Then they would empty the kitchen cupboards of food for Fran to take to the homeless shelter along with any of Daddy's clothes that might be suitable.

"That may well be enough for today," Andrew said. "Leave the spring cleaning for the weekend when Alice can help."

"How come you've been able to take a day off work?" Fran asked.

"I've decided to step back a bit from the business, go part-time. It's taken a while to organise and I wanted to tell you face to face, in case you worried it was because I'm ill. I'm not, I'm perfectly fine, but the stroke-that-wasn't put the wind up me a bit. When I was in the ambulance I was thinking, 'Shit, what if this is it? I haven't done half the things I want to.' So from the end of the month I'll be down to three days a week and taking a load more holiday too. We're heading off to California to see Nick for the whole of July."

"Good for you. I felt so bad leaving you to sort out all the probate when I was away ..."

"Fran, you have the potential to feel bad about anything, and you know there was nothing to do. If I need to take time out, then you need to cut yourself some slack."

"You're right, and actually I have started to do just that. I've given myself quite a big talking to about putting myself first and sometimes I even manage it. But for now we have a job to do, so stop stuffing that cake into your mouth and let's get on."

They started in the hall, the faint lines around the space where the clock had been catching Fran's eye wherever she looked.

"Have you any idea what you'd like from the house?" Andrew asked.

"Not really. Maybe one or two of Mama's plates to remember her by, and perhaps that painting of Midhurst pond she bought Daddy for his fiftieth, as long as you don't want it."

Andrew shook his head. "I thought I'd go through his books. I'll have more time to read now, and if I remember rightly, he had quite a collection of James Bond hardbacks and loads of Dick Francis."

Fran smiled at him. "Good call. You might even find a first edition tucked away somewhere. You never know your luck."

It didn't take Fran long to go through the plates. She wasn't too keen on the overly floral designs her mother had loved, but there was a Wedgwood one depicting a swan tending its tiny cygnet that Daddy had given Mama for Christmas one year and she had absolutely adored. Although it wasn't really Fran's taste either, it brought back such happy memories she couldn't let it go.

Setting the plate to one side, she began to empty the sideboard of their parents' best dinner service and pack it in old newspaper ready for auction. Mama had collected it for years, buying a piece here and a piece there until she had the whole set, but who used dinner services like this anymore? Fran certainly didn't. A friend or two around for supper at the kitchen table was her lot. Perhaps she should do that more often, she mused. It would be a reason to replace her own slightly chipped crockery. She looked at the dinner service again, it was such a shame ... No, now she could afford it she definitely wanted something she'd chosen herself.

Andrew appeared at the dining room door, grinning. "Look what I've found. It was tucked inside *From Russia, With Love*, at one of the steamier scenes."

He handed Fran a note in her mother's writing:

Going to be the best Tatiana you've ever had. Bedroom. Three o'clock. I'm planning to enjoy your retirement too xx

Fran felt herself blush. "Well I never ..."

"It's kind of weird thinking of your parents being that sexy, isn't it? And in their sixties as well." He laughed. "There's hope for me yet!"

"But you and Alice ..."

"Oh, we're fine. Probably as loved up as you can get when you're both working full time and energy's at a premium."

"I'm glad to hear it. You've always seemed so right together."

He put the book down on the table. "And what about you? Wasn't there a man in the picture when you were in Dubrovnik?"

Fran shrugged. "We were just friends. He reminded me a bit of you, actually."

"What, desperately good-looking and charming with it?"

"A lot better looking than you." She prodded him in the stomach. "Keeps himself fit too."

"Oh, so you were such good friends you noticed those sorts of things about him?"

"Andrew, give over."

"I'm your little brother. I'm meant to be annoying."

Fran rolled her eyes and knelt back down to wrap the gravy boat in newspaper. "We'd best get on."

"There's something you're not telling me."

"Bugger off and sort out the rest of those books."

Once she'd finished packing the dinner service Fran moved on to the kitchen to make a start on the cupboards. The last few *čupavci* were on the table. Jadran again. And Andrew. Why had she shut him out like that? Wouldn't a man's perspective on this be useful? At least he might have an opinion on why Jadran's emails were so … impersonal, almost. If she could get to the bottom of that … if she had even half an idea of where they might go from here …

Before she could change her mind, she called up the stairs. "Time for a cuppa and a sandwich?"

Andrew's head appeared over the banister. "How about we go to the beach?"

"Good call. I'll dig out a flask."

They settled themselves on the top of the shingle bank, watching the clouds shift along the horizon. Unlike the rich blues and azures of Croatia, the scene in front of them was unremittingly grey; the gunmetal sea in the distance, the lace-edged waves raking the pebbles through the foam, the leaden sky.

"Looks like it'll rain later," said Andrew.

"Mmm." Fran raised her sandwich to her mouth, then stopped. "I'm sorry I was obtuse over Jadran earlier ..."

"It's none of my business. Unless, of course, you want to tell me."

"I think I do. I need some advice. From a male point of view."

"Well, I'm listening, but spare me the gory details. You are my sister after all."

"There's nothing *gory* to tell, as you so delightfully put it. We were just friends. Well, only a little more. There didn't seem any point when we both knew I was coming home, but the fact of the matter is, I really miss him. He's one of the good guys, Andrew, and at my age you don't find them on every street corner."

"And does he feel the same?"

"I don't know. While I was there, I thought so, but there's nothing to suggest it in his emails. He never writes about his feelings at all."

"That could just be a man thing."

Fran nibbled the corner of her sandwich. "I did wonder, but … he said before I left that we'd only really know how we felt about each other when we were apart."

"That sounds a bit cockeyed to me."

"No. It makes perfect sense. He was widowed almost twenty years ago: his wife and daughter were killed in the Homeland War and he hasn't dated since. And as you know, it's even longer for me. I assumed, after Ray, that that part of my life was over. I just couldn't believe I wouldn't mess it up again."

"But you weren't the one who—"

"Oh, I know that now. I've done a lot of thinking, Andrew. The real hard stuff. I've even been trying to be more selfish, well, self-centred anyway. While I was in Dubrovnik, I came to realise that I could be. You see, nobody actually needs me anymore and while at first it was downright scary, now I'm beginning to understand how liberating it is. I just feel a bit wobbly about it, you know, trying to find a balance.

"It was one of the reasons I came home early and why what Jadran said made sense. I was so scared I just wanted to be needed again, and that my feelings for him weren't real after all. I needed that distance too. And of course what I've come to realise is that I do love him." She laughed. "I've never said it out loud before."

"Fran, you need to talk to this guy."

"I know, but I'm scared."

"Because he doesn't mention his feelings in his emails?"

"Partly that, and partly because, well, I just can't see a way forward for us. We live fourteen hundred miles apart and I couldn't deal with an on–off relationship where we only see each other every so often. It's bad enough as it is."

Andrew wrapped his arm around her shoulder and gave her a squeeze. "OK, let's look at the options. First, you go back to Dubrovnik and—"

"No! Much as I love it there, I don't want to leave Michael and the girls again. Claire grew up so much while I was away and I couldn't bear to lose touch with their lives."

Andrew nodded. "I get that. I think I'd find Nick being abroad far harder if he had a family, but he and Julian seem happy enough with their chihuahuas. So, option two, Jadran comes to live here. You said he'd lost his family …"

"Yes, but he still has his siblings and a nephew he's really close to. A whole life, all his friends, his memories …"

"As do you. You can't put yourself second in this, Fran, and from what you've been saying you know that."

"If you'd let me finish …" She glared at him.

"God, you look like Mama when you do that. It's scary!"

"Then shut up and listen."

He made a zipping motion across his mouth.

"Jadran doesn't travel. Apparently he only ever left the country for work."

They fell into silence, listening to the crackle and draw of the shingle in the waves and the calls of the seagulls overhead. The sounds of their childhood.

"Can I speak now?" Andrew asked, and Fran nodded. "Relationships are about compromise, and if he won't give and take, meet you halfway, then he isn't worth it, and you'll need to face that and move on."

Fran picked up a handful of small pebbles and trickled them through her fingers. "Meet me halfway, you said?"

"I don't mean you settle in Switzerland or somewhere, though ..."

She punched his arm. "I know that, but you've given me an idea."

"What?"

"Not telling. Not yet, anyway. You're right – I need to talk to him first." She jumped to her feet. "Come on, those kitchen cupboards won't empty themselves." She all but ran up the beach, with more energy than she'd had in weeks, leaving Andrew to pick up the flask and Tupperware box, shaking his head but laughing all the same.

When Fran got home there was an email waiting from Jadran, as she'd known there would be. In some ways he was still very much a creature of habit, and as she'd driven back from Aldwick the thought had begun to gnaw at her, undermine her confidence. How could she ever, ever ask him to make such a cataclysmic change to his life? On the beach it had seemed so easy, but back in the real world ...

In her heart of hearts Fran thought she would probably be asking too much of him, but Andrew was right; at least she would know, and then she could move forwards. However painful that might be at first.

His email was full of his progress – decorating the apartment, how he had enquired about becoming accredited as a tourist guide specialising in the Siege of Dubrovnik – and how Vedran was revising hard for his exams. The tourist guide thing was frankly incredible; this was the man who, just a few short months before, had asked his nephew to tell her about his wife and daughter. So he really was making significant changes. Could he make one more? Could she ask him? Was she finally strong enough to take it if the answer was no?

The thought was frankly terrifying, but all the same there was a bubble of excitement inside her. It was how she imagined standing on a diving board would be, gazing down at the clear blue waters far, far below. She had climbed this high, risked this much … now she was here, how could she not jump?

But how could she? She re-read Jadran's email. Like every other he'd sent there was nothing personal in it, nothing emotional. Did that mean her first instinct was sound, that distance had made him realise there was only friendship between them? Or was Andrew right, that it was a bloke thing? Oh, god, she couldn't do this. And yet, she knew she had to for her own peace of mind. Which was, after all, the most important thing.

Instead of writing a proper reply, she asked him if he'd like to take an aperitif with her the next day, and sent instructions for joining Skype. Heart in her mouth, she pressed send. She still had the best part of twenty-four hours to bottle it. In the meantime she had plenty to do: battle into her wetsuit and go swimming first thing, then if the weather was fine, make an initial attack on her parents' garden. And right now she had to get ready to go out to supper with Parisa. Just as well they were eating in town so she didn't have to drive, she thought as she headed for the kitchen drawer to root out the corkscrew.

But as she gazed out of the window, wine glass in hand, she didn't switch off her computer. Would Jadran break his habit and respond? Her message would ping onto his BlackBerry wherever he was.

Before heading upstairs to change she glanced back at the screen and was rewarded.

I'd love to x

It felt like a promising start.

In the moments before Jadran's face appeared, Fran's barely-suppressed panic bubbled inside her like molten lava, making it hard to breathe. She was wearing the embroidered cardigan he liked so much, but was it over the top to dress up for a Skype call? She'd had her hair restyled since being home too, cut far shorter, although her unruly waves still took every opportunity to bounce back and she'd failed to find a reliable way of controlling them. Would he like it? Would he even notice?

But Jadran was smiling, not the small, tight thing he had used when they'd first met, but the broader version she had come to know and love. "Safranka! It is wonderful to see you."

"And you too. I've missed you."

He glanced down. Was he embarrassed? Was it not how he felt? "And I you." He almost whispered the words, his voice husky with emotion, then he cleared his throat and carried briskly on. "Before we raise our glasses, can you carry your laptop around and show me your house? I want to be able to picture where you are."

Why was he changing the subject? What should she do? For a start the place was a tip; her dirty breakfast things still on the draining board and washing strewn over every radiator.

She tried her best to smile at him. "I'm embarrassed to be honest. It isn't very tidy … I've been out all day."

"Then perhaps another time." Despite his words he looked a little disappointed.

At least if she was walking around they wouldn't be staring at each other from screen to screen while she gathered her tattered courage back together.

"I'll just show you this room and the kitchen. But you'll have to close your eyes to the dirty dishes." She swept the laptop off the table. "I've decided to renovate it anyway when we've sold Daddy's house. I've never had the money to do it before." And she prattled on about how she might knock the two rooms into one and put in a breakfast bar, and how she quite fancied white-painted cabinets, but wasn't sure how practical they were.

When she sat down again they raised their glasses to each other, chinking them against their screens. "So you have plenty of plans for your house?" he asked.

"Yes. I see myself living here for quite a while."

Was that a flicker of something in his eyes? Sorrow? Or relief? He was sitting back from his computer, cradling his beer glass, so it was hard to tell.

Right. If she was ever going to say it, it was now. No point in putting it off or this conversation would become beyond awkward.

"But I want to talk to you about the future too."

"It's OK, Safranka, I understand—"

"How can you possibly, when I haven't said anything yet?"

"My apologies." The small, stiff smile again.

"You told me that only once we were apart would we really know how we felt about each other, but our feelings are something we haven't talked about in our emails. I've been home for a month and it's about time we did."

"So you have reached a conclusion?"

"It's more that I have an idea." How on earth was she managing to sound so calm and practical when so much of her happiness depended on his response?

He leant forwards. "Tell me."

"I want to give us a chance. There's a huge gap in my life without you. You're a very special man and, if possible, I don't want to throw that away. But ..."

"Isn't there always a *but*?" He sounded so wistful for a moment she could feel herself backpedalling and agreeing to whatever he wanted. But that wouldn't do.

She took a deep breath. "The *but* is that I can't give up my life in England. I have a family and friends here I love. As you do in Dubrovnik. So ... so ... what I'm asking you to think about is, how would you feel ... if it works out between us ... splitting our time between both places? I know it's a lot to ask ... Gora said you don't like to travel so—"

"Oh, Gora's gossip! Much as I love her, sometimes I could kill that woman." To Fran's surprise, Jadran started laughing. "I don't suppose she mentioned that I used to travel so much for work that I didn't need to go anywhere in my time off? Right now there is nothing I would like better than to experience new things, new places. Especially if it's with you. Safranka, this is everything I have been hoping for and dreaming of since you left."

"But you said nothing in your emails ..."

"I knew you had things you needed to work out and I didn't want to put any pressure on you. Although, during the first week I have to admit I was close to booking a plane ticket and throwing myself on your mercy, even though I knew that wouldn't have been right."

"Oh, Jadran ..." Fran clutched her wine glass. Was he really saying these things? Did he really mean them?

"So shall I buy my ticket now?"

She shook her head. "Not right away. I've heard from the Daksa archaeologists. They're going to be reburying the bodies in early July and I'd like to be there. Andrew and I should have finished clearing the house by then, so how about I come to you first?"

"I can wait a little longer to see you now that I know. Thank you, Safranka. You have made me so very happy."

"Then that makes two of us." She raised her glass. "To new beginnings."

"And happy endings."

Chapter Thirty-Nine

Daksa, 24th October 1944

The moment he sees the pit, he knows. He'd known before, of course he had, except he'd refused to acknowledge it. But this is the moment he moves beyond any sliver of doubt. Ahead of him the mayor begins to remonstrate, the crack of something solid on bone a warning to them all.

His leg drags as they are herded up steps into some sort of building. Although he is shaking, he will not stumble. He will not fall. He will not beg, plead, or argue either. There is no point. This is the end; the end of it all.

He limps to the furthest corner, away from the group. He looks up to see an arched ceiling, revealed by the broken floorboards of whatever used to be above. The only light streams through the small square windows high in the walls. If only he could climb and look back to the city. Perhaps it is best that he cannot.

Three monks move amongst them. He is not the only

innocent man and for a moment there is a flicker of anger. If they had listened to him, he could have told them who was good and who was bad. He could have stopped the injustice. But could he have sent a fascist to his death? Even that he doubts.

A monk stands in front of him; tall, soft-voiced, a rosary in his hand. "Would you like to pray, my son?"

He shakes his head. "I am sorry. I do not share your faith."

"There is always time."

"It is not for me. But please, if you can, say a prayer for my wife, Dragica. She believes." His eyes fill with tears as he says it and he looks away.

The man puts a hand on his shoulder. "I will do whatever gives you comfort."

The act of kindness steadies him. Not all men are bad. He knows that really. He thinks of Vido, the truest of friends, of Solly. He thinks of the father who raised him alone after his mother died. For what? To finish like this?

He sinks to the floor, his head on his knees, the mustiness of the earth filling his nostrils. He is beyond hunger, beyond thirst. Dragica's face fills his mind; her smile lighting his darkness for a blissful, yearning moment before she vanishes. The reality is he will not see her, will never hold his daughter, again.

It is too much; too much. The agony in his leg he can bear. The pain of death even, the hot rip of bullets that will put an end to suffering forever. But what is beyond his wildest imagining of pain, is knowing that he will never see Safranka grow up. That is the hardest thing to bear.

What sort of child will she become? What sort of woman? He thinks of the night she was born and his wishes for her.

That there will be laughter in her life, and love. That she will grow to be fearless and brave. That she will never know the evil of persecution and war. That last wish is bitter indeed; will she be forever tainted by his death? Will she be branded a collaborator's child?

He hopes Dragica will do what's best. They spoke of it the night before he was taken. She did not want to accept that he might be held prisoner for a very long time. Neither of them had wanted to believe he might never come home. He should have been braver, done more than hint that there might be circumstances it would be better for her to leave. But he could not bear to see the anguish in her eyes.

The other men have spread around the room and he becomes aware they are scratching on the wall. When the end is near, the urge to make a mark on the world is strong. But he has made his; his legacy will be Safranka. He just hopes Dragica will make her understand that he wasn't a bad man.

His head drops again and he studies the floor between his knees. Beneath them is a sharp stone. He could scrape too, leave something. But what? Something to show he is not a fascist like the others. If he shared the monks' faith he could scrape a cross. If he shared Solly's, a Star of David. And yet ... and yet ...

It is the reason he is here. It is the one symbol that would set him apart from the Ustaše. A last protestation of innocence. For all anyone will see it on this godforsaken isle. But someone might. In the months and years that come, someone might find shelter here and wonder. He imagines that person, by some miracle, is Safranka and finds himself dashing away tears. He picks up the stone, heaves himself on to his hands and knees, and begins to carve.

Later they come for them. Five names are called out, including the hated priest. He walks with dignity at least, but leaves the others to help the man who has collapsed into hysterical weeping. His sobs mark their progress around the outside wall and are only silenced by the torrent of gunfire.

No one in the room speaks. He continues to carve the final downstroke of the letter M. His initials and the star. There is no time for more.

Next they call the monks. He stands too, follows them. As the guard makes to stop him, he shakes his head.

"Let me die with good men, not fascists."

Their eyes meet and after a moment the partisan nods. "It makes no difference to me."

So he steps into the evening sunshine for one last time, looks up at the sky, the flitting clouds, the birds wheeling above his head, the gentle wash of the waves on the shore. Then down at the earth that will soon cover his bones. He follows the monks around the corner of the building, leaving behind a future that will be his wife and daughter's alone.

Chapter Forty

Dubrovnik, June 2010

Fran settled in the shade of the orange tree in the courtyard behind Jadran's apartment. Its dark glossy leaves rustled as the slightest of breezes found its way over the walls from the sea, the buildings surrounding them muffling the city sounds. Above her, the uneven blocks that made up the buildings glowed golden on the upper storeys where they caught the sun, and a colourful counterpane flapped gently from a window on the top floor.

She stretched her legs along the stone bench and wriggled her toes. "This is blissful. A little oasis from the chaos outside. No wonder you've never wanted to leave."

Jadran smiled. "It never even occurred to me to. When I returned after the war it seemed obvious to move in with Leila's mother; we were both lonely and grieving, facing towards the past instead of a future neither of us welcomed. But we made the best of it, and when she died, I'd been here so long it had become my home as well. It's such a relief that you like it too – although that might change once you've suffered the old-fashioned plumbing."

"There are plenty of consolations." Fran thought about the rooms upstairs, all recently decorated in fresh, clean colours that lightened the heavy wooden furniture which sat so well beneath the high ceilings. Maybe the bathroom and kitchen did need updating, but that was hardly her call. She hadn't even been here an hour; what did she know?

The moment she'd stepped onto the black and white tiles in the communal hallway the hustle and bustle of the journey had begun to melt away and she'd started to relax. Coming back to Dubrovnik had been almost as nerve-racking as her first visit; there was so much more at stake. While she'd been waiting for her cases in the baggage hall, she had felt so sick she'd had to make a dash for the toilets, and although Jadran's welcoming hug had made her feel so much better, it was only once they arrived at the oasis of the apartment that she began to feel more herself.

After putting her suitcases in the spare bedroom, Jadran had suggested a cooling drink, and although Fran had been gasping for a cup of tea, the lavender lemonade he'd given her had been so very refreshing, and anyway they had quickly opened a bottle of wine. As Jadran fiddled with the stem of his glass she realised she wasn't the only one trying to hide their nerves.

"I hope you don't mind, but I have cheated for supper and bought a pizza and some salad from the delicatessen. I didn't want to spend your first evening cooking, when I could be spending it with you."

"That sounds absolutely perfect. Will we be eating outside?"

"Whatever you prefer. To be honest I rarely use the courtyard, except to dry washing, but I sense that might be about to change."

"I don't sit in my garden very often either, and not just because of the weather. It's one of those things it's far nicer to do with someone else, isn't it?"

Jadran put his hand over hers. "I am rediscovering there are an awful lot of things like that. Safranka, you don't know how happy you have made me."

Her heart felt so full of love she could barely answer but she both wanted and needed to reassure him. "And you, me. I never even dreamed I could fall in love at my age, or that I would even want to. But it has happened, all the same. It might not be straightforward, but right at this moment I feel as if we can make it work."

He leant in to kiss her and she swung her legs out of the way to sit closer to him. It was a first kiss all over again and the taste of him filled her; wine, mixed with the salt of the olives they'd been sharing, and something that was particularly his own. Something she had craved while she was back in England without even knowing it.

They kissed for a second time, drank more wine, kissed again, and finally ate pizza, their bodies touching at hip, thigh and shoulder on the old stone bench. Butterflies fizzled and swooped in Fran's stomach, but she knew she was hungry for more. Just how much more? Her bags were in the spare room, so what would happen now? God, it was frightening, but magically exciting all the same.

Jadran disentangled himself from their embrace. "Coffee inside?"

"Yes please."

She took a deep breath and, collecting their empty glasses, followed him up the uneven steps to the first floor apartment.

As she waited on the sofa, Parisa's voice filled her head, telling her to go with the flow. There was no need to rush, they had weeks ahead of them, months. With any luck, a whole lifetime.

When Jadran sat down next to her they kissed again, longer, deeper, and her arms crept around him, easing his shirt from his belt to reach the warm flesh beneath. Fine hairs covered his back, soft to the touch, and she felt his goosebumps ripple beneath her fingers.

His hand moved slowly from her shoulder to her neck, stroking the nape under her hair and caressing the tip of her ear. No one had ever touched her with such gentleness and care and, wherever it took them, she didn't want it to stop.

They were half-naked, their coffee cold on the table, when Jadran pulled away.

"Safranka … how ready are you? I don't want … I don't want us to do anything you're not comfortable with. There is no need to hurry, we have all the time in the world."

His eyes told the story of his touch, rich with honesty and love.

"I … I don't know, not really. I don't want to stop, but all the same I don't … well … I have no idea if my body … I mean … what's even possible at my age."

There. She'd said it. It was out in the open and if she'd broken the moment …

But Jadran laughed softly. "Then that makes two of us." He

stood and reached his hand down to her. "We may not be as young as we were, but we're not too old either. Perhaps just a little out of practice. We'll find our own way. Trust me."

His grip was warm and firm around her fingers.

She nodded. "I do."

Jadran's weight was heavy on the side of the bed and before Fran had even opened her eyes she could smell coffee.

"So this is the morning you decide to sleep in." There was a laugh in his voice as he bent to kiss her. "I'll have my shower now, while you wake up."

He was right. It had taken her almost a week to adjust to sharing a bed with him. At first every movement, every sound, had woken her, sometimes lying there for hours, listening to his even breathing and occasional snores, feeling his warmth beside her. It was good, very good (well, perhaps not the snoring) and something she had never thought she'd experience again. One of the many, many things in fact.

Grinning to herself she wriggled up the bed, pulling the sheet with her and picking up the cup from the bedside table. Whoever thought people in their sixties were past it? The more they'd got to know each other's bodies, the more comfortable they'd become. All right, not everything worked quite as smoothly as it had done in their younger days, but the intimacy, the emotional closeness, seemed more intense than ever.

And now finally, finally, she had actually slept more or less through the night, and on a day she didn't have time to lie around in bed either. She leant over to check Jadran's watch –

ten to nine. They were meeting Eli and Elvira for coffee in a café near the Green Market, so as soon as Jadran had finished in the bathroom she'd need to get a wriggle on.

She loved going to the market and had been gratified when the women had remembered and welcomed her. The produce now was subtly different and the meals she created were based around enormous overripe tomatoes, slightly bitter pale green peppers and dark, plump aubergines. She'd also struggled home up the slope with a huge pot of fragrant basil, which had joined the geraniums in the courtyard, releasing its scent whenever she brushed past.

The trickle of water that served as a shower ground to a halt. Jadran had been right that first evening, sorting out the plumbing was top of her list. Their list. As he started to whistle, she reached for her dressing gown and swung her legs out of bed. She didn't think she'd ever become used to wandering around the apartment naked in the mornings as he did, however beautiful Jadran told her she was. Some things were non-negotiable. Some things were just the way she was.

While he was shaving she just had time to check her emails. Claire was waiting for the results of her school exams so she was anxious to see if there was any news. But the only fresh item in her inbox was from the Daksa archaeologists, attaching her father's autopsy report. She hesitated before clicking on the file; she had asked them to send it as soon as it was ready, but now it was here, she wasn't sure she wanted to read it at all.

Jadran appeared behind her, his towel wrapped around his waist. "Any news from Michael?"

"No. Just this."

He rested his hand on her shoulder. "You haven't opened it?"

"I've only just read the email. But honestly, I was prevaricating a bit … and anyway, it's bound to be in Croatian."

"Which you could probably manage quite well …"

"Not if it's technical jargon."

"So would you like me to tell you what it says?"

"Yes please."

She clicked on the file, then sat back and rested her head against his arm. The final piece of the jigsaw she was ever likely to find and she couldn't imagine it would tell her anything about the sort of man her father was. But somehow she felt she owed it to him to know all there was to know, and then he could really be put to rest next week.

Leaning over her to see the screen, Jadran hugged her to him, his body slightly damp against her cheek.

"So, he died from a single bullet wound to the back of the head, which sounds brutal, but it does mean he would not have suffered."

She nodded. There was a strange lump in her throat, making her feel slightly sick, as she tried not to think how he must have felt in those last moments before the shot came. But it was beyond her wildest imagination.

"Now, a little about him they could tell from his body. A bit less than 1.7 metres, so not a tall man and small-boned generally, with a badly worn knee joint and evidence of muscular shrinkage, probably caused by childhood polio." Jadran paused, then said slowly, "Safranka, he would have walked with a limp."

Why did that feel important? It took her just a moment to remember, but even then she could barely believe it. "Like the man who rescued Elvira."

When she looked up at Jadran he was beaming down at her. "Exactly like him."

She gripped his hand. "Do you think ..."

"Yes. Yes, I do. This time the odds are on his side." And he held her to him as she sobbed.

Eli and Elvira were sitting at one of the tables under the neat rows of square umbrellas that had filled the fringes of the marketplace since the season began.

Eli stood and shook Jadran's hand, before kissing Fran shyly on the cheek. "I am so pleased you have decided to return."

Jadran grinned. "For a while, at least. At the end of the month we go to England until the autumn. It won't be so hot – or so crowded."

The waiter arrived to take their orders then Fran turned to Elvira. "It is lovely to see you too."

The woman's lipsticked smile was broad. "I hope if you are going to be here more often we can become friends."

"And we have some news," Eli interjected.

"News? As it happens, we do as well, but you go first." Fran laughed, but she was sure it was caused by the electric fizz of excitement that had been running through her since she'd got over this morning's shock.

"Well," Eli continued, beaming at her, "a couple of weeks ago we had a service in the synagogue when the rabbi visited us from Zagreb and of course Elvira came. Then afterwards ..." He turned to Elvira. "But it is your story to tell."

Elvira shook her head. "As if you ever let anyone tell a

story when you know it as well, Eli, but I will try. After the service we had a small reception in the museum. I hadn't been there in years and I was absolutely amazed to see a photograph of my father's Bar Mitzvah ..."

"You know, the one I showed you, of Solomon Goldstajun," added Eli, earning a sharp look from Elvira.

"Eli had not realised there was any connection because he did not know my birth name. But there he was. It was very emotional." She looked across at Fran. "You lost your father young. You will understand."

Fran nodded, suddenly filled with sorrow. Elvira would have memories, and although they would have brought her pain, at least there was something to hold onto, whereas she ... even now, she only had shadows. But of course, Elvira was a link to her past as well; although she did not know it yet, because she remembered Fran's father too.

"Anyway," said Eli, "of course I showed her the picture you found in the old album of the two boys—"

Elvira cut across him. "As you know, it was small and the quality poor and my eyes are not that good, so I asked my nephew to enlarge it. He is a genius with such things and made some sort of digital magic, so we have a better image. Of both boys. And Eli said you thought the other looked like your son so we knew you would be interested." She reached into her handbag and put the photograph on the table, twisting it towards Fran.

As she leant forwards to look at it, it was all she could do to stop her fingers from trembling. Surely, given their fathers had been friends, this could very well be hers. She studied it minutely, aware of three pairs of eyes looking at her. The nose, yes, it was rather like Michael's, but for the first time she could see the child's eyes. Eyes just like her own, dark and round. But no, they couldn't be, it would be too much to hope for. The boy was trying to look away and the photo was black and white, so anyone's eyes would look dark. She was seeing things that weren't there. Did she want them to be that much?

Jadran leant over her shoulder. "Safranka, look. Next to the younger boy, on the ground. Isn't that a crutch?"

Elvira nodded. "I thought so too. And of course the Ustaše who helped us to escape walked with a limp, and my mother had said he was a friend of my father's. Fran, do you possibly think ..."

Fran's mouth was so dry she couldn't speak. Was it possible she was looking at her father? Common sense told her she had to be, but on top of this morning's revelation it was almost too much. Mama's hero, albeit as a child, was right in front of her.

Jadran put his hand over hers. "The autopsy arrived from the archaeologists this morning, and that was our news. Safranka's father's leg was damaged, probably by childhood polio."

Eli had a triumphant look on his face. "That makes perfect sense. We know from death records there was an outbreak in 1926/7 so it must have come from that. This is so exciting, Fran, this has to be your father, it must be. We have found him for you after all."

She gazed at the picture, still unable to form appropriate words, her spinning world grounded only by Jadran's touch.

Elvira reached out and held her other hand. "It must be such a shock, but I have so much to thank your father for, Fran. He gave me my life and I mean that. I read ... I read in the paper they are burying the victims of Daksa next week and I would love to be there if it is allowed. I want to pay my respects."

Still choked by the lump in her throat, Fran nodded. Finally she was able to tear her eyes from the picture and look into Elvira's face. "I would really like that," she croaked. "And I expect he would as well."

Dubrovnik, July 2010

The four of them met on the harbour at Gruž to wait for the chartered boat that would take them to Daksa, Eli having insisted on coming too. Already the day was hot, the sun glaring from the concrete that surrounded them, and one of the archaeologists was moving between the groups of mourners to hand out bottles of water.

Fran turned to Jadran. "I'm not even sure if *mourners* is the right word. Most of us are too young to have actually known the people who died in the massacre."

"It's hard to think of a better word though. I suppose we are all here to pay our respects, to remember them, but how many genuinely mourn their passing sixty-five years later I do not know."

Elvira frowned. "I think I do. Of course I only have the vaguest of memories of your father, Fran, but I certainly feel sad this is how he was repaid for his courage and kindness."

Fran nodded. Over the last few days she had veered between sorrow, anger, then thankfulness for the way her life had worked out. The freedoms she had enjoyed in England, with another good man as a father. But she still wasn't ready to share any of that with anyone other than Jadran, so instead she said, "I'm wondering … if Mama had lived this long, would she have still mourned him? She would have lived a whole new lifetime since."

"And that will be the way with most people here," said Eli with a slight bow of his head.

During the short boat journey Fran and Jadran stood at the rail, his arm around her shoulder and hers around his waist, as they watched first the grey mass of the quayside slip past, and then the elegant single span of the Franjo Tudman bridge, its cables gleaming in the sunshine high above them.

"It will be good to see my father laid properly to rest," she told him. "I mean, I haven't a clue whether he was religious, but it feels respectful for him to have a proper burial and a final resting place, not just that horrid pit they were thrown into." She shuddered.

"That can be the way in wars."

She looked up at him. "The awful things you must have seen."

"Yes, but now I can let them go." He kissed her gently on the top of her head and she leant further into him, his warmth comforting her as much as she wanted to comfort him.

The boat was tied up near the lighthouse as they had done themselves on the day they first met. This time a proper gangplank had been secured, and they took their place in the line of people filing ashore and onto the path through the trees. Over the summer a covering of grass had grown and the branches and shrubs seemed to have encroached a little more, blocking out any trace of sunshine.

The archaeologists led them past the barn-like building she and Jadran had explored to a space freshly cleared of vegetation. She felt his grip tighten on her arm when they first saw the rows of freshly dug graves, into which the coffins had already been lowered. Neat wooden shapes, each containing what was left of a man. Next to her, Elvira let out a small gasp and Fran knew how she felt. Seeing them lined up like that brought it home how horrific the executions had been, and Fran had to work pretty hard to remind herself that this was bringing closure and peace.

She focused her attention on the grey stone cross at the far end of the clearing, flanked by four slabs engraved with the men's names. Whatever they had or hadn't done, no one could ever forget them, not now. That her father, who had saved Jewish lives, had died and was buried amongst fascists was not lost on her, but if Jadran was right, he probably wasn't the only innocent man in the rows of coffins. An elderly woman nearby smothered a sob; she was one of the few old enough to have genuine memories, and Fran's heart went out to her. If she had known her father this would have been a very difficult day indeed.

Fran understood little of the service, which was in any case mercifully brief. Jadran explained it was non-denominational, although the man officiating was Catholic as a mark of respect to the monks and the priest whose bodies were being committed to rest. After a long moment of silence, the archaeologists began to lead the congregation away from the gaping holes in the ground. Some paused to look for a nameplate on a coffin, but not Fran. It was done. Her father was at least buried with some sort of dignity.

On the grass outside the barn refreshments were being served, but Fran wasn't hungry. She'd had enough of this place, of the dark cypresses rising around them, the voracious laurels and clinging ivy encroaching on the ruins. The muted cocktail party chatter and clink of glasses seemed completely incongruous. She had seen her father finally laid to rest, and now she wanted to leave.

Straight after the service Eli had made his excuses and disappeared to look around, but now he returned, a gleam of excitement in his eyes.

"Fran, Fran, come with me. You must see this."

Curious, she followed him up the steps into the barn, the cool, damp air a welcome respite from the heat outside. Beams of light reached the walls from the broken windows above, the faint mouldy smell wrinkling Fran's nose.

They followed Eli to the far corner. "I've been looking at the graffiti."

Elvira looked around and shivered. "The swastikas ... all that Neo-Nazi stuff ... it's frightening."

"No, not that. The old markings near the floor that were made by the men who were executed. I overheard one of the archaeologists talking about them on the boat and I wanted to see if I could find Fran's father's. Of course there are many swastikas amongst them too and for a long time I thought he hadn't left his mark, but it's here, on its own in this corner."

Using the torch on his phone he swept the lower reaches of the wall. "There – can you see?"

Fran and Jadran crouched. The letters B and M were uneven, and next to them was a Star of David. Fran felt her mouth drop open in disbelief.

"Why..."

"To me it is a message to future generations," Eli said. "A single Star of David against all these swastikas. One man's testimony that in darkness there is always light."

Elvira stifled a sob. "And to show that mistakes were made."

Jadran nodded. "It seems to me it was a way to protest his innocence. To show he was different to the others here."

Fran reached out and ran her fingers over the rough marks in the stone. The M was barely finished, its final downstroke no more than the tiniest of scratches, as though he had run out of strength. Or time. She traced them again, touching where her father had touched all those years before. For the first time she felt close to him, as though he was only just out of reach. What had she missed, not being brought up by this man? Who might she have been? But no, she couldn't go there. What was important was who she was. Hadn't Jadran almost said as much the first time they'd come here?

On her knees on the uneven floor she reached inside her dress for the necklace her mother had brought from Dubrovnik all those years before. Until today she had never worn it, and she doubted she would again, but it had felt like the right thing to do.

She leant into the wall, touching its Star of David against the carving and whispered, "*Tata, razumijem.*"

Jadran touched her shoulder. "Are you all right, Safranka?"

She nodded as he helped her to her feet. "Yes, I am just telling him I understand."

He wrapped her tightly into him. "I'm sure he knows."

"I hope so. He gave me life, after all. A different life to the one he intended, no doubt, but a good one all the same. Maybe better than I would have had growing up here, who knows? But more than that, he brought me back, and without him I never would have found myself, or just as importantly, you."

"You are at peace with it? You can accept what happened?"

"It is easier because I did not know him. But yes, I think I can."

He squeezed her tighter. "The past may make us, Safranka, but it is the future that is important."

She looked up at him, laughing. "Even at our age."

"Well given your insistence that we're practically geriatric, we must not waste a single moment."

He took hold of her hand and led her into the sunshine, where she looked up at the cloudless blue sky above her head. People were drifting towards the boat and she stood for a moment, drinking in the birdsong and the wash of the sea.

Yes, here her father was finally at peace. And so was she.

Acknowledgments

Incredibly sharp-eyed readers with laser memories may remember the scenes in *The Olive Grove* when Damir visits Vesna's home on the mainland and looks out on Daksa. While I was ferreting around trying to discover the island's name I came across accounts of a massacre there in 1944 and saved them to my research bookmarks, just in case. But the story was so haunting it was one that, over time, I realised I had to tell.

I know there may be readers who will be disappointed this book isn't a full dual timeline like *An Island of Secrets*, but the reality is that there isn't enough information available about the Second World War in Dubrovnik to make that possible. Initially I thought there was so little that Branko's story could only be hinted at in a prologue and epilogue, but even as I wrote those opening paragraphs, he was demanding to be given a proper hearing.

So I dug and I dug, finding out just about enough from Jewish sources and a few paragraphs describing the arrival of the British in Michael McConville's *A Small War in the Balkans*. With a bit of imagination – and after all, I am a storyteller – that was sufficient, but I was lucky enough to discover a letter from one of the partisan commanders who arrived in Dubrovnik in October 1944 that gave me a few more incredibly useful scraps.

This was always going to be Fran's story though. This was

something my wonderful editor, Charlotte Ledger, and I agreed on from the very start. So many women in their sixties face what Fran faces, building a life of their own after years of having everything on hold while caring for family members, and I have wanted to create a protagonist in that position for years. Charlotte was brave enough to encourage me to put her centre stage.

Because it had worked so well for me before to visit Croatia, once I had a solid draft behind me, I took the same tack this time and there are a whole barrel of thank yous relating to the trip. First, Andy Smeed-Curd at Completely Croatia, definitely my travel agent of choice, for once again using his expertise to tailor everything to my exact requirements; ensuring that I was well-placed to visit Trsteno Arboretum, Lopud, and Dubrovnik itself.

At Lopud, the monastery was an important setting for me, but it is now an incredibly high-end holiday villa and event space called LOPUD 1483. The general manager, Klara Šoštarić was hugely helpful and managed to squeeze in my visit between rentals. I was shown around one Sunday morning by their security guard Alan who was a font of knowledge about not only the monastery's history but the island's as well.

I had discovered from Jewish sources that Lopud was one of the places Dubrovnik's Jews were interned by the Italians on German instructions, but I didn't know where. Although the monastery was a partial ruin at the time, I had a gut feeling it could be there. Watching a video about its restoration, I saw preserved graffiti on one wall, which read 'IL DUCE'. I just knew I was right.

Except I wasn't. Alan told me that the monastery had been the Italian headquarters, but the Jews were held in a hotel, which I later discovered was the Grand. Cue rewriting of Branko's story (more than once!), and it perfectly illustrates my point about the research material being difficult to access.

Part way through our trip we moved on to the mainland, and some of my research at least shifted to Jadran's own wartime past. Here I owe huge thanks to two extraordinary men who lived through the Siege of Dubrovnik and were more than willing to tell their stories. First, Krešimir Pehar, who runs Dubrovnik 4U Transfers and who became our guide on Mount Srđ, where we visited the Homeland War Museum, although I learned just as much about the war from him. Second, Mato Knego, a veteran who now works as a tour guide. His openness and honesty during our walk around the old city will haunt me for a very long time.

There is a big thank you to Darko Barisic (as ever) who as well as patiently answering all my questions, generously gave us the use of his apartment in Cavtat. It was one of the highlights of the trip to see him again after almost three years.

We had the warmest of welcomes in the Jewish museum (unlike Fran's initial experience) and, in fact, everywhere we went. The one place we didn't get to visit was Daksa. It is still unbelievably hard to find anyone who will take you, so I had to rely on internet resources and, anyway, there was a part of me who wanted to leave the men buried there to rest in peace.

Closer to home, big thanks to my friend and beta reader Sally Thomas. Her insights were invaluable in shaping the final draft. And the constant support I have received from other writers, in particular Kitty Wilson, Cass Grafton, Susanna Bavin and Alexandra Walsh has been brilliant too. Thanks also to the wonderful group of people who attended Rosanna Ley's writing retreat at Finca el Cerrillo in March 2022, in particular my walking buddy Angela Petch, who helped so much with ironing out the finer points of the plot.

As well as Charlotte at team One More Chapter, Julia Williams's insightful comments helped me to make the book so much better, as did Michelle Griffin's meticulous proof read, and some of the wonderful things they said about Fran's story will remain with me for a very long time.

Last but not least, my husband, Jim, puts up with a great deal, and in particular suffered extreme heat in Croatia on my behalf. I could do none of this without him, and this book is dedicated to his father, John, and his partner, Joan, who, since my mother-in-law, Marjorie, died in her early sixties, have been living proof that new love in later life can be anything you make it.